Ben Alderson

A DECEPTION OF COURTS

REALM OF FEY BOOK 3

ANGRY ROBOT

ANGRY ROBOT
An imprint of Watkins Media Ltd

Unit 11, Shepperton House
89 Shepperton Road
London N1 3DF
UK

angryrobotbooks.com
twitter.com/angryrobotbooks
Lots of lying

An Angry Robot paperback original, 2024

Cover by Sarah O'Flaherty
Edited by Eleanor Teasdale and Shona Kinsella
Set in Meridien

ISBN 978 1 91599 870 5
Ebook ISBN 978 1 91599 877 4

Printed and bound in the United Kingdom by CPI Group (UK) Ltd, Croydon CR0 4YY.

9 8 7 6 5 4 3 2 1

MIX
Paper | Supporting
responsible forestry
FSC
www.fsc.org
FSC® C171272

Merlin, thank you for keeping this service alive in your heart, and thus, in mine.

CHAPTER 1

The rancid stench of shit, ale and coal-infested smoke burned away at my nose as I navigated my way through the slums of Lockinge. Flies pestered me with their buzzing, but I'd grown far too familiar with their presence, I hardly bothered to swat them away.

With my head kept low and hood pulled over my brow, not even one of the human patrons – cursed to dwell within the city's slums – noticed me. In their eyes I wasn't out of place, and neither was the equally concealed figure at my side.

Nefarious happenings were expected in these parts of the human city.

The Cage, as the slums had been aptly named, was rife with strangers harbouring secrets and dangerous desires. No one looked for too long, for fear of being bottled by a drunk or captured by a vagrant, only to be sold in one of the many back-alley markets.

Although the dirtied streets and shoddy residences were full of humans at the best of times, the Cage turned out to be the best place for a group of fey, a mutated human, and a nest of assassins to hide out in. Which had been exactly what our band of unlikely allies had been doing in the weeks following the events with Aldrick and his demonic apparition of Duwar.

Hiding. Biding our time. Waiting for the moment to strike.

If Althea had gotten her way, we would've been back in Wychwood by now. Elinor Oakstorm, mother to the deceased Tarron and Lovis and widowed queen to Doran Oakstorm, had returned to Wychwood safely, as her letter four days prior had confirmed. Accompanied by Cedarfall guards, the Queen of Oakstorm was required back in her court. A court that'd believed her dead, killed by Hunters, many years ago.

Information my brief stay in Lockinge Castle's underground prison had uncovered was not the case at all. That *prison* being the very reason I'd yet to return to Wychwood.

Elinor's return home had many benefits to our cause. Mainly to rally the aid we required in the human capital city of Lockinge. Which, to Althea's great disdain, was where we'd been hiding after we had escaped Aldrick's clutches.

Truth was, I slept better knowing Elinor was far from Aldrick. Her innate power of healing was crucial to Aldrick's ability to mutate humans into powered beings. Without her blood, Aldrick couldn't kill then reanimate any more unwilling humans, like he had done to Duncan.

Duncan. The thought of his name alone conjured the feeling of his calloused hands rubbing up my back and his full, wet lips tracing secrets into the skin of my neck.

Every day that passed only added to the ever-growing panic in my chest. I expected him to break beneath his change, but his resilience surprised me every day. The iron-willed Seraphine, our gracious host who so happened to be one of the lead assassins in the infamous Children of the Asp guild, had gifted him an iron bracelet – thin and delicate – much like the one my mother had left me as a child. It kept Duncan's new power buried. But I could see, deep in his verdant eyes, it lurked. Waiting, like a snake, to strike.

Deep in the belly of the human city wasn't the place for explosions of unnatural lightning. It would've given us away before we wanted it to. And the little time Duncan had without the band, his magic seemed to control him more than he had control of *it*. I knew there'd be a time to understand what had happened to him, but until *my* plan was complete, those wonderings would have to wait.

A shrill cry of a bird tore me from my mind, back to the moment at hand. I didn't need to look up to recognise the call. Lucari, Kayne's hawk, sliced through the night sky, a smudge of grey and white against the backdrop of obsidian. The creature moved with such speed that the drunk men who sang from the steps of derelict taverns would blink and miss it.

Sober to the bone, I knew what it meant. Lucari's two sharp calls gave an obvious message.

Our time of waiting was almost over, and the time for action mere moments away.

"You know, Robin, it is not too late to put a stop to this. If you tell me you have changed your mind, I will stand by you and help you come up with another solution."

I peered to my side, catching the glint of bright eyes beneath the faded burgundy cloak. Even within the shadows, Althea Cedarfall's presence burned as bright as the inner flame which sang in her soul. Cedarfall power – fierce as a raging flame.

She'd yet to reveal what she had promised the Children of the Asp in return for their help in rescuing me from the clutches of the Hand. Then again, I too had paid a price for their continued help – one I was not ready to reveal either. That was the thing about me and Althea, we were both as stubborn as a rock amidst a river. I was just thankful she was at my side tonight.

Sighing, I lifted my gaze to the dark outline of the castle far ahead. Lockinge was built on an incline of land. Seraphine had explained that the humans once believed the castle itself was constructed on an extinct volcano as a tribute to the Creator. A way of ensuring they were as close to his heavenly domain as possible.

Just the thought alone made me cringe. The castle was once a signal of faith and love for the Creator, but it now housed the one person hellbent on bringing forth a time of demons and their vengeful power.

"There's nothing more important to me which would make me put a stop to these plans, Althea. We've worked too hard, I'm going to see them through."

Her fingers snaked from beneath her cloak and into the sleeve of my under jacket, where she found my hand and held it. The moment of her touch was brief yet comforting. "This could end terribly; you understand the risks, don't you?"

Of course I did. I exhaled, my breath clearing space within the dank, heavy air. "And it could also work. It *has* to work."

When I slept, I ran over my plans. During my waking hours they lingered clear in my mind. There was not a moment of the day or night I'd wasted, always thinking about what waited before me.

"Your belief inspires me, friend. Let us do it. Not that you need a reminder, but I am by your side until the end."

As I had said many times over the days, I repeated two words that began to lose all meaning. "Thank you."

My mind, as it did during every moment of silence I was awarded, drifted to the warren-like caverns far beneath Lockinge's castle and to the countless fey trapped there. How could I have returned to Wychwood knowing what was left behind? The answer was simple: I couldn't.

I thought of Jesibel often. Her face burned hot in my mind whenever I contemplated giving up on my wild idea of saving all of them from Aldrick. She, like the others trapped within the Below, had been stolen from her home and used like cattle. All so Aldrick could see through his fucked-up wishes to create an army of powered human beings that would help bring forth a promise of a demon in a world that had turned its backs on its gods.

How many Icethorn fey had been captured because of my family's death? If I'd returned to Wychwood, I would've been taken to my court only to find it empty and void of existence. Because they were here. In Lockinge, buried beneath the ground with iron cuffs around their necks.

I was a king now. Whether I completely believed it or not, it had to mean something. If not to myself, then to the people who relied on me to save them.

My mistakes and grief had led me to this place. I refused to leave it without taking what was rightfully mine.

"You came back for me. What I am doing for those in the Below does not differ from your choice of always standing by my side."

Althea kept pace at my side, boots slapping into puddles of Altar knows what. "I know. Which is precisely the reason I have not snatched you by the short and curlies and dragged you back to Wychwood against your will. This *is* the right decision. Dangerous, yes. Slightly fucking stupid, but excellently planned, also yes."

"Your mother is going to kill me when we get back, isn't she?" I exhaled, mind flashing to Lyra Cedarfall, who was a projection of what Althea would look like in the years to come. Burning red hair, eyes glowing with authority.

My comment was not made to make Althea laugh, but it did. She released a gleeful bark into the night, throwing her head back as she did so. "Not if you are successful. It is not her you should be concerned with anyway. Gyah will ruin you if this all goes wrong. She has grown rather protective of me since our short and unpleasant stay in Finstock."

I found that Althea spoke of Gyah a lot. As though her mind was occupied with her personal guard, a feeling I understood well. It warmed my stomach, watching how Althea's face would brighten at the mention of the Eldrae. Her admiration was abundantly clear across her expression whenever Gyah's name crossed her lips.

"Remind me to keep poking at what's going on between you both," I said. "When this is all over."

Althea punched a fist into my shoulder, even gently her strength was paramount. "If we survive, then I may just tell you all the juicy details. On the agreement of a trade with the details about you and your *Hunter*."

"Duncan," I corrected for the hundredth time. I'd yet to hear Althea call him by his name, always referring to him as the title we first met him under.

"Yes, General Rackley, which... speaking of the devil."

My heart lodged in my throat as two shadows peeled from the wall of a building ahead of us. We slowed, hesitant at what waited before us. If it wasn't for Lucari, who swooped down from a great height and perched on the shoulder of the shorter figure, I would've thought they were a threat, when in fact, they were both the complete opposite.

In my eyes, at least.

Wooden shutters flapped in the icy winds, groaning and screeching on hinges that wouldn't survive the night. Plaster crumbled away in patches, littering the cobbled street beyond it with snow-like mounds of worn paint and brick dust. The abandoned building didn't look like much else compared to the darkened homes which leaned on it from either side. There was no marker to suggest it was one of the many burrows the Asps used as a place for hiding and scheming. Not so abandoned after all. But after tonight, it would never be used for anything again.

I thought of the thin, tired mattress floors above us. It'd been rolled out beside a cracked oil lamp within one of the top rooms of the building. I felt no love lost for the idea of it going down in flames. Literally. I thought of the down-turned mirror, which had gathered dust since our first night. Since seeing Duwar, I found looking into mirrors difficult now. Each time I passed one, I expected to see a molten, horned god staring back at me. Thankfully, Duncan made sure this was one less concern by removing the few that'd been hanging within our base.

One of the many things Duncan had done for me.

"Any sign from the castle yet?" I spluttered, practically falling into the outstretched arms of Duncan. He held me close, my cheek pressed into the leather belts strapped across his chest in three lashings.

It was dark within the shadow of the building. Not even the moon dared to provide me with enough light to see him in all his glory. So I used the rest of my senses to admire him. I inhaled deeply, allowing a moment to convince myself it was only him and me with no needs and wants. If I kept my eyes closed long enough, I could've pictured us during another time, another moment. One which didn't include the impending doom of what the night was to bring.

"Not yet." Duncan's deep voice rumbled through his chest and into mine. "However, Seraphine has confirmed the Hand has left Lockinge. But until the signal reaches us from inside the castle, we must wait. It's imperative that Aldrick is far away if we dare hope for success."

I pulled away from Duncan and looked back up toward the ugly outline of the castle far ahead. There was a tower which reached skyward, far taller than any other beside it. The point flirted with the dark clouds, which, now and then, would conceal the pointed tip from view.

As Duncan had already confirmed, the tower was dark. My sight might've been stronger if my blood was full fey, but I could still make out the slit-like etchings across the tower's walls. Windows. Dark and lifeless. Much like the rest of the castle had been since the night when Doran's gryvern attacked. Part of me had hoped Aldrick's silence resulted from the fact he had died beneath the mirror Seraphine had pushed atop him.

But our intel suggested otherwise.

Aldrick was a weak, crazed man. His power was to leech into minds, smothering will and control. His magic was strong as a web woven from iron, rendering anyone he desired completely powerless. He could enthral us all if we got close enough again, which was why it was essential to my plan that Aldrick left Lockinge before we snuck back inside.

I buzzed with nerves. Not wishing to even blink for fear that I would miss the tower glow with firelight in signal.

"We are perhaps a couple of hours away from Wychwood ships reaching us," Kayne warned, expression stiff. Lucari lowered her beak and dropped something small into his hand. "If anyone else catches wind that an armada of fey ships are hidden on horizon of the human capital, it will spark a frenzy before we have a chance to even begin."

I looked Kayne dead in the eyes every time he spoke, which was rarely. There was still trepidation in the way he looked at me. Unlike Duncan, Kayne's years of brainwashing had yet to vacate his gaze. We were close, but more time was needed. No matter if he may have believed he hid it well from me, he was wrong. Trust went both ways, after all.

I'd shared my concern about Kayne with Duncan, who'd planted a kiss upon my forehead and promised me his friend could be trusted. Until he proved otherwise, I would have to let the red-haired Hunter prove himself to our cause. I couldn't deny that his skills as a Tracker had been essential in getting us this far. Without Lucari and Kayne's knowledge of the city, we wouldn't have heard the whispers suggesting Aldrick prepared to leave Lockinge.

But his involvement didn't mean that the moment I felt he was a threat, no matter his friendship with Duncan, I *would* destroy him. The wary glint in Duncan's dark emerald stare spoke volumes. He understood that, and didn't waste breath arguing against it.

"Show me what has been sent," I said, trying to keep the harsh command from being too prevalent in my voice.

Kayne nodded, unkempt ginger curls falling across his brow. He outstretched his hand, unfurled his pale fingers and revealed the twig with three distinct golden leaves.

Leaves from the city of Aurelia.

Althea's breath caught in her throat. "It *is* them."

I felt a swell in my chest as I regarded my friend. There was no concealing the smile that leaked across my face. "Elinor did it, just as she said she would."

"Never underestimate the bond of friendship. My mother and Elinor have been close since childhood. If there was ever a connection powerful enough to send ships to sea for us, it would be them."

Kayne fisted the golden leaves, crushing them to powder in his palm. Elinor's letter from days ago had promised her aid, but seeing the hue of the leaves and the golden dust it left stained across Kayne's fingers, it all became extremely real.

There was only a flash of excited anticipation before it all came crumbling back down upon me. Reality did that, ruined a moment, sharpened the sense. Without it I might've lost myself in my hope, rather than the hard work still ahead of us.

Winds shifted, bringing with it a sharper scent which cut through the smells of the slums. My eyes stung. I blinked it away, unable to stop myself from wincing as the acidic scent invaded the back of my nose and throat, clinging there.

"Everything is in order." I stepped away from the building and swallowed the urge to cough violently. "But if the signal doesn't come from the castle, then we take faith in Seraphine's confirmation Aldrick has left the city, and we move. Too much is riding on this to turn back."

Soon enough, the horrific smell from the building would alert the intoxicated nightly wanderers of the Cage that something was wrong. This wasn't the only building which bled such an aura. Spotted around the Cage were other empty Asp buildings, each one soaked with oil.

Ready and waiting for that one signal. Everything hinged on it.

I fixed my gaze back on the dark tower and waited. My anxiety was reminiscent of being suffocated. It felt as though a strong, gloved hand pressed down over my mouth and another pinched at my nose. The more time passed without the signal, the stronger the drum-beat of anxiety became. Someone was speaking, but my mind thundered as if an army of horses stampeded through it.

"Robin?" Duncan said, his tone suggesting it wasn't the first time he'd spoken my name. "Tell me you are still with me…"

I ripped my attention away from the still-dark tower and looked toward Duncan. Even with the iron bracelet around his wrist, I was certain I felt the crackling of sharp, white-hot lightning dancing across his concerned gaze.

His hand worked circles into my back to calm me. It worked enough for me to fake my reply. "I'm fine, just focused."

"You have a lot on your mind, but don't allow it to drown you. Speak to me, share the burden."

I swallowed, feeling as though knives filled my throat. "If I fail them–"

"If it brings you comfort, the fey in the Below will know no different," he replied quickly. "Focus on what you can control and not what you can't. Okay? Keep a clear head."

I forced a smile. If Kayne, with his judging stare, or Althea, with her obvious distaste for the man who touched me, were not at our sides, I would've kissed him. Gods, I wished I could. The promise of losing myself to him was the reward I'd give myself when this was all over.

"Better?" he asked, dipping his face toward mine.

"Much," I lied.

Perhaps fate was willing to join our band of unlikely allies. It wouldn't have been an impossible thing, considering the group I stood a part of. A king, a princess, a Hunter and a mutilated human. Fate would've felt rather at home among our ranks.

Which is why she picked that moment to reveal herself.

Three quick and high whistles broke through the night. Shivers prickled across my skin as I threw my attention back to the tower in time to see golden, beautiful fire spark into existence. The glows of wondrous flame danced from within the tower. To anyone else looking up at the castle, it would've seemed normal. The occupants of the castle were simply choosing to occupy the tower this night. But to me, it was the signal we'd been waiting for. One Seraphine had planned with the few remaining Asps who still were inside the castle.

When the Hand leaves Lockinge, the tower will burn.

It felt as though time slowed to a near stop as I watched the tower begin to burn.

Then another fire started. An explosion rocked the Cage, brightening the night sky in a cloud of vicious flame. The sound was so jarring it restarted my heart, allowing the adrenaline to flow like a wild river through my blood.

Far in the distance, buried deep within the belly of the slums, an Asp hideout erupted in flames. I blinked and could imagine brick and glass raining down upon the empty streets, heat searing across the dirt-covered roads.

Screams from unexpecting humans.

Another explosion followed. This time from another pocket of the Cage. Then another. And another. One by one, the slums of Lockinge shook beneath the destruction of fire. One small spark, that was all it took, and the oil-soaked buildings burst into flames.

"Should we toast to our success?" Althea asked from my side, lifting something before her. Carefully held between two fingers, she displayed a corked vial of brown liquid. Part two of our plan.

"I think that would be a splendid idea," I retorted, joining Althea and taking an identical vial from my chest pocket and holding it up.

One by one, the others followed suit, drawing free a vial of tonic. Our corks popped in tandem, discarded on the cobbled street without a second thought.

Seraphine had explained many times how she didn't succumb to Aldrick's mind control during her infiltration into his inner circle. The tonic the assassin twins ingested daily – *Mariflora* – was basically a flower ground up into a paste and diluted with liqueur. The flora, although native to a particular woodland in the Elmdew Court, was currently being farmed in the basement of one of the buildings that now burned deep in the Cage.

After tonight, we wouldn't need to take the necessary precautions to keep Aldrick from grasping control of our minds. We would be far from this wretched city by morning, as long as we were successful–

No, Robin. Focus.

"Bottoms up," Duncan said, winking at me. My breath hitched in my throat; scarlet threatened to overcome my cheeks.

"You wish," I whispered.

"Oh, I do." Duncan's tongue departed from his lips a second before he pressed the vial to them and cocked his head back.

"Fuck," Kayne grunted, shaking his head like a dog. "Disgusting."

Althea squinted at the vial, not an ounce of disgust across her face. In fact, she brought the empty vial to her mouth and licked the dribble of tonic that escaped down its side. "Grow a pair, Kayne. I'm sure you've had worse in your mouth."

The Mariflora burned down my throat, not leaving an inch untouched. It took effort not to choke on a laugh as I watched Kayne's face turn as red as his hair.

At least he had sense in not joining a verbal duel with Althea. No one would win against her.

"Now we've all had some good-old liquid courage," I said, my mouth feeling like I was breathing fire. "Care to do the honours, Althea?"

She no longer held her empty vial. In its place was a bud of golden fire. It threw light across her concealed face, highlighting the wolfish grin contorting her freckled, beautiful face.

"I cannot even express how much I have looked forward to setting this place alight." Her fire grew in size, sharing in her excitement.

"Oh, we know," Duncan added, with a friendly roll of his verdant eyes. "It's all you've been talking about since you first stepped foot in it. Not up to scratch for a princess, is it?"

Althea's grin intensified, flashing teeth at Duncan, who only returned her smile – even if that was not the reaction she was looking for. "I prefer my beds off the floor and covered in at least eight pillows."

"Then light it up," I said, secretly feeling the same as Althea. Even if the fire did burn away the grime, mould and stench of the building, I didn't think my skin would be rid of its memory quite so easily.

"With pleasure…" Althea lifted her arm back as though the fire in her palm was a ball, and she was ready to throw it. "Time to break into a prison and free some fey."

I nodded, grinding my teeth, body vibrating with the need to see this to the end.

Althea rolled her shoulders back, tilted her head downward and flashed teeth, offering us all a warning. *"Run."*

CHAPTER 2

It didn't take long until Lockinge was bathed in flames. And the more those sparks ignited, the harder it was to clear the smile from my face.

Smoke billowed from the countless buildings engulfed in the raging inferno. The heavy presence blanketed the already obsidian sky until the moon and stars were no longer visible. If it wasn't for the mask of dark material I'd pulled across my lower face, I would've tasted ash and charred oil across my tongue, because the air of the city was thick with it.

Duncan kept pace beside me, thick-muscled arms pounding at his sides. Kayne led the party with his hawk slicing through the sky. Althea drew up the rear, though I couldn't see her as my focus was pinned on the castle ahead. The slapping of her footfalls and laboured but controlled breathing informed me she was close.

Even as humans flooded, sleepy-eyed and terrified, from their homes, I couldn't help but delight in my excited exuberance.

It's fucking working.

I only risked a moment to glance over my shoulder to see our plan in fruition. Stretching wide across the cramped, dark streets and lanes of the Cage were buds of tangled flames as every dwelling belonging to the Asp burned.

The sacrifice of the Asp's many hideouts was meant only as a distraction. Something to draw the Kingsmen and Hunters from the castle to investigate the destruction and manage the chaos. This was our way of clearing a path to allow entry back into the castle grounds and back to the place we'd not long escaped. Our return was solely for one purpose. To break into the prison and free the hundreds of fey trapped far beneath the city.

And the flood of armoured men and women, each displaying the white-splashed symbol of the Hand across their chests as they ran through the main streetways from Lockinge, confirmed the plan was working.

My ears still rang with the explosive blast Althea had created once she threw her conjured flame toward the building we'd called home during the past weeks. No love was lost for the cold, mould-covered rooms and the rats that had attempted to evict us. Even as we passed through the middle sector of the city, keeping in the darkened side streets, I recognised the small inkling of guilt for the lives of the creatures that would now be burned meat back in the slums. Their deaths were the sacrifice that had to be made for saving the others.

Sacrifice, the harsh truth of the word, being something I was all too familiar with now.

There was only so much I could've prepared for. And even more steps ahead of us were out of my control. I couldn't let the pessimistic worries cloud my judgement. There were only so many times I could've mapped out the precise route through the city toward the castle. My mind had reeled with my desire to free the fey from Aldrick's capture. For weeks, it was all I could think of. From the moment Seraphine smuggled us back into Lockinge until now, my focus was on them.

Sometimes, when the winds changed, I could still smell the sewers upon my skin. Clambering through the thick, unknown substances begrudgingly flowing into the ocean through a series of cavern-like tunnels beneath the city. We came back into Lockinge, covered in shit with even more to deal with.

It would all be worth it. At least that's what I convinced myself of over and over during the nights I lay sleepless beside Duncan on the roll-out mattress back in the now burning building.

First, I asked Elinor to secure means of travel for the countless number of fey we would save. Ships, and a lot of them at that. A way of returning the fey home. I'd believed it would have been the hardest challenge ahead, but I was wrong. Convincing Seraphine to give up the dwellings the Asps owned within the city took the most effort. I did it because there was no other option, but the cost was great. No matter how many times Althea asked, or Duncan raised a brow in inquiry, I didn't reveal what I'd traded for their help. But as it was with the guild of assassins, nothing was free in life, only in death was money as useless as breath.

Seraphine had lost everything with her sister's death. Aldrick had taken her twin from her and left her as one piece of a set of two. But coin still bled a darker red than the blood of family. I was a fool to even think the assassins would have helped out of the desire to do what was right. Just as Seraphine had said to me when I first requested her help, the words were still clear even now.

Saving the world from a demon god does not save us from poverty. That's another war entirely.

Right and wrong were simply two sides of the same coin, and the Asps didn't care which side it landed on, only that it landed in their palm.

I felt as though we'd been running for only a moment before we came to our agreed meeting place. Kayne pressed himself into the side of the merchant's building before it gave way to the main street. It gave the best view of the main parade that led toward the castle. The same parade Duncan and I had been dragged up when we had first arrived in Lockinge. Back when I didn't know the Hand's true identity. Before he revealed himself as the very creature he'd petitioned his followers to hunt, capture and kill: a fey.

"How many do you see?" Duncan asked, hardly a hair out of place. He didn't look as though he'd run up the harsh incline of a city, whereas I fought the urge to fold over to catch my breath.

Kayne was silent for a moment, craning his head around the corner of the apothecary shop that provided us shelter. This was the last place to hide before we had to begin the more tiresome fight toward the castle's entrance. "Forty," he replied, "maybe fifty, from what I can see. Not counting those surveying the walls or watching from within the bastard castle."

"Fuck," Duncan groaned. Reminiscent of another time and place when he had expelled the same word under different circumstances. "I thought more would be drawn by our distraction."

I pressed up behind him, running a hand up his hard back and lacing it over his shoulder.

"We planned for more," I whispered. "But that is what a contingency plan is for. Don't worry, this isn't going to halt our next step, just… make it slightly more difficult."

Staying positive was the only option for success, I had to keep the morale up.

"And hoped for less," Althea interjected, pulling down the covering of material from her mouth. "What are the chances we are up against powered-up humans? Because that is what *will* affect our success rate."

Duncan stiffened beneath my hand. I squeezed my fingers into his shoulder, hoping to provide him with some grounding comfort.

"Your guess is as good as mine," Kayne replied. "I could get a better grasp of the number if you let me send Lucari to scout–"

"No," I snapped, swallowing the urge to shout. "She is important to us, I can't risk Lucari. The second someone spots your hawk, it will give us away. Lucari stays with you until we are so close to the guards that your sword has already pierced through the first chest you find. Only then can she be free to tear their faces off."

If my hearing was as strong as Althea's, I would have been certain to catch the sound the lump made in his throat as he swallowed. His silence spoke volumes. I could see the trepidation in his unblinking eyes as he wrestled with himself internally. Lucari meant a lot to Kayne, and to my cause.

"No one is forcing you to take part in this, Kayne," I said, stepping closer to him. "I will not think less of you if you sit this one out."

Kayne was facing the real possibility of fighting those he once fought besides. This was a big ask – I recognised that.

Kayne kept his chin raised, looking down the point of his freckled nose at me. "I've made my choice. And I'm here, aren't I? If I didn't struggle with the concept of killing innocent people, I wouldn't be human."

He used his words with intent, and I felt their stab.

"Innocent isn't a word I would have used to describe them," I replied.

"Regardless of that. I fight with you."

Relief unfurled in me. "Will you feel the same if you face someone you once knew? If the person at the end of your blade is another Hunter you were close to? I need to know that you will slay anyone who stands in our way."

My eyes flickered between his, trying to catch some hint of cowardice. If there was any of that emotion lurking, Kayne did well to keep it concealed.

"Robin," Duncan said, using my name to draw me back to him. Like an anchor, the deep alto of his voice had the power to gather me in his hands and make me feel safe. "Do you trust *me*?"

"I know where you are going with this," I replied, losing myself in his deep, forest stare.

"Then you don't need me to remind you that I trust Kayne, so put your faith in me. Regardless of what his thoughts are toward your..." *Kind*. He wanted to say it but held back as he caught daggers from Althea. "What I'm trying to say is Aldrick is our common enemy. Fey, human, he is a threat to us all. Ensuring he cannot do what he has done to me again is the first link in the chain that we must break. We can only win if we work together."

"Ever considered trading in the hunting of *my kind* for a living and giving speeches to the downtrodden instead?" Althea questioned, head tilting sideways an inch. There was no denying the sharp steel in her voice. I winced as she sliced through the sudden tension between us. "You'd do well at it."

"Please. I haven't allowed for time to argue," I said, before Duncan could retort with whatever lingered across his full lips. Turning my attention, I regarded Kayne and Lucari a final time. The hawk scrutinised me through beady, wary eyes from her perch upon his shoulder. "Kayne, I trust you will do the right thing when presented with it."

He nodded, gaze sharp as a blade.

"Then there's only one way to find out," Althea replied for him, pushing past us all so she could get a look at the next barrier we had to get through. "So, who's ready for some rough and tumble?"

Duncan grinned, raising his hand to the two-handed hilt protruding from the cloak upon his back. It was his way of confirming he was, in fact, ready.

Kayne followed his friend, drawing out the twin swords resting patiently on his belt, twisting each in a full arc at his side as Lucari chirped with equal readiness. "I'm in."

I had weapons at my hip and others strapped around my arms and thighs. Seraphine had taken a keen interest in training me in the art of sharp objects, even though my best weapon lingered in my blood. Magic. I may not have been accepted into the guild with my skills, or lack thereof, but I was more confident with the handle of a blade in my hand than I had been before.

Although tonight, those were not my weapons of choice.

Nor was a blade or axe something Althea planned to use. I recognised the heat spilling from her skin as it reared its presence to the surface. Magic sang in the air, delighted for the release. We would fight with the power Aldrick longed to harvest – turning what he desired most back on his hard work.

Although I'd yet to release the hold on my magic, I could feel its hunger for revenge. It comforted me.

"Before we go," Duncan muttered, pulling me tight to him. "One last thing."

Our entanglement had been reserved from public displays of affection. It had not felt right to flaunt it around Althea, or Kayne for that matter. They both knew about us, but still, there was an unspoken rule which kept distance between us when others were around.

A rule which Duncan swiftly broke before we threw ourselves into the pending fight. He pressed himself to me, sword gripped in his hand to stop himself from reaching out for my face, as I was confident he wished to do. With a quick dip of his head, I found his lips pressed to my own.

A wave of serene peace rushed over me. Before I closed my eyes, I caught the deepening of the single, lined scar which ran from the corner of his eye to the corner of his lip. It was one of many imperfections I obsessed over. I didn't need to run my finger down its trail to know just how it felt to touch. That feeling was already embedded deep in my mind.

His kiss was soft and far too quick. It wasn't ridden with the usual tangling of tongues and nipping of teeth at lips. It was pleasant like a compliment, one which warmed my soul.

When Duncan pulled away, I gravitated toward him. My weight fell against his rigid, firm stance. He breathed out a sigh that sang with a smile.

"My king," Duncan said.

"Shouldn't you bow when speaking to me?" I whispered.

Duncan's bright eyes flashed as he winked. "There will be time for that later, once we free your people and amend some wrongs."

I stood, dumbfounded, as Duncan drifted away from me, nudged Kayne on the shoulder and strode out in full view of our enemies. For a moment, I almost called for him to stop, forgetting that this was all part of the plan. *My* plan.

With the confidence of royalty or someone who simply believed he belonged somewhere, Duncan strode toward the murmuring guards, who soon noticed him. Highlighted by the backdrop of the burning slums of Lockinge, Duncan called out with a voice conditioned with command from years of being his prior deadly self.

General Duncan Rackley, the Hunter.

"Aren't you going to see what all the fuss is about?" Duncan's shout carried through the night, hardly muffled by the drawing of swords or the twang of bows being pulled taut. "Your city is burning, and you're standing around like you don't have a care in the world."

"Halt!" a Hunter shouted.

Duncan didn't stop.

Come on.

Althea gripped the back of my cloak to stop me from running out.

Where are you?

"Wait," Althea hissed into my ear. "Just wait."

"What was that?" Duncan shouted back at the Hunter. "Come a little closer and say it again. This time, put some effort and inject some confidence into your command... perhaps I might believe it."

"Another step, and you'll find yourself pierced with arrows like a turkey during yule."

"Where is she?" I asked Althea, finding words difficult as my heart thumped in my throat. Duncan was drawing their attention to him, but that was useless if our guest never showed.

"Seraphine will come," Althea replied. "Have faith in her promise. She has not let us down yet."

Faith. Such a strange concept. It did little but encourage hate and spill blood. I was certain there was a beautiful side to such a thing as faith, but I'd yet to find it.

I bit down on my lower lip, filling my mouth with the sharp taste of copper. It was the only thing stopping me from giving in to my anxiety and shattering.

"Now, now, I have only come to have a chat. Hunter to Hunter." Duncan was out of view, but his voice was ever more powerful. "How about it, a little heart to heart. Me, you and… my blade?"

"Hurry…" I said, my inner thoughts now controlling my words. Ice crackled across my closed fists, numbing my palms as my nails dug into them. An icy chill wind gathered from the dark street behind us and pushed at my back as though to urge me forward.

A whistle cut the night just as it had back in the Cage. I could have fallen to my knees as another returned the call, then another and another, until the sky was full of signals.

"NOW!" Althea cried, but I was already running.

Lucari squawked, unleashing her cry of war as she took flight alongside Kayne, who followed with blades raised, into the main parade.

I released the magic I held, called out in silent prayer to Altar for support and lead my allies to battle. All in time to witness the Children of the Asp reveal themselves among the crowds of unprepared Hunters. One by one, the assassins drew their blades, spilling the blood of our unexpecting enemies all across the streets of their oh-so-great capital.

CHAPTER 3

Conception of this plan started three nights ago, which so happened to be the last time I'd killed a Hunter.

Even as the one I held onto in the present time, skin turning to diamond glass before he could do so much as scream, I still felt the remnants of blood from my last victim across my hands. No matter how many times I scrubbed at them, the feeling of sickly warmth refused to leave.

After tonight, I would need to bathe in the ocean for an eternity to rid myself of the feeling death left in its wake.

Unlike the nameless Hunter, whose body shattered into thousands of star-like pieces across the courtyard before Lockinge Castle, the one I'd murdered those nights ago had a name. One I refused myself the peace to forget, even though the dirty pig deserved it.

Peter Torr. He was a stout human man with black hair thick with grease. When he ran his hand through it, his fingers looked wet. He bore the symbol of his master, the Hand, across his chest, wearing it with pride. His stained tunic had wrinkled when he sat down in the dirtied tavern in the Cage. I imagined Peter simply expected that the mark upon his tunic would've benefited him a night of free drinks and free sex with any of the tavern's patrons he so wished.

It was Seraphine who had provided insight into his whereabouts that night. And she had been right. Peter sat upon one of the rickety barstools, its legs screaming with protest at his unwanted weight. Big meaty hands slapped upon the bar as he demanded the attention of the young barmaid who pulled pints of ale for those who had the money to pay for them.

I sat and watched him in the darkened corner of the stale-smelling tavern, hood drawn over my head to hide the points of my ears from view. Before the Hunter had entered, I felt a thrill of being out in public after days holed up with Duncan, Althea and Kayne in the dwelling that had become much more a prison than a home. That bubble of excitement for being free popped the moment Peter barrelled in with his slurred yet demanding voice.

"Fill it all the way," he spat across the bar, making the young barmaid wince. From fear or disgust, I was at too much of a distance to be sure of which. I determined it was likely both. "Bet you're good at that, girl, aren't you? Getting filled up... and I can certainly do that for you."

I couldn't hear what she mumbled in reply. But I did witness the wash of red pass across her face, and how she moved quicker to give the Hunter what he wanted just so she could get away from him.

Peter drank and drank. The more time passed, the more I convinced myself just how easy this would be. I still couldn't touch a single drop of the amber-hued liquid in my tankard for fear I'd vomit or grow hazy, when all I needed to do was focus.

Seraphine, as I learned to trust, was right about a lot. Perhaps that was what being an Asp was, more so than hidden blades and sleight of hand. Information. Knowledge.

Four drinks. That was all Peter handled before he dug his cumbersome hand into the pocket of his trousers and produced the very thing I'd come here for.

Keys.

I found my lips turning upward as he did what Seraphine had warned he would do. Men. Predictable creatures. Not all, but most from what I learned.

From his pocket, with swollen hands, Peter pulled free the large metal hoop and upon it, three slim keys hung. I recognised them instantly from the night in the cage when Duncan had allowed Althea, Gyah and me to free ourselves of the iron collars that strangled our throats.

For the first time since ordering the ale, I gripped it and brought it to my lips. Over the lip-worn rim of the tankard, I couldn't take my eyes off them. Starving, I felt my desperate want for the keys constrict like a serpent deep in my stomach.

I needed them, and I'd do anything to get them in my hands.

Peter swung the keys around as though they were a trophy. A sign of dominance that he was a Hunter and everyone around him was lesser than. My heart gave a leap of hope that the surrounding humans viewed Peter with equal disgust. Then I remembered it was because of his state and persona and likely nothing to do with the fact he hunted, captured and killed fey for simply existing.

I itched to throw myself at him. Take the keys from his hand and leave. Or take his hand with them, for it would stop him from doing whatever he contemplated when he glanced toward the barmaid as she passed.

But I waited. Patiently, as I had every day since returning to Lockinge. My end goal was more important than rushing, and I had prepared far too long to waste this moment and ruin it.

Peter left the tavern after his sixth tankard of ale. His sloppy feet stumbled over one another as he moved onto the street. Like a shadow, I followed. He was singing when I stepped up behind him, close enough to taste the sweat that oozed from his hunched, round form. He awkwardly fumbled over his words. In his drunken state he could hardly pronounce the lyrics clearly. He would never have known I was there. Peter didn't stop his slurred song until my blade pressed to his throat. It was impossible to discern if he gargled from the shock of the dagger slipping across his neck or if that was an ale-induced hiccup.

Peter Torr bled out into the night, unable to sing or scream as I tore away the hoop of keys he held defiantly on to. His wide eyes had stayed open as gargling sounds erupted from the dark slice across his throat. Blood-slick hands grasped at the gash as though he could pinch it together to still the bleeding.

His efforts were wasted; the damage was done.

Peter watched me as I sauntered toward Duncan, who had lingered in the shadows of the tavern's back alley. I felt no remorse as I lifted my red-stained fingers to display the keys to him. There was no praise waiting for me in that alleyway. Not that I required any.

Now, three nights later, as I swiftly threw out my hands toward another Hunter who ran at me with his sword held high, I discovered the guilt. It had been hiding this entire time.

It had buried itself in my gut like a barbed knife. If I reached for it to pull it free, I would have suffered more pain and discomfort. So, instead, I pushed the guilt deeper and deeper with every life I took. But the weight of the keys in my breast pocket helped dampen the feeling, if only slightly.

It's for a greater cause, I reminded myself.

Wild, frigid wind conjured around me and burst forward with a gesture of a hand. It ripped across the ground, encouraging jagged shards of ice to race and burst up from the cobbled streets. The Hunter wasn't prepared as my ice devoured his feet and lower legs. It was so sudden his bones snapped through his skin as his momentum was ruined.

My attacker folded in on himself, dropping his sword, which skirted to a stop beneath my boot.

"You will only be remembered for being on the wrong side of history," I said, breath fogging beyond my lips. Then I blew out, forcing as much breath as I could muster to cover the Hunter's face until his skin hardened and lungs turned to shards of cold stone.

Two down, countless more to go.

Althea was a tempest of fire. Her flames hissed like snakes as they met the skin of those foolish enough to choose her as their victim. In contrast to the cold surrounding my body like a shield, I recognised Althea's power pressing against me with demanding force.

I winced against her heat, as bright as a dying star. A vortex of boiling flames that danced to her bidding. They took the Hunters and left them as husks of blistered skin and charred bone.

Althea truly was an unstoppable force. The wicked smile that glowed across her face told stories of just how desperate she had been to do this. Like a bird finally released from an iron cage, she was free to unleash her magic and send a message to those who opposed her.

My distraction in the raging inferno meant a Hunter got too close to me. A blast of air sliced the side of my face as she swept a blade down toward me. I side-stepped, gasping at the sudden presence. I slipped across the ice-slick ground and lost my footing. If I hadn't, the blade would have found itself buried in the soft skin where my neck met my shoulder.

Duncan must've heard my sharp intake of breath. Such a small sound beneath the thundering of death and chaos, but he heard it, because he was on me in seconds, parting from the darkness with his long sword swinging with precise aim.

Unlike the Hunter, Duncan didn't miss his target.

Her head tumbled from her shoulders, dark blood spurting skyward from severed veins. There was so much blood. It spilled and flowed as though Duncan had opened a river and let it flood across her corpse. She stood, animated, before crumpling to the ground where her body joined the others that had fallen to our attack.

"Did she hurt you?" he asked, jade eyes wide with terror. I felt them search every inch of me for a sign that the Hunter had touched me.

I shook my head, unable to form words, as Duncan's frantic worry mutated into a wild fury. My stomach jolted just watching him as his mind sped through the different circumstances in which those last moments could have ended.

"Good," Duncan exhaled, face pale. Then I noticed the droplets of blood that trailed down his face like rain. There was no knowing if it was his or that of the woman he had felled. "Stay together now. I don't want you straying too far from me again."

I raised my chin, ice crackling around my fingers and tracing my wrist like the bracelet that Duncan wore to keep his new power contained. "It was a moment of distraction. Not weakness. Let the bodies behind me be the proof that I do not need someone to fight for me."

"I fight for you because I care that you live, not because I don't think you are capable."

Another Hunter had appeared like a phantom beyond Duncan's shoulder. He had not noticed, succumbing to the same distraction that had almost cost me my life. Before the blood-covered dagger could plunge into his back, I threw myself into Duncan's unexpecting arms, shot my hand out over his shoulder and took the Hunter by the chin.

"He," I hissed through gritted teeth, "is mine."

Human skin turned grey beneath my fingers as I forced my freezing power across it. *Into* it. Soon enough, I could tighten my grip, and my fingers dug into glass-like skin. I tugged, and the lower part of the Hunter's face came away in my hand with little effort.

He stumbled back, eyes wide and bleeding red. Then he fell – dead.

"What were you saying about staying together?" I whispered into Duncan's ear before drawing back, half a face still in my hand. Each tooth fell away from the mass of frozen flesh. They pattered across the street like hail, thudding mutely across the blood-soaked cobbles.

"My point proven," Duncan replied. His torso stiffened beneath mine, which pressed into him. I revelled in the feeling, allowing myself only a moment of enjoyment during such an event.

Then we were apart. Without another word, we threw ourselves back into the fray of battle, this time not straying far from one another.

It was impossible to find Seraphine among the small but deadly crowd of Asps that had exposed themselves. The assassins were deep in the courtyard, focusing on the wall of Kingsmen that had taken the rear of the fight, whereas the Hunters were left to us to pick off one by one.

Lucari shrieked, blood dripping from her beak as she dove and sliced down upon the heads, faces and necks of the Hunters she could reach. I still knew little of the bond between a Tracker and their hawk, but Kayne had explained that the tips of the hawk's claws had been painted with liquid iron and left to dry. Its purpose, not that he needed to elaborate, was to weaken the fey the hawk found and to allow time for the Tracker and their group of Hunters to catch up with them.

There was something poetic about Lucari turning her sharp metal claws back onto the very humans she had once served.

Aldrick *had* to be far away from Lockinge for my plan to work. But I almost wished he could see us now. Tearing through his misled followers. When he heard of this, I hoped he felt the blow. If I focused too much on the death left in my wake, the kindling of guilt would've hindered me. Instead, I focused on the fey I was doing this for.

It was not long until every Hunter, who didn't have the sense to flee into the burning city, died. Breathless, I stepped over the corpse of a silver-clad Kingsman whose face had been shredded; by a knife or claws, I could not determine. Bile burned the back of my throat, but this was not the moment to show regret.

I had a group to lead. Then, in the dark of a room where no eyes were on me, I would grieve the lives lost – enemies or no, death was a hard thing to deal out.

"Is that all of them?" I muttered, unable to even comprehend the blood that flowed from the bodies into the grooves of the cobbled streets, where it ran like rivers between each stone.

"For now." Seraphine's cool voice set my nerves on edge as she peeled away from the wraith-like bodies that patrolled the dead, digging swords into hearts or necks just to make sure they had died. "There is over three times the number of Hunters we have just dealt with currently sleeping throughout the castle's corridors. We need to be long gone before the drug wears out of their systems. Before sunrise."

"And you are confident the dose is strong enough?" Althea asked, skin still sizzling from her expenditure of power.

"Princess," Seraphine began, eyeing Althea with well-earned caution. Her dark hair was tucked into the hood of her cloak, allowing only her eyes and bright features to be exposed to the night. If one were to illustrate an assassin without ever seeing one in the flesh, they would have painted a detailed portrait of the woman standing before us.

"'Althea' will do just fine, *assassin*," Althea replied, lips curling.

"The dose is strong enough to put the giants of old tales into the deepest of sleep. So, yes." Seraphine bowed her head slightly, not drawing her eyes away. "Althea."

"Then we move on to the next step," I added, desperate to keep going.

The assassin smirked. Her beady eyes traced me from face to foot and back again. "On your request, we move, my king."

I was her current employer, not her king. No matter how I had tried to express my desire for the Asps to work alongside me, not for me, Seraphine still treated me like her boss.

There would be a time I would truly express how uncomfortable that made me feel, but now was not it.

"Enough time has been wasted," I said, eyes drifting toward the gleaming gate that would lead us upward through the interconnecting courtyard and toward the entrance to the prison. "Kayne, send a signal to our ships. I need them aware of every failure and success until our very heartbeats are in sync."

The whistle Kayne conjured, as his teeth bit down on his lower lip, was no different to a nod in agreement. Lucari dropped from the sky, landing on the leather band around his forearm. Kayne replied, "See that you all make it out alive."

"Suddenly care for the fey's wellbeing?" Althea questioned.

My skin prickled in reaction to Althea's backhanded question.

"How about I please you with an answer when you return?" Kayne bowed, stiff and forced, but still a sign of respect.

Althea's head tipped in some form of acceptance.

I couldn't fathom that we had made it this far. I had hoped for success, but standing amid the dead with mere moments until we reached the prisoners, I could hardly contain myself. Part of me longed to release a cry of victory until every star could hear what I had done. My bones trembled with anxious energy which wouldn't calm until I unlocked every iron collar and saw every captive fey on the Cedarfall ships.

As if reading my nervous energy, Duncan reached out a hand and gripped my shoulder. "We are almost there, Robin. You've done incredibly so far."

We. Such a beautiful and frightening statement, but I was pleased to hear it. Either way, I needed them all. This would have been impossible without my unlikely band of allies. Each of whom looked at me expectedly amidst the sea of bodies.

I was a king, and it was time I faced the responsibilities that came with that title.

I didn't wear the Icethorn crown but I felt the burden of its weight upon me. A constant reminder which ensured each foot stepped ahead of the other. Deep in my mind, there was another face. I had thought of her every day. *Jesibel.*

Duncan, Kayne, Althea and even Seraphine knew of the fey woman I'd met within the prison. Her face represented all those captive. It was always at the forefront of my mind, as this plan had materialised out of a single idea.

Free them. Save them.

"In and out," I said to our group. My features hardened into a mask of determination. As I had before, I conjured an image of Jesibel in my mind, as if I included her behind the intention of my words. "Our people have been kept from their homes, their loved ones, for long enough. It's time we set them free. As they should be."

Althea bounced between one foot and the other. "It's prison break time."

"About *fucking* time as well," I exhaled, brows heavy with worry but lips quirking into a grin. "Remember, stick to the plan. And take as many Hunters down as you can."

CHAPTER 4

The huddle of human guards didn't have the chance to notice our arrival until it was too late. We dealt with them with ease – and by dealt with, I meant slaughtered. With every life taken, my skin itched with the guilt harbouring in my soul. Duncan took the lead down the remaining steps. Blades met flesh, and blood splattered violently across the sand-dusted ground. Their dead bodies were left stationed beyond the iron gate at the bottom of the steep, narrow steps. Although the Hunters didn't notice our swift arrival until our blades had already pierced their chests, the imprisoned fey saw everything. And yet not a single one gave us away until the job was done.

Deep in the underbelly of Lockinge, the Hunters wouldn't have heard the struggle that'd occurred far above. The prison felt like another realm entirely, hidden away beneath rock and stone. The world above could've been destroyed and the hundreds of captives in this place would never have known.

I surveyed the crowd of fey before me, eyes scanning frantically across every face. Even if I didn't wish to admit it, I already searched for Jesibel among them. I was thankful that Althea took charge, snatching a key from a slaughtered human and stabbing it frantically into the lock. She was careful to close it behind us. Until we spoke our piece, no one could leave. Everyone, for the success of our plan, had to be on the same page.

No warning could have prepared her for what waited beyond the gate she opened. Althea knew what lurked down in the pits of Lockinge, but the scowl she wore suggested she couldn't have imagined this. There were so many people. Perhaps even more than there had been when I'd last visited.

"Please, gather around and listen," Althea shouted as she swept into the prison, us following in tow. Her voice brimmed with command, but there was a soft undertone that couldn't be ignored. It had its desired effect. The fey closest to the gate parted, like water around a stone, as she made her way inside.

I sensed their desperation to flee now that the chance was there. I just needed them to hold off a little longer.

I watched from behind Althea as the expression on the fey's faces relaxed in recognition. Unlike when they looked at me, they saw Althea for what she was; the princess of the Cedarfall Court.

A cacophony of confused murmerings and shouts greeted us.

"We *are* here to free you," I called out, arms raised as if that could calm the crowd. Slowly, I watched the faces morph around me. Hope sparked behind tired, glazed eyes. "But to ensure each of you makes it out of this place alive, I'm going to need you to listen. For those who cannot hear, spread my message."

Althea stepped aside, turned her body, and gestured me forwards. As her attention shifted to mine, so did the multitude of captives. "King Robin Icethorn speaks to you, listen if you wish to survive."

That did it. Like a ripple across a lake, some order settled over the gathered crowd.

I swallowed the lump in my dried throat. There was an overwhelming urge to bring my fist to my lips so I could cough and clear it. I feared worse and expected I would give in to the violent crash of waves in my stomach and vomit from anxiety alone.

Althea had told them who I was, and now they looked at me expectantly. Pushing my discomfort to the attention aside, I lifted my chin and adorned the mask of the king they expected.

"We thought they'd killed you, Robin," one of the fey admitted. It was a man I recognised from my short stay. He pushed his way through the wall of bodies, to the annoyance of those around him.

The last time I'd seen him, he was gasping for breath after Jesi had sprung upon him, slapping his neck and breaking his nose all within a blink. His dark beard was as wild as before, and the shadows of a blue bruise still haunted his now crooked nose.

I stiffened as he approached. Duncan noticed and stepped close to my side, which had the fey male coming to a halt. Then he noticed Kayne, Lucari and, worst of all, Seraphine, who lingered at the back in hopes she would be forgotten.

"He's finally sent for us all, hasn't he. Is the Hand tired of keeping us down here? Has he come for his final tithe?"

"We have nothing to do with the Hand," I replied, watching as the stillness of the crowd slipped into disorder. "We come on behalf of Wychwood."

"The realm that chose to forget about us? What good are they to us?" he barked two questions in quick succession, spit flicking over his dried lips where it clung to his wiry beard. The man lifted a calloused finger and pointed to Seraphine, who hardly recoiled at the hate that contorted his face. "She always comes to collect us. The Twins only come when the Hand needs us."

I pinched my eyes closed, wincing at the reaction I imagined would cross Seraphine's face. Twins. Not anymore. Her sister had died all those nights ago. It was a topic that Seraphine had warned to be left alone. I only hoped, for our sake, she didn't react.

"Why not ask your prison guards why we are here?" Seraphine snarled. "Oh wait, they are dead, aren't they? Shame, perhaps they would have clarified that we are here to save you, you ungrateful–"

"Not," I said, making my word as sharp as a newly forged blade, "now."

"What do you want with us… *king*?" the man spat, still treating me as anything but the title he used. That word felt more like a curse. I couldn't blame his distaste for royalty when, collectively across the courts, they had done little to help him or the rest of the captured fey, who had been abducted, forgotten and killed over the years. I didn't have the time to tell them the truth – that Wychwood never knew of the Below's existence.

"Your name?" I asked, offering a steady hand. "How about we start there."

He contemplated my question, confusion sparking across his fatigued gaze. "Names are earned."

I nodded, almost expecting his reluctance. "Then let me do exactly that." My hand snaked into my breast pocket. The slim, crafted key that was a newly made copy of the one I'd pried from Peter Torr's dying hands met my fingers and slipped into my grasp. I pulled it free. His shoulders broadened as I stepped toward him, eyes locked on his freedom.

"What are you doing?"

"Earning your trust." I spoke as loud as I could muster, wishing that enough of the fey could hear me, and then spread my words throughout the crowd. "I made a promise to return and free you all. This is no place for the fey to be kept, and I wasn't willing to turn my back on you. I couldn't go on living my life pleading ignorance to what I found during my last visit."

Wide-eyed, the fey looked down the length of his swollen nose as I raised my steady hands towards the worn iron cuff at his neck. It took a moment to find the small hole which the key could enter. It'd been rusted over from years of being left. But I found it and with little force, the key fit inside, turning with ease.

It seemed the entire prison inhaled at the same time, including myself. I withdrew my hands and allowed the cuff to break apart. It fell to the ground in twin pieces with a satisfying thud.

He stood there, dumbfounded, with his eyes fixated on the iron that rocked to a stop by his boots. If he blinked, he would have released the tears that clung desperately to his lashes. When he finally looked back at me, his skin had paled. Even his voice was broken as he spoke through a dry, clogged throat.

"Michal," he said. "My name is Michal."

My chest filled with an abundance of gratitude. I allowed myself a moment to swell with the realisation that I had done it. I had followed through and freed a fey. One of hundreds, but it was a start.

"Michal, I'm going to need your help if we are all to get out of here. I have ships waiting for us all to board, ships that will take us away from Lockinge for good. But, for that, we must work together."

Michal seemed transfixed by his newly gained freedom, dirt-covered fingers raised to his neck. Disbelief crackled across his face as his fingers met the red-raw skin hidden behind the iron for countless years. "Tell me what you desire of me, and I shall do it."

I placed my hand on his shoulder, thankful for the strength of his form. With my spare hand, I presented the silver key to Michal. Hidden within the inside pocket of my jacket, I had a fistful of spares ready to hand out. If we had a chance of getting out of this place quickly, then our small group would need all the help we could get. It is why we had many copies of the keys cut, each ready to pass through the crowd when the moment was right.

"Help me free as many of these fey as you can," I said, leaning my face toward his. The relief which filled me was so honest that it made my limbs shake. "Don't stop until every person within this prison feels the same elation as you. Can you do that for me?"

Michal nodded, breath hitching as the silver passed into his hand. "It would be my honour."

The crowd buzzed with uncontrolled energy at what they had witnessed. I already heard the whispers spread like wildfire throughout the chasm of prisoners. Those closest to Michal begged him to free them first, swallowing him entirely into the throng of bodies until I could barely hear him over their pleas.

I gathered steel inside my lungs as I took a gathering breath before throwing out my shout across the cavern for all to hear. "Once the iron is removed from your necks, please gather yourselves by the gate. I know you wish to leave, but you must wait until we are all ready. There is no knowing what waits for us when we depart, so it is best we do so together. We are broken when separated but unstoppable as one."

Out of the corner of my eye, I caught Duncan looking at me. I felt his stare before I saw it. Like phantom fingers, his eyes trailed me from foot to head. His prideful grin echoed in the glistening damp that clung to his dark eyes. My heart skipped a beat, and I packed that image of him away into the back of my mind. It was a vision I wished never to forget.

Time was inconsequential within the cavern beneath Lockinge. It should have mattered, but it didn't follow rules. There was no telling how long it took to work ourselves through the crowd. Althea, Duncan and I pushed ourselves deeper into the crowd, my hands aching as I gripped the key, moving it from one iron cuff to another. It took no time at all for the pocket of spare keys to empty as others like Michal joined our effort.

There were tears. Shouts of glee. Some fey fell to their knees, and others displayed flashes of unlocked magic. I thought I heard the roaring of a beast, followed by the blur of deep, russet fur passing among the crowd. Looking through the moving swell of bodies, I was confident I'd seen a bear. Powerful, thick limbs pounded atop the ground, which quaked beneath their force.

It was a shifter. A fey with the ability to transform into its animalistic form. The clamour shook the dust from the cavern's walls.

Althea noticed it, too, tears glistening like jewels across her hazel eyes. Pride swelled in every line and crease across her face as she moved her key from neck to neck until the ground was littered with broken castings of iron.

I risked a look toward the gate of the prison. Kayne and Seraphine controlled the crowd, which boiled with the desire to escape this place. They had been forced up a few steps beyond the gate but did well to handle the crowd.

An undeniable panic ate away at my nerves. I half expected a surge of Hunters to flood down from the ground far above and into the prison to stop us. Every passing moment that they didn't arrive did nothing to calm me. It only prolonged the impending doom of what could happen and urged me to work harder, faster, as I moved deeper into the cave.

My mind was a storm. Destructive and powerful, unable to focus on a single person as faces blurred before me. With every person I worked to free, another was at the forefront of my mind. A name slick across my lips.

Jesibel.

I searched for her. Looking to Duncan and Althea to see if they were the ones to find her and take the iron from her neck. They both knew of her. She had been pivotal to my brief stay in the prison. Her name is embedded into the story of my visit and the connection with Elinor.

I knew I wouldn't have survived without her intervention all those weeks ago. And every day since, her face had been embedded in my mind like a knife in the flesh of an enemy. Obsidian eyes and midnight hair, Jesi represented the Icethorn Court and everyone who had been exposed to this treatment after my mother and her family had been killed by Doran's gryvern. I was doing this for her and every soul that had been affected by the chaos of the realms.

Yet I could not find her.

If I added that concern to my shoulders, I would have crumpled before unlocking the final cuff. I had to have faith that she had been freed by Althea or Duncan and that we would be reunited once we left Lockinge far behind us.

Relief had yet to settle. I expected to meet resistance. Not that I hoped for the worst, but everything had gone too close to plan. It unnerved me. I massaged at my lower stomach, turning to work out the knot that had settled within it. Duncan stood like a statue of stone at my side with his hand on my lower back. Even with the material separating his touch from my skin, I still recognised the slow, circular motion his thumb made.

"I am so proud of you," Duncan whispered to me. I tried to allow his words to fill me with some sense of clarity, but they did not. "It would have been easier to turn your back on these people and place your hope for their rescue in others. I admire the choices you have made."

"Don't speak so soon," I replied. Michal was close to my side, helping the older fey and making it his sole purpose to make sure no one was left bound. I nodded at him, face stoic, as he passed. "Until every single one of them has boarded our ships, I will not mark this as a success."

Duncan's hand lifted from my back. The lack of his touch had me turning to look at him, which was exactly what he wished for. He took my chin between his thumb and forefinger, lifting my face to look at him. The prison was engulfed in chaos. I heard some commotion toward the gate, but hoped Seraphine was keeping order.

We were so close to success.

Duncan lowered his face towards mine, cool breath brushing across my skin as his lips closed in on me. I exhaled, expecting to feel the brush of his feather-soft mouth upon mine. But the feeling did not come. I opened my eyes to look deep into his. The green was so vivid this close that I could have felt as though I was lost in a forest with no way out.

Not that I would have ever wished to escape his entrapment.

"Take a moment and allow yourself to truly understand what you have just accomplished."

"We," I muttered, gaze flickering between his mouth and his narrowing eyes. "Nothing about this has been solely my doing. Without you, Althea, Seraphine and even Kayne... well, I would have failed before even beginning."

"There is something endearing about your inability to see what you are capable of, Robin, but one day you are going to learn to reflect on your actions and recognise the effect they have on others."

I lifted onto my toes, reaching a hand up to the back of Duncan's head. My fingers coiled through his thick chestnut hair; my nails traced dangerously across his scalp. I felt Duncan melt into a bundle of pleasured shivers.

"Do me a favour and tell me this all again when we reach... home," I said, staring deep into his soul.

"Is that what you are calling it now?" Duncan tilted his head, allowing my hand to bring him closer to me to close the small gap that was left between us.

As my lips pressed into his, I replied, "Maybe."

The kiss was brief but deep and passionate. I allowed myself a moment to forget the world around me and focus only on the man in my hold. Duncan, who had turned his back on the indoctrination that he had been subjected to, fell willingly into my hands. We had found each other during a time when neither of us was looking. I would never let go of him, even if there was another name that still lingered at the back of my mind.

No. Don't. I pushed the thoughts back, keeping them away like wolves from a burning torch. *Not him.*

"Are you ready to see this through?" Duncan asked, pulling away. My hands tickled across the short hairs that shadowed his jaw until he fell completely from my touch.

The corner of my lip turned upward as we both looked toward the stairwell. My stomach jolted as the darkness beckoned me forward. Far above, the fey would soon file out into the courtyard littered with the slain bodies of Hunters and Kingsmen. How would they react when they looked up to see the sky and the stars and feel the kiss of freedom as the night wind enveloped them in its embrace?

I looked back to Duncan, feeling the swell in my chest and allowing it to steal away my anxiety, if only for a moment.

"Stop!" a high-pitched scream sounded, and I swore my blood turned to ice. I spun around to face the sound, only to see the crowd swell like a tidal wave, right in the direction of the gate.

A crack followed, then the Below silenced. The peace lasted only a moment before fey, mere moments before we'd be ready to lead them to freedom, surged at the gate. Magic cracked the air, splitting it in two. And all I could do was watch as the fey broke through Seraphine's one-woman guard and ran away from me, directly toward impending danger.

CHAPTER 5

The dawn sky fought through thick clouds of smoke which did their best to block out the rising sun. It left the world awash with the brush of dark russet. Beyond the impenetrable clouds of ash, the dawn fought hard for its rightful place. Although the hue of deep orange and red replaced the usual blues, it still allowed some light in to know that we had spent far longer than expected in the deep caverns of Lockinge's prison.

It was the perfect backdrop for my crumbling plan. All my hard work literally running away from me, and there was nothing I could do to stop it.

The muscles in my legs screamed as I ran out of the Below, lungs aching, back bowing as though I carried the weight of the world on it. And in a sense, I did. Because my world, everything about my life over the past three weeks had led to this moment.

I should've known they wouldn't listen to me, but gods know I wasn't going to give up now.

It was clear the moment Duncan and I escaped the staircase and flooded out into the chaos beyond that ruled the human city.

The courtyard before the rise of Lockinge Castle bustled with fey gripped in the throes of panic. I pushed through the swell of the crowd, suddenly aware of the stench that poured from the bodies of the captured fey as the winds whipped among the crowd. The smell of stone and musk did well to combat the heavy presence of burning wood and charred stone that wafted up the incline from the slums. The Cage still burned, hot and violent.

It was impossible to understand where I was when the majority of the bodies around me towered far taller than I. But Althea's booming voice acted as my guide. The harder I worked through the squashed bodies, the louder her shouts became.

"Stop!" Althea roared. "It is not safe for you out there."

I saw her the moment I broke free from the wall of fey. Her skin was pale, her eyes wide as concern practically poured from her. She did not shout at the crowd that I had fought my way through but toward the outlines of figures that broke away from it, and ran toward the city instead of away from it.

"We need to stop them," I said, stumbling toward her, my heart lodging in my throat. I dared not blink and miss the fey running away from me, toward danger I couldn't save them from.

Althea raised her hands and placed them at the back of her head. "There was nothing I could do."

"How many?" I asked, breathless.

"I don't know, Robin, they just ran. There was no stopping them."

There was a part of me that longed to remind her she was wrong. She could have, in fact, stopped them. My mind raced with ideas of how her power could have conjured a wall of flame and kept the fey penned within the courtyard.

But what difference would that be to the prison they'd just been in.

I gave them freedom, but expected that to come with them handing their free will to me.

From one captor to another. Aldrick's voice taunted across my mind. Since his power had invaded me, he'd occupied my thoughts countless times, even if it was only the memory of him rather than his amplified, controlling presence. I knew it was not actually him this time, but more a figment of his presence that lingered on my consciousness like a demon upon my shoulder, whispering into my ear.

In fact, it was Kayne's voice that tore me from my destructive thoughts. Looking sidelong at the wall of the fey, Kayne had gripped one by the forearm as though to stop her. "You've been told to follow orders. Heed them or–"

"Enough," I snapped, grappling with the understanding that I was failing.

The young woman in Kayne's grasp fought hard to get free so she, like the others who tried to break away from the remaining crowd, could flee into the city in hopes of freedom.

Kayne saw the powered fist fly toward his face a moment too late. As he gripped for his nose, catching the burst of red gore in his hands, the fey woman escaped and ran for the raised gate, following the small group that fled.

Time seemed to slow as I made my decision deep within my subconscious. I followed the woman as she ran for her freedom. A shiver of cold passed across my arms. My breath thickened into a silver cloud beyond my parted lips as I moved my eyes ahead of the woman and toward the open gate.

Althea made it two steps forward, hoping to catch the fearful woman before I opened the floodgates to my magic and let it free.

Duncan called my name from somewhere close, but it was faint enough that I could ignore it. All I could focus on was the fey now steps from leaving the courtyard to join the others who had fled, not from danger, but into it.

I dropped to my knees and slapped my palms across the street. The moment my fingers touched the stone, my power left me with a raging hunger.

I closed my eyes as euphoria filled me. In the dark, I saw an image. The bloodied bed of grass around the axe-scored stump of a tree. Another image came next of the spreading ice as it crawled up the legs of the executioner, turning skin to glass and blood to rivers of frozen diamonds.

When my gaze flew open, I could hear the body of the executioner as it snapped in half and crumpled before me. This moment was very similar to the time my magic first revealed itself in the field full of fey captives and Hunters who longed for fey deaths. I wasn't in control of my emotions or power then. Now, I commanded both as the rightful king I'd been forced to become.

Ice spread across the courtyard. It cracked across the stone, turning the ground white as it swept toward the gateway. The fey cried out as my power burst before her. It took effort to encourage it to flow around her whilst focusing on my end goal. The gate.

As my icy presence reached it, I threw my hands upward. I conjured a wall of pure, diamond-cut ice to fill the gateway until the city beyond could no longer be seen. Curls of mist danced across the view before me. Tendrils of frozen air stung pleasantly across my skin as I admired my creation.

You and I are no different.

"Yes, we are," I hissed aloud in response to my inner thoughts. "I do this to save them, not enslave them."

"That's enough, Robin. Keeping them trapped hardly sets the example of freedom that our effort has been focused on," Althea said beside me, her innate flame working to melt the ice closest to her feet. "There have to be other ways, Robin."

"No," I said, glancing only for a moment toward her. "For the safety of everyone, I cannot let them run into a city full of people that hate them. I've done what I had to do."

I could see from the pinching of Althea's mouth that she had more to say but kept it to herself. But the sharp glint in her eye also revealed that she would tell me, eventually.

Facing back toward the crowd, I looked over the wall of dirt-smeared fey as they, too, regarded me with an expression I had yet to see on them.

Trepidation.

"The city is full of people who would see you nailed on pikes for the birds to feed off your flesh. I cannot allow you to wander blindly into your enemy's arms. They'd treat you in far more hateful ways than the imprisonment you have experienced thus far. The freedom you seek is close, but we must act as one to see this through." I gave myself a moment to catch my breath, taking in the band of fey that had stuck with me. "Please, to those who still think running now is the best option, I beg you to listen. Know I don't wish to stop you from finding your freedom, but I simply wish to ensure you do so in a way that sees you survive long enough that Lockinge becomes nothing more than a terrible memory."

I waited for some reaction. All I could hear was the thundering beat of my heart in my ears. Urgency propelled me forward, looking toward Seraphine and the figures of her fellow Asps as they had wormed their way around the crowds to prepare for the last hurdle.

"Freedom *is* close," I repeated, hoping those at the back of the crowd would hear me once my words spread through it. "I promise."

"I'm sorry, Robin. They fought through me," Seraphine said as she came to stand beside me.

"You did everything you could," I replied, thankful for her help.

"I have instructed a small group of Asps to go searching for any strays. Forgive the fey for taking a chance to run, something we cannot blame them for. They've spent so many years down there, contemplating this day."

"I just don't want to fail them," I admitted.

"You haven't. It's not over yet." Seraphine shifted her gaze and whistled. The high-pitched sound cut through the murmuring crowd and stilled them into a state of momentary silence. More Asps began calling out with simple instructions and guidance about what was to happen next.

I stepped back and allowed the assassins to sink their claws of control into the fey and gather them in an orderly fashion that would see us toward the shoreline at the back of Lockinge Castle. To the boats that should stand by, ready to collect us and take us all home.

"You can't worry about everyone," Duncan said. I'd not heard him join us until his hand was upon my shoulder and his voice warming my soul from the outside in. "There comes a time you must accept that responsibility is something fragile."

"Whilst I accept the Icethorn crown, I can't accept that."

"I just don't want to watch it wear you down." The determination that crackled across his face had that effect on me. What had I done to deserve his loyalty after everything my presence had done to him?

I winked at him, feigning a confidence that was becoming second nature to me. "I like when you worry about me."

"Shall we turn the tables? I could go and help Seraphine's Asps in the city and see how you like it."

"I trust you don't need me to tell you how foolish you would be to approve that," Althea added, cheeks flushed as she interjected her opinion.

I nodded softly in agreement with her. "Duncan, you stay with me. I cannot save people if they don't wish to be saved."

"Then I wish them luck." He offered me a sympathetic smile, then lifted a gaze toward the expanse of fey the assassins had begun shepherding toward the direction of the castle's docks.

"They'll need more than luck," Kayne offered, still clutching at his nose. I could tell from the shadow behind his gaze that he meant every word with little sincerity. Already the freckles beneath his eyes seemed to disappear beneath the darkening bruise the fey woman had gifted him. Blood spread between his fingers, some even smudged across his chin.

"You know, mate, you should really get that looked at," Duncan said, knocking his friend with a bump on his shoulder.

"Fuck *you*," Kayne replied, searching the skies for Lucari, who would have squawked with shared anguish at his broken nose.

* * *

We made it around the castle without another issue to deal with. My mind, although still locked on the group of fey who left us, was thankful that those who stayed were not under threat. There were no Hunters who came out to stop us. The presence of Kingsmen was also non-existent. The further we made it toward the rear of the castle, the more dread settled within me. Amplified by Althea, who seemed to pluck the worry from my mind and speak it into existence.

"This should not be so easy," she said, keeping her voice low to prevent the fey from hearing her concern. "It doesn't seem right."

"Thank Altar it is," I replied, trying to force confidence into my tone whilst clinging onto the presence of my magic in case the moment required it.

"Admit it, something is not right about it," she continued. "The castle is *too* quiet. We have met no resistance when there have been many opportunities for it. I can't help but feel that Aldrick wants this to happen. He practically opened the door and allowed us in. He may as well have offered us a warm meal and a soft bed to sleep on."

I didn't wish to agree out loud for fear that what she spoke was true. Instead, I kept my gaze fixed on the mass of fey that thundered through a corridor deep within the castle. As Seraphine had previously confirmed, we passed heaps of humans who looked as though they slept on the floors, others in a deeper slumber with throats sliced and bodies covered in blood.

But where was everyone else? Where was the human king, who had become a puppet for Aldrick? He'd not been previously confirmed as another number of the dead in the days that followed our initial escape. What about the servants who should have filled a castle? Perhaps they were hiding within many of the rooms, or they had run when the first signs of our ambush had occurred. It could not have been the latter as the Asps hadn't seen anyone flee the castle when we'd been deep in the prison beneath. And the castle, as Althea had said, was far too quiet to suggest that anyone was within it at all.

Burying the dark thoughts deep in the pit of my being, I focused on keeping one step ahead of the other. We were so close to the promised freedom, the plan almost over. Focus was important to seeing it through to the end. Not looking back, but forwards.

"We cannot afford to contemplate failure," I said, pinching my nails into the skin of my palms. It was the only thing to keep them from shaking. "It's not an option. I won't allow it."

"Tell me that again when we are safely aboard our ships. I wish to never look back at this place again," Althea replied. "I'm ready for a proper bed, a nice meal and something to wear other than fighting leathers."

"I get the impression you still don't forgive me for refusing to return to Wychwood."

"It would have been a lot easier than this." Althea glanced my way, lips pulled into a thin line as she contemplated her next words. "But not nearly as thrilling. This will forever be the bravest thing I've known someone to do. I admire your decision, Robin. I only wish it never had to happen. All these years and the courts… we continued on, complacent with the shared belief that they'd all died. We failed them, over and over. *No more.*"

I raised a hand and placed it above the scar on my chest, the very one Althea had burned upon me after Tarron drove a blade of light through me. It felt like it happened so long ago. Far beneath the leather material, I recognised the scar, wearing it like a badge of honour. In a sense it was the day I died and was reborn into this new version of myself. "So much has changed in such little time. I'm scared to blink for fear of what else will happen."

Althea focused her gaze forward to the glow of light that signalled the exit that we moved toward. She didn't recognise this corridor like I did. Althea hadn't been with us as we escaped Aldrick. After Seraphine had buried him beneath the haunting mirror that'd shown a glimpse of the demonic presence which caused all of this. Duwar. The demon.

Talking with Althea did little to keep the dread that had lodged itself in my heart from piercing it completely. The scorned monster and its threat to both realms always lingered at the back of my mind.

It's that terrifying vision we witnessed that made looking in mirrors hard for me since then.

I wasn't a fool. I knew that when we finally left Lockinge upon the ships that waited for us just beyond that door, it wouldn't be peace we faced. The threat of Aldrick and his promise to bring forth the demon god into this world was genuine. Our next issue to deal with. Tonight was merely one step closer to solving the actual devil at hand.

"We must keep our focus on the horizon," Althea said softly. "One step at a time, and we will one day reach it."

I exhaled, feeling the pressure in my lungs fade. Duncan walked ahead of me, aiding an elderly fey woman by taking hold of her arm and offering her support.

He was my horizon.

As if sensing my attention, he glanced over his shoulder and smiled. Duncan kept me going, at least, one step at a time. As long as he was close, I had the energy to keep playing this part of king until it benefited those around me.

I returned his smile with one of my own. But the moment was severed when a hollow bang sounded far beyond the castle's walls outside the doors. Right toward the rear of the castle where the Cedarfall ships waited for us.

The crowd ahead came to a collective stop suddenly. My breathing hitched as though talons wrapped around my throat and squeezed. The shuffling of feet faded into silence as the thunderous song of my impending doom chorused in my mind.

There was another bang, this time louder, like the splintering of wood. And then I was running. My mind focused on the blue expanse that raced toward me. There was a ground-shaking boom followed by the splinter of wood as it exploded beneath the force.

I knew, deep down, before I burst out into the world beyond and looked at the ocean, that our ships were under siege.

But what I didn't expect to see was an armada of monstrous vessels cutting across the ocean toward the line of Cedarfall ships. Nor did I think it possible when I saw the white-winged figures filling the skies with hands full of gleaming weapons of gold splendour.

CHAPTER 6

Grand ships of perfectly carved timber were scattered across the ocean's disturbed surface. From my position, they looked like wooden toys floating in a tub of water, ready for a large hand to descend from the sky and move them.

I settled on a ship closest to the shore, vessels of russet-stained wood formed a walled barrier. Atop masts, Cedarfall banners trembled in the winds that whipped across the ocean.

I tasted the bitter salt across my dried lips, mixed with the harsh smoke that billowed from the ship's port side.

I should've felt a swell of relief at seeing the fey ships. Instead, heat coursed through my chest. Bile crept up my throat. I watched as the wall of far larger, far grander ships cut across the dark, foam-tipped waves toward the shallow waters.

Toward the fey ships.

I lifted a hand and covered my eyes. Squinting, I focused on the ivory sails, which billowed in the winds. Across the cream material was a symbol I recognised with sickening clarity. Not even its violent rippling could hide the mark of black stitching.

The wheel of the Creator. The same symbol I'd seen nailed above Abbott Nathanial's church. I distinguished its two inter-crossing lines, which overlapped the circular symbol and pointed east, south and west. The northern line tipped like an arrow and pointed skyward to the Creator's heavenly domain.

But that wasn't the only similarity to Nathanial's church. Because the creatures flying through the sky looked exactly like the depiction of the angel on his stain glass window.

"We're under attack," Althea gasped, eyes snapping from creature to creature.

She was right. I froze, not from horror, but the need to calculate my next steps carefully. Dragging my gaze from the wafting sails to the winged figures, I was transfixed as they swooped through the clouds as though the sky had birthed them.

They dove with grace. Like birds, they folded their feathered limbs and dove toward the ocean in a spear-like formation. Except the creatures didn't disappear beneath the surface of harsh waters. They cast their great wings out, catching them mid-fall, skipping across the ocean's surface like stones, directly toward the Cedarfall ships. The dull dawn light caught on blades. They glittered in their hands as though forged from light itself.

I heard them the closer they came. Their haunting cry of war carried across the winds like a siren song.

"What are they?" Kayne asked the question on everyone's minds, breathless at my side. Lucari flared her wings upon his shoulder but didn't dare become airborne. I didn't share the same connection Kayne had, but I sensed her fear as sour as my own.

"Gryvern?" Duncan questioned, equally taken aback by what we witnessed.

"No," I replied confidently. "Those are not gryvern."

I narrowed my eyes, trying to discern details which would help me give them answers. My mind was numb. All I could do was watch helplessly as the creatures speared toward the fey. Angels, that was what Nathanial had said he'd seen. Spoken to. I put it down to a senile mind, but now I wasn't so sure he was ever misled.

Seraphine was suddenly at my side, peeling from the swell of freed prisoners who waited, audibly panicked, by the display they too witnessed. "Well, looks like we have a change of plan.

Robin, we cannot risk the lives of those fey by taking them out of the castle to this, not until we know what we are facing."

Her words settled over me like cold rain, hissing off the anger boiling across my skin.

"Any insight you can offer?" I asked her, master of knowledge and secrets.

She shook her head, black hair cascading over panicked eyes. "I have no idea."

I believed her, and that only made this more horrifying.

"What's our next move, King?" Seraphine asked.

I gasped at the question, not yet sure. "We follow through with making sure we get these fey away from Lockinge."

"Our only chance of leaving Lockinge is moments from sinking to the bottom of the ocean. Look!" Seraphine pointed outward, turning my attention to something I'd already noticed. One of the Cedarfall ships lifted at an awkward angle as though a monstrous creature dragged it down into the deep. Whatever had caused the ship to sink had torn a mass of wood from its hull, leaving a gaping hole for water to gush into.

As though our attackers waited for our full attention, an explosive bang echoed across the waters. I snapped my head at the sound. A blur of black metal shot across the seas with furious speed. There was nothing I could do but watch as it shattered through the side of another Cedarfall ship.

In the distance, fey soldiers threw themselves into the depths as their ship broke apart in a storm of wood and flame.

"We have to stop this." My command burst out of me. A violent shiver took over my body as I witnessed bodies disappear beneath waves among the carnage. Our saviours had sailed all the way around the continent on my order. But, once again, I had led them to their deaths.

"Robin," Althea snapped, ferocity matching that which stormed inside of me. "Those are my people. Our people. I'm with you. We cannot turn our backs on them, letting whatever those are attack them the moment they're free. We've got to do something."

My jaw ached as I ground my teeth together. "We will do something. Together."

A plan formed in my mind. It was rushed. Given the chance, I would have likely discovered multiple problems with it. But I didn't have a moment to think when unknown creatures bearing the symbol of the Creator attacked us.

Duncan was already looking at me as though he sensed where my thoughts had gone. Deep lines furrowed across his brow as the winds whipped his length of dark hair from his face. The scar on his cheek created a devastating shadow from his eye to his lip, which curled into a sneer.

"Seraphine, keep the fey safe inside the castle until we have dealt with those opposing us," I said, voice firm as more pieces of the plan slotted together.

"On it," she said, before running off, spreading that command through the small army of her Asps.

"I know that look," Duncan said, frown pinching harsher, eyes never leaving me.

"Those *things* in the sky. I need you to bring them all down." My command was vague but clear to Duncan. His eyes softened, and cheeks flushed. Then Duncan followed my touch and glanced down at his wrist.

I held it in my hand. My thumb dusted across the thin iron bracelet that reminded me painfully of the one and only item I had been given by my mother.

"Robin. I – I don't think I can do it."

My fingers gripped tighter as I urged him to look back up at me. He needed to see the desperation in my eyes so that my plea made its way into his soul.

"You heard Seraphine, those ships are our only chance at leaving. The more we hesitate, the more will sink. We must stop this before any more are destroyed."

"Fighting Hunters and Kingsmen is one thing, but going against winged warriors is another," Kayne said, always the first to point out the flaws.

"Enemies," I reminded. "We planned to face enemies, and that is what clearly waited for us outside. The plan has simply changed."

"Kayne is right, Robin. There is no saying what we are up against," Duncan replied, chest heaving with each breath. He fumbled as he spoke. His hesitation poisoned every word that passed between his lips. "It is one thing trying to save the fey, but what if I hurt someone? I can't control this… power."

"I need you to try, for me, if not for them." I gestured to those around us. "Do it because I asked. You asked if I trusted you, and I do, Duncan. For the sake of everything we have put ourselves through these past weeks, please."

Sorrow creased Duncan's expression. He closed his eyes for a moment, stilling as though he hardly needed to breathe.

"Tell me you will try." I couldn't conceal my creeping panic as I spoke to him.

When Duncan finally replied, it wasn't with the resistance I expected. "You could ask me to jump from this very spot, and I would do it. How could I ever refuse you, Robin?"

It was more a statement than a question. I was his weakness, as much as he was mine.

"Thank you," I exhaled, not wanting to blink to miss the storm in his dark eyes.

Duncan sighed through a weak smile, one that never reached his eyes. He pressed a kiss on the crown of my head, holding it there for a paused moment.

I thought the spark I felt was simply from the shock of his touch. But as he pulled away, his eyes glowed a molten blue. His wrist was naked of the iron bracelet. I knew the spark was from something else entirely – magic.

The iron bracelet fell from his clutch, allowing the electrifying strands of his new power to coat his skin like snakes of bitter, fiery light.

"Go," he whispered, urging me away from his body, which ignited and crackled with snakes of purple light. "Run!"

Leaving him was the hardest thing I'd done, and yet it was my only option. I didn't stop moving, Althea alongside me, until I stood before the stretch of dark waters far beneath the castle.

Wild wind whipped at my black hair, obscuring my view of the battle across the ocean. Above me, ominous clouds flooded the sky at an unnatural speed. Thunder rumbled in warning, roaring as though a creature of nightmares hid among the clouds, waiting to burst through and devour the world.

Looking back up toward Lockinge Castle, I could see the heart of the phenomenon. Upon the worn stone wall of the balcony stood Duncan, with his hands raised to the sky, like a child willing their parent to pick them up. The bolts of blue-purple light that burst from his hands suggested something darker.

Duncan's mutation, a result of the concoction of fey blood Aldrick had inserted into his heart, had cursed him with powers that should never have been possible. He called for the wild storm to close over the world. He enveloped the world in shadows, only illuminated by sudden tongues of forked lightning. Duncan seemed limitless.

"It is working," Althea shouted above the storm. It took a strong will to look at her. Back straight, chin raised in defiance. The Cedarfall heir watched the horizon with boiling intent. One might've wondered if she was in control of the storm that brewed ahead of us from the look in her eyes alone.

I could see *exactly* what she meant. The white-winged creatures scattered across the skies as the bolts of lightning whipped down upon them. Duncan's lightning was chaotic, clashing into the ocean without prejudice.

Since our escape from Aldrick, Duncan had been adamant to keep his power buried by the iron bracelet. He told me he didn't want it – admitted his fear of it. But I knew he was wrong. He simply didn't trust it. Yet.

Duncan was uncontrolled and fuelled purely on desperate instinct – but his intention was exactly where it needed to be. And for that, I was thankful.

Although he looked like a god, calling down streaks of light from the skies as though they were his strings, and he was the puppet master of the storm, he'd reach his limit soon.

That was when Althea and I would act.

I bit down on my lip until I tasted blood. Although unpleasant, the distraction stopped me from looking back at Duncan.

"If this doesn't work, we risk everything," Althea reminded me, rolling the dark sleeves of her form-fitting tunic up to her elbows. Freckle-covered arms now exposed, she shook them as though stretching them out in preparation.

"And we lose everything if we don't take the risk," I replied, my heart jolting at the sight of the strange, winged creatures dodging with poise and ease through the lightning strikes. There was something familiar about them. I couldn't focus on one long enough to claim answers, for they swooped and dived, flying with a speed that made them blur into figments of ivory and gold. "I refuse to fail after everything we have done. For our sakes and theirs."

I thought back to the freed fey who waited in the castle. Kayne, Seraphine and her small army of Asps would have their work cut out for them, trying to keep some sense of calm among the crowd when a war quite literally raged outside of the castle's protective walls.

Suddenly the human city was now the safest place for them to be.

Confident pleasure sparkled in Althea's gaze as she locked her eyes with mine. She nodded first. I replied with a curt tip of my head. "Then let's not let them down," Althea said, rolling back her shoulders. "Ready?"

I took a step toward the water that rushed back and forth upon the shore. Foam and seaweed tumbled over with the tide.

"Set fire to the sky," I said, facing out at the waters toward the pandemonium. Duncan's power had separated the fight but had not stopped it entirely. That was our task.

"Oh, how I have wanted to hear those words."

Heat exploded behind me, but I was already running from it. I didn't need to look back to know that Althea had released her power completely, just as Duncan had.

And now it was my turn.

The shallow waters turned to solid ice beneath my feet. It was as though winter seeped from my body with no thought or physical action. My power devoured the ocean surface willingly, flooding across the dark blue until it glistened like diamonds. There was no room for hesitation as my boots met the layer of ice.

This was not just magic, it was the power of Icethorn – a gift of being its king.

I didn't stop running. There was only the single thought of keeping one foot in front of the other and the desperate need to ensure no more ships fell to this siege.

My feet slipped as I chased the spreading of my ice out into the ocean. Stiff wind lapped at my cheeks, causing tears to roll down my face, only to catch in frozen droplets before they reached my jaw.

The closer I was, the clearer I saw the creatures. Two arms, two legs. A body no different from mine – despite the magnificent feathered wings bursting from their backs.

Humans. They had to be human or at least something similar. Not like the gryvern, with their monstrous forms and leathered wings. And, like the sails marked with the symbol of the Creator, they also displayed the same mark upon the drapes of ivory material across their chests instead of plates of armour.

Althea continued throwing flames into the skies, lifting them higher and higher until they billowed far past Lockinge castle's tallest tower, scorching the clouds in thick plumes of smoke. My feet stumbled beneath me as I glanced back at her. From a distance, she looked more like a bird from stories old, thrusting wings of fire across the world until she burned it entirely.

Althea's display of power encouraged my own. I felt in competition, expelling the winter I housed within me and freeing it across the world.

My forced confidence didn't last long.

Slicing downward from the sky before me was a woman of ethereal power. Black skin glowed in contrast to her dove-grey wings. She moved with such speed that her outline became unclear. Until she stopped, throwing out her impressive span of feathered limbs to catch her downfall. Braids billowed around her frame like coiled strands of shadow. In her hands, she held a hammer of sorts crafted from gold. This close, I could see its surface swirled with decorative symbols. It took both hands for her to hold it, her muscles bulging with restraint.

"Halt this madness," she bellowed, hovering before me, feet barely above my floor of ice. I drank in the vision of her. She wore a garment that would have been well suited for a place within a church. Similar to Abbott Nathanial's shawl, except hers was cut to fit her body for not only the purpose of prayer but battle too.

"A madness it would seem you have caused," I spat.

She regarded me, golden eyes drinking in my body. "Never did we expect to find the fey allied with the Defiler. Is this what has become of the world since we left it in your capable hands?"

Her words didn't make sense, not as I was enthralled with the way her hands twisted around the leather-bound handle of her weapon. I felt her intent to use it upon me just as I felt the breeze her wings created.

"I don't know what you are talking about, but if you wish to save your… warriors, I suggest you stop this attack."

It was as if she didn't hear me, or at least didn't care for my threat.

"Where is he?" she asked instead.

"Call off your attack!" I repeated, feeling the edge of anger that provided me comfort and confidence in the face of this winged human. "I shall not give you the grace by asking you again."

I reeled back as she laughed, the sound so melodic and sweet.

"Is this the resistance the Defiler sends to greet us?" she asked. "Pathetic. We expected more from you."

"Who is this Defiler you speak about?" I asked, clawing at what she had previously said but not quite catching it. Still, Duncan's lightning raged on through the skies. It thickened in the air. The other creatures struggled to keep pace as his lightning exploded the world in light and heat.

"We have travelled too far to entertain such foolish questions." Her lip curled upward as she swung the hammer with ease. It must have been made from feathers or something softer than metal for it to move with such effortless grace.

I threw myself backwards, falling on my ass and skidding away as the hammer fell into the body of ice that my feet had not long touched. It exploded into shards, a vicious crack snaking toward me.

It took not but one brush of my hand and the water froze over, stopping the webbing of cracks from spreading any further.

"We do not wish to fight," I pleaded.

"That's a shame," she said, swinging her hammer again.

Refusing to back away, I lifted the chill of winter from the water and into the moisture-laced air. Like Duncan's power, it sparked, but from a destructive cold instead of boiling light. It met the head of her weapon and clashed with it. The force sent her off-kilter for a moment.

"Who is the Defiler you speak of?" I screamed my question before she could right herself and attack.

"Do not play coy with me," she spat, annoyance slashed across her beautiful face.

I took my chance of peace to speak before she swung the hammer downward. "Do you serve the Creator?"

Her arms tensed, wringing her hands upon her weapon once again as though it were a habit of comfort. "The Creator. Our Light. He has tasked us with stopping the Defiler from freeing the demonic entity Duwar with the precise instructions to take any life which dares stand in the way. Which, as it seems, is you."

I looked beyond her, to the shattered Cedarfall ships that scattered across the ocean, then to the winged beings that dodged Duncan's lightning as they continued their attack.

"You've got this wrong. I believe the person you speak of – this Defiler – is Aldrick."

"Aldrick," she hissed the name, proving it was not unfamiliar to her. "He will die for his treachery."

"A feeling we share. Make it known that we don't stand with him but *against* him."

Her expression didn't waver. It was stoic and unmoved, clear that my words did not have the effect that I wished them to.

"Lies born on the tongue of a snake. Enlighten me, fey. What serpent are you?"

I shook my head, ready to fall on my knees and plead for this to end. From the sickening distrust in her obsidian eyes, I knew it would not make her believe me.

"I'm Robin Icethorn, King of the Fey Court, and I beg you to hear my words and seek the truth in them. We are not allied with Aldrick… the Defiler, the Hand, whichever name you wish to best recognise him as. Those ships you send to the ocean floor are rescue vessels for the fey who wait, in fear and desperation, in that castle. Fey whom we have promised to save. And I swear to Altar, on the Creator, on anything worth naming, that if you stand in our way, I *will* stop you even if it destroys me."

My entire body trembled. I felt my chance for peace ebb away as she shifted her hammer in a sharp motion. This time, it wasn't the heavy head that she brought down to me.

It was the handle, as though she was offering her weapon to me.

I looked up the length of polished gold until my gaze settled back on her face. Her expression, although still filled with something that would spark fear in the weakest of souls, had seemed to soften.

"Take the hammer in your hands, and I will pursue the truth or unveil the deceptions you sputter toward me," she said, the bite in her tone almost softening. "Do it and you may save them all or seal the doom we have arrived to provide."

I didn't need to be told twice. Swallowing back my hesitation and pride, I reached out and wrapped my hands around the handle of her hammer. It was warm to the touch. Alive, almost.

The nameless warrior held the head of her weapon in her hands, tethering us both until we were connected by the length of gold. Instantly, I felt its hefty weight. If she had released her grasp on it I would've fallen beneath its mass, crashed through the ice at my feet and sunk to the bottom of the dark ocean with no hope of coming back.

"One question, that is all I will give you."

Nodding, I gritted my teeth and waited for what she had to ask me. I couldn't understand how touching a weapon would grant me the safety of my people, but it was a chance I was prepared to take for them.

"Are you allied with the Defiler, aiding him to bring forth Duwar to this realm?"

It was the easiest answer to give. My mouth opened so quickly that I hardly took a breath before. Then I felt it. A strange, drawing pull from within the weapon that tugged at my very bones as I spoke.

"We are not."

The winged woman hesitated, looking down at her weapon as my words settled over her. With bated breath, I waited for her to speak as she contemplated something silently. The sound of battle still raged behind her. It seemed louder than before.

"That is the truth," I reiterated, my fingers tightening their hold on the handle. "You would be the fool to think otherwise."

Suddenly, she withdrew the weapon from my grasp. The powerful pull I felt in my chest disappeared as my hands met empty air.

"The Creator has recognised your truth."

I expected something more, but then she turned, wings almost knocking me backwards. She faced the remaining Cedarfall ships and her own armada. Not once had I questioned her authority. It seemed to seep from her pores, leaving no room to deny it.

"Wait," I spluttered. "Do not do this."

"It," she replied, "is done."

She threw back her head and released a sound that I had not heard another person make before. It was a mix between a scream that had the power to curdle blood, but also a song. A pitched note that soon became one of many as the other winged beings stilled in the air and returned her call.

I watched, stunned, as the fighting ceased. The clouds broke apart, and the bolts of lightning diminished. My heart skipped a beat as I searched for Duncan on the wall far behind me, but I couldn't see him. His presence within the air faded quickly, so much so that I knew he had finally discovered his limitations.

"Robin Icethorn," she said, turning my attention back to her. Regret drew down at her face as she landed upon my stretch of ice to stand before me. In the air, she seemed tall, but standing before me, we were similar in height. "I fear our grave misunderstanding has cost you."

Fury coiled within my chest, but I forced it down long enough to get my next words out. Carefully chosen and full of demand, I spoke as softly as I could force. "As penance for your mistake, you are going to help me fix this. And then you are going to tell me exactly who you are."

CHAPTER 7

Hidden away within the great cabin on a Cedarfall ship, Duncan moaned beneath my caress, reacting as though my soft touch caused him pain.

His skin had drained of colour since I left him to unleash his magic. Its pale hue exposed a webbing of blue and red veins lingering just beneath the surface. It'd been a few hours since the attack had ceased, and still there had been little improvement in Duncan's health. But at least he was awake. That was something, I supposed. Although it took an immense effort for him to hold his eyes open for longer than a few seconds.

Despite the chill that clung to him, Duncan's body was coated in a thick film of sweat. Each time he gathered enough energy to open his mouth and speak to me, his jaw trembled and his teeth clattered. Exhaustion clung to every inch of Duncan's appearance, making it painful to look at him.

Duncan had tested his new powers to the limit. Powers that should never have belonged to him. And it'd weakened him greatly. It took both Kayne and me to haul Duncan from the outer boundaries of the castle to the smaller vessels that waited upon Lockinge's shore. I still felt the imprint of his slack, idle body across my side.

"You must stop doing that," Duncan whispered, attempting to push himself from the slouch he had slipped into within the chair. "You'll have no fingers left at this rate."

I pulled my fingernail from between my teeth. If Duncan hadn't made the comment, I wouldn't have even noticed I was chewing my nails at all.

Needing to give my hands something to occupy themselves with, I drew the damp cloth out of the bowl. I wrung the water out and then reached to hold it to Duncan's feverish forehead. "Duncan. It is not the time to worry about me. You are being unreasonable, and to make matters worse, you are in *no* state fit enough to refuse me."

Although his body was still weak, his demanding nature burned brighter than the midsummer sun. "I would hardly refer to it as being unreasonable. My duty is to keep you safe, so tell me why I can't worry about you?"

I wished to remind Duncan he wasn't my personal guard. But as the words dredged across my tongue, I held them back behind gritted teeth.

There was only one person who had that mantle, and I couldn't risk losing myself to the memory of him.

"Says the man who can't even sit up straight," I replied. "Duncan, please. I will be fine."

"I know you will, because I'm coming with you, Robin." Duncan shrugged off my attempt to trail the damp cloth across his sticky forehead for the fourth time.

"And what are you hoping to achieve with your stubbornness?" I asked, winning the fight with little effort as Duncan flopped back upon the captain's red velvet chair in the centre of the room. "You have taken yourself to the limit. Practically reached the edge and thrown yourself over it. Duncan, if you don't allow yourself to rest, then you will be no good to me, or anyone, for that matter."

He peeked open an eye and looked directly at me. Haloed by the shadows that hung with pride beneath his stare, the green of his eyes seemed equally dark. Never-ending.

"Just give me a minute, and I will be ok. I've been through far worse than this, trust me," Duncan said, glancing around the cabin with a single, raised brow. "Do you think the captain has something strong to drink? The right liquor, if sharp enough, could raise the dead... just imagine what it could do for me."

"I hardly think alcohol is your saviour," I retorted.

The truth was, I didn't know what would help him heal. Duncan was a rarity. A human with access to magic that should never have been his to use. There was no knowing how his body would react to the power, and from the state of him, it didn't look promising.

I glanced around the mahogany-decorated room. The walls had been hand-carved into one complete picture of a woodland, with trees, plants and small birds balanced on thin branches. The room itself was a work of art. Heavy crimson curtains did well to block out the light from the large bay windows that gave a view of the ocean beyond. Everything about the cabin was handsome, besides its scent. I'd taken to breathing in and out through my mouth. Anything to avoid the eye-watering aroma of salt and dried fish that seeped through the wooden body of the ship.

Duncan wasn't the only one who would benefit from a drink. If it didn't fix his ailments, perhaps it would solve mine. Even if the burn of alcohol allowed my mind to wander away from the winged humans for only a moment, it would be worth it.

If I wasn't worrying about Duncan, I was dreading the meeting that would soon begin. A meeting with the winged humans who'd almost sunk all the Cedarfall ships. People who now waited on their own vessels for us to arrive. It was hard to discern if my urge to vomit was from the gentle sway of the moored ship or what lingered far across the waters.

I'd never found the concept of answers so frightening. Selfishly, I didn't think I could cope with unveiling more secrets that each linked back to Aldrick and Duwar. It only solidified just how serious he was as a threat to both realms. If beings from another uncharted place joined the effort to stop him, Aldrick's scourge was more of a widespread threat than I first believed.

"Never mind the drink," Duncan said, drawing me back from my thoughts. He reached out a shaking hand and took my wrist. "I have other suggestions that may be a better remedy for me."

"What you need is a healer," I said, rolling my eyes at the mischief that oozed from him.

"What I need," Duncan winced as he attempted to pull me to him. "Is standing right before me. You, Robin."

I allowed him to guide me until I sat on his lap. Duncan was weak, his effort feather-light, but I desired to feel his reassuring touch, so I bowed to his wish. Duncan flinched as I sat upon his outstretched thighs. He didn't complain with words, but the shake of his leg and the way his teeth bit down into his lower lip suggested that it was a struggle for him.

"Be careful," I warned, wrapping my arms around his neck and resting them on his shoulders. "This isn't the type of resting I had in mind for you."

Duncan's hand wound itself around my waist and anchored me to him. As fingers drummed on my side, my anxiety slipped away. This was something we had learned in the weeks past. Using one another's touch to distract us from the world and its realities.

"Then we finally agree on something," Duncan replied. "I thought it was impossible."

"I know what you are trying to imply, and you are not getting anywhere with it," I said softly. Worried that if I spoke too loudly, it would shatter this moment altogether.

Just us, me and him in a room, pretending that the world outside it didn't matter.

"Let me indulge myself, if only for a moment," Duncan exhaled, resting his head back on the gold-painted wooden frame of the chair. His eyes were closed now, and he was smiling. Grinning to himself like a cat who had uncovered the lake of cream all for himself.

"Speak then, or forever hold your peace."

Duncan's fingers gripped tighter into me. My heart leapt wildly in my throat.

"There are so many things I wish to say. None that would be suitable in such a place. What I wish to do and what I will do are two separate matters."

I lowered myself to his cheek and pressed my lips to it. His skin twitched upon impact, and his smile widened. The kiss was brief, and yet exactly what I needed.

"That's all you are getting," I whispered, lips brushing the damp skin of his cheek.

"More," Duncan demanded. "I deserve it."

Lowering myself to his face again, I aimed my lips at the corner of his mouth, where the scar met his smile and gave the impression that it was never-ending. This kiss was as gentle as the first but lasted a heartbeat longer.

"Better?" I asked.

"Ask me after another," Duncan replied, gravelly voice rumbling with a chuckle.

"Do you enjoy demanding things from me?" I asked, smiling too as I moved back to his face again.

Duncan seemed to find some strength as he held tighter onto my back. I had no hope of escaping him, not that I cared to.

He raised his neck from the chair and opened both eyes. Our faces were only inches apart. "Believe me, darling, what I want from you is far more than closed-mouth kisses. Until I locate the energy to do what I desire, another kiss here will suffice."

He pressed a finger to his lips as though telling me to be quiet.

My mouth pressed to his for a final time, lips urging one another's apart as our connection quickly dissolved from its softness to desperation.

I groaned into Duncan's open mouth. His tongue lapped against mine, fuelled by the noise I made. My fingers coiled within the locks of dark hair, tracing across his scalp that conjured a shiver to spread across his exposed arms. He had hold of me, too, ensuring the kiss wouldn't end before he wished for it to. One hand grasped onto my side, and the other gripped the back of my neck with force. In that moment, he wasn't the weak man who'd pushed himself to the limits of his power.

Our kiss might never have come to a natural end if not for the knock at the door.

Reluctantly, I pulled away to a string of displeased groans from Duncan.

"It had to be too good to be true," Duncan growled, his grip on my side still preventing me from standing. "Let them in, and there is no going back. Tell them to fuck off, and we can continue where we *bluntly* left off."

Upon the door that led out to steps down from the main deck of the ship was a circular porthole of frosted glass. I recognised the shadowed outline beyond. They were tall. Wild curls of hair. Twin points of ears.

"Once this meeting is over with, there will be plenty of time during our journey to Wychwood where we can pick up where we left off." I patted his knee and stood. Duncan's hand traced the curve of my ass as he dropped his arm, reluctantly.

"I don't feel comfortable letting you go to them without me," Duncan attempted again, circling back to our original discussion. "Those people have proven themselves volatile. I don't trust them with the most important person in my life."

A warmth spread across my chest as his words settled upon me. I had my back turned to him as I faced the door that sounded with another knock, this time more impatient than the last.

"You can come in," I called out.

"Robin. Don't ignore me…" Duncan started.

I glanced over to him as the door screeched open, allowing the rush of salt wind to fill the room.

"If, and only if, by the time we leave you can stand without aid, then you may join me."

Duncan's lips narrowed into a thin line. It was the last thing I saw as I turned my attention to Althea Cedarfall, who led the party of three into the room.

"So, he didn't perish after all," Althea cooed, sparing Duncan a quick glance. As she did, there was nothing caring about her expression. However, when she looked back my way, her face lit from within as her freckle-covered lips turned upward.

"You would have liked that, I'm sure." I stiffened at Duncan's reply, but Althea showed no sign she heard as she continued.

"We have a matter of minutes before *Rafaela* sends a vessel to collect us. Are you prepared?"

Rafaela, the name of the warrior who had offered her strange hammer to me.

I opened my mouth to reply before Seraphine cut in. "Still think it's wise we tell them to drag their sorry arses to us. We shouldn't be at their beck and call, unless they are paying of course."

"Old habits die hard." Althea rolled her eyes, not even trying to hide her disagreement.

"I can't expect our people to welcome the humans aboard after what they've done." My hair had grown considerably over the past weeks, so that when I shook my head, dark strands of black fell before my eyes. It was becoming second nature to run my fingers upward through my hair to lay it away from my face. "It would be best that we discuss matters on their own ground. We may not trust them, but we know their enemy is our enemy. That must count for something."

"All the more reason for them to come here. Let them face us!" Seraphine added, leaning against the doorway to the cabin with her arms and legs crossed. "They should feel uncomfortable surrounded by the people they tried to slaughter! Three have died because of them. Forgive me, but breaking bread is not as exciting a thought to me as it is to you."

"I didn't realise that an Asp cares about anyone but their employer," Althea added.

"My contract is not yet up," Seraphine added, looking to me. "Until then, I care."

"Three have died?" I repeated, allowing the number to settle over me.

Seraphine's grimace was enough of a confirmation.

"At least," Kayne said from where he sulked at the door. "It may take some time to make sense of the census, but so far, three are unaccounted for."

I stepped forward, offering a hand toward the scroll that was gripped in Kayne's fist. "Who?"

Jesibel? Was it her? From the chaos after leaving the Below I'd still not had the chance to find her.

Kayne didn't hesitate to hold it out to me. "Before you ask, no, she is not on my list."

My heart sank into the pit of my stomach just like the Cedarfall ship that Rafaela and her fellow assailants had destroyed.

"Are you sure?" I asked, unable to take my eyes off the roll of parchment now in my own hands. Dark ink scribbled across the yellowed parchment. Names, so many names, hand-scribed in wonky lines. It all blurred as my eyes traced over the mess of ink.

"Checked it over more than once," Kayne replied. "Jesibel is not a name that has been given."

Kayne's efforts had been vital to our plan from the moment it was forged after our escape from Aldrick. Seraphine had no trouble trusting in him, like Duncan, either. It seemed only Althea and I still had difficulty in that department – although for Duncan's sake I fought to keep my distrust to a simmer.

"I promised her," I muttered, swallowing the lump that suddenly invaded my throat. "I said I would come back and I did. But if she is not here, then I failed."

Althea stepped to my side and placed a hand on my shoulder. Her touch made the scar upon my chest twitch.

"This is beyond all of our control," she said. "Like everything that is happening around us, we can only face forward and deal with it together."

Despite her attempt to reassure me, Althea's words didn't have the desired effect. Instead, I clung to the painful feeling that failing stabbed me with. Duncan noticed, laying a gentle hand on me for comfort.

"Those from the prison who cared enough to speak with me said something about Aldrick visiting the prison days ago." I was aware Kayne was speaking, but his words only tickled my consciousness. "They said he took a large group of captives with him. They never returned."

Could she have been one of them? Out of all those fey, how had Jesibel been among those he chose?

"And this is the first we've heard about it?" Duncan spoke up, leaning forward in his chair. "Seraphine, our eyes and ears. It doesn't seem like you to have something so important go unnoticed?"

I snapped my attention to the assassin. "If Seraphine knew, she would've said."

"That's right." Seraphine held my stare. Her jaw tensed; her eyes burned with determination. She no longer leant against the doorframe but stood tall and narrow. Her entire body was tense as she faced me down. "Is that an accusation hidden behind your words, Duncan?"

"I don't know, is it?" He glowered in return.

"*My* informants tell me the moment Aldrick so much as pisses. This, if you can find it in yourself to believe, is news to me."

I searched the assassin's face for a lie, but if she had one, she concealed it well. It made little sense that Seraphine would hide something from me. I was her sponsor, and that meant more than any bond to the Asps. With the price I paid for her aid, I knew she wouldn't lie.

"I believe you," I said, fingers strangling around the crumping parchment.

Her lips thinned into a line, but the lines across her forehead softened. "I'm glad you have sense, my king."

"I don't know what to believe anymore," Duncan added behind us.

"Finally," Althea added. "Something we agree on. There are currently winged humans waiting, not a stretch away from us. Now is not the time for distrust. As a group, we need to stand as one if we want so much as the chance to see this to the end."

Althea made sure she glanced at each one of us as she spoke.

"Althea is right. We stand firm together, unbreakable in the face of change."

"Said like a bona fide royal," Seraphine replied. "Your kind has a knack for motivational speeches, as I remember."

"Remind me, what court was your home before you defected to the Asp nest?" Althea asked, chin raised.

"Not yours, sweetheart," Seraphine replied, blowing a kiss that turned Althea's cheeks red with fury. "Elmdew, although the court of Spring is not exactly a home for me. It hasn't been for a long while. I turned my back on that place many moons ago."

"Which explains why you struggle with authority," Duncan added, closing his eyes. He didn't see her scowl, but smiled anyway.

"Seraphine, your insight has been pivotal to getting us here. I don't doubt you were not aware of Aldrick's last movements, but do you think your Asps can locate any hint of where he may have taken the fey? Just because Jesibel is not with us now doesn't mean I wish to stop searching for her. I made a promise. I take that seriously. Kayne, I ask that you investigate with the fey we saved; if anyone might know who was taken, it would be them."

Both the Asp and the Hunter nodded.

"What is to say he took them anywhere?" Althea added.

"He needs their blood, not their flesh. He may have drained his supply and taken it with him to conduct his monstrous mutations."

The thought alone had the power to unravel me. I refused to believe it was an option.

"I will send word back to Lockinge and to those who are staying behind," Seraphine said, shooting me a wary glance. "If there are bodies to find, they will locate them. Don't worry."

The ground swayed beneath me. I opened my mouth to speak, but it filled with a rush of sick that slipped over onto the floor. I folded over, hunched over my knees. Althea jumped back. Duncan called my name. But all I could picture was Jesi, a stranger who I had fixated on helping... dead.

"I'm fine," I gasped, as my allies tried to help me. Clearing my mouth, I spat the last dregs of bile and hardened my resolve. "Jesi's death is not an option I'm willing to accept. Jesi is alive, as are the others he took from the prison. If he has left Lockinge, he will need a lasting supply of blood to keep his power. He needs her alive." *So do I.*

"Then we will find them all," Althea said, eyes wide with determination. "Your promise to Jesi will be met. I guarantee it."

I couldn't explain aloud just how profound an effect Jesibel had had on me. She'd represented the Icethorn Court's people. Alone, lost and then stolen, whilst fleeing a broken court left in the wake of my family's death. It was up to me to put it right. Her face had been at the forefront of this rescue mission, and the burning hope I coveted in my soul had been doused completely by the realisation that she was still lost to me.

Seraphine shifted, sensing movement at the door before anyone else. "Time to go."

We all turned to the captain of this ship. Flanor was an older man with sun-spotted cheeks and meaty hands that looked as tough as the bottom of a boot. The Cedarfall captain had bright sun-yellow hair and a rugged beard that likely harboured stories from years at sea.

"A small boat cuts across the sea," Flanor said, throat thick with age. In his hand, he gripped a brass spyglass. "You asked to be informed the moment we saw them coming, and I have. The crew is growing restless at their arrival."

"We will be up shortly," Althea replied curtly, already pacing toward the doorway in which Seraphine prepared to leave.

Flanor bowed his head to Althea, offering her the spyglass as she swept to his side. "For giving up your cabin, Flanor, I will see that my mother thanks you generously."

His rosy cheeks swelled at that. "It's my pleasure, truly."

Duncan had slipped into sleep, his eyes fluttering. I was thankful he was not awake to argue his point again. It was easier this way – at least, that is what I told myself. Each step away from his tired body only clenched at my gut.

"Robin," Kayne said as I moved for the door.

"Yes?"

"I'm going to stay back with him," Kayne gestured toward Duncan, who had begun softly snoring. "It doesn't seem right to leave him alone among–"

"You don't need to say it." And he didn't. Kayne was the only one who still carried his sword on his hip. The handle was never out of reach. Duncan and Kayne were Hunters. Regardless of what had been done, I knew Kayne still felt that his presence among us was threatened.

He didn't trust us, and truthfully, I don't think the fey trusted him either. But I was trying, for Duncan.

"Perhaps you'll be more successful in getting him to rest than me," I said, offering a smile that was not returned.

Kayne's lip curled over his teeth, only slightly. I blinked, and his stoic expression returned. "You may think you need to tell me how to care for him, but you don't. I have been by his side far longer than you. Remember that."

I swallowed my words as Kayne stalked away from me. Looking around the cabin, I wondered if anyone else had heard. Althea had already drifted up to the main deck with Flanor, and if Seraphine had overheard, she showed no sign.

It took everything in my power not to look at Kayne as I walked away. As I reached the door, Seraphine blocked me. "Haven't you forgotten something?"

Seraphine tipped her head toward the grand desk that waited back in the cabin's heart. "If you are to meet with the humans, do so as you *truly* are."

There was an underbelly of discomfort when she spoke. As my eyes fell upon the item she spoke about, a bitter touch of ice spread over my spine.

The Icethorn crown sat within the open-lidded box. Elinor had made sure it was sent with the ships to collect us. Physically, it was worthless to our cause. But as a symbol, it meant everything. I last had it in the Cedarfall Court, so it must have been provided by Queen Lyra.

I had brought it with me to see Duncan, allowing it to become an afterthought the moment my eyes had settled upon him. Now, it was the brightest thing in the room.

"Feels like part of a costume," I admitted. "A rather pivotal accessory though, I can't deny."

"Dare I ask why?" she asked, pursing her lips.

"Because I don't deserve it." I turned my back on the crown and moved to leave, only to be stopped by Seraphine's firm hand upon my arm. "But clearly Elinor knows that wearing it will only solidify my authority around so many who may still not trust me."

"Oh, swallow your self-pity, Robin, and put the damn thing on," Seraphine scolded. "I am the last person who cares about titles and crowns, but what you have achieved is not something to be dismissed. And what you are going to continue to do suggests, even to me, that you are a king."

I held her stare until she dropped my arm.

"I've paid you to say this to me," I reminder her.

"Oh," she replied with a laugh. "I may do many things for payment, but lying is never one of them. Even you couldn't offer me something for the use of that skill."

"That's a comforting thought," I replied, slipping the silver-toothed metal upon my head. The crown fit perfectly. The cold kiss of metal flattened my blue-black hair down to my scalp and rested just above my ears.

"Glad to have been of service." Seraphine slapped my shoulder and looked me up and down with an expression I'd not seen on her before. I didn't have time to place it before she was moving.

CHAPTER 8

The tension in the dimly lit cabin was so thick that each inhale felt like breathing in mud. The small circle of candlelight was only enough to illuminate the three winged humans sitting on one side of the table and the three of us on the other.

"I speak for us all when I thank you for accepting our appeal for a meeting," Rafaela said, sitting straight in the backless chair that gave room for her folded grey wings behind her. Since having our interaction out on the ice I'd conjured across the sea, Rafaela hadn't changed out of her gold-hemmed robes of white. Rafaela's sleeveless tunic exposed arms crafted from defined muscle. She kept her hands joined and rested on the table before her. "And of course, our expressed and utmost sincere apology for what has occurred today. Of course, words are meaningless without action, so we have arranged for any supplies lost in the sinking of one of your ships to be reimbursed and provided at the end of this meeting."

"Thank you," I said, meaning it wholeheartedly. "Perhaps we can begin by discussing who or, pardon my rudeness, what exactly you are? As you can imagine, we are a little confused as to what exactly is happening." I tried to keep my face void of expression that would soon betray me and the discomfort I felt being in the presence of such powerful and unknown creatures.

"An understandable question. One of many I can imagine you have." Rafaela rolled her shoulders back, enticing her wings to shiver for a moment. "Although we can't blame you for your lack of knowledge. We were warned that this realm has forgotten of our existence, so your ignorance was expected. It would seem the lack of belief runs deep in both the fey and the humans."

"Answer the question," Althea added, speaking before I could utter a similar sentiment. *"Please."*

"Altar was not the only god to make beings in his image. It was clear the humans would not stand a chance against the power of the fey, in case they turned their power against them. So, the Creator crafted warriors of his own. We are known as Nephilim. Our purpose is to spread His word and protect it, no matter the cost."

"Angels," I said.

"Ah, so the knowledge has not been completely lost?" Rafaela asked.

"Not by everyone," I replied, aware of my friends side-eyeing me. "There was once a pious man who mentioned angels. I didn't believe him at the time, but I do now."

"Nephilim, angels," Seraphine barked, seemingly the most relaxed out of the three of us. Her boots were moments from resting on the glass-topped table as she slouched down in her seat. "Never heard of you."

"And that is precisely the problem," Rafaela confirmed, hardly caring for the assassin's presence. "Our kind were dismissed from your realms many moons ago. So many that even the moon itself has forgotten about us."

"Why though?" I asked. My voice filled the cavernous room and echoed back at me.

"I'm prepared to answer any question you have, but you will need to be more specific," Rafaela replied. She stood from her chair, her wings twitching with unspent energy. Even folded, I could recognise the pure strength and span of her feathered limbs. If she were to extend them here, they would likely break out on either side of the cabin's wooden walls.

"Why do we not know of you?" I extended my question, following her as she skirted the table toward us.

"You may expect a story of jealously, conflict of power or perhaps hate. But I'm afraid I'm going to disappoint you with the answer. The Creator simply did not require us in Durmain. After the great divide, it was agreed the fey would linger in Wychwood and the humans in Durmain. Our job, of ensuring peace, was not required."

"The humans are safe from us." Althea shifted uncomfortably in her chair. "It would seem it is the other way around now."

"Indeed," Rafaela nodded. "The Creator's word we had been entrusted to spread, had already spread like wildfire across the humans. Our purpose had been met."

"So, the Creator filed you away like ancient books in a long-lost library, ready to call upon you when the world finally forgot about him?" Althea suggested.

Rafaela shook her head, braids of deep brown hair twisting around her shoulders. "Not quite, Althea Cedarfall. The Creator does not wish to force his presence on humans. Faith must be found, not forced. If it was not for the threat of the Defiler's return, we might never have sailed across the seas to find this land again. Some of us even feel disappointed in our return, but we have a purpose."

"To spread his word?" I asked, but felt as though I already knew the answer.

"To protect them from our shared enemy," the other woman said. Her voice was light with youth. I could tell from her sharp tongue I had offended her with my suggestion. "Unlike the Nephilim of the past, our purpose this time is very different. Aldrick wishes to bring forth a threat that will annihilate the human race. We've come to make sure that doesn't happen."

"And what of the threat to the fey," I added, tension unravelling in my gut. "Do you care for us?"

"Of course we do, however, that is your responsibility, is it not? Powerful kings and queens, you already have the magic to protect the fey. We are but two sides of the same coin, wanting the same outcome."

"To spread his word?" Seraphine snapped. "Seems like a rather relaxed way of protecting humans."

"Did you miss the second task he bestowed upon us?" the younger Nephilim said, tilting her head to the left.

"Protect *His* word. What little of the faith remains, it is our duty to ensure it does not dwindle," Rafaela said.

"So, let me get this straight. You show up now because of Duwar?" Seraphine asked, brows furrowed and teeth bared.

Rafaela nodded, grimacing as the name of the banished god seemed to fill every quivering shadow of the cabin. "The demon god is coming. For the sake of us all, we must ensure the gate to its dimension is left untouched, secured and closed. Duwar's return will affect us all, no matter what lands we live upon. It just so happened that you found yourselves in the crossfire of our visit to meet with the Defiler's chosen subject. And for that, again, I apologise."

"Then you might like to know that you are late," I added. "Aldrick left Lockinge in search of the keys. If you were hoping to catch up with him, we better end this conversation and let you go."

"You know of the keys?" There was no disguising the worry in the younger girl's voice. I looked at her face, seeing how the emotion across it betrayed her. Her hair was golden, as though the sun itself laid its presence upon her head and gifted her with a head of its own light. Piercing blue eyes set nestled upon her face like jewels. Unlike Rafaela's wings, hers were a dark brown. Among their feathers, I could see other beige tones that reminded me of an owl. And her wide eyes only added to her appearance of wisdom.

"I know *of* them, but not what they are or where," I replied. "Aldrick enjoyed boasting about his plans but giving only enough away that still kept him steps ahead."

"He is blind in his search," she replied. As though reading my mind, she quickly answered my thought. "My name is Gabrial, and I am the Creator's script. Memory of his word in flesh."

"What an introduction," Seraphine mumbled beneath her breath. "Do you all have fancy titles?"

"Gabrial," Althea added in hopes of burying Seraphine's distrust, quickly drawing the young girl's attention from the assassin back to her. "Do you believe Aldrick doesn't know where to look for the keys that will unbind Duwar from his imprisonment?"

"Considering Aldrick had one key in his very possession and let it slip carelessly through his fingers, all without knowing, it would suggest he doesn't," Rafaela said. "I know Aldrick *thinks* he knows where to search, for the Defiler will whisper many lies in his ear. However, they are both as lost and blind as a lamb without its mother. But he knows they will be within Wychwood, so that is where he will start looking. And usually, when you look for something, you end up finding it. We are here to stop him before he does."

I stood without realising, mind focused on only one thing Rafaela had just let slip. "He had one?"

Gabrial smiled knowingly, tracing her bright stare from the crown upon my head to the polished toe of my boot. "Once he recognises a key for what it truly is, the rest of them will easily lay themselves before him for the claim. It is our duty to ensure he never discovers them."

"Then we must get to them before he does," I spluttered. "Destroy them so neither Aldrick nor anyone else weak enough to allow a demon to fill their minds can attempt this again."

Gabrial looked to Rafaela, who shared the worried expression. Without uttering a word, Rafaela seemed to communicate something to the girl.

"Destroying the keys is not an option," the third Nephilim said. It was the first time he had spoken, his deep voice a low rumble, like the distant song of thunder before a storm. As he laid his eyes on me, I sensed a mistrust in his stare that didn't waver.

"We would all be liars if we did not admit that destroying the keys would be the easier route to stopping Aldrick from freeing the Defiler," Rafaela added, drawing the focus back to her. "However, doing so would simply unlock further problems that even we do not have the power to stop. I'm the Creator's hammer. Enforcer of His word. And if I can recognise that destruction is not the way out of this, then know it for truth."

"So you *do* all have fancy titles?" Seraphine asked, her voice slipping into the moment of silence such that not a single person could pretend not to have heard it like the rest of her comments.

"My name is Cassial," the man with the slitted cloak and ivory-white wings said. "The Creator's shield, guard of His word."

His hair was midnight black, his face shadowed with a beard that matched. The silver of his eyes was so bright that they looked almost entirely white.

Cassial was clearly the oldest of them all, with a broad figure and towering presence that gave him the impression of being the offspring of a giant. His giant fists were balled at his side. One slam of them upon the glass table and it would have shattered into countless pieces, that I was sure of.

Seraphine pulled a face, brows raised to her hairline. "You must be special. I pride myself on having an excellent memory, but even I'm going to end up forgetting that. So Cassial will do."

"Our names will suffice." Rafaela smiled, her eyes glowing with genuine amusement. "But you are right, only the special ones have titles. There is a small selection of us, personally chosen by the Creator. Although, speaking of names, is it not your guild that run around under the guise of a snake?"

"We prefer serpent," Seraphine said, her amused stare giving away her enjoyment of the back and forth. "It has more of a bite."

"Oh," Rafaela sang. "I'm sure it does."

As they spoke, I blinked and glimpsed a vision of Abbot Nathanial. His body broken beneath the rubble in the church all those miles away. He was devoted to the Creator in a place where others were not. His memory alone had me turning on Seraphine.

"Seraphine, perhaps we don't offend our hosts, especially since we know what they are capable of?"

"Or that we may be looking at some of our most valuable allies," Althea added.

Seraphine stood abruptly. Her chair clattered to the floor. The sound of its fall was uncomfortably loud. She hunched over the glass table with her arms locked below her to keep her upright. The weight of her grief was so sudden and overwhelming that it almost brought Seraphine to her knees. I knew the feeling well.

A stain of scarlet crept up her neck and shaded her face with ferocity. "My distrust and annoyance that they have simply turned up now after already so much has been lost is beyond me. Do not ask me to show them respect when they have spent years hiding away in Altar knows where doing who knows what when I'm sure the Nephilim's presence in this realm may have prevented us from ever getting to this point."

"But we are here now," Gabrial said, attempting to calm the furious assassin.

"My sister died because of your tardiness," Seraphine snapped, eyes glistening with tears. "Forgive me if my welcome is not as warm as you were hoping."

I had no right to ask Seraphine to grasp onto her rationality when my lack of it had led me into Aldrick's hands. Grief was an emotion powerful enough to execute decisions without a second thought. It latched onto fury and fuelled it.

"Loss is the ugly truth of conflict," Rafaela said. A sympathetic warmth burned through her deep eyes as she refused to drop her attention from the heavy-breathing assassin. "I wish I could ensure you that our presence will prevent more, but I dare admit it will only incite further harm. The Nephilim's presence will enrage the Defiler. Make the demon desperate and rushed. Our being here presents a challenge, and the Defiler's desperate need to be freed will probably encourage them to counter that challenge."

Seraphine's gaze flickered across Rafaela. In search of what, I was unsure. But to my surprise, she took her seat again. "You are confident in your hopes of stopping Aldrick from releasing Duwar?"

Rafaela contemplated Seraphine's question for a moment, glancing across the other two Nephilim that sat, stone-faced, at the table. "There is no other choice."

"If that is the case, then we must work together," I said. "We could do with the help of those clearly well versed in battle."

"Strategy," Rafaela corrected. "And yes. We don't intend to leave your side for a moment, Robin Icethorn."

There was something off about what she said, but I couldn't place a finger on what that was.

"We know more about Aldrick and what he will do to ensure his task is completed. You have the knowledge of Duwar," Althea said, slapping her hand on the table. Smoke curled around her fingers as the surrounding air hissed. "Together, we have power. I like the sound of becoming allies."

"If you share what you know about the keys, we can help protect them whilst Aldrick is found and dealt with," I added. "Aldrick is a powerful fey with the ability to invade one's mind and control his victim from the inside. If we are to stand a chance at stopping him, it will be together."

"History has not looked kindly upon the union of fey and humans," Gabrial said. "As you are well aware, Robin Icethorn, previously Robin Vale. You are the son of such a union. You, more than anyone, understand the divide."

"I do." I speared my gaze across the long table toward the younger Nephilim, who seemed to study her open palms as though they were pages of a book. Her attention on them interested me like a moth drawn to a flame. Looking through the dimly lit room, I pondered why her eyes ran back and forth as though she read from pages. Then I saw it. Beneath her skin, moving with fluid grace. There were shapes I did not recognise. Until I focused harder and saw the shapes shift into words.

The marks were a darker tone to her skin, like ink upon pale paper.

"I don't remember telling you of my past though," I said, unable to draw my eyes from the Nephilim's skin.

"Nor do I know of it by asking you," Gabrial replied, lifting her attention to me for only a moment. "The Creator has humans past and present written in scripture. You, Robin, are as much human as you are fey. Your heritage places you in favour of the Creator. He sees your story and remembers it. As he does with all his children. I see your origin and everything that has come after it."

"Neat trick," Althea muttered, watching the scripture move like a raging river beneath the girl's skin. "Would come in handy if we come to an agreement of how we are to work together."

"All in good time," Gabrial said, her smile so genuine it almost stole my breath. "I'm memory of His word. My purpose, as the Creator's script, is to remember what was and is. History of all born in his image is remembered on my skin. Answers and memories that even you, Robin, have forgotten. Ah, see here when you were shy of your fourth year, and you fell from the tree and snapped your ankle. Your pain is remembered. As is the memory of when you woke to two intruders in your home who took you and sold you to the Hunters. I see, as the Creator does, everything. That is my burden."

My cheeks burned with the thought of the young girl seeing my past. What secrets and stories she could uncover with such a gift.

"We are all burdened," Rafaela added, walking back to her seat. "Given gifts which have a purpose in His name. Just as you, Althea Cedarfall and Robin Icethorn, have a purpose for the fey. Children of Altar—"

"It would seem you have a way of diverting the conversation swiftly away from the keys," I said, shaking off the confusion Gabrial's revelation had cursed me with. "I think we should focus on that."

"For good reasons," Cassial said, casting his silver eyes across the three of us.

"Robin is right. If you are unwilling to answer our questions, why call on our council in the first place?" Althea asked, tone suggesting her annoyance of the dance.

Unless they were keeping the knowledge from us because they didn't trust us with it?

"The human who waits on your ship," Rafaela said. "His story should have ended, yet still his lungs are filled with life. His heart beats, but not by the will of the Creator."

"Duncan." My body hardened in my seat, skin turning to cold stone. It was undeniable that the Nephilim shared an unspoken interest in Duncan, for they each glanced at one another.

"Duncan Rackley," Gabrial confirmed his name. "He should be dead, but he is not. We would like to know why."

"Can't you glean that information, Script of the Creator?" Seraphine spat, leaning back in her chair. It was a miracle she didn't prop her feet up on the table.

"His story ends with his death," Gabrial replied, unbothered by Seraphine's sarcasm. "I cannot see beyond it."

"Well, you can thank Aldrick for that," Seraphine added.

"And what are we thanking him for exactly?" Cassial asked, deep voice a rumbling groan.

"He is–"

"Again, we have danced away from the only topic that matters. And that is the keys." My mind wanted nothing more than to keep Duncan away from the line of focus. Whereas I could control what I said, my magic loosened at the mention of the man I'd do anything to protect. I felt the flow of cold air seep out of my mouth as I spoke. Rafaela looked at me and my display of power. A single brow lifted as she did so.

The concept of the Nephilim asking after Duncan did more than simply unnerve me. I felt a shiver of disgust at the idea of him filling their interest. Defensive jealousy was so intrusive that I lost control of the frozen power that twisted deep within me.

"We mean him no harm," Rafaela said.

"I wish to believe you, but you see I'm rather protective of what belongs to me."

"Understandable, considering all that you have been through. However, perhaps I can prove that we are no threat." Gabrial reached out a hand across the table. Ink swirled across her palm. "Let me show you."

I studied her palm, mesmerised by the words shifting just beneath her skin.

Her fingers curled, beckoning me to take them. Gabrial must have sensed my hesitation as she saw my hands grip onto my thighs in defiance. "The human side of you allows me to share the word with you. Please, if this does not help you to trust us, at least you can see that we do not lie."

I gritted my teeth. My jaw ached as I reached out for her hand. "I'm sure you don't need warning that if you do anything to harm me, I could shatter your hand with a single thought."

She sighed, her smile never wavering. "Not everyone is out to harm you, Robin Icethorn."

"We will see." I stared deep into her azure eyes as my fingers brushed her palm.

On impact, the world faded.

My mind was filled with images. I saw a young boy with obsidian hair throwing himself into the arms of a man. My father. Before my heart crumpled with pain, the image shifted like ink in water.

I saw... stones. Four black pillars formed around a symbol etched into the ground. This new vision felt different. I sensed power there. The image moved quickly, but I recognised the symbol of the Creator. It was scored on the ground between the four stone pillars. Except it was upside down. The northern arrow upon the wheel pointed south. Down.

The ground shifted beneath me. I felt myself fall sideways into the next vision before I could make sense of the first.

Out of the shadows, a balcony formed. Upon it, two men stood. One was small and the other was tall. The vision grew more defined until I recognised the steel-silver eyes and close-cut hair. As I recognised what I was being shown, I wished to pinch my eyes closed. To block out what was unfolding before me. As though sensing my wishes, the shadows exploded once again... but not before I heard two words spoken by the taller man.

Little bird.

I drew my hand back from Gabrial as though her touch burned me. She held her eyes on me. Her resolve was powerful across her youthful face.

"What happened?" Althea snapped, encasing me in a protective arm.

"I'm fine, Althea." I couldn't explain it. The visions, so real that I could hear, taste and smell my surroundings. "Impressive gift the Creator has given you," I added, eyes fixed to Gabrial.

"What did you see?" Althea asked, her concern rushing over me in a tidal wave.

"I showed Robin his past," Gabrial confirmed for me, likely aware I couldn't form the words to begin to explain.

"The stones," I said, wanting to divert the topic from the potential of slipping to the royal guard I fought daily to keep from my mind. "What are they?"

"Ah, so Gabrial has shown you the gate we have left behind," Rafaela said, patting her comrade on the back. "That gate is what our kind have spent centuries protecting. The reason why we have been too occupied to meddle in human and fey affairs."

"It will take more than that for us to trust your intentions," Althea said.

"I trust them," I added quickly, needing to diffuse the distrust between both parties.

Rafaela shrugged, fighting a smile. "Your internal concerns are for you to explain, not for me to speculate. We simply wish to understand what Aldrick is doing in his task of freeing the Defiler. Why he keeps your kind prisoners and how his followers have access to powers that should not be possible. Hence our interest in Duncan Rackley."

Before I could open my mouth to fight back on his behalf, Althea spoke for me.

"Perhaps we go and find him straight away. Then you can ask him yourself. If you say that Duncan is no longer human enough for you to see his story, then he is no longer your responsibility. Leave him to us."

Heat coiled in my chest at Althea's words. I mouthed my thanks, and she nodded. If there was anyone who could protect him as well as me, it was her.

"I have an idea," Seraphine spoke up, shattering the tension. "How about you tell us about the keys, and we will consider giving you what you need. A trade, so to say."

There was a silence in the room that stretched and devoured us all. No one dared speak first, not when it signalled the forfeit. I waited, willing to encapsulate every single Nephilim in the room in ice to ensure they could never even think of Duncan again.

"Your trust in us must be earned," Rafaela said finally. "Robin has made his stance on Duncan clear. We will not push again."

A warmth unfurled in my chest at Rafaela's words. My anger was now not with the Nephilim, but with the assassin who was still under my employment. It seemed she required a reminder. Abruptly, I stood, followed by Althea, who grimaced in silent agreement that this conversation had ended. "Thank you for your time. I have ships full of fey who I have promised to return home. You have a demon god to stop from destroying the world."

For once I allowed the illusion of the king to slip, giving way to the selfish man who lurked beneath. And that part of me needed to get Duncan as far away from these people as possible.

I turned on my heel and moved for the door.

"Unfortunately, I cannot let you leave." Cassial stood before it, his hulking frame blocking out the glorious light of late afternoon. His sudden presence was unexplained. He had shifted from his seat to in front of the door in a blink.

"Out of the way big guy," Seraphine growled, setting herself before me. Like Cassial, she had moved unseen and now held two curved blades in her hands. Weapons shouldn't have been brought into the meeting, but of course, the assassin had means of slipping in a few.

"I am afraid I am not able to do that."

Seraphine's lips curled over teeth. "I won't ask again, I will make you instead."

Cassial chuckled, glancing at the assassin's knives with a lack of fear. "Pretty. I use blades bigger than those to pick food from my teeth. What is it you wish to do with those?"

"I have a few ideas."

Althea was behind me, facing back into the room. Fire danced around her wrists, building its heat and intensity with each passing moment. "What is the reason for this?"

"Your protection," Rafaela added quickly, both her and Gabrial sitting calmly at the table as though we were not moments away from a fight.

"Do you need us to prove that we do not need it?" I asked, stepping to Althea's side. Ice crackled across my fingers, bringing the temperature of the room down.

"We do not wish to argue with you." Rafaela held her arms up at her sides in surrender.

"Had us fooled when you sank one of my ships," Althea reminded, knees bowing slightly as she readied herself.

"That was before we knew who and *what* you are."

"What we are?" There it was again, the strange use of words. It unsettled me enough to relax my hold on my power and command Seraphine to stand down. "What do you mean by that?"

Rafaela looked to Gabrial, who shook her head in silent refusal. Whatever Rafaela was about to say, she swallowed it, took a deep breath and shifted her gaze to Cassial. "Let them leave if they so wish, Cassial."

"That would not be wise," he replied, refusing to move. "You know it as well as I."

"They *may* leave, but… not alone." Rafaela's voice brimmed with control. The leadership she held among their group was clear. Cassial did as he was asked and stepped aside from the doorway, but not without a snarl at Seraphine, who, in return, snapped her teeth at him in play.

"Ready our fleet," Rafaela called out after us as we slipped out of the cabin before another could stand in our way. "It would seem our journey is not over yet."

"Where will you go?" I asked, turning back to see Rafaela's full attention on me. Although moments before I wanted to run from this room, there was a small part of me that knew these beings were the key to dealing with Aldrick.

"Wherever you go," Rafaela replied with words I didn't expect. "We shall follow."

I tried to swallow, but my throat seemed to have closed up. I only managed one rasped word. "Why?"

"Because you are crucial to ensuring Duwar stays locked in his dimension. Your survival is our survival." Rafaela stood, muscles flexing in her arms as she placed them at her sides. "As mentioned, we will provide any supplies lost. In the meantime, take the time you need to settle any internal grievances. When you are ready to discuss how we can benefit you, we will be here."

CHAPTER 9

I stared up at the ceiling, bedsheets sticky around my naked limbs. No matter my desperation for it, I had no hopes of getting back to sleep. The sour taste of the nightmare I'd dredged myself out of still haunted me. A dream of black stone pillars, winged humans and a demon god trapped behind glass.

The worst part of it was seeing Jesibel. The context was strange. But it felt so real. As though Jesibel made me recite everything I had learned whilst weighing up if my failing her was worth it.

Now, as I tried to steady my breathing, I focused on the carved details of the wooden ceiling and couldn't answer the question.

Deep in the belly of the Cedarfall ship, the air was thick with moisture. The cabin must have been buried beneath the surface of the ocean. Damp seeped through the oiled plank walls and filled the dank air entirely. The overwhelming scent of salt soon became an afterthought when my mind and stomach cursed the constant swaying of the boat. It was no surprise that I fought to keep down the measly plate of hard bread, cured meat and cheese that waited for us when we returned from Rafaela and her fellow Nephilim those hours before.

As they promised, small vessels overloaded with supplies had been brought to us. More proof that we could trust them. And yet, there was something about their interest in Duncan that made me want to keep a distance.

Duncan's rhythmic breathing was the anchor I required. It prevented me from losing myself in the maddening sway of the ship and the dream, which worked in tandem to curse me. I latched onto the deep, rasping inhales and the slight whistle he made at the peak of his exhale. His closeness didn't help the heavy, sweltering warmth that encompassed me. But I didn't desire there to be any distance between us at all. In fact, whilst one of my arms was resting behind my head, the other was pressed next to Duncan's with our fingers intertwined.

My hand ached from being linked with his for so long, but regardless of the discomfort, I kept it where it was.

It was better he slept. He needed it. Even if he'd put on a brave face and joined in with our conversation about what was discussed with the Nephilim, he still suffered. Duncan had fallen asleep only moments after his head hit the pillow. One minute we had been weaving out of conversation and kissing, the next, he was quiet. His dark lashes fluttered as he entered his dreamscape. I hoped his dreams were not as haunting as mine had been.

There was another part of the vision Gabrial had shown me, which I had kept from repeating. Although it had not infiltrated my nightmare, as if the information was not important to the phantom of Jesibel, now it was all I could think about.

Erix.

I would have lied to myself if I had pretended not to have thought of him often. The plans of freeing the captured fey had been more demanding of thought, but he always lingered. Now, surrounded by the ships that held those we had saved, my mind seemed to have found the capacity for Erix. Encouraged by the two tormenting words that would always remind me of him.

Little bird.

What happened to you? I screamed into the darkness. My fingers tightened around Duncan's as the feeling of panicked desperation for the answer overwhelmed me.

When Queen Elinor Oakstorm killed her husband, Doran, I wondered if it had somehow killed Erix as well. The gryvern had been an extension of Doran's will. His twisted offspring. And they hadn't been seen since they attacked the castle that fateful night, so I could only think they perished. What I hoped for was something completely different. Seraphine shared reports from the Lockinge civilians, which told of the gryvern fleeing, but that had been it.

A strong, loud part of me hoped Erix grasped enough control over his own will and body to get as far from Lockinge as possible. Or that he found peace, in whatever form that would have been.

Just as I often did and had grown extremely efficient at, I shelved the dark thoughts and moved on to others. The list of my torments was long and ever-growing, but they could wait until we saved the world from Aldrick.

I'd chosen not to tell Duncan that Rafaela inquired about him, as had Seraphine and Althea. Rafaela and her fellow Nephilim could look anywhere else, but Duncan was mine. I recognised the feeling for what it was – territorial. However, this was not a feeling I buried easily. After what I had lost, no one would take him from me.

I hated we were not already sailing for Wychwood, even though it had been my command that was given to ensure that. There was something about the Nephilim keeping me here – a conversation still left untouched.

Duncan shifted beside me, his breathing breaking its pattern. I turned my head to look at him, to find his narrowed, tired stare on me.

"How long have you been awake?" he asked, voice groggy.

I let out a sigh, suddenly relieved. Hearing his deep, rumbling voice edged with exhaustion was the relief I required from my mind. As always, it had the power to expel the tension that built up in my chest. "Unfortunately for me, it seems my head is refusing the idea of sleep. Sorry if I woke you."

"I'm only sorry you didn't wake me sooner. Come here," Duncan groaned as he encouraged me closer to him. "Would you feel better talking about it?"

He had let go of my hand to allow me to get as near as possible. My fingers were stiff; my wrist ached from being stuck in one position. All those discomforts melted away as my cheek pressed into the hard curve of his chest. Duncan had shaved the hairs from his torso with a wet blade only days ago. Already the hairs had grown enough to prickle me. Not that I cared. In fact, I was slightly disappointed when he had shaved at all. Although I didn't admit that to him. There was something about seeing his muscles sculpted by the shade of dark hair that set something ablaze in me.

"Oh, you know," I whispered, laying my hand on his stomach. He was warm to the touch, our bodies equally sticky. If he didn't look so exhausted, I would've suggested a stroll to the main deck for the welcoming kiss of fresh air. "Same old concerns about demonic gods and their mind-controlling puppets searching for the keys to bring forth a world of damnation and death. Nothing too consuming."

It was easier to blame all my anxiety on Aldrick instead of bringing up Erix, Jesibel, and the empty Icethorn Court that waited for me. Not to mention the Nephilim. There were so many other concerns that if I didn't slot them each into their own place in my mind and give them attention, one at a time, I feared I would implode.

Duncan pressed his lips into my hair and kissed the top of my head. He pulled back enough to speak but still kept close enough that his breath tickled my scalp. "One day, we will be sleepless for other reasons without a care or concern in the world."

I closed my eyes, trying to conjure up such a time. It felt impossible. "Say it again, and maybe I'll believe you."

"I believe it," Duncan replied as he lay back on the pillow. His eyes had closed again, but his fingers slowly trailed shapes upon my upper arm as he held me to him.

"How do you feel?" I was scared to ask for what he might reply, but I did so anyway.

"Don't you have enough to worry yourself with other than my well-being?"

I laughed, catching the hint of his sarcasm from the sly grin he forced upon his face. His dark hair had been swept from his forehead to reveal it glistening in the dull glow of the swaying lantern on his side of the room. Some colour had returned to his face, but he still looked fatigued.

"You are all I think of," I admitted. "Which is more a pleasure than a pain. Anyway, I need you to get better because you owe me something."

"I do?" Duncan's smile widened as he surveyed me out of one open eye.

"Yes, something that requires you at full energy... at least that is what I recall you saying. I mean, lots has happened since then. After a few minor hiccups along the way, my plan of emptying the Below has worked. That, and now there is currently a sea full of ships with winged humans who name themselves after the Creator's favoured inanimate objects... and not to forget the mystery of keys and missing fey. In fact, perhaps my mind is playing tricks on me, and you promised nothing at all."

Duncan's fingers no longer traced my skin but gripped it. His thumb pressed down into my arm with a pleasuring force. "No, no. I still seem to remember a promise."

"Enlighten me," I replied.

I longed for Duncan. His touch, his taste. There was a need to feel him, which I also caught in the glow of his eyes. Mischief and hunger coiled in his dark gaze made clear by the parting of his lips and the flash of his tongue caught between teeth.

"Are you using me, Robin Icethorn? Because if you only require me in your life to tire you out, I'm certainly up for the challenge," Duncan said, spare hand reaching down for the bedding that covered his modesty. At first, what I believed was a mound of material revealed itself to be a peak caused by the swell of his hard cock.

"You can hardly keep your eyes open," I said, trying to be coy but failing. "I hardly think you have it in you to ruin me."

"Ruin you?" His eyes narrowed.

"Was that not the promise you made, to ruin me? I could have sworn it was."

Words seemed to fail Duncan as his mouth opened and closed like a fish out of water. Giving up on finding the right thing to reply, he surprised me with strength as he rolled me on top of him.

A giggle escaped me as he forced me atop his waist, straddling his proud body with legs bent on either side of his hips. I felt him thrive beneath me, hips rocking in tandem with the ship's natural movement. The press of his cock upon the thin material of my undershorts turned my want for Duncan into a feverish need.

Part of me felt wrong about doing this here. With everything that had happened since my head last touched a pillow, this moment of distraction felt undeserved. As though this prize hadn't yet been earned.

But I couldn't wait for our return to Wychwood to take Duncan. Not when he was beneath me now, hands gripping my thighs and encouraging me to roll my hips upon his cock. His eyes had shed the tired gleam. He hardly blinked as he looked up at me. Waves of dark hair spread across the pillow, fanning out around his head like a halo of shadow.

"I missed this," Duncan whispered. "I missed *you*."

"How could you miss me when I haven't left your side?"

Duncan stared me dead in the eyes as though searching for my soul to judge it. "You might have been beside me, but your mind has been elsewhere. Every time I have looked at you, I have seen heavy clouds flooding your mind. I don't blame you, of course, not with everything you have done." Duncan lifted a hand from my thigh and brought it to my face. I kept still as his fingers glided across my cheekbone, inches from my left eye. "But now they're clearer than before. Not blue skies, not yet. But the clouds are thinning within you. I'm glad for your sake."

I couldn't face holding his attention, so I dropped my stare to the outline of his chest, where both my hands were placed. "I'm sorry."

"For what?" Duncan quickly asked, dropping his hand to my chin and lifting my face back up so I could not hide from him. "Focusing your attention on saving hundreds of innocent people? Never apologise for doing what is right. Not to me."

"I'm finding it hard to even imagine a time when things will be normal," I muttered. "It's like I'm punishing myself, constantly thinking about what comes next, and if I'm honest, I haven't thought this far ahead. Returning to Wychwood is the next step, but why does it feel like such an impossible leap to make?"

I felt as though I stood on the precipice, staring down at the sharp drop into nothingness. This far, everything we had achieved was because I took a leap into the unknown. But this one. This last jump to return to my court, empty and void of family and life, felt like the hardest part.

"Whatever is to come in the days that follow, know you are not alone. I'm here. You have friends and allies." Duncan buzzed with determination. I respected just how much effort he put into making sure it reached his eyes. For a moment, I believed his confidence in me. "Outside the doors to this room are hundreds of fey indebted to you. And I hardly get the impression Althea is going to leave your side again. I understand what Wychwood and the Icethorn Court represent for you."

"A lonely place. And I don't want those fey to fight for me just because they think they owe me. I am owed nothing."

"Respect is not a transaction, Robin." Duncan traced soft fingers over my skin, sending shivers down my spine. "And I refuse that statement that Icethorn is a lonely place. When we return, we do so as a family. Albeit a found family of misfits. A king to rule over reformed Hunters, mutated lovers, a nest of assassins and a host of fey who never believed they would find a home again."

I leaned over Duncan, lowering my face as close as I could to his without our lips touching. "How is it you have such words of wisdom in times when I need them most?"

"Perhaps our brief stay with Abbot Nathanial had a profound effect on me," he replied.

"He would be proud of you." I blinked, drinking in every detail of his face. From his dark lashes that framed his forest-green eyes, to the scar that linked from the corner of his left eye to his lip that deepened when he smiled. The way the stubble of his beard sharpened his cheekbones and jawline as though a painter shadowed the right parts of his face to make him exude masculine beauty.

"Nathanial would be proud of *us*," Duncan said, reaching his hands over my shoulders and lacing his fingers behind my head. He wedged me in place, ensuring I could not move away from him. "And more importantly, I love you."

I practically sagged beneath the words, unable to keep my bones and muscles strong enough to hold me up. Duncan had a way of melting me into a puddle with his words and touch.

"I love you, too," I replied. "Which is why I would do anything to protect you. Anything."

Before he could question the hidden meaning beneath my promise, with fierce lust, I crashed my lips into his. The kiss was sudden and full of passion. Duncan kept his hands behind my head, keeping me to him. Although, there was no way I would break away from him. Not now, not ever.

Our tongues encouraged one another into the dance. I tasted mint with the undercurrent of strong spirits. Whisky, perhaps. Its sharp bite glossed across my lip as his tongue trailed it.

Duncan brought his hips up beneath me. The press of his cock fuelled me. My fingers ran up the back of his head, coiling among his thick, chestnut-brown hair until I was locked in place. He hissed as I tugged, stretching the hair at the scalp to where pain and pleasure mixed as one.

He liked it. As did I. With Duncan, I had discovered ways of pleasure that he could provide me. Things I never knew were possible. There was a pride in uncovering a partner's desires, and this was one that shifted the control of sex into my hands as Duncan willingly gave himself to me.

I pulled at his hair harder, tearing his mouth from mine, leaving my lips tingling from his pressure. My jaw itched because his beard rubbed close against my smooth skin. Duncan cocked his head back, stretching his neck out as he expelled a groan that shuddered the very seas.

He knew what was coming.

I dove into his neck, tongue wetting his skin first to ready the place as I sucked and nibbled. I trailed the entire stretch of his neck until it was pink and moist.

Duncan's hands fell from the back of my head. His thick fingers trailed down my spine and found their place on either side of my ass. He pinched the fleshy skin as he gripped each cheek with desperation. I returned his rough touch with a sharp nip at the soft skin beneath his ear.

"You," Duncan said, voice deeper than it had been before. "Don't you dare move from this position. Am I clear?"

"Loud and clear," I replied, whispering into his ear. The brush of my lip against it conjured a shiver across Duncan's chest and arms.

"I'm going to fuck you where you sit."

Ensuring he knew that was what I wanted, I pressed myself down into his member. It twitched beneath me.

"Look at you, Duncan Rackley. It would seem the promise of my tight ass has brought you back to life."

"Such a naughty tongue. Perhaps I should put it to good use. You want me to fuck you, don't you, my King?"

I nodded. "I'm that readable, am I?"

"Indeed, you are."

Duncan's nails pinched into the skin of my thigh. I gasped before he yanked the remaining sheet off me, allowing the cold salt breeze to brush against the exposed heart of my ass. The pleasurable feeling only intensified as a large finger slipped across it.

"Remember, I'm still not feeling completely well," Duncan purred, eyes wide and burning with unbridled desire. His nail traced circles around the heart of my ass. The touch reduced me to a puddle of breathy moans. "I'm going to need you to do the work. Are you up to that?"

Just the thought alone had my knees trembling. It was a shame his cock would not greet the insides of my mouth because it salivated profusely. Such a waste of spit.

"I'll do my best."

"That is all I can ask," Duncan replied, lifting his fingers to his mouth. As he brought them away, a link of spit pulled between his hand and lips before snapping. My stomach hardened as his wet fingers wiped across my ass. I leaned forward, always breathless at his touch.

Duncan did it three more times until he offered his glistening fingers to my mouth.

"Spit," he demanded.

I did as he asked, glad to provide the lubrication that had filled my mouth.

Not such a waste, after all.

"Good boy," he said, his hand falling from view. This time his hand didn't touch me but himself instead.

The next moments happened so quickly. There was no warning as his thickness pressed into my ass and filled me. I called out, throwing my head back. Duncan entered me, urging me to sit back down until my cheeks pressed into his hips. I closed my eyes and arched my back instinctively.

"Ah," he moaned, biting down on his lower lip as his eyes rolled into the back of his head. "This is divinity in flesh."

He sat me like that for a moment, allowing my body to return from euphoria before continuing. Our heavy breathing synched. I was certain I felt the drum of his heart inside me, matching mine with every beat.

"I'm yours to do with as you please," Duncan said finally, lifting his hands from my ass and resting them behind his head. He wiggled into a comfortable position beneath me, the muscles in his stomach rippling. I counted six mounds, with hints of two others that hid beneath my thighs. It was so easy to lose myself to him. To distract myself with the way he had been crafted. The faint marks of scars, new and old, only added to the patchwork of stories that covered his skin. I loved every single one and wished I had time to kiss them all.

"I like it when you command me," I said, admitting my deepest inner thoughts. I spent all day playing king, commanding others, pretending to be something I naturally was not good at. But with Duncan, I gave up all that control to him. It's what I loved about our time together.

"Okay, Robin," Duncan spoke my name, drawing my attention back to his face. He had done little work so far, but still his forehead glistened with sweat. "Ride me. Do it until I fill you. Pleasure me, and I will do the same for you in return."

Living to please him, I did just that.

He didn't reach for my cock, not as I expected. I pouted down at him and, as though he could read my mind, Duncan added. "You won't need to do anything but fuck my cock, and I promise you, you will race toward the end without touching yourself. Do you trust me?"

"More than you could imagine."

"Good." Duncan smiled. "I'm all yours."

And he was. All of him, body and mind. He was mine.

I bounced upon his length. At first, the movements were small as I grew familiar with his stretching presence inside of me. Then the momentum built. I threw my ass down upon his cock, lifting it higher and higher with each thrust so his entire length could fill me. The wooden bed creaked and screamed. It echoed that of my legs, thighs and knees, which cried out.

But I didn't stop. Not as Duncan lost himself in the maze of pleasure, hardly able to keep his eyes open as I fucked myself upon his long, thick cock.

Deep inside me, the tip of his member found the point of divinity and slammed into it over and over. Soon enough, the world fell away from me as I could only focus on that feeling and ensuring I didn't let go of it.

"That's it," Duncan encouraged from beneath me. As though he knew I had found what he had suggested. He willed for me to grip a hold of the feeling and never let go. "Keep doing that, *just* like that. Fuck me. Darling..."

I think I said something in reply, but I was so far into the mysticism of his sex within me that everything seemed muffled except Duncan's voice. His deep tone guided me through it, only making the force of his cock inside me more intense.

Suddenly, I took a deep breath of freezing air. No longer did I linger within the divine feeling inside, but I became it. I shouted out as the pleasure overwhelmed me, spread its warmth across my stomach and raced down the end of my member until it burst out of its end.

I knew that Duncan also found the same blissful ending. As the ring of my ass tightened around his cock, and I slowed my bouncing, Duncan was calling out with the same groans as me. His were deeper but equally uncontrolled and overwhelmed with gratification.

It took a moment for the chaotic feeling to dissipate. I left the dream-like state and returned to the world, exhausted, happy and fulfilled.

Still, with Duncan inside of me, he brought me down to his mouth and kissed me softly. My damp palms spread across his chest.

"You did not lie," I said quietly, forehead pressed to his. "If I was not so tired, I would demand you show me that again."

I had finished without the need to touch myself. The feeling was impossible but possible. Clear from the spread of cloudy liquid that dripped from the tip of my cock onto Duncan's lower abdomen.

"We have an endless amount of time ahead of us," Duncan replied. "And I have an equal number of things to show you until you grow bored."

"Duncan, I will never grow bored of you. Not in this life or the next."

"I demand that you repeat that to me every morning and night," he replied through a yawn. "Just so I never forget. If you can't get some sleep after that, then I have failed my duty to you."

Duncan pressed a final kiss to my forehead and helped me off him. I rolled next to his side, unable to forget the physical memory of his cock inside of me. Nor did I wish to forget it.

"Promise?" I asked, glad my eyes fluttered closed, and my mind was empty of anything but him.

"I promise."

This time, when I closed my eyes, swept away by the rush of tiredness, there were no stone pillars or wings to greet me. No Erix or Jesibel. Just quiet and endless nothing. If only I could sink my fingers into the peace, because it wouldn't last for long.

CHAPTER 10

Two long days, and equally drawn-out nights, had passed since I last spoke with the Nephilim, yet their words grew louder in my head. Perhaps it was because my dreams repeated them. Over and over, replaying the vision Gabrial had revealed to me. If I could've gotten sleep uninterrupted by the same repetitive nightmares, I may have been able to concentrate on other matters. Alas, I found no reprieve when my eyes closed.

The yawn racked my entire body. My mind sluggish and footing awkward, I stumbled into the crowd that dominated the main deck.

It was impossible to discern the time of day when impregnable clouds blanketed the sky with a multitude of greys and silvers. I only hoped the rain, which had held off this far, would leave us be. It wouldn't be good for the morale of the sailors, finally preparing to embark on days' worth of travel.

Today we would leave for Wychwood. It would've been sooner but Seraphine's Asps had found fey stragglers in Lockinge and escorted them to us. I first didn't leave because of the Nephilim, but was glad for the hesitancy because I still held out hope that Jesibel would be found and returned to me.

A hope that was quickly dwindling when every small boat arrived and she was not on it.

Seraphine had accepted the summons I sent for her only an hour ago. She surveyed every Cedarfall soldier that passed us with eyes narrowed in distrust. I quickly learned that unless you were putting money in her pocket, she wasn't going to trust you. The assassin stood tall, both feet on the deck. Wisps of her thick hair caught in the wind, tugging free from the loose braid that snaked down her spine. She wore matching form-fitting trousers and a top made from the same cut of black material. It extenuated every length, curve and muscled mound of her body. The outfit was held together by a web of leather straps that concealed weapons in almost every place she could reach on her person. Perhaps her decoration of blade and steel was the reason no one seemed to approach her.

"How long ago did you get back?" I asked, my back pressing into the polished wooden railing that overlooked a drop into the dark azure of the ocean.

"Not too long ago. I didn't think that I had to check in my every movement, Your Highness," she replied, tone equal parts dry and distant. "Usually, my sponsors are not so suffocating."

"Touchy. Sounds like you have had a long night," I retorted, trying not to show how her tone chipped away at my ability to keep the poison from my tongue. "Are you annoyed at me for something, or more pissed that you came back empty-handed?"

"So, you heard?" Seraphine shot me a displeased look with a raised brow.

"I've learned gossip spreads quicker than scurvy on a ship," I replied. "That, and I keep checking over the census, hoping more names are added to it."

"Not the name you were hoping for I'm afraid." Seraphine exhaled, neck clicking from either side as she continued watching the busy crew. "Lockinge is lost to bedlam. Humans enjoy the lack of authority in the city. The few Hunters who stayed have now fled. The humans' king is nowhere to be found. I give it until nightfall, and the city will be lost to chaos that even Aldrick couldn't grasp his hands back on."

"Where have they all gone?" I asked, fighting the urge to chew on my already ruined nails.

"Called back to their master like good mutts."

"Then we send people to follow the Hunters, find out where Aldrick is?"

Seraphine shot me a smile. "Already on it."

"I knew I could trust you," I said, wondering if she even cared.

Turns out she didn't, as she replied, "You're paying me well, what can I say, I am yours until the contract is complete."

Which meant that when we landed back in Wychwood, Seraphine was no longer a crutch I could lean on.

"Don't remind me, I might just cry. I've grown rather fond of your company," I said, nudging her shoulder.

"I said you pay me well, but not enough to suffer through your sarcasm, King. It's high time we get out of human waters, and back to familiar ground."

"It didn't feel right leaving without at least trying to find as many who ran as possible," I said, reaching into the pockets of my trousers as though searching for something.

Seraphine shrugged. "A lesson in life is you can't help them all. Trust me."

"Then I'm wondering why you seem concerned about the humans and Lockinge?"

The corner of Seraphine's red-stained lip turned upward. "Believe me, Robin, I couldn't care less if the city burns to nothing but ash. But I understand the importance of balance, and it does not sit right with me that Aldrick has swept in behind a veil of lies and deceit, only to leave again with nothing but turmoil behind him. It has little to do with my care for the humans and everything to do with fixing the damage left by a common enemy."

"Even if the humans don't recognise Aldrick as that very thing, their enemy?"

"Oh, they will if he succeeds with his plans and the world becomes a playing field for a demon god," Seraphine replied. The humour that had not long graced her expression melted into something darker.

"Do you think Aldrick knows about the Nephilim?" I asked, tipping my head to the quiet outlines of boats that waited across the landscape behind our fleet. Two days, and we'd heard nothing from them. I hadn't seen nor had report of much activity from Rafaela and her fellow winged-human holy warriors. They had kept themselves quiet, but regardless of their silence, their presence was still felt. Even now, one glance across the sea, and their fleet still lingered.

"The Nephilim were never mentioned," Seraphine added, stare glazing over in thought. "Not that there was much conversation when my sister and I aided him. From what I can say about Aldrick, he is one-dimensional. He has little ability to focus on anything but the task at hand. It has consumed him."

I looked across the deck, eyes falling upon a familiar figure. Duncan moved among the crew, a large sack gathered on each of his shoulders. Extra supplies Seraphine had returned with.

The change in his body had been impressive. Now, he almost seemed stronger than before. Duncan's health had improved dramatically. Each morning, he woke with more colour in his cheeks and more desperation in his touch.

He'd not yet noticed me, but my attention gravitated toward him naturally. Duncan was laughing at something a Cedarfall soldier had said. Perhaps they joked about how Duncan could carry twice the weight without showing a sign of struggle, whereas the soldier was practically dragging one sack across the deck like a stubborn child in the throes of a tantrum.

"I get the sense that Aldrick knows more than we think he does," I replied. "We have underestimated him this far."

"So you believe Aldrick knows about the Nephilim?" Seraphine asked, drawing me from my distraction.

"His timing is all too sudden. Aldrick showed no signs of completely abandoning Lockinge. Even we believed he would only leave long enough for us to have a small window to get in and out. For such a great fortress, I don't understand the reasoning in his plans to leave it behind. Hardly protected at that. Unless he was running from something."

I noticed Seraphine's lips pinch into a pale line. Her brows drew downward, casting lines of concern across her forehead. "Speculation. I know everything he does. I would have known if he was preparing to flee."

"Would you?" I asked, discouraged by her blatantly inflated ego. "Then give me an explanation that makes sense."

"You haven't paid me enough for explanations," Seraphine retorted.

"Not this again." I rolled my eyes. A sour taste pinched at the insides of my cheeks. What more could Seraphine have asked for in payment than what I had already given her? Just the thought of the price I had paid was enough to encourage a storm in my stomach.

"Someone is looking better though." Seraphine changed the conversation abruptly. I believed she had the power to read my thoughts. "Amazing what sleep can do for the body after it nearly destroyed itself using power that doesn't belong to it."

"Yes," I replied. "Thank Altar for sleep."

Not that I could relate. I had very little of it.

"You know, I pity you, Robin."

Her comment slapped my cheeks red. "Pardon?"

"What will the courts think of King Icethorn when he opens his home to Hunters and assassins?"

"Would you keep your voice down?" I hissed, eyes flickering around the deck for anyone who may have heard.

Seraphine delighted in my reaction, both corners of her lips turning up into the brightest of smiles. "You haven't told him, have you?"

I turned my back on Duncan and faced Seraphine directly. I saw her gleeful expression and the outlines of the Nephilim's ships far in the distance behind her. "There has not exactly been the time to discuss such things with Duncan. Not that it would matter to him. As you so put it, I am the Icethorn king. My decisions are mine solely to make."

"Such an awfully long-winded way of saying no."

"No, then. Happy?"

Seraphine took the end of her braid in her hand and twisted it around her fingers as she studied me. "And Althea, did you ask for her judgement before you signed into my deal? Nothing better than some royal advice when making a deal with the Asps. I know members of the Cedarfall family are well attuned to how we work. That, and I have Asps everywhere. They burrow into every nest, all but yours. Until now, of course."

"Would you stop!" I hissed through gritted teeth.

"Robin, please let me watch when you tell them. I'd love to see their faces when you reveal what you gave us–"

The sky exploded with a thunderous crack. The force of the noise rocked the world. We were all awarded a moment of peace, trying to work out what had happened. But then the sound occurred again, this one far louder than the last. The boom burst within my ears, rocking my skull with the force. One moment I watched Seraphine's smile grow, the next, my face was pressed against the damp floor of the ship's deck with nothing but the crystal ringing filling my head.

I forced myself up, hands pressing against the slick wood, as more sprays of cold water rained upon me. Spread across the deck were bodies. Some were still, with wide eyes looking skyward. Others writhed across the ground, hands pressed to their ears or their mouths. It was strange to watch someone scream without a sound. I focused on a soldier closest to me. His lips were moving, but I couldn't hear anything above the ringing in my skull.

In a stupor, I sat myself up. Lifting my hands to my ears, I felt warmth. When I pulled them back, the tips of my fingers were coated in blood. The ruby glistened like jewels against my ivory skin. Rivers of it raced down my hand, circling my wrist before dripping upon my wet trousers.

Suddenly, two firm hands gripped my shoulders. I was aware of the touch before my mind could provide me with the command to look up.

Duncan knelt before me. His pale lips were moving, but I couldn't hear him. Not clearly, at least. I narrowed my gaze on his mouth and could hear a faint but muffled barrage of words. They seemed to be buried so deep beneath the incessant ringing that I could hardly focus enough to understand.

I almost laughed. The feeling was strange, but it seemed easier to give in to deliria and laugh at my confused state instead of allowing panic to overwhelm me.

Something beyond me, somewhere in the distance, caught Duncan's attention. He looked up to the sky, falling back away from me. I watched as the horror crept across his expression, his mouth gaping open in a silent scream, his eyes unblinking.

It was his reaction that tore me from my feverish state.

I followed his line of sight and looked up. Far above us, a wave of obsidian cloud rumbled across the sky with momentum that shouldn't have been possible. No storm moved so swiftly, devouring light as if it fed on it. Billowing and monstrous, the cloud passed overhead and moved toward Lockinge. It cast a shadow across the ground.

The ringing in my ears calmed. Another sound replaced it.

"What is…" I began, swallowing my words as the Nephilim joined the view with their wings outstretched, in contrast to the dark state of the sky. I blinked, capturing the image in my mind like a painting.

Rafaela took the lead of the flock, slicing in an arc toward our ship, which the rest of her kind followed. Even from a distance, I felt her stare upon the place I sat slouched. She held her golden hammer between two powerful hands, ready to use it.

"Robin, we need to get everyone off the deck," Duncan said, although more a command. Panic edged beneath each word, still muffled but now clear enough to make sense. He knelt before me once again, his entire focus on me. His verdant eyes flickered between the dripping blood from my ear to my red-stained fingers on my lap.

"What happened?" I replied, breath caught in the back of my throat.

Duncan traced his hand across my face. His touch felt cold. I recognised a slight tremble in his fingers. "Nothing good if they are coming."

I winced as Rafaela was suddenly in the air above us. She buffeted her wings, slowing her descent before her boots smashed onto the deck.

"Are you well, Robin Icethorn?" Rafaela strode forward, offering me a hand. I caught her eyes flickering toward the blood that dribbled out of my ears. Her attention lingered on it only for a moment, genuine concern etched across her face.

"Been better," I replied, contemplating taking her hand or not. My decision was made for me when she retreated. "I get the impression you know what caused that."

Rafaela nodded ever so slightly, biting down on her lower lip before responding. "I think it best you see to yourself and your people, and then we discuss matters in a place without an audience."

"Can we wait for answers?" Duncan asked, annoyance rolling off him. "Seems something that dramatic needs an explanation immediately."

I tried to catch my breath as it suddenly felt as though it had tried to escape from me. Panic clawed its way down my throat and made its presence known among my bones and blood.

"Something terrible has happened." Rafaela said. "Nothing good will come of speaking about it and causing hysteria to spread among your people."

"No shit," Seraphine groaned. Until now, among the chaos, I had forgotten about her. She was hunched over at Rafaela's side, shadowed by the proud wings. Red leaked from the corner of her mouth, only visible for a second before Seraphine cleared it with the back of her hand.

"Where is Althea Cedarfall?" Rafaela asked, ignoring Seraphine's glower.

I pressed my fingers to my temple, trying to calm the thudding that had overcome me. "She... she was on another ship with Kayne–"

Rafaela was airborne before I could finish. Duncan raised an arm against the force of wind her wings conjured. I turned my face into his chest, pinching my eyes closed. One moment she was there, the next, her outline fading across the sea of Cedarfall ships in search of Althea.

Something about her sudden, desperate departure only fuelled my worry. I pushed myself from Duncan's embrace and moved for the railing to follow Rafaela's flight. "If something has happened to Althea..."

"She'll be fine," Seraphine replied out of the corner of her mouth. "It is best you show those watching that you are calm too. There is nothing more detrimental to leadership than allowing panic to seep beyond your own control. Deep breath, turn and face them, and show that everything is in order."

She was right. All eyes were on me, and I quickly sensed the mask of king returning to its place upon my face.

"What if it isn't?" I said out the corner of my mouth, gripping onto the railing for support.

"Until Rafaela returns, we will not know exactly what has happened," Duncan added, laying a hand on my shoulder and squeezing.

I looked between them both, unable to stop myself from speaking aloud what my mind had already made up.

"Aldrick." I spoke his name as though it was the most disgusting thing to grace my lips. "This is his doing. It has to be."

Seraphine looked out across the sea toward Lockinge and the rolling dark wave that had thinned into what looked more like mundane storm clouds.

Duncan didn't offer me a lie to douse the flames of panic within me. But he also didn't shy away from my gaze, instead greeting it with haunting defeat. "I think he found what he was looking for."

"A key?" Seraphine spat. "How could he find something when we don't even know what it is yet?"

Something that the Nephilim had said repeated in my mind as though Seraphine's comment had dredged it from the deepest parts of my subconscious.

"Not what," I said, fighting the urge to empty the contents of my stomach into the ocean beneath me. I had to be strong, if not for myself, but every fey watching for me to lead. "But who?"

CHAPTER 11

I stared out the circular porthole, marvelling at the blue sky. There was no longer even the wisp of dark cloud. The sun beat proudly upon the ocean, making its surface glisten like diamonds. The gentle lull of water against the boat and the quietness of the deck beyond the room only added to the atmosphere of serenity. If I closed my eyes and placed my hands across my ears, then I might've even tricked myself – convinced myself that I wasn't in this cabin, listening to the Nephilim as they turned everything we knew on its head with a single sentence.

"Aldrick *has* discovered a key," Rafaela said, confirming what I'd already worked out. A worried scowl set into her face as she rested her weight against the hammer. "We hoped Aldrick searched blindly for them, but it would seem he has obtained access to information that shouldn't belong to him. Information that left these realms when we departed."

"And you are certain his discovery caused the phenomenon?" Althea asked, sitting straight-backed in her chair. Her entire posture was rigid and stiff, whereas I felt the urge to give myself to the exhaustion and crumple in on myself.

"What happened was only a warning. A sign that the bindings keeping the Defiler trapped have weakened," Gabrial added, her gaze never leaving the skin of her arm. Symbols and words flowed, moving in tandem with her eyes which scanned her skin like the page of a book. She studied them, brow creased in concentration. "Much like Robin, Aldrick is half-fey, meaning his story is scripted among the Creator's words. I can see what he has achieved and how. There is no denying his success." When Gabrial lifted her attention from her skin and sighed, a single tear rolled down her cheek.

"And our failure," Cassial growled, mountainous arms crossing his chest.

"What can you see?" Seraphine asked, unable to hide the demand in her tone. "If he has one, then there are three more to get. Surely, we can keep Aldrick away from the rest of the keys?" The assassin lurked in the shadows of the cabin, fiddling with a short, serrated knife to keep her hands busy. "Or lead him to us if they share such knowledge."

"Exactly, Asp." Rafaela wrung her hands on the handle of her hammer. "However, it would seem that Aldrick is already aware of where the remaining keys are. Keeping the information from you will be of no benefit to us anymore–"

"Rafaela," Cassial growled. "We haven't discussed this."

"Cassial, please calm yourself down," Gabrial replied, clearly unconcerned by the bloodthirsty assassin who stalked her as a cat did its prey, nor the mountain of a man imposing over her.

"Tell us how we stop him," I said, finally breaking my silence. "What good is waiting around discussing matters when we need to find and stop him? As Rafaela said, if he has one, he knows where to get the others. It is clear you know where the keys are and keeping them from us will benefit no one. Aldrick *knows*. Level the playing field and tell us what you are keeping."

Gabrial and Rafaela shared a look. Cassial grunted in his own form of silent communication.

Duncan had remained as quiet at my side, silently surveying the shifting tide of tension within the cabin. He placed a hand upon my shoulder, setting in closer until his stomach brushed against my back. At first, I wanted to refuse his wish to join this conversation, especially with the way the Nephilim's gazes always seemed to linger on him. But there was no keeping Duncan away, not after what had happened. Besides, I needed him with me.

After all, it was his choice to make, not mine.

"Believe us when we say that we have no interest in allowing Aldrick to lay his hands upon another key," Rafaela said.

"And there is no saying what will happen if the gate keeping the Defiler imprisoned is weakened again." Gabrial lowered her arms beneath the table, that single tear slipping off the tip of her button nose.

I wanted to ask what she cried over, but the time wasn't right.

"Where's this gate we are so concerned about?" Duncan asked, taking the words out of my mouth. "If such a place exists physically, should it not be guarded at all times?"

"Oh, it is." Rafaela tilted her head, eyes trailing Duncan from head to foot. "The Isle of Irobel is not only our home but the very land in which the gods fought and won against the Defiler. Generations ago, when mortals and gods communed with ease, the Creator sent the Nephilim to live and guard the gate, never to leave unless the threat of the Defiler's freedom became a possibility. Although we can be killed by mundane means, the Nephilim live far longer lives than humans or even the fey. We were made for this task."

"I would suggest keeping conversations of your weakness at a minimum," Seraphine added.

Rafaela shot her a look, her head tilting inquisitively. "Are we not allies, Asp? Why should we concern ourselves with sharing such knowledge when all in this room trust one another, do we not?"

It was a loaded question, and from the way Seraphine shifted her eyes to me, I knew she'd just opened the playing field for me to provide an answer. "Yes. We are allies. To be honest, we need as many as we can get if we are to face Aldrick."

All I could think about was what Duncan had said about the fey we freed being the ones to fight for us. Why risk the lives of people I'd just saved, when there was a ready and waiting army just before us?

"I agree with Robin, but allyship comes with trust," Althea said, turning the focus to her. "So, I have a few questions, if I may."

Rafaela waved a hand for her to begin. "Be our guest."

"Does the fact that Irobel is not charted on any map have anything to do with upholding the same air of secrecy for both your kind and the gate itself?" Althea asked. "I can only guess that removing all traces and stories of Duwar from both the fey and humans' histories was important to upholding his imprisonment. But the lack of education about Duwar has only led us on the path of being unprepared. Frankly, our lack of knowledge has set us up to lose."

Rafaela nodded, mouth edging into a frown. "If anyone ever said the fey were not clever beings, they were wrong."

Althea's rich eyes narrowed on the Nephilim. "Care to clarify if that's a compliment?"

Rafaela placed a hand over her heart. Regret pinched at the corners of her mouth. "I did not mean to offend you, Princess Althea Cedarfall."

Althea sucked her tongue across her teeth. The smack of it was the only sound she replied with.

We weren't off to a good start. For the sake of our next steps, I had to take over.

"Gabrial," I said softly, trying to ease my way through the tension. "Can you tell us how Aldrick found the first key? If you share the knowledge, it will help us keep him from the rest."

"*That* is not information necessary for you to be privy to," Cassial snapped, tensing his broad frame as he spoke. It seemed even the veins in his neck bulged as though strangled between muscles.

I got the impression that talking to Cassial was more of a challenge than the rest of them.

"Cassial, if Aldrick has discovered the truth, then there is nothing stopping us from sharing it with them. We can agree on that, can't we?" Gabrial looked to the brooding male, exuding the same demeanour of power without all the muscle and brawn. "As Princess Althea has suggested, perhaps we have been led down this road of failure because of secrecy. It has not brought us any luck thus far."

I could see Cassial's desire to refuse Gabrial, but one look at Rafaela, and he seemed to retreat. "So be it. On your head be the Creator's judgement."

"I *am* the Creator's judgement," Rafaela reminded, her tone overbrimming with the allure of a leader. "I say we tell them the truth."

"The floor is all yours," Althea said, displeased by the sibling-like quarrel. Or just displeased with Cassial, because her stare only fixed on him with a look of pure contempt, enjoying every moment of him being put in his place.

Rafaela cleared her throat, just as Gabrial nodded at her to begin. "It was Altar who forged the lock upon the gate, after agreeing with the Creator to banish Duwar. It weakened both gods greatly, not just in power but their relationship. Duwar was the thorn keeping them apart. Both gods lost immense levels of power trapping the Defiler in his prison, which can be felt to this day with their lack of physical presence in the realms. In a weakened state, both Altar and the Creator used the remaining essence they held and crafted physical beings in whom they could entrust the banishment of the Defiler to last eternally. The Creator, as we explained, crafted the Nephilim in his image. From his tears, we were made. Just as Altar created the fey from his blood. Altar tricked the Creator though. He took his essence, the keys to Duwar's gate, and placed it in four of your kind. Burying his power within them with the purpose of stowing it and spreading it out as a fail-safe to keep the gate sealed. What I'm sure your god didn't account for was that those four beings he had chosen would take their new power and use it to fashion a realm to benefit them. All whilst forgetting their initial purpose."

A deathly quiet settled over the cabin. I could've sworn I heard every person's heart beat in tandem. I took a breath, only to find my heart bundled in my throat. I almost choked on it. Rafaela's words repeated like a puzzle that I attempted to piece together. The edges of my vision darkened as the world seemed to melt away. When I blinked, it seemed the darkness only insisted on drowning me entirely.

"I don't understand what you are alluding to," Seraphine snapped.

I wanted to look at Althea, but I was frozen in place whilst my mind pieced together the meaning of Rafaela's story.

"Yes. What is it you're trying to imply?" Duncan added. The warmth of his voice reminded me of my control. As always, it calmed me. At least enough to lean into his hand that was spread across my shoulder.

"The fey courts," I said. "We're the keys Aldrick is looking for."

As if my words were the crack of a whip, the room exploded in mummurs and questions.

"Yes, that is correct," Rafaela said. "Robin Icethorn, you are a key. One of the three left remaining. Althea, your mother is another..."

Aldrick had a key and it slipped through his fingers. It was me.

"Which leaves Elmdew and Oakstorm," Althea muttered, gaze lost to a place upon the desk before us.

"From our understanding," Gabrial added, "the Oakstorm key has recently exchanged place from Doran Oakstorm to his wife Elinor upon her return."

"Yes, Elinor claimed it," I confirmed, thoughts drifting to the instructions I had shared with her. Instructions I had to uncover myself when claiming the destructive power of the Icethorn Court, which I now recognised as something else entirely.

Gabrial said softly, whilst spreading her sorrowful stare across the room. "I believe you have a ritual for such a transfer, although the meaning has been lost to you, masqueraded beneath royal protocol. Although Robin, from what I've gleaned, you weren't blessed with such a ritual. You faced the raw power of Altar's essence and claimed it yourself, did you not?"

"If there was a passing of a key, I would know about it," Althea snapped, eyes wide as she tried to make sense of the revelation.

"Forgive our choice of words," Rafaela said. "We refer to Altar's essence as a key, but it is not shown in the shape or form that you expect when linked with such a word. It is power unlike anything you can understand…"

"Power that could destroy a realm," I said, remembering the bundle of pure magic that chased through Icethorn's skies before I accepted it. "Elinor returned to the Oakstorm Court to claim it."

"Except, it is not *power*." Rafaela's grip tightened upon her hammer. "It's the *key* to keeping a demon from entering this world and destroying it. Hence the word. Althea, you would know about the succession rites of your court. Can you understand any part of it that could suggest the transference of a key from one to another, without realising the potential of power you accept?"

The Cedarfall princess pondered the question. Through her widened eyes I could practically see the cogs turning. "There is something. A short practice where the head of the court presents a labradorite carving to their chosen heir. It's all I can think about."

I'd never heard of such a rite before, but then again, my true family died before they had the chance to reveal such things to me. "What is that?" I asked.

"Labradorite is known as Altar's bones. It's the same stone that signifies the separating borders between each realm. It is what keeps the power in…" Althea blinked, realising something. "Because it *contains* power."

Gabrial smiled, a proud grin one would expect a parent gave their child when doing something impressive. "Exactly, Princess Cedarfall. As the queen or king who carves their chosen statue out of labradorite, it contains the essence – Altar's key – and then is given to the next. Although you do not remember the complexities to the rite, that is what it is for."

"We wear them, for two weeks before we are crowned," Althea said.

"Thus soaking the essence into yourselves without knowing," Rafaela added. "Like water to a sponge. Although, you know what happens when the rite is not complete – as Robin Icethorn's story proves."

"Wait." I gargled on the word. Dread traced its talon up my spine. A wave of pure sickness overcame me. "If a key has been destroyed, then…"

Althea's chair screeched as she pushed out of it. Her force was so great that the chair tumbled, crashing into the ground away from her. We both worked it out at the same time, blinded first by knowledge, but even that couldn't keep out the root of the conversation.

Aldrick had destroyed a key. Gabrial had shed a tear when she told us – as though she was grieving over something. No, not something. *Someone.*

"Who did he kill?" I spat, slamming ice-cold hands upon the table until ice webbed out across it, devouring wood within seconds.

Heat flared at my side, more magic spilling free into the air.

"If a key has been destroyed…" Althea's eyes filled with furious tears, but her resolve kept them from spilling. Her entire body trembled, encouraging streams of heat to twist from her skin. Cassial flinched from her suddenly. "I hardly imagine the fey he has encountered would give the… power. The key, whatever it is. They wouldn't have given it to him willingly. Who did Aldrick kill – is my mother still alive?"

Rafaela recoiled at Althea's cracked shout. More of her heat pumped into the air, encasing the cabin in an unbearably sweltering fog.

Unable to let her suffer alone, but aware her lack of control could destroy us all in a single moment, I moved to her side. As my arms wrapped around her, I brought my icy chill to encase my skin, just to protect myself. Our powers clashed in a hiss, but I didn't let go.

"Your family is safe," I whispered into her ear, trying to convince her and myself. "I believe it."

"Robin is right. The Cedarfall court has not been touched by Aldrick. At least, not yet."

Then who? Elinor? The Elmdew kings? I felt guilty in the knowledge that I put more hope into it *not* being Elinor Oakstorm.

"If he touches them..." Althea didn't need to finish her threat for me to understand it.

"I know," I replied. "And I will be with you when he burns."

"Aldrick has not destroyed a key, he needs them."

That calmed Althea down, settling my own maelstrom within me. "Then no one has died?"

"Unfortunately they have. Aldrick will not destroy the essence, because he requires it. However, its host, they are only a barrier in his way," Gabrial confirmed. "Destruction of such a power is detrimental to his end goal."

"I will ask you again," Althea seethed. "Who has he killed?"

Gabrial stood slowly from her chair, pressing her hands dutifully before her as though holding a flower between each palm. Across her skin, the symbols had stilled, fading to a faint silver until they looked more like old scars. Regardless, I knew they were there, waiting to be read by the Nephilim when required.

She lifted her azure stare, expression not matching the words that followed. "King Peta Elmdew and his husband, King Consort Dai. The spring court has fallen. I am so sorry for your loss."

Gabrial lowered her chin, falling quiet. In the wake of her revelation, there was a heavy weight that set upon us all. Her silence allowed us to take in the knowledge that Aldrick had succeeded in killing the Elmdew kings. And that truth settled over my conscience like molten ash.

Gabrial's previous sorrow made sense now. This explained why her stare lingered on her skin, rather than us, at the beginning of our conversation. She had known. Maybe even seen what Aldrick had accomplished.

If it had turned her to tears, I could only imagine how horrifying the truth really was.

"Can you... show me?" I asked. My throat burned with anguish. It took effort not to give in and allow it to overcome me completely.

Rafaela read Gabrial's body language and spoke for her. The younger Nephilim dropped her stare, and retreated further to the side of the room.

"Their death was not kind, Robin. Witnessing it will not bring you anymore answers to what we have given you." I read the emotion in Rafaela's open stare and knew her refusal was a way of protecting me. "It would seem that Duwar shields Aldrick. Gabrial can only see glimpses of what has occurred. What she can glean seems to be what Aldrick wants her to see. How he has got such knowledge of the keys, and of us, I cannot yet comprehend."

"We aren't going to let him win," I said, gaze lost to a place on the wall beyond Rafaela's head. "Every move, every step. Aldrick is always ahead. So, we must find a way to leap ever further, to put him on the back foot for once."

Not one disagreed with me, and yet I still couldn't say exactly how we were to do this. But the seed was sown, I wasn't prepared to give up so easily.

"Can you at least tell us how this has happened?" Duncan questioned. "Only days ago, Aldrick was in Lockinge. Knowing just how he has gotten so many steps ahead will help us navigate forwards. Please, Gabrial. We appreciate this is hard for you, truly. Any further information will be greatly appreciated."

If there was no other reason I required Duncan in this moment, it was for how he spoke to Gabrial. Careful, and with respect. He was far more skilled at keeping his emotions in check than I was.

"I will try." Gabrial cleared her throat, then lifted her reddened eyes back to the group. Gone was the sadness. Now anger replaced it. "Aldrick's personal ties to the Elmdew Court root deep. Reading his past is messy, as though it has been tampered with. It would seem he left Lockinge long before you think he did." I shot my eyes to Seraphine, who hardly masked the abundant surprise from Gabrial's explanation. "Aldrick, alongside an army of mutated humans, crossed the Wychwood border and infiltrated the court. What I know, which is the clearest part I can see, is that Aldrick used his power to ensnare King Peta and make him give up his power somewhat willingly. What followed is…" Gabrial smacked her hand to her mouth. Her skin took on a greenish sheen.

"That's enough." Rafaela shot forward to fuss over Gabrial but was waved off. "No more."

"I am fine," Gabrial spluttered. "I just… give me a moment."

Edging on the side of caution, I thought it best the conversation was taken away from what Gabrial had learned. The horror she'd seen had affected her greatly. It aged the young girl before my eyes, a heavy burden to witness the death of a person, whether she knew them or not.

Empathy was a unique gift, and Gabrial was overcome with it. I told myself that there would be a time we would demand answers, but for now, it could wait. Our focus had to be honed.

"What does this mean for us?" Althea asked, red-rimmed eyes lifting, the faint crackle of heat still emanating from her skin.

"It means that Aldrick is going to stop at nothing to get the remaining keys," I said. "But we are going to stop him."

"Yes, we are." Rafaela locked her golden stare upon me, fixing me to the spot with her determination. "Robin, Aldrick is going to come for you. For all of you. But I... we will not allow that to happen. Going forwards, any step made, we do it together. If you will accept our help, we cannot make you."

"We accept," I said, with the confidence of the king I was becoming.

My hand shot out toward Rafaela, such a human gesture but one that the Nephilim recognised because she took my hand in hers, her grip iron-clad. "Then let us form a plan, ally."

CHAPTER 12

Three excruciatingly long days of travel – that's how long it took my body to finally adopt the natural sway which mirrored the ship's as it sliced across the ocean. The terrible sickness, which the sailors had warned about, had barely passed. In its wake, I was left with a thudding ache deep in my skull. It sang in synchronicity with the smashing of water against the ship's hull.

I spent more time on deck, surrounded by open salt winds, than in the dark pits of the cabin in which Duncan was currently left sleeping. I wished for him to be well enough so I could share his gentle warmth with the freedom of the sea.

Dawn had barely graced the skies with its brush of lilac and rose. It was common that the deck was full of life before the sun rose. The buzz of the fey snatched away the peace I craved. I grew used to slipping out whilst they slept. Moments like this, small pockets of quiet when there was nothing but me and my thoughts, were not as terrible as I once believed.

The silence gave me time to contemplate what had passed and what also waited for us when we arrived in Icethorn in a matter of days.

However, today I wasn't the only one who frequented the early hours of the day to bask in its clarity. Rafaela weaved throughout the thin wisps of cloud with her wings outstretched, casting a shadow across the deep azure waters below. As we did each morning, we recognised each other's presence with a glance and then left each other alone. She kept to the skies above her ship; I kept to monitoring mine.

Rafaela and Gabrial had joined our journey to Wychwood, whereas Cassial stayed in Lockinge with an army of Nephilim. Quietly, I was glad he didn't follow. Cassial hoped to gain control of the human city. Faith in the Creator had dwindled to a dying flame thanks to Aldrick and the wildfire that was his lies. However, Cassial believed in the power that was spreading the word of the Creator back among the humans. I imagined once the humans saw the winged warrior, they wouldn't need much reminding of the faith they'd not long traded for Duwar and his promise of power.

It wasn't every day angels from scripture turned up at your doorstep.

Neither Rafaela nor Gabrial had even given thought to joining Cassial. Both had made it their duty to protect the remaining three keys, plain and clear. Which meant, proven by the shadow I'd gained, Rafaela never strayed too far. When I was awake, she was awake. Even hidden within my cabin with Duncan's limbs entwined with mine, I sensed her.

My stomach groaned, sending a sharp stab of hunger across my torso. I pressed a hand to it, massaging the ache in hopes it faded. It wouldn't be long until the mess hall would be overcome with food and I'd eat with those manning the ship. I wouldn't touch a morsel of food before, choosing to break bread with the fey I'd saved. If anything, I told myself it would help build respect – reminding them that I was no different to them.

Luckily, it wasn't required to stop along the Durmain coastline to restock since leaving Lockinge. Rafaela had seen to us being stocked up with food and supplies, ensuring we could keep moving toward our destination without delaying.

That wasn't the only reason I was glad we didn't need to stop. We didn't know what lurked along the human landscape. Their hate for our kind would take longer to repair, and it was best we returned to our realm as soon as possible. Both to return the fey back to their rightful homes and to enter the chaos that was left in the wake of Aldrick's destruction of the Elmdew Court.

Every day that passed was another day closer to Aldrick becoming a threat to another court. I only hoped the birds we sent with messages reached the courts before Aldrick's force did.

Footsteps sounded across the deck, distracting me. It was unusual for someone to be up so early. I turned, gathering myself, and prepared to leave the sailors to their tasks, but it was Kayne who emerged from the shadowed stairwell. A look of surprise splashed across his freckled face, telling me that he didn't expect to find anyone awake.

I offered a smile and made a move to leave.

"Rushing off?" he called after me, voice thick with a yawn.

Suddenly, I felt awkward. I fidgeted with my hands, kept in place as Kayne stood at the exit of the lower decks. Tall, thin as a reed with long legs and arms, which he stretched away, the tiredness settled in his bones.

"I left Duncan a while ago. It would be better that I'd returned to the cabin by the time he wakes up," I replied, trying to read the trepidation in his narrowed eyes. "Unless you would prefer my company?" *Which I doubt you would.*

I hardly had shared a word with him in days, and not by my own choice. Kayne laughed but said nothing to combat my question, proving my theory right.

Lucari gleefully swooped from his shoulder, wings flapping in a blur as she shot skyward toward Rafaela, giving chase. Once the hawk drew close to the Nephilim, she recognised Rafaela wasn't willing to play and quickly dipped away from her. Her squawk practically screamed with fear.

"Can't sleep either?" he asked, breaking the silence between us. I hated how tense he was when he spoke to me. I wasn't the one starting the conversation, and yet I still felt like it was an agony getting any more than a few words out of him at a time.

"Not really. I've been awake for hours, something about the swaying that really fucks with my stomach," I replied, feeling the usual awkwardness that thickened the air when Kayne was around. After our last interaction, it seemed Kayne did everything to only be around me when Duncan was there. Even the hesitant glint in his eyes revealed he would have preferred I'd not seen him. "How about you?"

"All I will say is the moment my feet touch the solid, unmoving ground, I might just cry," Kayne said, focusing his attention on his hawk and not on me. "I've heard we have a couple more days of this hell to get through."

"If winds permit, we will reach Wychwood late evening in two days. At the earliest."

"Oh, I can just imagine the warm welcome now," Kayne said, not bothering to conceal the roll of his eyes.

"You were a Hunter. Forgive the fey for treating you with caution, which I am sure you can understand they'll have…"

"I sense a but coming on."

"*But*, they will learn to trust you like I have."

He shot me a look, brow furrowing. "Do you?"

"I hope so."

Kayne huffed, stretching his neck backwards and then to either side. Besides what his words suggested, nothing about him seemed concerned. "Duncan will expect the welcome too, right? What is to say you are not leading us blindly, to reach Wychwood only to be met with a trial for our heinous crimes?"

"After everything we've been through, you still don't trust my intentions," I replied. I savoured the harsh copper tang as my teeth gnawed down into the inside of my cheeks. The pain and taste were the distraction required to not say what I truly wanted.

Kayne shrugged, smiled and walked right past me with the confidence of someone knowing where they wished to go. Which, on a deck surrounded by stretches of ocean and nowhere to go, confirmed he just wished to get away from me.

"Is there a problem?" I asked, rooted to the spot.

"I don't know, should there be?" Kayne said, shrugging broad shoulders.

"No. Kayne, I don't understand your hostility toward me. I don't want to have this relationship with you," I said, chasing after him like a fool. In another world, I would've walked away, cursing his name under my breath. But Kayne was Duncan's closest friend. His brother of soul, not blood. It was imperative we got along.

And I needed Kayne for other means. Selfish, yes, but still important. Kayne's skills as a Tracker were highly desirable for the problem I had: locating Jesi.

"Do you want me to pretend to like you?" he asked.

My throat tightened. "Ah, so he finally admits it."

"I thought I'd made it obvious. Guess I should've tried harder."

"If you don't care about me, then why are you here, Kayne? Nothing was stopping you from leaving. You could have turned your back on all of this, but you helped. Is it to boost your ego or make yourself feel better for the terrible things your time as a Hunter has caused?"

Kayne spun on me. All of his humour melted from his face. I rocked back a step. "Do you truly need me to spell it out to you?"

"Well, it might help me understand you."

Kayne's chest rose and fell with each breath. His eyes bulged, veins protruding from the temples of his head. For a moment, I thought he was going to expose all his truths, but then his chin dropped to his chest, and he took a shuddering inhale.

When he looked back again, he was in control. "I'm sorry, Robin. It's been a long couple of weeks and... I shouldn't take it out on you. I've never been good at controlling my tongue like Duncan."

I searched his tone for insincerity but came away empty-handed. "If there is something you wish to get off your chest..."

Kayne shook his head and continued before I could prod again. "There is no excuse for my behaviour. Duncan would tell you, I'm a prick. Born and bred. Ignore me. And maybe don't tell Duncan. He'd tear my throat out if he heard how I spoke to you, and I am rather fond of it, so please, you know, maybe keep my sudden, unfair outburst between us."

I zipped my finger across my lips and threw it over my shoulder in a gesture. "Not a word." *At least not yet*, I thought.

Kayne sighed, genuinely relieved. "Great."

"Great," I echoed.

Kayne whistled for Lucari to return to him. "Best be off. I find the best time to sleep on the ship is when everyone else is awake. Less snoring to keep me up. A bit more rest might even improve my mood."

He went to move past me, but this time I stopped him. My hand pressed against his chest. "I need to ask something of you before you leave."

Kayne glanced sideways at me, then down to my hand, before he stepped back to remove my touch. There was no ignoring the grimace that lifted his lip into a snarl. "Should I be worried?"

"Maybe. It's about Jesibel," I said, repeating her name as though everyone else was as familiar with it as I was. Which, in this case, Kayne was. After he had taken the census of the fey names, he knew who it was I longed to find among the lists. "You're a Tracker. You have more skills when it comes to locating someone, especially a fey, than anyone else I can think of. Lucari has helped you find hundreds of fey in the past, and all for the wrong reasons. What if I asked you to help me find one, but for the right reasons?"

Kayne paused, digesting my words as though they were something hard to swallow. He chewed on the insides of his lower lip, stare tracing every inch of my face as he conjured his response. "I can't do that."

My heart sank into the pit of my stomach like a stone in a river of anxiety. "Would you rather I beg you?" I said with urgency. "Because I will."

Kayne shook his head gently. "It's not safe for Lucari to travel such long distances without me. There's no saying that she will find Jesibel alive alongside Aldrick. But doing so will only allow Aldrick to use Lucari like a beacon as she guides him back to us. To *you*."

He almost seemed pleased with his excuse. A flash of pride passed across his eyes, if only for a moment. It was soon replaced with an emotion more empathetic, like forced relief. He wasn't quick enough or slick enough for me not to notice.

"I'm worried about her, Kayne," I forced out, almost ready to tell him how she invaded every dream I'd had in the days past. If only to free myself from her haunting presence, I longed to do something, anything, to help find her. "How is it that even the fey we saved have no idea if Aldrick took her. They can name other fey, but not Jesi. She can't have just vanished."

"Have you ever contemplated that she doesn't want to be found?" Kayne asked, and I felt the blood in my veins chill.

Unable to formulate a reply, Kayne took my silence as a means to end the conversation. "Are we done here?"

I swallowed hard. "Very much."

Before I would actually get on my knees and beg, I turned my back on Kayne, feeling the pressure of another's attention on me. As I looked skyward, Rafaela was looking in our direction as though she had heard the entire interaction.

"Robin," Kayne called out a final time. "I *am* sorry for, you know... earlier."

I had to stop myself from turning around and shouting at Kayne. His refusal to even consider helping me had encouraged a lump of frustration to fill my throat. If I had unclamped my closed lips, what I had to say would not have been so kind.

I flashed Kayne a fake smile to complete our conversation just as a noise sounded from the sky above us. When I glanced up at Rafaela, she was no longer looking at me. Instead, she glanced toward a dark mass in the distance, one that flew above the line of clouds with incredible speed.

My blood thrummed with ice as the shadow grew larger the closer it became. Although I couldn't make sense of it, I knew it was a threat as my magic naturally rose to the surface. Beast or not, I'd protect this ship with everything in me.

The mass moved with speed, slicing above the cover of the cloud.

Rafaela had stopped flying. She hovered in place with the hammer gripped in her hands. She unleashed a throaty noise which carried across the sky, much like the sound she'd made to call off the attack on the fey ships days ago. The purpose behind it soon became clear as more winged Nephilim shot skyward from their ships to join her. This time, it was a rallying cry.

Each held weapons that caught the light of dawn and winked with the kiss of illuminated gold.

"What is that?" Kayne grumbled, hand raised to his brow. "Has another key been…"

"No," I said, sure of myself. "This is different to before–"

A sky-splitting roar bellowed over us.

My next words shouted over the roar. "Get Duncan."

"It looks like it has…"

"GET DUNCAN NOW!"

A deafening snarl drowned out my shout as the shadow closed over our fleet of ships. Between the weaker wisps of cloud, obsidian scales flashed. Great wings cast darkness over the boat, blocking out the sun completely as it moved overhead. My eyes took in leathery wings double the size of the sails that flapped behind me. A tail as thick as the trunk of the oldest of trees.

My mind drifted to Gyah, pulling forward an image of her in her Eldrae form. But this was not an Eldrae. Fearsome and deadly, its presence weighed down on the world. It let out another sound, grumbling from the pits of its hulking body.

The Nephilim readied themselves for an attack.

Kayne hadn't moved. Lucari was silent as death on his shoulder.

I gripped the edge of the railing, ice crackling across the wood. Not once did I take my eyes off the creature as it flew overhead. It was a risk to even exhale for fear of drawing attention to myself.

As suddenly as the monster's presence became known, it passed. Flying out of sight toward the faint outline of land in the distance.

I was left gripping onto the splintering railing, with the inability to move. Part of me waited for the monster to turn back around, realising what it had just passed over. Surely it would come back to devour us. But I got the sense it didn't attack because it didn't bother itself with us. Not because it wasn't our enemy, but because we were not a threat in its eyes.

I don't know what truth made me feel better.

"Do not worry, the Draeic will not return," Rafaela confirmed, knuckles pale beneath her tension as she leaned against her hammer.

I turned to look up at her, blinking away the shadow the beast had imprinted into my consciousness. "Draeic, yet another name for creatures we've never known existed before."

"It is a demon, Robin." For the first time, I saw fear in the Nephilim's eyes. "I had hoped such nightmares would be kept at bay, but the Defiler is making the most of the weakness Aldrick has gifted to the gate. I imagine more will come if they haven't already."

I didn't recall stories of demons such as the one that had just passed when Duwar had been mentioned. From my knowledge, although limited, I understood Duwar was banished to another realm. But the echo of the beast that still rang in my head had proven otherwise.

"What was it exactly?" Kayne asked, voice on edge with a subtle tremor. His skin had turned ice-white with fear. "And why is it all the way out here? I thought the gate was in Irobel?"

"There is much we don't know about the Defiler. There's no saying what the demon god has accomplished during their banishment. But the Draeic are like hounds. Pets, if you will. They go to where they are called."

"To Aldrick," I muttered, aware that my breath fogged beyond my lips as my power coiled out of my control.

It took a moment for my mind to catch up. I still reeled from what I had witnessed. Commotion spread across the ship as the fey tumbled out to find out what had happened. Across the sea, I saw the smudge of figures leaning over the railings in search of the thing that had woken them.

"It's going to him, isn't it?" I said, cautious. I didn't want to spark fear among the crowd. "He is behind this. The keys, the gate. This is just another string he can add to his bow. Soon enough, the bastard will have enough to balance the arrow that destroys us."

"It would be the most plausible of answers," Rafaela replied. Lines had etched themselves across her forehead. Deep-set and aggressive, so much that they looked like physical scars of her concern.

I knew that feeling well enough to recognise it.

"Are you all right?" I asked as Rafaela dropped her wide eyes to the ground.

"If... if that monster made it this far from the gate, it means it got past the Nephilim stationed there."

The sudden understanding of her visible distress became clear to me. She was concerned for those she'd left behind. "I am sure they are–"

But before I could finish consoling Rafaela, her wings burst outward. It took only two powerful flaps with undeniable force and she was skyward, shouting down one last command. There was not an ounce of sadness or concern left in her eyes. "We must reach Wychwood. It's no longer safe. Robin, urge your ships forward, use your power to buffer the sails with the winter winds coursing through you. We must *not* allow for any further delays."

CHAPTER 13

Drifts of snow fell upon Duncan's head, tangling with his dark hair. I was mesmerised by him. Intricate flakes caught in his eyelashes and littered his broad shoulders, soaking into his leathers, making them glisten in the dull light. For those that fell upon his skin, it took a moment for them to melt upon impact with his warmth. Once evaporated, they left a glistening sheen of moisture across the sharp lines of his face.

The muscles in Duncan's jaw were set with concentration. His brows furrowed over narrowed eyes as he tried to make out the shapes through the mist and darkness before they revealed themselves as our ship drew closer to the land. "You've done us all a service, Robin."

"I only did what was required," I replied, although my body sang with my exhaustion. If I wasn't sleeping, I was doing as Rafaela requested, calling upon cold winds to rip across the ocean and press our ships forwards.

I wasn't the only one. A handful of fey with elemental magic had helped, too. Some guided waters to help push our ships. It was a joint effort, and one that had worked.

After days of travel, Wychwood finally loomed before us. It was only a shadowed smudge across the horizon, hidden by a cloak of late dusk and the blizzard that ripped across the landscape. Regardless of our inability to see what waited for us ahead, I knew with no doubt that we were in Icethorn territory.

I *felt* it, deep within me. The cord that tied me to these lands had thrummed back into existence earlier that very afternoon. And it tugged within me ever since. From that moment onwards, I could think of nothing but reaching our destination and letting my feet touch solid ground. My land. My home. A place I had spent little time in yet was intrinsically linked to. It was as though my skin was Icethorn's earth, my blood was its waterways and my bones were the rocks that stitched it together.

I raised my face skyward, closed my eyes and exhaled. The kiss of cold snowflakes against my face was refreshing and calming. I smiled against their graceful brush, revelling in the cold bite that pinched my cheeks and turned them red.

"You're smiling," Duncan said.

I tilted my face until I could see him again. He was looking at me with the same intense concentration he gave the land ahead. His gaze flickered between my eyes and my lips as though he couldn't decide which was more interesting than the other.

"Regardless of everything we've left behind and still have yet to face ahead, the relief I feel knowing I'm almost home is enough to make me feel happy," I admitted. "If only for a moment anyway."

A silver cloud of breath burst beyond Duncan's lips as he sighed. His hand snaked around my side and pulled me in. His warmth was as clear as one of Althea's conjured flames. "It's one of life pleasures to see you smile, Robin. Now I know what to do to grant you one, I will utilise the knowledge going forwards."

Duncan turned his attention back to the view ahead, clenching his jaw and sealing his lips closed once again.

"Is something bothering you?" I asked, sensing something brewing beneath Duncan's surface.

His fingers drummed across the side of my waist. "The unknown has always been a terrifying concept to me. And we are about to dock into the heart of it."

Reluctantly, I tore my gaze from his tense profile and scanned the shadowed outline of my court. "At least we will face it together, right? As much as this place is my home, it is still a strange place. My experiences in Icethorn have not been as... welcoming as you'd expect."

I almost lied and said memorable. The memories I had of my court were not kind. But the potential was there.

Icethorn had been the place I'd built a pyre and burned my father's body to ash. Another image overwhelmed me, a memory of kinder times that now spoiled in my stomach. Erix and me in Berrow. Both of us, entangled as one as a winter storm whipped the abandoned town beyond the rundown house we hid within. Such little time I had spent this side of the Icethorn border, and it had brought nothing but a discomfort in my gut.

And yet I was smiling, because reaching Icethorn meant I'd won at something. I'd saved the fey from Aldrick.

"You're shivering," Duncan accused. He didn't ask if I was cold, because that wasn't why my body shook. He knew that my affinity to winter prevented such an ailment. "Here."

Duncan lifted the thick cloak and draped it across my shoulder, its brown and grey fur edging nestled into my cheek. I pressed in closer to his side. He closed the heavy swash of material over me like a wing and kept me in place. It wasn't the warmth of his body imprinted on the cloak that comforted me, but the concept that it was his.

I was his.

"I wish I could promise you that everything will be all right," I replied, fingers weaving among his, which lay upon the ship's railing. "But lying to you is not a habit I wish to take up."

"Nor do I want you to ever feel you need to lie to benefit me."

I'd not exactly lied to Duncan, but neither had I been entirely truthful. Something about what he said wedged its way into my soul like a splinter of iron. With everything going on, I didn't wish for the added discomfort of half-truths.

"Has Kayne spoken to you at all?" I asked, pondering our last encounter days prior. I hadn't seen him since.

"Nothing of credit. But I plan to interrogate him when we reach safe land. He's been avoiding me. I don't think there has ever been this distance between us."

"That's odd," I said, feigning ignorance.

"I know. To be honest, I'm not sure what I have done, but it must be something. At least he has the fey to focus on. It seems he is making up for lost time. Never thought I would see him so interested in helping before."

Guilt uncoiled within me. I was the reason this barrier had built between them. Even if Duncan didn't recognise it yet, I did.

Noticing my lax expression, Duncan dipped his chin toward me. "Should Kayne have said something to me?"

I contemplated lying, but that would go against everything I had promised him mere moments before. "A couple of days ago, I asked for his help with locating Jesibel. He refused. It's nothing serious, but I get the impression if someone else asked the same thing of him, he might've been more willing to offer his help."

Duncan paused, taking a moment to read the underlying accusation woven through my comment. "You think Kayne has an issue with you?"

"It doesn't matter if he does or not." I shrugged, feeling strangely awkward discussing matters of Duncan's closest and oldest friend. Especially with him. I hadn't even voiced my concern to Althea. I waited to see how Duncan reacted to the conversation. Searching for a hint that Duncan may already know what I was suggesting.

"It matters to me, darling."

I offered him a smile, trying to reflect the emotion in my eyes, but failing. "I think I'm just being sensitive?"

"What, you, sensitive? No." Duncan winked. "Care to tell me what he has said to you?"

I tore my hand from his and placed it over his chest. His heartbeat thundered up my arm. Duncan might've pretended he was calm about the topic, but the way his body reacted suggested otherwise. "Nothing to merit you worrying. Forget I said anything. What matters is I trust Kayne. He's been pivotal in seeing our success up to this point. Perhaps what I asked of him was too much. I'm just surprised he didn't bring it up with you, that's all."

Duncan's mouth twitched. "If you ask me to talk to him, I will. Just say the word."

I shook my head, looking back toward Wychwood. "I shouldn't have brought it up. It's nothing, really. Kayne said it would threaten our position if Lucari is seen by Aldrick, and he is right."

Duncan didn't reply again, and I was glad of that. Swaddled in warmth, we both watched the Icethorn Court draw nearer.

Our destination was clearer to see now. The closer we moved toward Wychwood, the easier it was to pick out details. Towering, verdant pines tipped white with snow. Sharp cliff faces of stone that rose from the sea and stretched toward the darkened sky. I scanned for a beach but couldn't see any location that suggested where we would dock. The only variation to the sheer face of the cliff was what looked to be a cove. The shadowed mouth was carved into the face of the rock itself. Jagged rocks extended beyond the water's rough surface like reaching claws. There was no chance of our ships getting close enough without finding one of those stone claws piercing their hulls.

Talking of Kayne, Lucari screeched as she flew, dancing among the drifts of snow. Unlike the hawk, the Nephilim didn't fill the skies. Instead, they stayed in their ship, which stalked our fleet like it was its shadow. Since the winged monster had cut across the skies, I hadn't seen Rafaela take to the skies at all. But her presence was always close, standing guard on the deck of her ship, her attention never once straying from our direction – from me.

"Boys." Althea announced her arrival, interrupting our silence with her presence. "Enjoying the view?"

The wind caught strands of her red hair and tussled it from her shoulders. Dark splotches hung beneath her eyes. I had noticed more, with each day that passed, that Althea's skin had taken on a slight green tinge. Although she did well to hide it, Seraphine had reported having seen Althea bent over the railing as she spilled the entire contents of her stomach into the ocean. When I asked if she was okay, she waved my concern off with a hand and threw herself back into the briefing of her conversations with our captain. Anything to divert the attention from the way the sea made her sick. To Althea, showing such sickness translated to exposing weakness. And, surrounded by Cedarfall soldiers, she'd never have allowed that.

If I was to learn anything from Althea, it was her steel resilience.

"Just relieved we have almost made it," I said.

"Because of you." Althea nudged my shoulder, pale lips cracking when she smiled. "Captain has assured me that this is the agreed location for our arrival. We are to anchor out at sea and move to land in smaller vessels."

"And we trust his judgement?" Duncan asked dryly. "The man has had one hand gripped on the wheel and the other on the neck of a bottle this entire journey."

"Got us this far, and in one piece, Hunter. I suppose you think you would do better? General was it, or did they call you captain in your ranks, too?"

"General," Duncan replied coyly.

"Ah, yes," Althea brushed her hair across her shoulder. "How could I have forgotten?"

I cleared my throat, demanding their attention. "Althea, not that it is my turn to belittle the captain, but I thought we were meeting our welcome party on the black sand beaches you spoke of?"

"We were. But plans have since changed, Robin. With everything that has occurred, I took it upon myself to alter our arrival destination rather last minute. I didn't like the idea of our plans becoming known by being exposed to the open for so long. Never know who is listening."

Aldrick. That was who she spoke about, I knew it without asking.

"Good decision," Duncan replied.

"Why, thank you." Althea mocked a bow. "I do live to please."

A stone dropped in my stomach. It was impossible to ignore the feeling. "We have an uncanny ability to hold information back from one another, don't you think?"

"You trust me, don't you, Robin?" Althea asked. "Because I've learned to trust you and all your quirky ways."

"Of course I do."

"Then the answer is mutual," Althea replied, eyes wide in genuine shock. "If it makes you feel better, no one knew but the old drunkard over there." She gestured toward the captain, who was singing a sailor's song as he navigated the lead ship toward Icethorn land. "Surprise."

A loud snapping of metal sounded from deep in the ship's belly. It vibrated through the damp, snow-covered wood we stood on as the anchor finally dropped into the dark waves. The same sound echoed across the ships that followed behind us.

Our ship jolted forward, groaning at the sudden tension as the anchor met the ground far beneath the dark waves. Duncan's hold on me tightened. If it hadn't, my ribs would have slammed into the railing.

"I cannot believe I am saying this aloud, but we actually made it!" Althea said, glancing between the both of us. "For a second, I didn't think we would."

The deck came alive with fey. By the last day of the journey there wasn't a soul who didn't help. Some began lowering the sails and masts, whilst others prepared themselves in smaller groups to await travel to shore. With each passing moment, the ship slowed gradually, coming to a final stop just shy of the claw-like rock formations surrounding the cove entrance.

"Please tell me someone is aware of your little detour?" I asked from beneath Duncan's cloak.

Althea's face beamed as she looked toward the cove. Her lips were pulled upward, her chin raised proudly beneath bright, gleeful eyes. "Oh, someone certainly knows."

I recognised the look on her face. A mixture of elated excitement followed the blush of her cheeks and the way her posture straightened. Althea's dirtied fingers gripped the railing. She leaned over to get a better look toward the cove.

"In fact, I can see them," she spoke into the roaring winds. "Look."

I squinted, trying to make out what she could in the distance.

"Stay close to me, Robin," Duncan whispered into my ear. "You'll be welcome, but I haven't earned that right yet."

"Nothing will happen to you," I replied. "I promise."

It was the easiest promise to make.

Althea raised a finger and pointed to the shadow-filled cavern beyond the crashing waves. The harder I looked, the more I recognised that those *shadows* seemed to move. A bud of flame illuminated the three distant figures.

"There she is," Althea sang, practically leaning over the bannister. "There's *my* woman."

My eyes landed on the very person Althea spoke of. Gyah Eldrae stood forward from the light. Even from a distance, I could see her burning smile. Beside Gyah was a vision of Althea, except much older. Queen Lyra Cedarfall was here to welcome us home, too. My heart swelled at the sight of them both, but it was the third person who forced my heart up into my throat. I blinked at the prickling sensation that filled my eyes as Queen Elinor Oakstorm extended both arms out to me and waved. If there was not such distance between us, I would have thrown myself into her embrace.

"We made it," I whispered, allowing the tear to fall from my eye.

"Yes, we did," Duncan confirmed, beneath the gleeful squawks of Lucari, who shot across the sky with anticipation. He leaned in and pressed a lingering kiss to my cheek. "Well done, my darling. You're home."

"No, Duncan." I glanced up at him, unable to hold the smile of relief from my face. "*We* are home."

CHAPTER 14

No one else seemed to notice Seraphine and the surviving Asps melting from the crowd of disembarked fey. I did. Likely because I expected it, the end to their service coming the moment our ship anchored off Icethorn shores. The Asp faded into the surrounding night, all without a second glance.

I thought she'd have at least said goodbye. To my discomfort, I was proven wrong. I reminded myself that her presence had always been a transaction. It was never personal. She owed me nothing. Our debt was now paid, just as our contract stated. As soon as we reached Wychwood, I'd only ever see her again if I'd the money to pay.

Since this time, it wasn't coin that had been exchanged for the Asp's assistance.

I was the only one who knew of the assassin's next destination. It was the price I paid for Seraphine's help and sacrifice. Being in Lockinge, I found it easy to offer the Asps a new place to nest. It was the only price she would accept since the rest of their dwellings were now husks of scorched timber and stone.

I paid with something far more meaningful.

The offering meant little to me before. But now, standing on Icethorn land with its spiritual presence thrumming through me, I felt otherwise. Too late, I reminded myself. There's no going back now.

I couldn't grieve over what I'd given them when I'd barely seen the place of residence before. It had only ever been a speck in the distance, the promise of a past I never had the chance to experience. Before Erix had been the one to point it out, I'd never have even known its name. Imeria Castle. Even now, weeks later, it was Erix's voice chiming through my mind as he spoke the name of my mother's home. Somewhere I could have claimed as my home. Except home was a place that earned that title. Which is what made it so easy to give this away.

I'd have to tell my allies soon enough. When one of them noticed Seraphine had disappeared, they would ask questions and I couldn't pretend not to have the answers. If I even attempted to mislead them with a lie, Althea would see right through it. Part of being a king was standing on your decisions with confidence – a skill I was growing rather used to.

Perhaps they'd react better if I told them first, before Althea, Duncan or the rest of them found out by other means. I hardly imagined they'd think well of me for forfeiting Icethorn's castle to the Asps.

But it wasn't *my* home. It was the gravesite for everything I'd lost before I even knew I had it. The human village of Grove still laid claim to that title. And I'd never want to return there, either. Not without my father beside me. Even in some warped reality, if he was still alive, I don't think the welcome would've been merry after what I'd done to James Campbell.

Forcing the tangle of thoughts to the back of my mind, I focused on what was ahead of me.

"The shifter looks like she wants to claw the skin from my face," Kayne said out of the corner of his mouth, daringly glancing toward Gyah, who had her arm wrapped protectively around Althea.

I stood between him and Duncan, watching Gyah and Althea reunite. There wasn't any point telling Kayne that he was wrong. Every time Gyah laid her golden eyes upon him, I sensed her desire to carve the skin from his body and devour it. Her intention was evident.

"Don't worry about her," I said. "She has better taste than the likes of you."

Apparently my attempt at lightening the mood had failed. Kayne grunted, not bothering to offer me a reply. I clawed back the desire to tell him I was joking, because I hardly imagined that would've made a difference.

"Mate, the last time she saw you was on the better side of a Hunter's cage," Duncan added, leaning around me to give his friend a wink. "You can hardly blame her for wishing to eat you whole."

"Explain the smile she gave you, then," Kayne replied. "Last time I remembered, you were beside me outside that bloody cage."

Duncan shrugged, looking rather pleased with himself. "Perhaps she's an excellent judge of character.

"Believe me when I tell you this, Duncan." My heart swelled in my chest as we drew closer to her. "Gyah's smiling at you for an entirely different reason than you think. I wouldn't think you are above the potential of a late-night snack."

The fierce Eldrae was adorned in the deep, autumnal-coloured outfit of a Cedarfall guard. Her belt was decorated with the hilts of weapons, each one a story of her skill. Even beneath the sea of snow-covered pines, the breeze was confident enough to twist her burgundy cloak at her back, mimicking the wings that hid within her concealed Eldrae form. Snowfall covered her hair in silver stars before melting into nothingness. As more snowflakes fell upon her, Gyah's skin glistened as though she was painted by jewels – until Althea gently caught them with her thumb and brushed them off.

I'd seen Althea focused before, like when she'd fought against a group of Hunters the first time I'd met her. But in the presence of Gyah, it was as if nothing else mattered to the Cedarfall princess other than the woman beside her.

"Interrupting anything?" I called out, feeling heat rise in my cheeks as they both settled their gazes on me.

"No," Althea replied.

"Yes," Gyah said in the same breath.

They both stood beyond a sharp-tipped tent, far larger than the others we passed. A village of them had been erected beneath the cover of Merrow Forest, which Althea had explained was only a short ride to Imeria Castle. Logically, she believed it would be our next destination, but I had yet to tell her that she was wrong.

Gyah released her passionate hold on Althea and threw her arms around me. "Come here you reckless fool." Her powerful limbs squeezed me around the middle, forcing a laugh out of me. "It's really good to see you in one piece, Robin. Although, between you and me, I can't say the same for the two stragglers behind you."

Although the way she said it suggested her words were only meant for me, Gyah made sure to raise her voice so Duncan and Kayne could hear.

"It's good to see you too," I replied, resting my chin on her shoulder as I returned her embrace. It was a surprise when tears prickled in my eyes, a stinging at the back of my throat almost choking me. "Sorry for the delay, although I'm sure you know all about it already."

"Oh, I do." Gyah pulled back as quickly as she had hugged me. Gone was her smile. Instead, she regarded me with a sudden snarl that made me think I'd said something wrong. There was no time to register as her fist pulled back and delivered a swift thud into my shoulder.

"Fuck," I groaned. It hurt a lot, but even I knew she'd held back her full might. "What was that for!"

"*Never* do that again, Robin." Gyah pointed a finger at me. Her tone oozed authority.

Duncan shifted a step closer, but I shot him a look which told him to stand down.

"You're going to have to be a little clearer than that," I replied, as pins and needles raced down my shoulder to the tips of my fingers.

"We are a team. We decide everything together. If you ever put me in a position to choose you or Althea again then I promise my fist will connect with your face the next time. Am I clear?"

I nodded, watching Gyah's body tremble with tension. Her eyes looked heavy, her lips drawn with lines around them that had not been there the last I had seen her. "Is now the moment to say that I think your decision will always and only ever be Althea?"

"Shut up," Gyah snapped, eyes narrowed. "Although, you're not wrong. But still, shut up."

"I'm sorry," I said, massaging the ache out of my shoulder to no avail.

Althea slipped a hand into Gyah's fist, preventing her from striking again. Upon contact of her soft touch, Gyah melted from her sudden fury into something more tepid. "You better be."

"I am."

"Do you know what, Robin, I hate nothing more than when people need to say sorry. It suggests they have something to be sorry for, which you, Robin, seem to do a lot. Leaving you that night was one of the hardest things I've done and I'll never forgive you for making me choose."

"Turned out okay in the end." I looked around us, to the fey bustling through the crowds, carrying wooden bowls of food, dressed in fresh clothes. There was no denying the morale of the camp was light.

Gyah's expression softened, her body leaning into Althea's side, not for support, but to eradicate as much distance between them as possible. "You're lucky for that. Any other outcome and I would've torn the muscles from your bones. Which, by the looks of it, you have a little more of than when I last saw you."

My body had changed from training with Seraphine and a few weeks of decent meals. I felt stronger because I had to be, for the people I'd done everything to save.

"And you..." Gyah snapped her attention to Duncan. He recoiled slightly from the beast lurking in her gilded eyes. "Where *do* I begin."

"Perhaps this is the best moment to reintroduce myself?" Duncan added, stepping to my side with a hand extended to Gyah. There was no denying the slight shake of his fingers, but I gave it to him, he didn't back down. His confidence, although forced, matched Gyah's demeanour. At least he didn't share the same hesitation that Kayne still showed as he sulked behind with Lucari chirping quietly on his shoulder.

If anything, Gyah would smell the fear off Kayne and relish in it.

"No need, Hunter, I remember you perfectly fine."

Althea leaned into Gyah's ear and whispered something. I couldn't make out a word, but whatever she said caused one of Gyah's brows to rise as she looked over Duncan with a scrutinising stare.

"We will see," Gyah said, replying to whatever Althea had said. Her words were entirely out of context.

Duncan lowered his hand awkwardly, fingers flexing as he put them back to his side. "So, what a lovely reunion, but I think we have a few details to smooth out before we set up bed for the night."

"A few?" Gyah barked. "And the award for biggest understatement goes to you, Hunter."

"Duncan," he added. "If you wouldn't mind, I'd prefer that."

"If you both don't mind sizing one another up, my mother is waiting inside there with Elinor Oakstorm." Althea gestured toward the large, pitched tent behind her. It was more like a small home than any tent I'd seen before, but then again, it was put up for royalty. What else did I expect?

"Let's not keep them waiting then," I said, gesturing for us to all move on.

"Ah, ah, ah, Robin. This audience is for you, and you alone." Althea wrapped a hand around Gyah's shoulder. "Whilst you put on your big king pants to discuss matters privy to the heads of courts, the rest of us will share a strong cup of ale to celebrate our return to Wychwood."

"You're not coming?" I asked, already knowing the answer but wishing for her to surprise me.

"Never has there been a moment where I was glad not to be wearing a crown. Robin, good luck, and we'll have a mug ready for you when you finish up."

I glanced at Duncan, who nodded in silent confirmation. "Go. I'll look after Kayne. I will make sure he's got some meat left on his bones once the shifter has finished with him."

Gyah snapped her teeth in jest, and Kayne actually flinched. It was hard not to laugh, but that wouldn't help my attempt at befriending him.

Anyway, it wasn't Kayne I was worried about.

Duncan took my face in his hands and brought his lips down on my forehead. When he pulled back, he spoke through a gravelly whisper. "*I'll* be fine, Robin."

"Come on, you unlikely band of allies," Gyah practically shouted. "Let's see if my enjoyment of humans improves after something strong to drink."

"Careful with him," Duncan said, cocking his head in his friend's direction. "Kayne's not accustomed to powerful women."

Kayne swallowed hard, freckled face burning scarlet. "That's not true–"

"That much has been clear," Althea snorted. "We wouldn't want to break him, Kayne has proven rather useful over the past few weeks. It's nice to have another redhead around, reminds me of home."

With that, the four of them sauntered away from the tent, three more willing than the other. I would've given anything to join them. Instead, I looked toward the tent and swallowed the stone of dread that had lodged itself in my throat.

Now was not the time for laughter between friends. I shed that skin, adorning the mask of king, as I lifted a hand to the dark grey material of the tent's entrance. For a few more hours I'd don my crown and be the person I was trying hard to convince myself I was. Not that it would matter. If I couldn't trick myself into believing it, how in Altar's name could I deceive the formidable women who waited for me inside?

Jewels of orange flame flickered from the central brazier, emitting warmth and enough light to matter. It cast shadows across the leaning walls propped up by thin poles of wood, which caused the material of the tent to bow between each rod. I was glad to have something in my hands, to stop them fidgeting. Already the skin around my nails was ruined from the incessant chewing. Thank Altar for the warmed cup of leafed tea that helped, the taste of wild berry a welcome relief from the salt that had invaded my mouth from the days of travel.

I found my attention drifted between the two queens until I felt more like a fly on the wall than someone with something to add to the conversation. My eyes fell upon the makeshift table, landing on the tea-stained maps, candles covered in cream wax and a single sword with a spiked sun carved into the end of its handle. The weapon belonged to Elinor, but was currently being used to hold down the curled edges of Wychwood's map. But as the orange glow licked across its sharpened edge, there was no denying its more useful purpose.

"Robin, you have had the most interaction with the Nephilim," Queen Lyra added, lifting the lip of her mug to her lips. Unlike Elinor and me, Lyra did not need to blow at the boiling, berry-infused water. She seemed to enjoy the scolding presence it left as it trailed down her throat. Perhaps the fire within her body enjoyed such a feeling. "What do you have to say about them as a threat to the fey? Now they have reached our land, they have become the minority. It would hardly take much force to deal with them before their interest in us sharpens to something less friendly."

"They aren't our enemies," I replied, trying to match the authority that coated Lyra's voice. "Aldrick is."

"The Nephilim are the unknown," Lyra added. "And I do not like the idea that an entire realm has dwelled out across the oceans for as long as the time of the gods."

I straightened my back in the chair, feigning authority in my tone. "If the Nephilim were an issue or threat, there have been years they could've meddled. And they haven't. I'd suggest we don't waste our time worrying about powerful allies who have promised to help us with nothing in return. Our focus should be on our shared enemy."

"Robin is right. Now is certainly *not* the time to create new enemies, Lyra," Elinor said, offering me a motherly smile.

I was glad to see that Elinor Oakstorm looked a world better than when I last saw her. Her skin glowed with the kiss of sun; her cheeks flushed with the red of apples. A tiara held back the mane of dark curls. The metal band was made from a gold, but woven to look like the knot of a vine. A pointed crystal sat upon her brow, decorated at its side by flowers made from yellow and red metals. Elinor certainly looked comfortable beneath the weight of her signifier, and I *certainly* preferred seeing it on her head instead of Doran Oakstorm's.

But that didn't stop a sliver of discomfort every time she blinked, flashing those piercing blue eyes through dark brown eyelashes. I couldn't help but see Tarron in her expression. Even though her smile warmed me from the inside, as though she conjured rays of sunlight and bathed me in them, it was a reminder of what price she'd paid to sit here as queen.

"The Nephilim are responsible for the death of a few of my soldiers. They have ensured that some of my own have not returned home as I promised they would," Lyra reminded. "Forgive me if I am not welcoming them upon the shore with open arms."

"I don't think they are expecting such a welcome either. They've not left their ship since arriving," I said, mind drifting to the ship and the two-winged warriors upon it. "Lyra, I trust the Nephilim. During a time when such a thing is hard to find, I'm confident they'll help us with our fight against Aldrick. We could do with all the force required to prevent another court from falling."

My words were meant as the painful reminder to what happened to the spring court.

"I hate that he has a name now," Lyra said, lowering her cup to the table as a grimace sliced across her freckled face. "Makes the Hand seem mortal, when in actuality the man is nothing but a monster."

"Names also have power," I replied, mind wandering to the echo of those very words I had heard before. "And we will need an abundance of it to go against him. Having the Nephilim by our side will help when the time comes. They know more about how to stop him than we do, we need them on that basis alone."

"Which is exactly what we must discuss." Elinor's eyes scanned the map, resting upon the marker for the Elmdew Court. "The longer Aldrick is left to his own devices, the closer he is to making his next move. And, considering my court rests closest to Elmdew, all signs point to him paying me a visit first. Frankly, as much as I wish I was, I'm not prepared."

"Then I put forward that we pay Aldrick a visit in Elmdew and evict him with fire before he has the chance to move," Lyra snapped, leaning forward on the table with both hands. "You may not be ready, but we have the numbers."

My nose itched with the kiss of smoke.

"Careful, my friend," Elinor added, looking down at the tendrils of flame and the sudden scent of charred wood that followed. "Before you do the same to us here and burn us out of this tent."

Lyra reluctantly pulled back her hands, extinguishing the small flames from her fingers with a single breath. "Enough time has passed where we have allowed that *man* to infiltrate a court and hold claim to it. He has killed our friends and forced innocents from their homes whilst keeping the rest as prisoners of war. In honour of Peta and Dai, we must deal with this threat once and for all. With force."

There was no denying the boiling, raw emotion that rolled from Lyra in waves. Regardless of if she had her flames in control, her magic was potent in the air.

Elinor laid a hand upon Lyra's, curling her fingers and holding on. Her touch emitted a golden glow that encased Lyra's skin and melted into it. I'd seen this healing power before, but it was not a physical wound Elinor wished to treat.

It was the internal wound of loss. And from the way Lyra's eyebrows softened, her mouth smoothing out of its pinched shape, and her shoulders lowering from the sigh she expelled, I could see that Elinor's power was helping.

"There is another problem we must remember," I said, drawing both of their attentions back to me. "By us going to Aldrick, we will give him exactly what he wants. We hold these *keys* to open Duwar's gate. We are exactly what Aldrick wants. If we do so, the realms will face a far greater threat than Aldrick. I can't help but think that Aldrick has not yet acted again because he is expecting us to go to him. He is lying in wait, not wasting his energy or forces until he needs to."

"Robin, I am impressed with your line of thought. You are right." Elinor smiled, her gaze lingering on me. When she spoke, she did so from a place of pride, the emotion so powerful I felt it career into me. "I can only imagine Aldrick's reaction when he figured out the truth of these keys he so desperately searched for. He had us both in his grasp, only to lose us. In a strange and twisted way, it brings me great joy to imagine him in his moment of dreadful realisation."

"The question is how did he find out," Lyra said. "How did he work it out if no one but the Nephilim seemed to have the insight? This is not knowledge that the courts have, and yet the moment the Nephilim come he suddenly works it out. See where my distrust comes from?"

"I do." I inhaled sharply at a sudden pain in my finger. Looking down, I saw the skin around my nail bed swelled with ruby blood. I'd not even noticed that I'd put my cup down. "Then we invite them off their ship and give them the chance to explain themselves. I'm merely passing on information, they would be better to explain."

"Aldrick is, I hate to admit it, a detailed man. He has means to information about Duwar, and that was before the Nephilim arrived. His information is coming directly from the demon. If he knows about the keys, surely it is through his connection to it?"

"Although I don't believe the Nephilim are involved with Aldrick finding out about the keys, I also do not think Duwar has anything to do with it. If so, Aldrick wouldn't have let me slip through his fingers." I offered a forced smile to Elinor, keeping my hands beneath the table. "We can speculate all night how Aldrick has gained such knowledge. It won't help. What might help is waiting on the Nephilim's ship. One of them, Gabrial, can read the past of humans from a script that presents itself on her skin. Aldrick is onlyhalf-fey, which means he's not above her prying. If anyone can help us gain information on Aldrick and put us, finally, a step ahead, it would be her."

Elinor's brow peaked at something I said. "Every movement of Aldrick is recorded?"

I nodded, noticing the same silent intrigue on Lyra Cedarfall as she gripped her cup again. Her fingers glowed a deep red, all to heat the tea she held, which soon hissed when she brought it back to her lips. "Unknown warriors beholding unknown magic. How many more surprises will we uncover until you see what I see?"

Lyra's distrust was evident. It would be foolish of me to disregarded it, but I also couldn't stoke the flames.

"Gabrial may be able to shed light on Aldrick's doings. That's the insight we will need to keep us a step ahead of him."

I purposefully left out the bit about Aldrick messing with what she was able to see, but I trusted she'd find a way around it soon enough.

"What do you propose then, Robin?" Lyra asked over the rim of her cup. For a brief moment, I caught respect in her gaze as she regarded me, not as Robin, but as a king who sat before her.

I took a deep breath in, making sure my answers were in order. I'd had days to contemplate our next steps, and to ensure I had the support of my fellow courts, I needed to be convincing.

"Aldrick must be stopped before he gets his hands on another key." *Before he kills one of us like he has with Peta and takes the key, willingly or by force.* "When he left Lockinge, he took some fey he'd imprisoned. What's clear is that Aldrick will continue to mutate his followers, providing them with powers until he has an army to match ours. But I think he's hand-picked them for his own benefit. And now he is in the heart of a fey court, he has access to more supplies of fey blood. The murder of Peta and Dai and the lack of the Elmdew power will mean humans can pass into the land freely. He will create his army. I don't require Gabrial's ability to know that for a fact. I suggest we fuck up his plans. What we don't need is an army to deal with. If we stay together, we will be stronger combined than separated. Then, with the help of our own numbers and the Nephilim, we can deal with him once and for all."

Lyra leaned forwards, lips curling into a smile. "And what do you suggest."

"We draw him out," I replied. "Greet him – not with the separated might of our powers – but with the joined force of all of Wychwood. Aldrick had the element of surprise to take down King Elmdew, but that is no longer something he has access to. We know his plans, so we best him at them. But we must stay together, the three of us cannot be apart. Otherwise he will pick us off, one by one."

"You suggest we abandon our courts?"

I shook my head. "That's not what I'm saying..."

"Then where do we go?" Lyra asked after sharing a quick glance with Elinor.

I wanted to answer her, but I couldn't find the words.

"I never imagined a day when we would sit together, discussing the potential of our realms becoming the playground for demons." Lyra stood up from her chair, gripping the back of it until her knuckles paled. "Yet our skies have already seen the likes of winged monsters, and I fear they are only the beginning."

"And time isn't exactly a luxury we have at the moment," Elinor said, looking between us both. "Especially in my court."

I deflated before the queens, trying hard not to show it in my posture.

"As much as I recognise the points you make, Robin, I have a family and a court full of innocents to protect. I cannot be seen to leave them and hide. There has to be another way."

"I agree," Elinor said. "My borders are flooded with Elmdew fey seeking refuge and protection. Besides the threat of Aldrick taking occupancy as my neighbour, my court hasn't entirely accepted me as queen yet. Doran's poison had seeped far inside the council. If I leave now, then they will waste no time jumping in and filling the place I leave behind, regardless of the Oakstorm power I have claimed."

"Then that leaves us with two options," I said, bristling at the idea that Elinor was coming up against resistance from the people she'd do anything to protect. "Kill or be killed."

"What if the keys are destroyed?" Lyra asked.

"The Nephilim have sworn to protect them. It's not an option."

Lyra's gaze narrowed, clearly not believing what I said was right. "I think it is best we invite the Nephilim from their ship and question them directly about the knowledge. Then we can make an informed decision on how we deal with Aldrick."

"I'll speak with Rafaela," I replied, short and cold. If there was ever a time I wanted to shed the skin of a king and pick up a mug of ale, it was now.

"Keep us informed with your progress," Lyra said, taking her moment to stand. "We shall hold council with the Nephilim before I leave for Cedarfall and return those fey you have freed back to their homes."

"If they let you leave," I added. "The Nephilim have become more of my shadow since meeting them."

"They are welcome to come with me, Robin. But regardless, I *will* be leaving. We cannot stay here. Our power may be what Aldrick desires, but it is the only play we have to keep our courts safe from him."

I swallowed the urge to remind Lyra that Peta had the power, and he was dead. Surprise attack or not, Aldrick was powerful. We shouldn't underestimate him.

"Will you be returning to Imeria?" Elinor asked, her question catching me off guard. I looked at her, searching her azure eyes for a reason she might already know the answer.

"I have decided those fey who wish to stay in Icethorn will be taken to Berrow. They can dwell there for the time being." The words came out before I could stop them. "Icethorn has been left empty for a long time. Before I know if Imeria and other places are safe, it is best they stay somewhere I can vouch to be free of dangers."

It was not completely a lie, simply the truth bent. I'd decided, as part of the plan those weeks ago, that if we returned to Wychwood, it would be better to keep the fey in one place.

There would be few, certainly not enough to fill an entire court, but regardless, I vowed to protect them. I could do so confidently if they were all together. However, I had no intention of ever returning to Berrow myself. Not with the ghost of memories left behind. Not when Erix's presence was smeared all across it.

"You have a fortress at your disposal," Lyra added. "If you wish to keep your people safe, then open your gates and let them fill Imeria's rooms. Altar knows you have the space."

I couldn't form a reply. It jammed in my throat. Lifting the now-cold tea, I took a swig, hoping to help clear it. The silence soon became so taunting I was forced to reply. "I... can't do that."

"Don't be ashamed if you hold little care for Imeria, but as king, it is your rightful home." Lyra placed a pointed nail on the map, directly over the very place we discussed. "You *must* claim it. I know Julianne would have dreamed of a day of seeing you, her son, walking the halls."

Elinor's eyes bore through me, searching for the reason why I reacted in such a way. Even if I wanted to, I couldn't hide from the truth forever.

Swallowing my guilt, I raised my chin and revealed the truth before it consumed me. "Imeria is not my home. It never was, and now never will be. It was the price I had to pay to even have the pleasure of having this conversation with you."

"Price you had to pay, what does that mean?" Elinor reached out for my hand, but I flinched away at her touch.

"What have you done, Robin?" Shock dripped from Lyra's tongue as she questioned me.

Lifting my chin, I forged my expression to a mask of iron and replied, "I'm not the only one in this room who's had the pleasure of making deals with the Asps. I couldn't offer them coin, but I could provide them with security. Imeria belongs to them now, not me."

"You threw away your kingdom, and for what?" Lyra blinked as she spoke.

"A castle, not a kingdom. I gave away a place of stone that meant nothing to me. And now I have an entire nest of Asps at my disposal, close enough to call on if and when required. I think, given my options, it was the best I could do. We all have a price to pay, and this was mine."

I waited for them to argue. To tell me I had made a terrible choice and to demand I claim it back. But they didn't. Neither Elinor nor Lyra provided judgement. I waited and waited, but it did not come as words. However, the look they both gave me spoke volumes. Lyra's eyes were overwhelmed with disbelief and fury, whereas Elinor regarded me with understanding.

"Speak with the Nephilim," Lyra said finally. "As Robin has said, let us deal with Aldrick before any more lives are lost. Then we will discuss what it means to be king and how best to make a decision in the future."

Her words stung far greater than any slap.

"Lyra, that is not a fair assumption," Elinor said.

"I am merely responding to facts, Elinor."

It was as though someone had stabbed me in the gut and turned the knife.

"I'm sorry, Lyra." I stood, body shivering with unspent tension. "Do you care to remind me what you have done in your attempts to free the fey that belonged to your court?" Anger twisted inside me, a cold blizzard of fury. "If I am not mistaken, you were complacent as the fey disappeared over the years, whereas I was not."

Elinor stood and moved from the table next, and I followed suit. "Please, that is enough."

"I do not deny that your actions have been valiant, but wearing the crown means you make a decision that benefits the many and not the few." Lyra drew back, her posture rigid from the same tension that thrummed through me. "Remember that the next time you make decisions."

"How about you tell that to the Cedarfall fey who fill this camp? Explain the meaning behind that to them and see if they understand why it took years to save them," I snapped.

Lyra didn't reply. I saw in the creases that spread across her forehead that she had something to say. Whatever it was, it never left her pale mouth. Before I could retract my words, Lyra bowed and left the tent swiftly, not without leaving a scolding kiss to the air around me.

I was left looking out after her, hating the internal, scoring pain born from knowing I'd disappointed her.

"I believe the decisions you make are for the best of not only your people but you, too, Robin," Elinor said softly, laying the motherly touch of her hand upon my shoulder. "You are the heart of this court regardless of the crown you wear or the throne you sit upon. You should also remember that."

I leaned into her, resting my head on her shoulder. Her arm dropped around me, keeping me close. I allowed myself a moment of selfish indulgence. Closing my eyes, I imagined my father and how similar his caring affection was to what Elinor provided me.

"Thank you for having faith in me," I said. "Even if my decisions don't make sense to you, they make sense to me."

"And what matters is you stand by those decisions." Her hand rubbed slowly at my back. Up and down. Elinor's fingers glowed golden as they dampened the turmoil of emotion, untying it from its knot within me. Clarity overcame me so suddenly that my intake of breath was the freshest and lightest it had been in months.

"I can speak on behalf of your mother when I say that she would be so proud of you," Elinor said. "Take that, keep it close, and remember it with what is coming."

"From the moment this all began, I've been lost. Lyra sees that."

"We all feel lost sometimes, Robin," Elinor admitted. "Recognising that is the first step back toward finding your way out of the maze."

I closed my eyes, allowing her words to settle over me like snow, where they then melted into my bones.

"Don't fear the journey. Feel privileged you are on one. Many have already lost their chance to live. In their honour, ensure you make a difference. Live the life they are no longer fortunate to have, continue the Icethorn legacy so we can save its future against our new threat."

CHAPTER 15

I found my friends by following the outburst of drunken laughter through the camp. The tent they were huddled within rumbled with the sound, and I paused outside for a moment, letting their glee sink into my bones and rid the horrible feeling left over after my audience with the queens.

My hesitation lasted a moment before I swept in to join them. As I pulled open the entrance, I was hit with a wave of warmth mixed with strong alcoholic spirits. My eyes practically stung as I entered, but my mouth watered with the need for my own drink.

The commotion of my arrival did little to conceal Kayne's reaction when I announced myself. I'd seen his smile which faded when he saw me. And since then, Kayne had stayed silent, lips barely twitching as I fell into conversation with them all.

Frankly, I didn't have the care or energy to worry about his feelings right now. I just wanted to drink myself into oblivion.

Kayne sat next to Duncan, so close that my stomach had burned slightly with an emotion that left a sour taste on the back of my tongue. My gaze shifted to the touch of their thighs and the way Kayne leaned into Duncan's side for support. Anyone would have believed Kayne was struck by Duncan's lightning by the way he jolted away from him as I entered the tent.

Duncan didn't seem to notice anything was wrong, but Gyah did. The face she pulled suggested so. I smiled weakly to acknowledge her, knowing this conversation would be saved for another time.

I threw myself into debriefing them about my conversation with Lyra and Elinor, aided by the cups of ale Duncan continuously poured out for me. Kayne hardly touched his drink. I tried my best to enjoy the conversation, but I could only focus on Kayne's stare, burning holes into me.

By my third drink, I was relaxed enough to ignore the Tracker and his disdain for me.

It was no surprise when Kayne stood from the cup-strewn table and announced he was retiring to bed. Relief cooled through me like a fresh breath of air as he prepared to leave. I was the only one not to bother telling him to stay.

"One more, Kayne, come on. When have you ever turned down a drink?" Duncan drawled, sloshing amber liquid out of the cup that he swayed.

"Lucari will need tending to." Kayne dismissed Duncan. "Strange place and all that."

"She is likely off terrorising the local rodents," Althea said, words slurred. "You can leave her to her own means for another drink, can't you?"

"If anything, I better save those rodents and get Lucari to deliver Robin's invitation to the Nephilim before I sleep."

Althea hiccupped as she spluttered. "If they don't arrive by morning, it will be my hangover-fuelled wrath upon your head."

"The Nephilim will receive it." Kayne's hand patted his pocket. The back of his freckled hand flattened the small roll of parchment I'd given him when I arrived. "Night all."

I kept my cup lifted to my lips, hoping it would prevent my need to bid him goodnight. The truth was, I didn't particularly care if it was good or not. As long as he and his stalking gaze gave me a reprieve, that is all I cared about.

"Rest well," Duncan called, as Kayne took his leave. "Hope the head is okay come morning."

"You know me," Kayne muttered, offering Duncan a wink. "When has my head ever been bad."

I almost choked on my drink. Gyah too. My stomach twisted at Duncan's knowing chuckle. "If you ever want to get to sleep tonight, perhaps we don't test that theory, friend."

What the fuck did that mean?

Gyah leaned into my side. The moment Kayne was out of earshot, she spoke aloud for the rest of us to hear. "Am I missing something? Because you look like you're about to vomit or scream."

I swallowed hard, tasting bile just as Gyah had said. "It's nothing."

"Refill anyone?" Duncan asked, leaning forward with the jug that was far lighter than it had been when I joined them. His arm flexed as he filled Gyah's cup. Some ale spilled across the lip, spreading across the veins of the wooden table.

"I thought I was the only one who didn't like the Tracker," Gyah whispered, looking daringly at me. "But you look at him like you want to knock a fist into him. You've all been stuck together for so long."

"I said it's nothing, friend. Leave it."

Not satisfised with my response, Gyah looked to the remaining group and lifted her voice so we could all here. "So, what has Robin done to piss Kayne off so much?"

I blanched on the spot, the blood draining from my face. A dribble of ale burst out of my mouth, which I quickly cleared with the back of my hand and forced out a laugh.

Duncan said nothing but leaned back on the bench. The presence of his arm across my shoulder was so sudden. Even our seat creaked with the movement of such a powerful body. "Kayne has never been the best at making friends. Unless those friends have feathers and claws."

"He didn't seem to have a problem before the princeling walked in."

"Gyah," Althea hissed, unable to hide her smile. "I think you mean *kingling* now."

"No." Gyah pulled Althea in close and pressed a sticky-lipped kiss upon her cheek. "That doesn't have a ring to it."

"I'm tired," I whispered into Duncan's ear, doing a job of distracting him with my hand as I ran it up the inside of his leg. He stiffened in his seat. The skin across his arms prickled with a wave of pleasured bumps. "And cold. How about we crawl under some fur and warm ourselves up?"

In other words, can we get away from this conversation as soon as possible?

"Hmmm, how peculiar. Robin Icethorn is cold." Duncan pressed a kiss into my cheek, his posture slopping. "If you are just trying to get me alone, say it. Or if you are looking for some warmth, I certainly have a few suggestions."

"Now, that is something I never, ever want to hear again," Gyah said, grimacing. Althea giggled through a haze of ale. "Before I am actually forced to slice my ears off, might I suggest we depart, dearest?" Gyah offered me a smirk as she spoke to Althea, who was leaning on her for support. "The weeks you have been kept from me have left much room to catch up."

"Catch up, is that what we are calling it?" Althea stood from the table with such speed that it answered Gyah's question. She swayed dramatically, stopping only as her hands slapped down on the table. Ale sloshed, and cups toppled over, and the tent erupted in drunkard cheers. "Would my guard do me the honour of escorting me safely to my tent? What with everything that is going on out in that world, I fear I might not make it there in one piece."

"Oh, but of course. I take my job seriously after all," Gyah replied.

With poised grace, Gyah swept Althea from her feet and threw her over her shoulder. Althea slammed her fists into Gyah's broad back, giggling and kissing. The Cedarfall princess was so lost in a fit that she kicked over another mug, spilling ale over my trousers.

"Night, boys." Gyah's lip pulled away, flashing teeth. "I hope you sleep as deeply as we will."

"Sleep is certainly on the agenda," Duncan replied, lifting his cup in a toast. "Just not straight away."

I clapped my hand over his mouth. "Would you stop."

Duncan's tongue writhed across my palm, spreading goosebumps across my arms.

"Go," I shouted to Gyah, "before he embarrasses me any more."

"Exactly why I'm beginning to like him," Gyah said, then left swiftly with a squealing princess still flung over her shoulder.

Relieved by the sudden quiet, I folded myself into the crook of Duncan's arm and chest.

"So, we made it," he said, looking longingly down at me in his hold.

"Made it alone?"

"That, and the fact I've tried to get into Wychwood for years, but to no avail. Who knew it would take me falling in love with a fey to gain entry?"

"Your motives are different this time, I hope."

"They couldn't be more opposite." Duncan ran his long fingers down the curve at the back of my head. His focus fell on my obsidian hair, which he brushed away from my forehead before planting a soft kiss upon it.

"Before I take a leaf out of Gyah's book and snatch you into my arms and steal you to bed, I want you to know that I will speak with Kayne come morning. Whatever tension he holds onto must be left here before we head for Berrow."

A chill raced down my spine. "And I thought I had a lucky escape from this conversation."

"Not so easily. Robin, you mean more to me than I could even begin to describe."

"I sense a *but* coming on," I replied.

"Not a but, an *and*." He lifted my hand and pressed a kiss to my knuckles before continuing. "*And* Kayne has been in my life for as long as I remember. Our friendship is important to me; however, if he makes you feel uncomfortable that isn't what I want. Friend or not, I will not see you slighted by him. You deserve his respect after everything you've done."

"Can I make a suggestion?" I asked.

"Anything."

"I think I should be the one to speak to him first. Before you need to get involved, give me one more chance to see what the issue is and find a solution."

If I could find a solution to Aldrick, at least I could fix something so mundane.

Duncan shook his head, verdant eyes not wavering from me for a second. "That stubborn mule of a man will listen to me. Let me understand what is going on in his head. You have enough to worry about without a sulking man-child."

A powerful throb echoed across my skull. I winced, pressing my fingers to my temple. The dim light of the candles became too bright for a moment. I blinked at the halos that seemed to duplicate as my vision blurred.

"Something I said?" Duncan asked, brushing his fingers beneath my chin.

I exhaled, feeling the sudden presence of pain evaporating as quickly as it came. "I'm just tired. There's so much to think about at all times. My mind is struggling with the weight of it all, if I'm honest."

I thought the drink would've helped my racing mind, but it only made the anxieties worse.

And I had not had a decent night's sleep since the prison break. Not with the invading dreams that greeted me every time my eyes closed. I hoped tonight would be different with all the alcohol that danced through my veins.

Although the idea of dreaming displeased me, I couldn't survive to see Jesibel there again.

"Here." Duncan offered me my mug of ale, which I gladly took from him. I inhaled the scent of buttery honey mixed with the sharper undertones of clove. I gulped down the remains of mine, relishing in the numbing sensation that filled my throat and spread like wildfire through my insides. All the while, Duncan continued to watch me with the same look of concern he always seemed to relate to me.

"Don't look at me like that," I said, lips glistening with ale.

Duncan took his thumb and swept a dribble which escaped the corner of my mouth. He traced it over my lower lip. The sticky residue only lasted a moment before he dipped in close and pressed his lips to it.

He exhaled into the kiss and I pushed in closer, deepening it until my body hummed with want for him. The empty mug was forgotten as my hands ran down the length of his arms, fingers rising and falling over mounds of muscle.

I recognised that my touch caused the dark hairs across his forearm to stand. My fingers traced softly until I reached his wrist and they tangled in metal. As soon as I touched the thin iron chain wrapped around Duncan's wrist, I felt the drawing pull of my innate power fall away from me.

My stomach jolted up into my throat. I tore my hand away as though lightning had struck it. Which would have been a better feeling than the draining power of iron.

"You are giving me a look that I'd rather you didn't," Duncan said, lips bruised pink from our kiss. His dark eyes glanced down at the cause of my reaction. He winced as he recognised the iron bracelet. "I don't want for you to worry about me, Robin."

"Well, I do." Ice cracked in my bones, fuelled by my anger. I recognised the emotion for what it was and didn't hide away as the feeling devoured me. "But if you wish to lighten the load on my mind, then do yourself a favour and face the powers you have been given. Hiding behind iron is not the answer."

A deep sadness glazed across Duncan's eyes, darkening them to pools of almost-black. He glanced down at his wrist again, wincing to himself. The iron bracelet stood out as something that didn't belong. And it didn't. I wished to tear it from him and allow him to face his truth. His new truth.

"I don't trust the person the iron keeps contained. This power isn't a gift. It was forced upon me. What it stands for, what I am... it ties me to Aldrick, and that sickens me."

"How can you say that when you don't allow yourself to even know this new version of yourself?" I asked, watching my question sink deep into him. "What you did in Lockinge, it is the type of power that will come in handy in the days to follow. No, you didn't ask for it, but what better excuse than to turn it against the man who changed you?"

My hands shook with the desire to touch Duncan again. I shifted across the short distance that had grown between us and eradicated it completely.

"I'm not ready, Robin."

"Trust me, that's a feeling I know all too well," I said, taking his hands and gripping them as though he hung from the edge of a cliff, and I was all he had to hold to keep him from falling away from me. "Listen to me, Duncan. I want you to hear properly what I'm about to say to you."

The scar down the side of his face flexed as his expression hardened into something of focus. He lifted his eyes to mine. They alone had the power to send a powerful buzz of lightning through my blood.

"You have my full attention always, darling."

"Good. Then you'll have no excuse to disregard my words again." I cupped his face in my hands, feeling the sticky warmth of his skin. His cheeks mushed slightly beneath my palms, but I didn't stop.

"Duncan, I understand you have been through a transformation you never wanted. I know what it means to you. This feeling is only something else we have shared. But not all change is full of fear and dread. I had to learn that the hard way. The blood that brought you back from death, that gave you another chance, is mine. I'm in your heart, just as you are in mine. Always and in ways that no one else can understand. Not anyone in this realm nor those that wait beyond the veil of time. The power does not link you to Aldrick, it knots you to *me*."

Slowly, the mask of steel that Duncan had erected crumbled. His brows softened, his forehead folding with lines. His beautifully carved lips parted. A strand of his chestnut-brown hair fell over his eye as he shifted in his seat. I reached up and brushed it away, tucking it neatly behind his curved ear.

"With everything I've done in my life, I can say confidently that I don't deserve you. But I am selfish enough to admit I'd never let you go either."

"Be selfish all you want." I leaned in. "I'm not going anywhere."

There were many things I loved about Duncan. Namely how close he made me feel to my own parents. I'd not told it to him before, happily keeping this feeling as my own little secret, but I coveted the ties of our story to theirs. Hunter and fey; two odds falling for one another. One day I'd tell him the importance of our differences. Of course, he knew about my father and mother, but not the echo of how his physical presence was such a daily reminder.

How he made me feel was like ripples across a lake when a stone was thrown onto its calm surface – Duncan was the stone.

"Is this the perfect moment for me to carry you to bed?" Duncan whispered, breath tickling my face.

"Take the bracelet off," I replied. "Then I'm all yours."

Duncan spluttered, exuding a deep chuckle that warmed my skin from the chill of the Icethorn Court that invaded our tent greedily. "Is danger one of your kinks, Darling?"

"If I feared you, then yes. But I'm not scared of you, Duncan. Not before and certainly not now."

"What if I hurt you?"

I held his gaze as my fingers reached back for his bracelet of iron. The moment the tips touched the metal, I felt the drawing, draining pull. This time, I didn't pull away. "I would forgive you."

"Wouldn't it be better if I wasn't put in a position that required the need for me to apologise to you?"

I shook my head. "For a man with such big balls, you're scared of a little lightning?"

Duncan smirked, exhaling a long breath out of his nose. "Never have I heard little in relation to me before."

"Exactly," I replied, weaving my fingers beneath the bracelet and folding them over until the thin chain bit into my skin. "Facing your truth is the first step to living with it."

"I love you," Duncan breathed.

Before I changed my mind, I ripped the bracelet from Duncan's wrist, snapping it into two pieces which fell from my fingers onto the floor at our feet. "And I love you, all of you."

Duncan lowered his chin, pinched his eyes closed and gave in to the heavy breaths that took over his body. His face screwed up as he waited for the lightning to come.

I felt his power in the surrounding air, hot and crackling. Small veins of light danced across the layer of his skin. The hairs on his arms stood to attention. I gripped his hands and squeezed, urging him to calm himself.

"Duncan, you control the power. Remember, it doesn't control you."

It took a few moments of tension until Duncan gathered enough of himself to look back up at me. The glow of his green eyes intensified as his power coiled within them. He hardened himself before my eyes, his strong chest rising and falling as he focused on putting a lid on the power.

I waited for him. Giving him the moments to regain authority. "You can do this."

Before long, the strands of purple light faded, the air returning to normal.

"Would you look at that," I said. "Duncan Rackley is finally free."

"As long as I have you, I'll always be free."

I narrowed my eyes on him, contemplating just how many things I wanted to do to him now he'd accepted his fate. "Now, back to the conversation of carrying me to bed–"

Outside of the tent a scream pierced the night. The sound ripped claws into my heart and shredded it to pieces, snapping our attention to the exit. I couldn't explain it, but the noise was filled with grief. It hit me in the chest, powerful, dreadful, so strong that it encouraged my eyes to fill with tears without me understanding what it was I cried for.

Even after the howl stopped, it still rang in my ears. The sound drew me to my feet. Duncan, too. The peace lasted a moment until the sound came again. But this time, when the scream returned, it was not one of grief. It was born from anger. Burning, overwhelming fury that thorned itself into my soul and made me prepare for action.

I'd heard the sound before, once, upon the oceans when the Draeic flew overhead.

It was a cry of war.

Not a warning or a threat – but a promise.

And I knew exactly who'd expelled it.

CHAPTER 16

I gazed down upon Gabrial, refusing to look away, my body equally as rigid and cold as her corpse.

Her remains had been laid out across the table for all to see, blood soaking into the wood and staining the air with the harsh tang of copper.

The blood was everywhere. Once-golden hair was now stained russet, her roots were so dark with gore that it looked as though her scalp had turned to obsidian. I was thankful for the two identical pins that'd sewn her eyelids closed. When she'd first been presented to us, they'd been wide and all seeing. It had taken a lot of encouraging for Rafaela to release her. She'd clung on to the body of the smaller warrior, the pain etched into her face with lines so deep they could've been scars.

Rafaela was drenched in Gabrial's blood, too. Her once-white tunic was splattered with the gore, spreading across her torso until it looked as though it was Rafaela who bled. But there was no denying that Gabrial was gone.

Before Elinor saw to Gabrial's eyes being closed, I knew I'd never forget how little white was left in the young girl's eyes. They were stained black as though her pupils had ruptured and the colour bled out of their confines.

It had been hours since Duncan pried the dead body from Rafaela's grasp. Since then, Gabrial had been cleaned and cared for. Her skin had been washed, and her body prepared for her death rites. Although, little could be done for the ribbons of skin that'd been clawed from Gabrial's body. The bleeding had stopped, but the damage was unrepairable. It was impossible to know what had been skin or torn strips of clothing. Face, chest, arms, neck, legs, hands. There wasn't an inch of Gabrial's body that'd not been tortured.

Her only discerning feature was the symbols across her now-greying skin – marks that would never reveal another human's story again.

Rafaela's fellow Nephilim had done well to fold the wings beneath Gabrial's small, broken body. But there was no hiding the patches of missing feathers or the irritated gashes that sliced across the bone-like frame of the wings. Whoever – *whatever* – had done this to Gabrial, had made sure they left their mark.

And as if the horror she'd been through was not enough, it was believed her tongue had been gouged from her mouth first. The fey healer found only the stump of flesh in her mouth. Not that it made anything better, but it was believed Gabrial had died from suffocating in her own blood. I only hoped her death was swift and provided her peace from the mutilation she'd fallen victim to.

Rafaela had hardly made a sound since she brought the body to us. I had to convince myself that she'd not turned to stone from grief. Every time the Nephilim took a breath in, as though she'd forgotten how to do so for too long a period of time, I felt the chill of relief. The only noise she made was a guttural growl when anyone got too close to Gabrial. There was no denying the fear in the fey healer's eyes as she tugged the white sheet up to cover the horror completely, finally removing it from view.

Gabrial's body had been discovered when Rafaela went to tell her of the summons Kayne had sent, the note tied around Lucari's leg. When Kayne was told of the circumstance, he paled so white I saw webs of blue veins beneath his complexion. Especially since Lucari hadn't returned since.

He knew this looked bad for him, but there was something telling me that he wasn't to blame. For Duncan, I'd keep Kayne safe from speculation until we all figured out what had actually happened.

"We are truly sorry for your loss," Queen Lyra Cedarfall said, her strong voice settling across the deathly silent room. Her words were meant for Rafaela, who showed no sign that she'd even heard the fey queen. "It saddens me we have met one another under such circumstances–"

"Gabrial is not *lost*," Rafaela spoke for the first time in what felt like hours. And she sounded as broken as she looked. "Gabrial is dead, returned to the arms of her maker before time. I do not want apologies. I want *answers*." Slowly she lifted furious eyes, settling them on everyone in the small crowd. "Now, I ask you… why is my sister dead?"

Why? Such a clear question, to the point and precise. Yet why was it the hardest to answer? That word alone opened a multitude of further questions. None of them we could answer, no matter how we wished to do so.

"I don't have the answers for you, Rafaela. But I swear it, with everything we have at our disposal, we'll help find what did this," I replied, tearing my mind from the haunting memory of Gabrial's flayed, greying skin. "I understand our promise may mean little to you, but I swear it."

Duncan placed a steady hand on my shoulder. I was thankful for how anchoring his touch was.

"This is Aldrick's doing, I don't think we need to waste time thinking otherwise," he said, placing his spare arm around Kayne's shoulder, protectively drawing him in close. A twinge of jealousy was born from his actions, and I couldn't lie to myself, seeing it displeased me. But I swallowed my pathetic misplaced emotion. Now wasn't the time for it.

"For our sakes, I hope you are wrong, Duncan," Elinor added. "If Aldrick's influence can reach this far, we have no chance against him."

"I dare the Defiler to stand before me. In the Creator's name, I will avenge her." Rafaela trembled on the spot, standing so suddenly that her chair clattered against the floor. "By nightfall, I demand the culprit to be presented before me for judgement. Turn your camp upside down, I do not care. But you find me who did this to Gabrial, I demand it."

"You think it was one of us?" I asked, sensing the accusation in her words.

Rafaela cast an accusatory stare across the room. Her full lips were drawn into a tight line, draining the colour from them. "I don't know what to think besides how specific the murder was. It was to weaken us, to keep us on the back foot. Gabrial is dead because of what she can provide – could provide us."

Rafaela was right. Gabrial had been killed because of the insight she could've provided regarding Aldrick. Without her, our ties to getting information had been completely severed. It was an unsettling thought, but not as damning as the idea someone in this camp was not working with us, but against us.

"Why did you request our audience?" Rafaela asked, snapping her eyes from Lyra, to Elinor, and then to me. "Was it to break bread and discuss unimportant matters, or was it because you recognised what Gabrial could do for *our* cause?"

I couldn't find the words to reply, knowing what Rafaela was suggesting. It was Lyra who answered, and even her voice shook with knowing.

"Robin informed us Gabrial had access to insight on Aldrick, an ability to read his past and present." Lyra kept her posture rigid, refusing to back down against Rafaela's clear insinuations. "Yes, we required her for her gifts, but do you really believe we are the ones who... murdered her? As you said, she was an important asset."

"She was more than an asset." Rafaela's cheeks blossomed with heat, staining her skin a rich crimson. Then she turned her attention on Kayne, just as I expected she would. "You sent the summons, where is your bird now?"

"I… don't know." Kayne stifled a sob, catching it in his fist as he, too, worked out why Rafaela believed Gabrial was murdered. "Lucari did not return."

"Then I trust I do not need to explain any further as to where my suspicions have found themselves." Rafaela's jaw trembled as she gritted her teeth. Muscles hardened in her jaw, matching the fury in her bright, accusatory stare. My eyes flew to her hands as they were gathered like boulders at her sides, for a moment I feared for Kayne's safety.

I stepped forwards, drawing out of Duncan's touch and positioning my body before them both. "We can throw accusations around, or we can spend our time getting the answers you need, Rafaela. There is no good to come from pointing the blame. What is important is we ensure this does not happen again. Clearly, we are not safe here, not anymore. Perhaps we never were. Not with this unknown killer among us. It is important everyone is questioned regarding their whereabouts."

"Unknown," Rafaela barked, eyes widening at the word. "Find me that bird and let us see if it really is unknown."

"Lucari wouldn't have done this," Kayne snapped. "If you think she is to blame, or even if I am, then why would I be stood here? If I was guilty, I'd be long gone."

"Kayne has spent most of the evening with us," Althea said, actually standing up for the Hunter. "In fact, there is someone who has suspiciously faded off into the shadows."

Rafaela's attention snapped to the fey princess, tongue lapping at her lip as if she hungered for the information. "Who?"

"The Asps. They haven't been seen since we docked," Althea said, looking directly at me. "This stinks of the bite of an Asp. Their loyalty lies with those who fill their pockets with coin. It wouldn't take much of a price for Aldrick to pay one. Perhaps Seraphine would be the first person we should investigate, since she's seemed to disappear at the right hour?"

"No." I shook my head, the word practically exploding out of me. "Aldrick is behind the murder of Seraphine's twin sister. Historically the Asps have not been the most trustworthy of people, but there is no amount of coin that Seraphine would accept to ever work for Aldrick."

"You sound sure," Rafaela said, disbelief evident in her tone.

"Seraphine is *not* behind this. I – I can vouch for their whereabouts, and it is not anywhere near here."

This was the moment to tell them that, as a condition of giving Seraphine and her vipers Imeria Castle as their new nest, it was actually a place of retirement. They got my stronghold, as long as they never accepted a job again.

"It's too messy of a kill for an Asp," Gyah said, golden eyes coiling with contained power. I sensed a beast lurking within, one wishing to be freed. To hunt whoever did this and bring Gabrial to justice. "If they're smart enough to conduct this atrocity, they will have the sense to never return to the scene of the crime."

"We will see," Rafaela snarled, her red-stained eyes filled with tears of fury and pain, landing back on Kayne. "The moment your little bird returns, I wish to see it."

"What if Lucari is dead too?" Kayne swallowed hard, unable to conceal the fear on his expression. "Has anyone contemplated that the same thing that killed Gabrial, has hurt my... my Lucari?"

Duncan drew the broken man to his side. "Lucari is a smart creature."

Elinor cleared her throat. "And Lucari is not the only creature with claws."

"What are you suggesting?" Rafaela paused, her eyes narrowing on the Oakstorm queen.

"Wychwood is home to many monsters. Some I'm more familiar with than others."

I knew exactly what Elinor was suggesting. "Gryvern. Do you think they..."

"I do not know what to think," Elinor said. "Doran's creatures have disbanded since his death, but they are still monsters. We should not ignore the chance that there is a flock nearby."

"If there is," Gyah growled deep in her throat. "I will find them."

All this talk of deceit, murder and monsters had me worrying for an entirely different reason. Had Aldrick found a way of getting control of Doran's creations? It would made sense – or was it easier to point the blame in any other direction than Kayne's hawk?

"Rafaela, I invite you to stay with us in my court," I said, demanding her attention. "I think we all agree this is Aldrick's doing. Until we can root out the infection among us, it isn't safe for you. Our focus must remain on him until we determine what our next steps are to be."

"What is there to determine, Robin Icethorn?" Rafaela shouted, her voice booming across the tent, the heavy canopy material flapping as though she'd brought on a gust of storm winds. "Aldrick must die."

"And he shall," Lyra announced. "But decisions of war cannot be rushed, nor is it decided between such limited company. We must return to our courts and prepare our people. We must brace our borders, sharpen our weapons. There are more ways to win a battle than with brute strength and power. We must be cautious–"

"No," Rafaela interrupted. "Gabrial has not died for you all to separate like lambs in a field, practically inviting the wolf to take you out one by one. What is important now is keeping you safe, preventing the keys from falling into Aldrick's hands." She took a hulking intake of breath, her wings twitching with unspent energy. "He must be stopped before he has any more of a chance to release Duwar. Gabrial's death will not be in vain."

"I'm sorry, Rafaela," Elinor interjected. "But this is far greater than Lyra, Robin and me. We have people to protect.

Innocents, like Gabrial, to keep from the same fate. We cannot abandon our courts and hide from Aldrick, as much as that seems like the only option."

I watched Rafaela closely as she pondered Elinor's words. She didn't blink, didn't release the tears she clearly fought hard to kept at bay. I sensed it, because it was a feeling I'd experienced before – Rafaela teetered on the edge of a knife. If she fell, it was into the abyss of sadness or fury. We were a matter of seconds from determining which side claimed her, it all hinged on how this conversation ended.

"As I've already petitioned, I'm with Rafaela on this. We should *not* separate." Every eye in the tent snapped to me. I straightened my back as much as I could, lifting my chin, imagining the crown atop my head. "But... I understand why we must."

Rafaela exhaled the breath she'd been holding. "Then it seems you've made your minds up. If you no longer require the council you have requested of me, I will leave."

"Rafaela, if there is anything you need from me," I said, reaching out with the overwhelming urge to supply her with the comfort of touch.

Rafaela offered me a sympathetic smile that revealed she was thankful I'd at least tried to help. When she turned her attention to the queens, that expression faded back into a mask of displeasure. "Queen Cedarfall and Queen Oakstorm, you will be provided with Nephilim to protect you on your return to your courts. Do as you wish and prepare your people. Time is sensitive. There is no knowing when Aldrick will act again. If you know what is good for you, you'll not refuse this offer."

"I get the sense it's not an offer, but a command. One, as you said, we would be foolish to decline," Elinor bowed her head, although her eyes never strayed from the Nephilim. "I accept."

"As do I," Lyra added.

"We wish to depart within the hour." Elinor straightened. "Thank you, Rafaela. After everything you have lost, we appreciate your help."

"Your escorts will be ready. But do not thank me yet," Rafaela replied through a grimace. "Even we do not have the power to save ourselves from Aldrick, let alone you."

With those last words, Rafaela knocked past me as she turned on her heel and swept toward the tent's exit. Before anyone could speak, she threw out her wings like a shield on her back.

"What would you like us to do with Gabrial?" I called out before Rafaela could fly away. "I'm not aware of the Nephilim's customs, but if you wish us to prepare a burial or ceremony, we shall do it. Whatever you ask."

I wondered if she heard the guilt in my offer. Gabrial was dead because of us, after all. Her blood was as much on our hands as it was on Aldrick's. If we'd not required Gabrial's gifts, perhaps she'd still be breathing, smiling that kind smile. But alas, those chances for life had been taken from her.

"There will be no need for a burial," Rafaela replied, voice cold as the winter winds invading the camp. "In the eyes of the Creator, it matters not in what state the body is left behind, but the memories and marks the person left upon the world. Gabrial will be with him now. Allow her body to perish, knowing her soul thrives in paradise."

There was no denying the slight choke as Rafaela spoke. Then she was gone, tearing out of the tent and leaving a gaping hole from her presence. As the canopy flapped open, it invited the chill of the dawn to invade within. I could've stopped the icy winds if I wanted to, but I didn't. Its presence was comforting to me. The sting of ice on my cheeks did more to wake me than anything else could've at that moment.

Silence thrummed across the tent behind me, surrounding the body of the dead.

I turned on the small company, taking time to look at every single one of them. "Ensure that whatever has been discussed here does not spread across the camp. Now is not the time to create hysteria. If we allow for chaos, we will lose control."

No one disagreed.

"There is still the issue of whoever killed Gabrial." Gyah glowered, the only one brave enough to look at the covered body on the table. "If the killer is still here, I would like to dine off their flesh. I will scout the area until we have left, if you permit it, Robin."

I could taste the indignation in Gyah's comment. As though the scaled creature hidden beneath her skin spoke for her. But more so, there was no denying how important her request for permission was. It was a sign, to everyone in this room, that it was me who Gyah looked to for command. Not her queen, who stood on watching. But me.

"As much as I share in your sentiment, I cannot risk you leaving alone," I replied. "We stay in pairs at all times. No one is safe. Aldrick has invaded, and I hardly imagine he will retract his claws, knowing Gabrial is dead. His presence is still among us. I *know* it. And now there is the issue of us needing information about him, or we will forever be chasing his tail, guessing his next moves too late."

Althea noticed something in me, just as I knew she would. "And, from that look in your eye, you have a plan, don't you?"

It was the easiest answer to give. I just hoped I had enough to tempt an Asp out of their retirement. "Oh, I do."

CHAPTER 17

I tugged on the leather reins, willing my mount to slow to a stop. Ahead of me, parting though thick winter mist, was a haunting shard of ice and stone. The last I'd seen Imeria Castle was from the edge of the village of Berrow. From a distance, it had looked big, but with it before me, I couldn't fathom its sheer size. It speared skyward, stabbing through grey clouds, an imposing monstrosity that represented the family that died inside of it.

I could hardly believe that a place like this could ever exist.

Streams of frozen winds slashed across the many turrets. It danced cautiously around the castle's edge as though even the elements feared the building. Icicles, far larger than me, hung from beneath balconies like pointed teeth. It wasn't a place of warmth and life. From the outside, I could feel just how vacant the place was. Even the cobbled stone road which led us here was buried in inches of snow and treacherous black ice.

"Are you sure they are inside?" Duncan asked from beside me.

"I am," I replied, my breath forming in a cloud of mist beyond my lips.

Imeria Castle had been crafted upon the face of a mountain. Harsh, raw rock mixed seamlessly with white polished stone that enticed natural light and refracted it in a myriad of hues and colours.

My neck strained as I looked up its entire length. I cast a hand over my eyes to block out the light. There was no knowing where the castle stopped as its tip was concealed among the heavyset clouds.

I could just about make out the dark stone which crowned the furthest northern spire. The obsidian spike's never-ending surface reminded me of the lake between the Icethorn and Cedarfall Courts. The Sleeping Death, as Erix had once explained. A body of water that seemed more like a realm of pure darkness.

Erix had been on my mind a lot today. There was nothing I could do to rid myself of his memory. And for the first time, I didn't want to either.

"No wonder you gave it away," Rafaela commented from her mount, a stained brown stag with two oversized antlers that dripped with icicles that were not there when we had left the encampment earlier. "It's not exactly a welcoming place. Perhaps your acquaintances left the moment they arrived. Anyone with sense would know this is no place to call home."

At least the Nephilim shared in the same feeling as I did.

"Oh, no, Seraphine is here," I replied, leather gloves squeaking as I gripped tighter on the reins. There was a small part of me that wished to remind Rafaela that Imeria had been a home once before. But I felt the need to advocate for the place was counterintuitive. I'd given it away, I couldn't start regretting that decision now. "Compared to the hovels the Asps had been previously living within, Imeria is the pinnacle of luxury for them."

There was the soft patter of hooves upon the snow. To my left, Duncan rode forward on his black steed. He chose the horse over the stag, commenting on how his thighs wouldn't feel so offended if he rode on something he was already used to.

"I think it's the second most beautiful thing I've ever seen." Duncan gazed up at the castle through the shadows of his hood. It was drawn low enough to cover his eyes but did nothing to conceal the purse of his lips. They revealed exactly what he felt as he looked upon the castle.

"What's the first?" I asked.

He shot me a look, one that already told me I knew the answer before he said it. "You."

Before Rafaela could comment, not that she would, Duncan made another point. "Forgive me for admitting this, darling, but I can see why Althea is royally fucked off with you."

"Comforting," I replied.

Even now, miles away from Althea, I could still imagine the steam of smoke that'd poured from her ears when I told her my truth. I couldn't have hidden it from her any longer, not when she asked why we were not all going to Imeria together. Her face bloomed a deep scarlet when I explained the reason. Seeing her reaction was exactly why I hadn't told her the price I paid for the Asps' help.

Which was equally why I didn't tell her the price I was *about* to pay, requesting their aid once again.

"So, this is what your ancestors did with the power gifted to you by Altar," Rafaela said, kicking her heels into her stag's side to urge it onward. "You crafted shrines for yourselves and titled yourselves as kings and queens. Unsurprising."

"Need I remind you I didn't ask for any of this?" I spat, my attitude as sore as my backside was in the saddle.

"Nor did Gabrial." Rafaela glared forward as she spoke. Her golden hammer had been strapped vertically down her back, laid perfectly between her snow-coated wings. Even with the weight on her back, and the added pressure left on her shoulders since the murder of her companion, Rafaela still kept rigid and straight-backed.

"Let's get inside, shall we? If we are lucky, Seraphine will have something to warm our stomachs," Duncan announced, hand resting on his abdomen.

"I think we will be lucky if they even let us inside," I grumbled, announcing my trepidation.

"Regardless of your contract with the assassins," Rafaela added, her determination burning around her skin like a halo of heat. "This is your home. Your land. They can open the door willingly, or we will be forced to break it down."

"Let's hope it doesn't get to that," Duncan added.

I looked at him, scanning the glint in his eyes, hoping to read his emotion. "Do you think I've made a mistake coming back here for them?"

Duncan hesitated long enough for my stomach to drop. "I will always support your decisions."

"That doesn't answer my question," I replied. "If someone in our circle killed Gabrial and has done something to Lucari, then the Asps are the ones with the power to wait in the shadows and find them."

That wasn't the only reason we'd come. Retired or not, I had to hope Seraphine still had Asps in every corner of every court – including Elmdew, where Aldrick currently resided.

"It is not me you need to convince, Robin." Duncan pursed his lips and turned back to the castle.

"Then why does it feel like I do?" I knocked my heels into the stag's side and began following Rafaela. She'd already trotted toward the half-raised gates at the end of the path. I didn't blame her for wanting to get away. Hearing us squabble was not what she would have wanted to hear, not after what had happened early that morning with Gabrial.

"We are not done talking," Duncan said, grunting as he put his horse in chase.

"Since this visit was one of the only things Kayne has ever agreed with me on, I would've thought that automatically gained your seal of approval, Duncan."

"Lucari is missing. Of course Kayne is going to want you to do anything to find out what has happened to her."

"And what of Gabrial?"

He didn't reply. I didn't need to look over my shoulder to know that Duncan's lips were left parted but soundless. There was a part of me that wanted to dismount and continue this argument. But then I would have to face the root of this problem. My vulnerability drove this wedge between us. I understood that. Which is what kept me trotting forward, biting down hard on my tongue.

Running from my insecurities was far easier than facing them.

"Have you come all this way to claim Imeria back from us?" Seraphine asked from her seat upon a silver-coated throne. My mother's throne – my throne. "Because I could have saved you a journey if that is the case. I thought you were a man of your word, Robin."

The assassin was laid across it, legs kicking over one arm as she leaned back on the opposite. Her posture screamed disrespect. I glanced at her muddied boot, smudging dirt across the pristine leather of the chair's arm. I wondered if her playful chuckle was offered because she gloated at the scowl her actions painted across my face.

From the moment we'd dismounted and entered Imeria, greeted by the assassins who melted from the shadows, I was furious. The emotion was misplaced, but I couldn't dampen it.

"My word is my bond," I replied, voice echoing across the towering, empty room. "This is not my home, not now, not before."

"Then do you care to tell me what it is you want? I can see the request haunting those pretty black eyes of yours. Telling like the glare of a magpie. You need something from me." Seraphine swung her legs over and slammed her boots to the ground. The Asp leaned forward, resting elbows on her thighs and placing her head in both hands. "Which is strange because you, of all people, know that we have retired – as per your own request. We've shed the skin of the Asps and now live humbly in our new home."

"A home that will be destroyed the moment the Defiler is freed," Rafaela shouted, wings flinching with the urge to spread and demand the space as her own. Her grip on her hammer hadn't wavered from the moment we stood before Seraphine.

"Which is exactly why I have permitted your entrance. Retired or not, I'm still flattered you've come all this way for me."

I couldn't fight the curl of my lip, nor did I try to. "Once an Asp, always an Asp."

"I've changed, Robin," Seraphine said, whilst watching Rafaela with a wary eye. "Out of the kindness we are attempting to adopt, I can offer you all a full belly and a warm bed for the night. Then you can be on your way, taking your burdens with you."

"Respectfully, we have not come all this way for you not to listen," Duncan added.

"Human, perhaps you need me to repeat myself. As I have already said, you are each welcome to stay in our home, but you *will* leave come morning."

"Name your price," I spat, nails slicing into my palms.

Seraphine slapped her palms across her thighs and spat on the floor between us. "Do not bring the chaos that follows you to our door."

"You know why we are here, and you are scared, understandably," Duncan said, stepping away from our line, closer to the assassin queen. I was certain I heard the rumble of thunder far beyond the thick stone walls, but no one else seemed to notice. "We are all frightened. The least you can do is hear us out."

"I already know what has brought you here. Old habits die hard," Seraphine replied, unable to hide her smirk. "We may have retired from our former duties, but we are not stupid enough to close our eyes and ears to what is happening around us."

The sinking feeling of realisation itched at my skin.

"So then, how many of you stayed behind to spy on us?" I asked.

"Enough to know what happened to Gabrial. So, have you come to lay blame on us for her death?"

I scolded myself for not noticing. How had I been so blind to trust that Seraphine would have withdrawn all her assassins when she had left for Imeria? Regardless of if she still revoked her former duties, they were ingrained into her blood just like this place was for me. "Well, are you to blame?"

"Of course not," Seraphine shouted, evidently offended by the suggestion.

"Care to touch my hammer, so I can seek the truth of that?" Rafaela said.

"We both know that isn't required, Nephilim."

I fought the urge to take my attention off Seraphine and indulge myself in studying the room I stood in. A place my mother would have once walked. I blinked and could almost see her, in my mind's eye, sitting upon the throne in Seraphine's place.

A brown sheet fluttered on the wall behind the throne. Now and then, I would see behind it, to the smashed glass window that Seraphine had attempted to cover. There was no hiding how the material caught on the jagged shards of glass that still clung to the frame, ripping holes that hinted at the grey-covered sky beyond the castle.

I didn't need to ask to know that this destruction was caused by the gryvern when Doran sent them to kill my mother. From the small glances I allowed myself on the walk to the throne room, it was clear the window behind the throne wasn't the only sign that a struggle had infiltrated this place. It scarred the walls, floors and pillars. Marks made from claws. Old stains splattered against walls, even the air was kissed with the memory of death.

Sensing my discomfort, a hand slipped into mine, drawing me out of my imagination. I followed the gloved hand up to the person it belonged to. Duncan's concern was palpable across his handsome face.

One squeeze from his fingers was enough to refocus me. "I'm here."

I forced a smile whilst the Nephilim and assassin entered a silent battle.

"Seraphine, if you know, then let us skip this part and get to what we've come here to uncover," I said, confidence borrowed from Duncan's steel gaze and firm touch.

"Your question would be wasted–"

"Who killed her?" Rafaela growled, slamming the butt of her weapon against the floor, cracking stone.

The sound rippled across the room, encasing us all in the tension that seemed to have grown thicker since we arrived.

"Unfortunately," Seraphine replied, narrowed eyes scanning the group. "I cannot provide the solace you require, Nephilim. The murderer of your companion is unknown to us, we only know it happened. The person who took that girl's life is skilled at hiding from shadows. But I'm aware you believe Aldrick is behind it, and I think we can all agree that he is."

"That's not good enough." The room shook as Rafaela stomped her foot down. Dust rained down from the vaulted ceiling, coating our hair and shoulders like snow.

Seraphine stood, then walked carefully down the cracked, worn steps until she was level with the three of us. It was the first time I'd seen her dressed in such luxurious clothing. Naturally, my eyes scanned her strong limbs for weapons, yet I couldn't see even the hint of any upon her.

This wasn't the assassin I had come to know. As Seraphine suggested, it seemed she truly had shed that skin.

"Gabrial was killed because of what she could provide you in the war to come. Her insight into Aldrick was invaluable, and whoever murdered her knew that. Which means you are once again blind to his movements and decisions. However, Gabrial isn't the only one with the ability to see doings at such great distances... is she, Robin?"

"No, Seraphine. She isn't."

"So, go on then, spit it out," Seraphine sighed, rolling her eyes as she looked back at me. "Ask me what it is you came all this way for."

I swallowed down my concerns, knowing Seraphine would sense even the smallest hint of trepidation. If I needed to convince her to extend her aid, I had to do so with confidence.

"Have your people retreated from Elmdew, or do you keep them there as a fail-safe as well?" I asked, smiling as the reaction that passed over her face confirmed what I needed to know.

"Aldrick brainwashed, used and ultimately caused the death of my sister," Seraphine spat. "She does not have the luxury of retiring alongside me, to experience the life which we dreamed of as children. I'd be a fool to completely withdraw my players from this game, Robin. Of course, I have my people in Elmdew just as I have them in Oakstorm and Cedarfall. I may have hung my daggers away, but I am still cautious – I know that the fight is not over."

"Then help us," I pleaded. "If not by locating the person behind Gabrial and possibly Lucari's death, but also by stopping Aldrick. Send a command to the Asps you have in the courts and ask them to guard the keys. Guard *us*, protect us. We started this together. Let us finish it as one."

"It will take more than that to convince me."

Duncan's skin crackled with lightning. It hissed in the air around him as he spoke. "Not all of us have the indulgence of hiding behind stone walls."

"Hiding?" Seraphine barked a laugh, twisting the skirts of her emerald silk dress as she turned back to the throne. For a moment, I wondered who that dress had belonged to before. Had Seraphine raided my mother's belongings, or had they already been pillaged by thieves in the years the court was left unprotected? "We're not hiding. We are enjoying the retirement your king offered us."

"And you can still have it," I snapped. "But what good is living a life of peace if the world beyond is in chaos."

Seraphine sighed, flicking dark hair over her shoulder. "Has anyone ever taught you the importance of grovelling when asking for a favour? Insulting me will not provide you with the answer you have travelled all this way for."

"Then what will?" Rafaela asked above the rustling of her feathers. "Name your price."

"That is not something you can afford," she replied. "Let alone Robin."

"Name it, give me the chance, and I will find a way–"

"Robin, enough!" Duncan snapped, blue light flashing in lines across his skin. "You have sacrificed more than you have needed. I'll not see you part with anything else to the likes of these scum."

"Listen to your keeper, Robin." Seraphine leered, now sitting back on the throne. My throne. The one my mother had sat upon when this castle was more than empty rooms and scars of destruction across every place I looked.

"You *are* frightened," Rafaela said, her smile terrifying. "There is no shame in that. You should be."

"Don't speak on my behalf–"

A sudden flash of golden light glowed across Seraphine's face. The hue smoothed out the snarl that had set across it, Seraphine's eyes fixating on the cause of the light, which was held in Rafaela's two firm hands, levelled between them.

The hammer. It was pointed toward the assassin, exuding a warm power that seemed to have some hold over Seraphine. The creases around the assassin's eyes melted away, and the black of her pupils grew in size within her eyes.

"You fear for the chosen family that you have filled this empty castle with," Rafaela said as she drew out Seraphine's truth. "Already you know grief, as do I. And you, like the rest of us, will do anything to protect those around you. But I will show you what will become of this world if you do not help. All your wishes will mean nothing…"

I watched in awe as Seraphine's disregard crumbled, and she wept. Her eyes filled with tears that fell freely down her face. Her lips were moving, repeating a word that I could not hear. The strange, enforced trance lasted only a moment. Rafaela retracted the hammer and slammed the head into the floor at her feet. The glow dissipated, returning the room back to its ominous hue.

Seraphine leaned forward, gaze fixed on the floor. Her chest rose and fell dramatically as though each breath was not enough to sustain her.

"What did you do?" I asked, looking sidelong at Rafaela, who seemed to wait for something further to happen. Seraphine was hunched, trying to catch her breath as wide eyes loosed tears in a never-ending stream down her paled face.

"I simply showed her what my hammer can. The truth. I gave Seraphine a glimpse into the future, one that her lack of help with ensure."

"A vision?" Duncan asked.

"Yes." Rafaela nodded. "One of destruction."

Seraphine slowly lifted herself up, although the weight of what she'd witnessed still bore down on her. Her wide, unblinking eyes overflowed with horror as her tears continued to spill without sign of stopping. Yet, when she spoke, it was nothing but the voice of the assassin I'd come to know. "I'll help you claim the answers you seek."

My breath hitched in my throat, surprised at just how quickly these tides had changed.

"Thank you," Rafaela replied, bowing her head, lowering her strange weapon back to her side.

I looked between them all. Duncan was stoic, clearly struggling with what he'd just witnessed.

Seraphine levelled her eyes with mine, locking me in place.

"Robin Icethorn, we will find the perpetrator who murdered your allies. But understand, when the answers you seek are not what you wish to hear, do not return to my home again.

As Rafaela here understands, the truth is not always what we wish to know."

"And... what of my other requests?"

"It will take some days to get answers back from Elmdew. In regards to protecting the Oakstorm and Cedarfall queens, I will make that request of any remaining Asps who've yet to vacate those courts. They will stay back and keep a close eye on those you wish to protect, until this hell is over."

It was my turn to bow, overcome with gratitude but being careful just how much I showed. There was a weakness in relying on others, but a strength, too. I just hoped it was worth it.

"Thank you, Seraphine. I am truly sorry I have had to bring this to your door again."

Getting information from Elmdew, and knowledge into what happened to Gabrial, was only the beginning of what I came here for. But knowing Elinor and Lyra would have the added protection of the Asps and Nephilim shielding them when returning to their courts made everything worth it.

It was a risk coming to Imeria, but it had paid off by the skin of my teeth.

Without Rafaela, I fear I'd not have been so successful.

Regardless of our success, I couldn't sleep. The little rest I had fallen into was riddled with Jesibel once again. It always felt so real. The dreams more tangible as time passed on. I was left to stare up at the darkened ceiling, trying to shake the discomfort from the dream I'd just woken from. I still sensed Jesibel's fingers rifling through my head. Picking at visions, one at a time. Gabrial, Seraphine, Imeria Castle. It was as though she wished to haunt me, punishing me for failing her by making me relive everything terrible that had happened.

Sleep had joined my growing list of enemies. I couldn't face closing my eyes again for fear of what I would find.

Duncan's broad back faced me. The moment his head hit the worn, dust-ridden pillow, he'd fallen easily into the peace sleep offered. He'd not moved a muscle since.

I had busied myself with tracing my nails across his skin. Faint pink lines were left in my wake. I watched as they faded within seconds before my eyes. At least those marks did. The other scars that littered Duncan's body would never be scrubbed away.

I thought of Gabrial and the words that stained her skin, telling stories of others, whereas these marks, the ones that crisscrossed in silver, puckered lines, told of Duncan's story. The pain he was subjected to during his time as a Hunter. Each etching was a symbol of his defiance. Some were not as pronounced as others. Across his right shoulder blade was a thicker, angrier scar that bumped beneath my finger as I ran over it. I drew my hand away as though it had burned me like fire.

Unlike the other scars, this one was a memory of the pain. Pain I'd caused him. What his ultimate defiance, falling in love with a fey, had resulted in. Even if I vowed to make sure he'd never face suffering at my hands again, I couldn't shake the knowledge that everyone around me was at risk.

And yet, selfishly, I wouldn't send him away.

I rolled over, ignoring the exhaled moan of Duncan who, somewhere in his subconscious, recognised the withdrawal of my touch. Unable to subject myself to my traitorous thoughts a moment longer, I swung my legs off the bed and stood up.

Beyond the narrow, long windows was a sky blanketed in the darkest of black. Thin wisps of cloud passed across the moon that looked hauntingly large this far up in Imeria Castle. It cast its ivory glow into the room, bathing everything around me in an ethereal glow.

I wondered what this room had once been used for. Who dwelled in it? It was far too small to be used as a chamber room. I imagined it was well-suited for a storage room, but I couldn't be sure.

Wherever I looked, questions haunted me, forever unanswered.

I snatched the cream tunic from the bundle I'd left on the floor. Pulling it back over my head, I didn't bother to work the ties around the neck. Instead, I left them loose to allow the kiss of chilled winds to devour my skin and wash the sticky sense of exhaustion that laced it.

Once I was dressed, I padded across the cracked, slabbed floor to the door. I clung to the aged wood that creaked as it swung open. Glancing back at Duncan, who still hadn't stirred awake, I gave myself two options.

Crawl back into the warmth he provided to the thin sheets, or wander through Imeria in search of the ghosts and memories that would make me feel something for this place.

I pulled the door closed behind me, shutting away the easier of the two options. I picked the latter and left Duncan alone.

Imeria Castle was a maze of empty rooms, narrow corridors with ceilings hidden by shadow and grand, glassless windows. Beyond them was a view of the Icethorn Court, which stretched like a patchwork of white, grey and silver for as far as the eye could see.

My thighs burned as I paced up endless stairs and down hallways that led to more hallways with closed doors on either side. The light grey carpet runner provided my bare feet with some warmth. Like most of the castle's aged decor, it was ripped and frayed.

I steadied myself by placing a hand on the wall. My fingers trailed over marks and scars as I dragged my touch along it. I didn't take long to see hints of the battle that'd been waged here. The slaughter of the family I'd never know. I saw three equally long scratch marks gouged deep into the stone, snatching my hand away as a bout of sickness uncoiled in my stomach.

Bannisters had snapped, exposing sharp splinters of wood that gave way to a great fall to a landing beneath the curved stairway. In some places, I had to take care not to walk over shards of glass hidden beneath flurries of snow let in from the destroyed windows.

Time had not been kind to Imeria, just as the gryvern hadn't been when they came and turned this place into what it was now.

A graveyard for my family. A place where the Icethorns should've all perished.

I would've thought I'd feel closer to my mother, walking on the same floor she had once walked. Treading in the same places she had. Occupying rooms where she had lived a life. But the truth couldn't have been more opposite.

I kept going, losing myself from the room I'd left Duncan in. I paid no mind to how I would make my way back to him. Somehow, I knew I would find him in this place or another. My main desire right now was fresh air, a place outside of the suffocating depression that hung in the air around me.

Reaching the top landing of yet another staircase guarded by towering walls covered with crooked, empty, gilded frames, I was greeted with a rush of wind that pushed the hair from my forehead. It was just what I needed.

Ahead of me was an arched doorway that led out to the exterior of the castle. Two doors clung to the wall for dear life. It was a wonder the hinges hadn't given way as they looked moments from falling to the floor completely.

Outside was some sort of grand balcony overlooking the Icethorn Court. I walked toward it, noticing the outline of a person sitting perched over the low stone wall that circled the balcony. Twin dove-grey wings fluttered in the winds, a golden hammer leant up against the wall.

So, Rafaela couldn't sleep either.

I walked cautiously behind her. I didn't wish to surprise her for fear she might fall over the stone wall she sat on, so I cleared my throat and announced my presence.

"Do Nephilim need to sleep?" I asked.

"We do," Rafaela said, all without looking back at me. "And what about fey kings, do you require rest or are you above that?"

"Good question," I replied. "Can I join you so I can unpack the answer?"

"This is your home; it would be rude of me to decline." Rafaela glanced over her shoulder briefly before returning her gaze to the stretching view. Before I could remind her that Imeria no longer belonged to me, she spoke again. "Your realm is beautiful, Robin. I keep looking, thinking I'm going to find the end on either side, but it seems to never stop."

"Your homelands must be beautiful, too," I said, really wanting to divert the topic from me and Imeria, or my responsibilities. "Do you miss it?"

"The Isles of Irobel are impressive, likely more so if you ever saw them. Collections of islands, small and large, scattered across the ocean. But the view is nothing like this. If you climb the tallest tower erected in my lands, you can see only sea glittering in the distance on all sides. Irobel has a beginning and an end. But Wychwood feels other. It is… grand. I suppose because I have never felt so small before."

"The world is a big place," I replied, unable to ignore how vulnerable she was being with me. It tugged at my heart, making the lump in my throat grow. "Your presence has proved that."

"Knowing just how big it is simply adds to the pressure of keeping the realms, and everyone in it, safe from imposing danger."

"A feeling we both share."

Rafaela's wing shifted slightly, giving me room to stand at her side. I was aware as she fanned her wing back out behind me, concealing the view of the castle. It was like having a great shield at my back. Which, in some sense, was exactly what Rafaela was. I only wished someone had been able to shield Gabrial from what happened to her.

"We will find out who was responsible for Gabrial's murder," I said, finding the need to promise again. "I swear it."

A sad smile crested over Rafaela's face. "You didn't get the chance to know her well, but Gabrial was the most excited of us to finally leave our home and explore what was to offer beyond it. And yet she was hardly given the chance to experience any of it. A world she treasured unconditionally. A place she didn't know, a place she had only dreamt of, and yet she would have given her life to protecting it."

My throat scratched as though full of sand. I gripped the stone wall as if the wave of Rafaela's grief had the power to take my legs out from beneath me.

"I wish there was something I could say to ease your pain."

Rafaela lifted her chin and kept her stare fixated on the furthest points she could see. Her voice didn't tremble when she spoke, nor did her eyes fill with tears. There was strength in her sadness, a peace that I marvelled at.

"Gabrial is with the Creator now. Knowing that gives me a sense of peace." The hint of a growl worked into her voice. "However, when my hammer crushes the skull of the being that killed her, that will also help alleviate some of this pain I find lingering inside of me."

I expelled an awkward laugh, unable to shield myself from the brutal honesty of her threat. "If anyone can find the being behind the attack, it will be Seraphine. Although there is something I feel as though I should share."

"What would that be, Robin?"

"I don't wish to tell you what will or will not help your grief, but I have searched for revenge and the bliss I believed it would gift me. But that wasn't what I found when I went looking. The promising allure of revenge is a lie. It does nothing to help the pain."

As I spoke, I remembered James Campbell. I thought of his shattered remains smashed across the ale-slick floor of the pub. Then of Doran, whose body slipped beneath the water as Elinor killed him. I hadn't recognised any peace on her face afterwards.

"What I'm trying to say is death is not always the answer," I added.

"You are right, Robin; it is not always the answer, but sometimes it is. That is my purpose as the Creator's hammer. He made me a warrior of his image and gave me the responsibility to punish those who require it. Just as you didn't ask for the power that Altar gave upon your bloodline, I did not ask for this. But I at least accepted it without question. I claimed it. Aldrick will not be the only one to fall beneath my truth."

"When does it end?" I asked. "What waits for you when the world has been cleansed of its threats, and you face freedom?"

Rafaela shrugged, lips twitching as she regarded my question. "That all depends on the Creator's will."

"That hardly sounds like freedom."

"Living in one's truth *is* freedom, Robin. A lesson you have recently learned. I, too, discovered my truth many years ago when I was born with a different name in a body that did not match the beauty of my soul. I am who I am because of choosing myself. Freedom is a concept I know well, in every sense of the word."

My breath clouded before me, matching the frigid air in defiance. "Then I hope we give the rest of the realms the same chance to experience the beauty of such a thing."

Rafaela offered me a smile. "As do I."

Something moved in my peripheral, just behind the top of Rafaela's head. She noticed my gaze shift and turned to look behind her to see what I had seen. Before I could follow, it was gone.

"I think that's my sign to return to bed and force myself to sleep," I said, patting the stone wall before making a move to leave. "I'm so exhausted that I'm seeing things. Rafaela, try to get some rest, too. Please."

"That is not exactly an enticing concept. Your beds aren't designed for bodies like mine." Rafaela threw out her wings. The thick carpet of feathers across them flickered as the breeze whipped at them. "Rest will come once Aldrick is dealt with."

"Good point, but–" I swallowed my words as a sound echoed across the barren landscape surrounding the castle. Rafaela's head snapped, looking out over the dark, searching for something.

The noise was like that of thunder. I expected to see the flash of blue-white light spear across the skies. A shiver passed across my arms, sending each individual hair to stand.

"Get inside," Rafaela said quietly, hunting the dark for the cause of her sudden panic.

"What is it?"

Rafaela's wings pounded with one fell swoop, and she was up, standing balanced upon the stone wall she had been sitting on. She reached down, plucked the hammer from its resting place, and clenched it in both hands. "Robin, do as I say. Go."

That's when the sound came again. This time it was louder. Closer.

Three dark shapes cut across the night sky, blending in with it seamlessly. If it wasn't for the moon refracting its light across Imeria's surface, I don't think I'd have ever made them out. Beasts. No, monsters, flew toward us.

"If you're not going to run, Robin..." Rafaela bellowed, wings already beating, feet lifting from the ground. "Then you must fight with everything you have in you."

It took little time for the creatures to cover ground and grow closer. I stood, rooted to the spot as the demonic monster I had last seen flying across our ship days ago hurtled in our direction.

It was the Draeic. Except this time, it wasn't alone.

CHAPTER 18

I tracked the Draeic, their speed horrifyingly impressive as they barrelled through the night. Magic flooded my veins. My nerve endings sparked. I tried to breathe, but a serpent had coiled itself around my chest and squeezed. I didn't need air in my lungs when my pure, undiluted power fuelled my body.

Let them come.

The world slowed to the detailed ebb of clarity. Rafaela's command rang continuously through my mind. *"Fight with everything you have in you."*

I glanced back toward the castle, *my* castle, and imagined talons tearing through the stone. My ears mocked the sound of the destruction. I heard the monstrous tails, thick as the oldest trees, wrapping greedily around spires, snapping them like dried twigs beneath their weight.

I wouldn't allow it. This felt like a test, Altar seeing me steady on my path as king but needing proof I was worthy. I'd show him – I'd show the world what I was capable of.

Although my mind screamed for me to do as Rafaela commanded, to run back into the safety of Imeria's walls, my heart refused, the decision further confirmed by my iron will. It kept me rooted to the spot as the violent beat of wings and thunderous roars grew louder as they flew closer.

Cold winds ripped around me. I heard their whispers of warning – their chants. The wind longed for me to let go of the power that shook within my core as though breaking free from a cage. This was my home. I'd not been here to stop the first unwanted assailants when they came, killed and left this court in ruins.

For their memory, I wouldn't run and hide.

History would not repeat itself this night.

The gale forced my back as though a hand urged me to face the incoming attack. My feet barely touched the floor as they lifted me. To its power, I was nothing more than a puppet tangled at the end of their strings. The sudden release intoxicated me until I felt as though my very being was no longer my own.

Because it wasn't.

My body was a vessel, a gift that was granted to keep the demons at bay. I supposed I would start using it for its true purpose by sending them back to the dark pits they'd desperately crawled from.

"I'm not leaving," I growled, more to the universe than Rafaela. Icy winds enveloped me, picking my admission and amplifying it. It tore the dark locks of hair from my forehead as it picked up in a frenzy.

Rafaela hoisted her hammer above her, gritted her teeth and then nodded. In a blink, she shot skyward. Rafaela was airborne, charging toward the three creatures with a scream of war. I admired her strength and prowess, it inspired my own.

This was my land, regardless of how, on the surface, I was disconnected from it. Deep down, swirling among the power my bloodline permitted, it was mine.

No longer held aloft by the welcoming torrent of my conjured winds, my bare feet pressed back to the cold stone as I prepared myself. Even at a distance, I could hear Rafaela's war song.

The Draeic were equal in size, but each born from different shades of night. Their hulking bodies were covered in an armour of sharpened scales. The closer they grew, the more I could see a form of what seemed to be light exposed beneath their layer of scales. Crackling red fire. As though lava flowed beneath, shown only through the cracks. Much like Duwar had looked when he presented himself in the mirror, standing proudly behind Aldrick. The monsters belonged to him.

My eyes devoured the creatures, searching for a weakness. The one that flew to the left of the formation struggled to keep height. It was subtle but enough for me to notice.

Its leathery wings were covered in tears and jagged holes. Moonlight easily speared through the thin membrane that stretched between their boned frames.

I wouldn't allow them to get any closer.

She met one of the Draeic head-on with equal confidence, hammer swinging in a blur of gold, colliding with the side of the creature's maw. There was no sign of hesitation as Rafaela's stone-grey wings carried her toward them. The hammer ruptured against scale, the Draeic roaring in agony, thrown into the front of another one of the creatures. They collided with a sky-shattering boom.

Wasting not another moment, I ran. This time to the outer edge of the balcony that we had, not moments before, been talking together by. The peace of our conversation was a distant memory. The harsh presence of stone pressed into my hip as I leaned as far over the edge as I could until all I could see was the darkened drop below.

Instinct drove me. I pushed my power into the surrounding air, and it welcomed me. Like a leech upon flesh, the winter air drank from me. I envisioned every flake of snow and ice entrapped within the winds that whirled around the castle. Honing my focus was as easy as conjuring a thought. Every one hardened and sharpened in my mind's eye, forming the snow into intricately crafted blades.

I blinked, and the dark glittered with static flakes that hung like stars across the landscape. There were so many of them that I couldn't fathom a number large enough to guess. Then, with clear precision, I guided the winds and pushed those crafted blades of ice straight toward the Draeic.

Another boom echoed across the landscape as Rafaela's hammer crashed into the snout of one beast again. Beside them, she looked small, but her strength was mighty. Unrelenting just like the storm I'd conjured.

My assault met the third of the Draeic. I felt every shard tear through hardened skin with the ease of a knife through butter. Over and over, I willed the ice to return, ripping, scratching, stabbing. A gust of silver wind engulfed the large beast completely in a vortex of my blizzard.

I revelled in the monster's howls as my power tore it to shreds. It was ripped part, bit by bit, caught in a web of my own making. My body tensed against the power, arms still outstretched, as I forced more of my essence into the winds until it was as much a part of me as my own hands.

A sudden, sharp tang of copper filled my mouth. My teeth bit hard down into the sides of my cheeks as I focused on destroying the creature. I brushed my tongue over the mess of flayed skin, using the pain to hone my focus.

I knew the very moment the Draeic stopped struggling within the vortex of ice and ruin. There was no noise anymore, no struggle. Only the continuous roaring of the Draeic Rafaela still fought. I couldn't look to see if she needed help, not until I was confident my victim would no longer be a threat.

A sudden heavy, unwanted rush of tiredness overcame me. Fog shrouded my mind, the world spun out of control. I withdrew my power, falling over onto the stone wall of the balcony as my knees gave way. My lungs burned as I inhaled frozen air deeply, forcing as much breath back into them as I could muster.

Something warm trickled down from my nose. Lifting a finger to check, it came back red and wet with blood. But all of my discomfort was not strong enough to stop me from witnessing the annihilation my power had achieved.

Lightheaded from the draw back of my power, I watched the Draeic as it fell from the sky. Its body was a bloodied, broken mess of limbs and bone. Meat hung from its corpse. The wings were so torn that even if it had survived, they wouldn't have kept it airborne.

I glimpsed its gouged eyes and shattered jaw. Then it was gone. Falling into the dark. Its death was so terribly silent, until the shattering explosion of its body meeting the ground far below echoed up the sheer face of the castle's walls.

My relief was short-lived as Rafaela's scream cut through the daze of power and tiredness. I looked up to see her body, grey wings folded protectively over her, hurtling through the night. From the arcing swing of one of the monster's spiked tails, I knew it had hit her.

I screamed her name, my voice filling the dark void between us. No room for thought, only action, I released my power again, recognising the slight strain on it. I thickened the air, trying to soften the inevitable fall. There was resistance, but it worked enough to give her the time she needed.

Just before Rafaela slammed into the castle walls below the balcony, she threw her wings out and regained control. Blood smeared her cheek as she looked up at me. I spotted a dark stain spread at the side of her waist that she had not seemed to notice or care about.

Everything that followed happened so quickly.

Rafaela flew upward, wings cascading powerful gusts down upon me. "I need to get you out of here."

"No, I can stop them."

Rafaela's bloodshot eyes suggested she didn't believe me. "You can't. They are Duwar's creatures – made of dark power – the more you use against them the more it will drain you."

Was this what was happening to me? How I'd reached the limit of my power so quickly.

"This is my domain; I'll not let them take it!"

"A wasted wish if you are dead." Rafaela glanced behind her, and we both watched as the remaining two monsters righted themselves and focused back on the castle. Not on me or Rafaela, but on the towering walls behind me. Globs of saliva dripped from their maws; ferocity twisted like red fire in their large, snake-like eyes.

"You," Rafaela shouted above the roars of war the monsters released, "are my priority."

My thoughts drifted to Duncan. Had he woken to the noise and thought it was more sinister than a crash of thunder? I wondered if Seraphine glanced out her window, expecting a storm, instead finding winged monsters claiming the sky of Icethorn as their own.

How much time had passed since we had first been attacked? I had to hope they were aware, preparing themselves for the horror that would follow if I failed.

"We destroy them," I snapped, lip curling over bared teeth. "It's the only option."

Rafaela just looked at me, her brow creasing as she came to her own conclusion.

I longed to tell her I could deal with it, but every inch of my body ached. The power I had exuded had taken it out of me. Looking at the two monsters that flew with frenzied determination, I knew deep down I couldn't take them. Not like I had with the other – not without them draining me.

I watched in frozen awe as the two creatures careened toward me. They showed no signs of stopping, no signs of slowing down.

"You'll one day forgive me for this," Rafaela said a moment before she flew directly toward me.

Rough hands grabbed at my body, and the ground fell away from my feet. Rafaela's nails pinched into my skin as she tore me from my castle and threw us both into the air. I gripped onto the bloodstained ivory shawl she wore and screamed.

Winds swallowed my cry with their own. The sound ruptured against my eardrums. My eyes streamed with tears from the slapping of cold upon my face.

"Wait!" I shouted, unsure if Rafaela could hear me above it all. It was one thing running, but leaving Imeria behind, forgetting those who still were inside of it... "Rafaela, release me."

Her hold on me only tightened, until I felt as though my ribs would snap. I struggled to breathe as the pressure worsened. It then filled my head. The higher she climbed into the sky, the more I felt the hands of air press into me, the harder breathing became.

I forced my eyes open, streaming tears, and glanced back toward the two remaining monsters.

They didn't follow us in chase as I expected. Yet there was no relief as I realised it. Because they never wanted me – that wasn't why they were sent here.

I finally discovered what the Draeic desired a split second before they got their wish.

Both remaining monsters split apart at the last moment, before smashing straight into Imeria's outer walls. Their power and speed gave the impression that they melted through stone as they disappeared into the castle's body. But that was wishful thinking.

It took a moment for the explosive sound of carnage to reach me.

Rafaela slowed in her flight. I felt the breath leave her lungs as she looked down at what had caused the noise.

The monsters hadn't been sent here to claim me. This was a suicide mission – and they had succeeded.

An entire side of Imeria Castle buckled and fell before our eyes. Towers folded in on themselves, walls exploded outwards, unable to hold the weight of stone above them as the two gaping holes the creatures left weakened them to the point of no return.

Soon the sky was full of dust and rubble as the castle continued to break and shatter, a cloud of it rupturing up from the distance around and swallowing the entire castle – or what remained of it – from view.

My mind screamed for one person. Duncan.

He was in there. The castle was falling around him. I imagined him in the bed, asleep and unaware, as bricks fell upon him. It took everything in my power not to blink and see visions of his head caved in, his body squashed to a pulp by the mounds of the castle that had stretched above the room he slept in – the room I'd left him alone in.

As the castle continued to fracture, as though made from glass and held in careless hands, my heart shattered in a symphony. Each brick, each slab of stone that crumbled beneath me, matched that of the pieces my heart snapped into.

Pain reverberated through my chest, and my grip on Rafaela fell slack. She was saying something, repeating the same words over and over. But I lacked the care to listen to them. There was nothing I could focus on more than the massacre laid out beneath my dangling feet. Or from the cavernous hole of loss that returned, like a vagrant tenant, to my soul.

The light of dawn revealed every horrific detail before me. Shards of golden light cut through the wisps of clouds and graced the mountain of rubble that stretched ahead of me. Dust clung to the air, invading my lungs, and making it feel like each inhale was full of grit and dust.

I cared little about my pain compared to the sea of agony that had overtaken me. If anything would destroy me, it was the knowledge of what I'd just lost.

Standing on a boulder, I looked out over the remains of Imeria Castle, and cried for Duncan until my throat bled raw. His name was a blade in my throat, scoring deep marks into it each time I shouted for him.

Rafaela didn't try to stop me. Instead, she continued her solitary search among the ocean of broken brick and dust-covered ruins for bodies. Corpses. Death. One of the

Draeic had been completely buried, but another was still visible at a distance, a single ripped wing stretching out of a mound of stone like a sail of a submerged ship.

Now and then, she would find signs of what she searched for. A hand reaching out beneath a blood-covered stone. A face covered by a layer of dust, skin ripped and skull shattered. Seraphine's body wasn't found. There was a man Rafaela uncovered, his torso had been severed, spilling the tangled knot of innards out in a puddle of red and black gore where his legs should have been – legs that were never found.

What Rafaela did find was death in abundance. But never life – hours had passed and not a single person had been found alive. My hope, what little remained of it, abandoned me soon enough.

I was thankful Rafaela had run her fingers down the Asp's grit-coated face to close his eyes. They had still gleamed with the fear he beheld in the moments before he'd died.

In another life, I may have grieved the Asp's death, the one my presence had brought to his new home. But I had no room for him, Seraphine or the other broken lives the castle had stolen.

There was only room for Duncan. He occupied every part of me.

Each time Rafaela found another body beneath the rubble, she would look up at me and shake her head.

As frozen tears melted down my cheeks, I wondered if she looked for Duncan to ease her own guilt. The emotion was the clearest in her eyes. Unspoken but bitter. I recognised it well the moment she'd returned us to the ground as we watched and waited for the fall of my castle to calm.

It took hours to settle enough for it to be safe for us to begin our search.

Rafaela hadn't said it with words, but she carried the weight of death on her shoulders.

At some point, I noticed the thundering of hooves in the distance. Weakly, I looked over my shoulder to see a hoard of stags rushing toward us, a wall of them blocking the horizon. Althea rode ahead, her poppy-red hair billowing behind her as she cantered toward us. Toward me. Following her was a formation of Cedarfall soldiers, fanned out like wings behind her.

You're too late.

Rafaela was airborne again, ready to fight, until she realised who was joining us.

Althea threw herself from the stag's side, almost tripping at first, before running toward us. She navigated over the rubble, wide eyes not leaving mine as she did so. Shadows hung beneath them, telling a story of the worry she held inside.

"We saw it, all of it!" Althea shouted. "I thought... I thought... I thought you'd died, Robin."

There was a part of me that felt like I had perished, alongside those beneath the rubble of my castle.

"They're dead," I interrupted her, unable to bear the weight of her sorrow atop my own. "All of them. Duncan is..." I couldn't say it. Didn't dare speak it aloud in case it made it real.

"Robin." Althea clutched my shoulder, her touch rooting me to the panic glistening behind her eyes. "Duncan is–"

"Dead!" I screamed, ice bursting from beneath my bloodied, scratched bare feet. It devoured the stone I stood upon, coating it entirely and cracking beneath my weight. "Duncan is dead, joining the number of those who died for simply being near me. Why don't you turn back to Berrow and run before I bring your end? Go on... GO!"

Althea stood firm, unmoving, although flinching slightly as she studied my magic. Part of me wished to throw myself into her arms, but then I blinked and saw her body crushed beneath stone or her chest pierced with a blade.

If my curse was that anyone who loved me died, I would make her hate me, just to save herself.

"Robin, listen to me," Althea said softly, as though my name alone was enough to break me entirely. "Duncan is *not* dead."

A wave of rage flooded through my body. Overwhelmed by the feeling, I threw my head back and roared. I shouted to the sky until my throat stung and my fingernails were embedded in my palms. I didn't stop until every breath lodged in my lungs had been expelled, and the world trembled from the suffocating lack of air.

I fell forward onto my hands and knees. The ice and stone cut into my hands and tore through my dust-coated trousers.

Every passing second that followed, I waited for Althea to tell me she was joking, that this was all some fucked-up hateful punishment. But she didn't. The two words she managed were as broken as I felt inside. "Robin, please."

I took a moment to gather enough strength to lift my head and look back at Althea. My sobs were heavy and all-consuming. It was strange to hear my heartbeat thundering in my ears when I was certain I no longer had one.

"Duncan is alive. I do not know how to explain this, but he is in Berrow... someone saved him. It is best I take you to him."

CHAPTER 19

Althea lied to me. It was the only explanation I believed. No matter how many times I forced her to repeat herself during the journey to Berrow, she never seemed to make sense.

Duncan is alive. He is alive.

As she spoke, it was like a puzzle with missing pieces. The final piece couldn't fit together perfectly to form the picture she attempted to paint for me. My mind refused to believe her, protecting myself from the inevitable truth I'd soon uncover.

The journey to Berrow was swift. I was so completely consumed by my thoughts it was like I blinked, and the ruins of Imeria were far behind us. One moment I was stood overlooking the destruction, and the next I stood before the ramshackle ruins of a house. Snow drifted across the bowed roof. The wind screamed around the exposed, rotten beams. I kept my gaze pinned on the open door and the darkness that lurked within. And I waited. Waited to be let down or told this had all been one sick game. A way to play with my mind and break it into as many pieces as the heart in my chest.

What made this reality so terrible was I'd been here – to this house – before. I had stood before this building many weeks ago. And it had hardly changed since. The house was exhausted, leaning to the side as though it'd given up completely. It was a feeling I shared. The glassless windows looked like gaping mouths, the shadowed doorway a mouth ready to devour me whole.

Did it laugh at me or show surprise at my presence? If it was the latter, we shared in the emotion. I never wished to see this place again, and yet here I was, the same broken man, but under far different circumstances.

Erix had been the one to bring me here. Bruised and exhausted in a time when I'd not yet accepted my fate. We'd been real, in a place of ghosts, invading the home of someone who had been forced to leave it behind when the Icethorn power ravaged across the land.

I feared to blink in case the image of our bodies entwined with one another filled my mind. How we'd lost ourselves in a bed, using our skin and touch to fend off the cold night that invaded the forgotten place.

"If you need me, I will be waiting here," Althea said, waiting just outside the broken gate that hung determinedly to the rotted post at the end of the garden's path. Beside her stood Rafaela, a silent guard. The wound at her side had still not been dealt with besides being wrapped in a makeshift bandage of material she'd torn from her clothing. That was yet another issue she'd refused the offered aid for. Alongside her rebelliousness against healing, she had also refused to allow me to enter without her.

It took a little persuading for her to finally understand I wouldn't allow her to chaperone me into the home before me.

This was my problem to deal with – alone. A problem I'd believed would never dare show itself again to me. If it wasn't for the promise that Duncan was alive and well, lingering in the cottage's darkness, I would've already drawn a blade, stormed inside and faced the horror.

Faced *him*.

Each step forward was as though I was wading through knee-high mud. I persisted, focusing on the chipped wood of the front door and the suggestive flakes of old blue paint that'd nearly all worn away. The front door was open as if it knew I was coming.

I sensed a gaze scratching across me from someone unseen within the building. I searched the dark, empty windows and found them empty. But that didn't suggest the being inside was not watching me – waiting for me.

There was only one reason I didn't unleash the final dregs of power I'd recuperated after the attack with the Draeic.

Because Duncan was supposedly inside. And yet he wasn't alone.

Althea had assured me he was, and I fought hard to believe her. She told me over and over, never faltering, as I asked her to repeat herself. My heart told me I couldn't trust what she told me, at least not until I saw him myself. My mind raced with questions. I drowned in them. It was not only the promise of Duncan I couldn't trust, but the company Althea said he had inside.

One wrong move and I could truly lose Duncan forever. It was a concept I struggled to convince myself of. Not hours before, I'd believed Duncan was dead beneath a mountain of rubble and destruction. Except he wasn't.

Without a word, I left Althea, my focus on what was waiting for me inside the house. I sensed Duncan as I strode toward the door. His scent of fresh pine and scorched earth. I followed it. However, I couldn't ignore the other presence that coated him like a blanket of darkness. Something cold and evil.

Of course, *he* had chosen this place to hide within for a reason. He knew what effect it would have on me – to weaken me, soften me, attempt to make me forget all the pain that came after our last stay here.

And yet, besides my disdain, if what Althea said was true, the person I wished to never see again was the very reason Duncan was still alive. The more rational side of my mind reminded me that Duncan would have been lost beneath Imeria's castle if not for him.

Somewhere, deep within my chest, there was a spark of

gratitude. It was faint and could be smothered completely at any moment. But I couldn't allow myself to ignore it.

I was greeted by darkness as I entered. The floorboards creaked agonisingly, exposing my presence. A damp scent hung in the air from years of snow melting into the walls and floor of the house. I didn't remember it being such an unpleasant place before. Daylight sliced in behind me, exposing walls speckled with stains of dark mould. Before me, the staircase was a death trap. The corridor to its side, covered in drifts of snow, squeaked beneath my footfall.

"Duncan?" I called out in question, voice breaking. His name died in the stale air the moment it slipped past my lips. I almost gagged as the air took its chance to assault my throat with its clawing. Taking a deep breath in, I expelled as much of the hideous smell out of my nose as I could.

Then I heard him. His voice was as real as the memories that haunted this place.

"I'm here, my darling."

I stopped dead in my tracks, my heart almost bursting from my chest, threatening to suffocate me as it lumped in the pits of my throat.

It *was* him. Duncan. The deep, rumbling tone of his voice caused shivers to pass over my arms. I waited patiently, holding my breath to keep as quiet as possible for him to speak again. This could've been a trick of the mind. A way of my memories conjuring a response and luring me to danger.

My knees buckled when Duncan called out for me again. "Come to me, darling."

I walked faster, following the same steps I had once before. Duncan's words had led me to a room that sparked discomfort in my mind. My skin itched at the memory, but I couldn't dwell on it. Then I heard it, the shuffling of someone else, the reminder that Duncan was not alone.

Fury twisted in a blizzard within me.

My foot kicked at the door, wood buckling beneath the

force, throwing it open with a crack. I hardly flinched as it slammed into the wall. Light followed behind me, slipping into the room, exposing every untouched detail.

It was the man who sat on the bed before me who demanded my attention first. Duncan. His back was straight, his hands gripped onto each side of the worn mattress as he looked upon me.

"I understand this is going to be a shock," Duncan said, mouth pursed as he regarded me, an unwanted strain to his posture. "But I'm going to need you to listen before you do anything you'll regret."

As my eyes fell upon my love, drinking him in, finally accepting that he was alive, I almost didn't accept his plea. I didn't care.

"Tell me this is real," I begged, gripping onto the door frame to steady myself. My nails bit into the old plaster of the walls until it crumbled away. "Say something again, so I know this is not some illusion cast to punish me."

I wished to run to Duncan and throw myself into his arms. A sob built in my chest. It crawled its way out of me, exposing the weeping child I buried inside. I found something I had believed was lost forever, and I promised I'd never let it go again.

"I'm alive," Duncan sighed as if even he couldn't believe it. A dark lock of hair fell across his eye as he turned his attention to something unseen in the shadows of the room. When he glanced back at me, his stare screamed with pleading. "But you must promise me something."

"What?" I gasped, tears sticky on my face.

Duncan's eyes shifted toward the corner of the room, laying briefly upon the shadows clinging like a blanket. "Promise me you will hear him out? I'm only here, alive, because of him – I owe him that much."

The shuffling of heavy feet sang from the shadows. A part of me registered the twisting of ice that crackled around my fingers as I flexed them to my side. It would only take a thought, and the ice would be directed toward the lurking presence – a presence I'd known would be here before I entered the building.

"I can't make promises I'm not sure I can keep." I stared intently at the corner of the room where the figure lurked. "Come out," I commanded, voice crackling with power. My attention was fixed on the way the darkness rippled as a body peeled away from its concealment. "Slowly."

And like a dog on a leash, *he* listened.

The hulking, tall figure stepped into the light, placing himself between Duncan and me. Regardless of my forced bravery, I couldn't stop myself from choking on my breath at the sight of him.

Erix stood in front of me. Steel silver eyes bore into me, invading my soul in search of something. "Hello, little bird."

This version of Erix was unfamiliar to me. He was taller than I remembered, as though his body had been stretched and pulled, his arms longer, his shoulders broader to accompany the wings that hung from his back like a cloak of leather. There'd been a time when I had his outline memorised, the way his shoulders dropped like the edge of a cliff to the narrowed, hard shape of his torso and waist.

Just like the last time I'd seen him in this very place, this very room, Erix was without a shirt. Tattered trousers hung off his legs, torn and ripped in places, adding to his dishevelled look. I believed the grey, almost silver sheen of his skin was because of the lack of natural light within the building. But as I shifted my body, giving way for more of the daylight to stream into the room, I was proven wrong. His skin kept that colour, a result of the curse his father had imposed on him. His affliction, his truth.

Erix hung in the horrific balance of fey and gryvern, not quite one nor the other.

"Please," he gasped, flashing the two sharpened points of his canines catching his bottom lip. "Say something..."

My heart hammered in my ears, my jaw dropping open and eyes widening to the point of discomfort as I took him in. He held his hands before him in such a mortal stance that it seemed wrong for the way he'd changed. Even more so since I had last seen him in the clearing, the night Duncan was captured by Hunters.

Far behind me, winds plagued by ice raced to greet me. They screeched through the house, crawling across walls and floors until they built at my back.

The last I had seen Erix, I promised him death if I was ever disgraced by his presence again.

"Don't do it," Duncan said firmly. He'd moved so quickly, seemingly unbothered by the gryvern's proximity. In a strange turn of fate, Duncan placed himself before Erix, who hadn't taken his eyes off me this entire time.

I fisted my hands, severing the connection to my power and leaving the snow and ice to fall naturally across the aged flooring of the corridor.

"Robin's reaction is justified," Erix whispered, looking to the floor, his shoulders hunched. "I'm exactly the monster he expected to find."

I couldn't stop myself from snapping. "That's just the issue, I never expected to see you again. And yet, here you are."

"And thank the gods he is here," Duncan said, briefly looking behind him toward Erix. "Without him, I wouldn't be alive. Remember that."

"What are you doing?" My words were more like a sob as I looked from Duncan to Erix.

"I owe him a life debt," Duncan answered, stepping toward me, arms outstretched. "So I'm keeping it, making sure he survives this conversation long enough for it to actually begin."

He swept me up in his arms. I was so overwhelmed by his touch that I buried my face in his chest, inhaling the reality of him until his scent lathered the back of my throat. The powerful wrap of Duncan's arms was more than enough for me to finally give in to the weakness I'd fought away since Althea had told me he lived.

I melted into him, closing my eyes, allowing myself a moment to believe that we were alone in this room.

"He saved me, Robin," Duncan said, his hold constricting around me.

"I know," I replied, voice muffled. "But... he... you know what he's done."

"We all made mistakes, but at least we can attest to them being our own fault. You know Erix was not in control – you've said as much yourself. Come on, Robin. Be rational. Look at me." Duncan pulled back, gripped my face in his grit-covered hands and held me so I couldn't do anything but see his desperation glowing within his eyes. "I owe him my life. And because of that, I cannot let you harm him. Not until you listen to what he has to say."

Duncan was alive because Erix had saved him – that was a fact. Althea had told me as much. I replayed the sickening feeling that coiled within me when she told me. Of course I hadn't believed her. Even with both of them before me now, the concept was impossible to grasp.

I wrapped my arms around him, wishing to melt into his body and never come out again. "I don't think I can do this, Duncan."

"This is going to be hard," Duncan began, pulling away from me but keeping a firm hold on my upper arms. "But Robin, you've faced worse. Think over everything you've achieved and tell me you are not strong enough to get through one conversation?"

The gryvern lingered in the corner of my eyesight, not once retracting his silver eyes from us for a second. I wondered how he felt as he watched me in the arms of another man. Just the concept made me want to push free of Duncan immediately.

"I'm in control, little bird," Erix said, averting his gaze from the two of us.

Erix's voice was the same as before. The confident, clear drawl as he called me by the nickname I had grown not to despise as I first had.

"Don't call me that," I hissed, unable to hide the shaking that exposed just how weak I was at the moment.

Erix's breathing hitched as though a knife struck him dead in the chest. "I'm sorry."

Duncan took my face in his hands, making it so I could only look at him. "Remember, Robin. The dead are told to blame the hand which holds the sword, and not the sword itself. Yes, Erix has done something terrible. He took something from you and doesn't have the power to give it back. But that's not a feeling I'm familiar with. And you. Erix was the sword, and the hand that controlled him has since been dealt with. Before you decide how you wish to serve him his justice, give him a chance to speak to you. His mind *is* his own."

"I... I thought you'd died," I muttered, picturing the destruction of Imeria Castle. "I really thought I'd lost you, Duncan."

"If Erix had not acted, you might just have. For that alone, give him a chance." Duncan took a deep inhale. "Please."

Swallowing down my anxiety, I managed a slight nod. Duncan exhaled through a smile, bringing his mouth down to mine. But before his lips could touch, I turned away, offering him my cheek instead.

"I understand," Duncan whispered into my ear, taking my hand and giving it a squeeze. Then he pressed a fleeting kiss to my cheek and drew back.

I looked to Erix, who never stopped staring at Duncan and me. Regardless of my feelings toward him, there was no reason I had to make him watch Duncan be intimate with me. Causing him pain wouldn't make any of this better. For from the grimace set into Erix's face, I could tell he'd expected such a show of affection.

Taking a deep breath in, I levelled my eyes, fixing them on Erix. "You can have an audience with me. Alone."

Erix's response surprised me. With a slight bow, he replied. "Thank you, Robin."

Satisfised, Duncan released my hand and made to move to the door. My entire body trembled at the sudden loss of Duncan's touch. He stopped at the door, offering me a final look. "I love you."

I opened my mouth to reply with the words Duncan deserved to hear, but they clogged in my throat. I couldn't reply, not here, not with Erix watching. He had hurt me, but he had also just saved the most important person in my life. There was a time for being a monster, and now was not it.

CHAPTER 20

I sat upon the far edge of the bed, discouraged by its presence but needing a place to settle myself as I allowed Erix to speak. Considering how the firm mattress beneath me made my skin itch with discomfort, I hadn't realised I fisted the sheets until my knuckles drained of colour. The last time I'd been here, on this bed, it was for different reasons. It took great effort to keep at bay the urge to slip into the warm memory. It called me in with its siren song, promising peace and comfort.

Erix hovered by the door. He paced, moving awkwardly with a body he was not yet used to. Longer limbs and the added weight of his leather appendages which hung from mounds protruding from each shoulder blade. It dragged him down, as though he carried the weight of all his guilt on his back instead.

The last I had seen Erix, he'd pleaded with me to kill him. He was frantic, and his behaviour erratic. Whatever had happened between then and now had smoothed out his cracks of sanity and given him, somewhat, a sense of humanity that he had barely clung to before. There was no denying he was different – more of his old self, and yet I still would be cautious.

Erix or not, he was a gryvern now – a new, mutated version of one.

"Say what it is you need to," I said, staring daggers at him, mapping out every move. "I haven't got time to waste on silence, Erix. And you can imagine, I have reasonability now, more so than you last saw me with."

Erix came to a stop, lifting his steel gaze to me. All my confidence melted away as he regarded me. The way his strong face softened spread warmth across my chest, how his fingers flexed at his sides as if wishing for something to do – to hold.

"This was not how I wished for us to see one another again," Erix admitted. "Truthfully, I'd come to terms with never seeing you again. Not that I haven't wanted to, but because that was what you asked of me and I was ready to respect that."

"What changed?" I asked.

Erix frowned, but only slightly. He fought to keep control of his expression. His face was almost untouched by his curse. Besides his ears, that were longer, and the grey sheen of his skin, it was mostly him. Erix. I focused on his wings to the drawn-out claws that protruded uncomfortably from his fingers just to remind myself of the monster he was.

"I recognised you were in danger, except I also knew you could handle it." Erix lifted his chin, steeling his expression. "I took something important away from you, I couldn't allow for that to happen again."

I swallowed the dangerous thoughts that mingled in my head. "And I should thank you for saving Duncan."

"You do not need to do anything you do not want," Erix added. "Not to me."

A lump filled my throat so suddenly that I almost gagged on it. Although my mind knew that Duncan was alive, it still took time for my heart to heal from the trauma that had taken tenancy within its remaining pieces. The physical grief that had attached itself to me was not so easily relieved. Even knowing that Duncan waited beyond this place for when I was done here, the feeling ebbed away from me slowly.

"After everything I have done to you, taken from you. This was the least I could do."

"How does your conscience feel now?" Tears stung the back of my eyes, but I refused to let them go. "Are you satisfied that debts are paid, perhaps relieved that your sins have been cleansed?"

I hated how I sounded, but more so how Erix flinched at the heat in my words.

"You are angry, understandably."

Angry, maybe before. The emotion that stormed inside of me was one I couldn't place with a name. "I saw you, before the Draeic attacked, didn't I? Back in Imeria. You were watching me. Stalking me. How long have you been lurking in the shadows, Erix?"

He rocked back, mouth parted, all without a sound coming out.

"You're right."

I blinked and caught a vision of Gabrial's body ripped to shreds and bloodied ribbons by claws. My eyes fell to Erix's hands, which he held confidently clasped before him. Had he been following me from Lockinge? Had he... killed her?

"The first time I saw you was in Imeria and Imeria alone," Erix said, as though reading the accusation in my gaze. "I suppose it is best I start at the beginning. It will help you make sense of how we got here."

Erix took a step toward me, his body language suggesting that he was going to sit beside me.

"Don't come any closer to me," I sneered, pointing a finger at the floor on the other side of the room. "You can talk fine from there."

Hurt speared across his face. Erix stopped and dropped his chin to his bare chest. Muscles rippled like water disturbed by stone. "I do not wish to make you feel uncomfortable."

"It's a bit too late for wishing such things."

I could've sworn I heard him swallow during the reverberating silence that strung out between us in these moments of tension. Having learned that Erix had stalked me, I was finding it hard not to convince myself that he was anything but Gabrial's killer. It made sense. Erix had killed before – what was stopping him from doing so again? How much was the Erix that stood before me in control of himself against the gryvern that stalked his own mind?

"I remembered little at first," Erix began, wringing hands before him. "But I am aware that my freedom, if that is what I can call this, started with pain. There was a time that I floated within the current of what I can only explain as darkness, pulled along by someone else's will and guidance. Then suddenly, that was gone. Severed. I remember my mind becoming mine again, and it was terrible. Memories and thoughts, they all came back without reprieve. I could not explain it then, and I still do not think I can, but it was like that presence just left in a single moment. I no longer sensed *him* inside my head." Erix knocked his fist into his skull as though his head were a door. "Doran was just gone. There was a period of time when I ambled through Durmain, unsure where to go, or what to do. Then I found Berrow. Berrow was like a beacon of light. I followed it. I came here without truly understanding why. Now I remember."

I pushed myself to stand, unable to touch the bed a moment longer. Wrapping my arms around myself gave me no comfort. I wanted to demand that he stop speaking, that listening to Erix speak was like torture. Because it was his voice. This was the man I'd last spoken with before he left me to go to Doran – before all the hell followed that decision. His voice buried claws into memories and dragged them to the surface.

If I closed my eyes, I could've conjured an image of me with my head resting upon his chest. I remembered the vibrations of his deep voice echoing across my skin.

"Do you want me to continue?" he asked, softly.

"Yes," I exhaled. "I do."

From the parting of his mouth, I could see that Erix didn't expect that answer.

"Berrow was so quiet. Peaceful, after a long time of my head being loud with commands. And then that all changed yesterday. Suddenly, the streets were filled with people. I saw Althea and Gyah and countless fey I did not recognise. I will not lie and say I did not look for you, because I did. Although

I could not find you, your presence... it was strong among them all. I heard your name, clear as a bell, even as some whispered it. They spoke of what you did for them – freeing them from imprisonment, just like you did for me, although a different kind of prison. Those fey who spoke about you could have been miles away, and I would still have made it out among the rest of what was said. I knew it was not right for me to stay here, not with the reality of them finding me. I am sure Althea would have enjoyed the chance to take my head and give it to you as a gift. So, I left. I should have flown west in search of somewhere else to dwell, but there was a part of my curiosity that drew me to Imeria. Perhaps I did not recognise it at the time, but I knew deep down that you would be there."

"And I was."

"Yes, you were," Erix said. "Over and over, I told myself to leave. I saw you with the winged woman and him. The Hunter. I saw you smile. It does not fill me with pride to admit that I stuck around longer than I should have. There were things I should not have seen..." Erix didn't need to finish his sentence for me to know he had seen me with Duncan in bed. "You were happy, but still there was something lost about you. I recognised it in your expression. But I also knew that was not my issue to concern myself with. So, just as I was about to leave you, I watched as you got out of bed and left the room. Just as I did to you, Robin, the greatest mistake of my life. One that will haunt me for the rest of my days."

I raised a hand sharply, cutting him off. "I've... heard enough."

What I really meant was I didn't have the strength to listen to the raw truth a moment longer.

"Please." He reached out to the air as if grasping the opportunity to speak before it slipped away. "I know you owe me nothing but let me finish. That is all I ask of you."

I gave myself a moment, trying to control my inner thoughts. Finally, beneath it all, I recognised the emotion inside of me. It was relief – relief that Duncan was alive but also that Erix had found his freedom.

"Why did you save *him*?" I asked. "Of everyone in Imeria, you chose Duncan to save. Why?"

"Because he means something to you."

His reply hit my chest like an iron bolt, striking deep into my soul.

"Everything," I corrected. "Duncan is everything to me."

Erix nodded, although I saw the pain and regret mix across his haunted expression.

"It was an easy choice to make. I was in the wrong place, admittedly, at the right time. No, it has not cleansed my soul of my sins or balanced the scales of justice. I did it because there was no other choice. My will is my own, Robin. This was my decision to make, my act – that is what is important. I do with it what I wish. That is what *you* have blessed me with. After everything, you gave me another chance and I have taken it."

"You have another to thank for your freedom," I said. "I didn't kill Doran."

"Then who?" Erix looked genuinely surprised.

"Elinor Oakstorm had as great of a reason for seeking revenge as I did."

Erix's jaw gaped open, exposing the slight points that each of his teeth had formed. In that moment, for the first time, his face looked monstrous. "She lives?"

"Very much so," I replied, glad for the change in subject. "A lot has changed since you gave yourself over to Doran."

"From those creatures that attacked Imeria, I gathered as much. I have never seen anything like them before. And the woman you fought beside…"

"Nephilim," I said, glad the conversation was shifting this way.

"Nephilim," Erix repeated, testing the word on his tongue.

"Have you ever seen one before?" I asked, reminding myself of the last question I had for him.

Erix's brow peaked. "No, never."

I tilted my head, watching him through narrowed eyes. "Which is strange because one of them was recently brutally murdered. We've since been unable to discover who would have the power to overwhelm a trained warrior whilst ripping her skin to shreds."

Erix caught on quickly. He recoiled, both hands raised in surrender, raising the very points of nails that had the power to do such a thing. "And you believe that has something to do with me?"

"I don't know what to think."

No, I hoped. But the killer was still out there, and Erix had a history. Perhaps I was searching for a reason to hate him, when in that moment, it was the furthest emotion I had for him.

Erix dropped to his knees, hands clasped together in some form of prayer. It was the same position I had seen Abbott Nathanial take up all those weeks ago. "I swear to Altar and everything beneath him, I have never seen or done anything against these Nephilim. There is nothing you owe me, Robin, but believe that I have not harmed anyone since my will was given back to me." He bared teeth, spittle hissing down his chin. "I wouldn't... I couldn't... *never* again."

No matter how much I wished he was lying, I knew Erix spoke the truth. I sensed it deep in my bones as his honesty flooded out of him. That didn't stop me from holding back my reservation. "Rafaela, the warrior I fought alongside, has the nifty ability to pass judgement. To seek the truth in places that truth wishes to hide. As much as I may believe you..." Erix's silver eyes widened. "It is not for me to deem you innocent or not... she can if you let her–"

"I will do it," Erix snapped. "I will do whatever is needed for me to prove to you I had nothing to do with this murder."

"Is that everything?" I asked matter-of-factly, hung up on the way he referred to me when needing to prove his innocence. Other's opinions didn't matter to Erix, but mine did.

"If you are satisfied with what I have had to say," Erix replied.

We stood there, staring one another down at opposite ends of the room. How had we got here? The thought was heavy with sadness and regret. If I didn't start walking for the door now, I might never have gathered the courage to do so.

I spun on my heel, turning my back on him, ready to flee. That was the moment the back of a hand brushed mine. A wave of shivers passed from where he touched me, encompassing my entire body within seconds.

"Robin?"

I stopped moving, finding it difficult to calm my breathing. "Yes?"

"You did not need to listen to me," Erix said. "It means a lot that you have taken the time to do so."

Seeing the pain in his eyes, they revealed that Erix had so much more to say, and there was even more I wanted to hear. But I had to put an end to this, before the interaction distracted me from what waited outside of this house.

Erix, even now, proved to be the distraction I once wanted, but now did not need.

"I hope you find some solace in this conversation wherever it is you end up next," I said, trying to keep my focus on the door ahead of me but wishing everything to look up at him one last time. "Rafaela will come in shortly to speak with you. Once you have proven yourself as an innocent party relating to Gabrial's murder, then you have until sundown to leave Berrow."

"I understand. Goodbye then, little bird."

I took one shaking step and stopped again. "What has happened to the other gryvern?"

"We've… they've dispersed. Sometimes I still sense them in my mind, but the connection has been quiet for a while now."

"Shame," I replied, mind whirling at the new concern of protecting my people. "We could have done with them for the battle to come. Monsters to go up against the monsters that will no doubt find themselves on our doorstep again."

"You really have changed too, since this all began." If Erix felt shame or discomfort for me referring to him as a monster, he didn't show it.

"I haven't had the choice not to," I said.

"If it means anything, the man I see before me is not the same one who told me he was frightened of the dark." Erix drank me in a final time, turning his eyes from my boots and back up to my face where they settled. "I am really proud of you."

My heart pranged in my chest, the feeling not as unpleasant as I would've expected.

"It's not the dark that scares me anymore," I whispered, forcing the words out before I could stop myself.

Erix fell into the question I had set up for him. When he asked it, I sagged forward with some feeling of relief. "What frightens you now?"

Just as he had, I allowed myself a final look at him. I glanced up at Erix, imprinting this new version of himself into my mind. We were so close that he stared down the arrowed point of his nose at me. His wings shifted nervously at his back, anticipating the response I had built within me.

"I'm scared to death of losing those I care about," I whispered, turning my back and severing our connection. Only when the bedroom's door was within reach did I finish what I had to say. "So, Erix. Do me a favour, and keep yourself alive."

As I walked out into the blinding light of day to Duncan, who waited for me at the end of the path, I was certain I heard a reply.

"For you, I shall. Little bird."

CHAPTER 21

I couldn't take my mind off Erix no matter how hard I tried to.

Duncan sensed it, so it wasn't a surprise when he didn't question me after I asked for us to be alone. My impactful yet brief conversation with Erix had a lasting effect. I couldn't think of anything worse than sitting before my friends and allies, pretending I could concentrate on the matters of demon gods and death. My mind was shrouded in heavy fog, and I needed a fresh breath to clear it. I longed for a moment of peace, locked behind a closed door, with no need to force a smile or pretend my mind was not preoccupied with other thoughts.

I was satisfied to know that Rafaela's wound was being seen to. Duncan had assured me that Althea and Gyah would keep a close eye on the matters of Berrow, allowing me time to work through everything that had happened. Not that I really cared for what Kayne was doing, but I asked anyway. He was important to Duncan, which meant he was important to me. Although my inquiry was wasted, as Duncan hadn't seen Kayne since we arrived back in Berrow. He shrugged as he confirmed it. His response was dismissive and misplaced. Clearly, there was tension between them, and I wasn't ready to unpack it.

The attack on Imeria and the death that followed did a number on me. Duncan as well. It surprised me that Kayne wasn't the first one to check on Duncan. Apparently, the ex-Hunter found it more important that the fey people he'd once sworn to hunt were settled in their new homes. There was a part of me that was thankful for him. Kayne provided more of his time to my people than I could have.

"I found this," Duncan said from the open doorway, leaning against the frame as he inspected a dust-covered bottle in his hand. He scrutinised the dark glass, lifting it close to his face... so close that his green eyes seemed to cross one another. "There is definitely something inside, and the cork hasn't spoiled. Should be good enough to drink. What do you say, fancy taking a risk with me?"

My chest warmed at the thought of a stiff drink. Not melted ice or water collected from a well in the heart of Berrow that needed boiling before it was safe to ingest.

"Trust you to find wine even in a place like this," I replied, cheeks prickling at the thought of taking my first swig. I had hopes it would help deal with my tangled thoughts of Erix.

"I'll take that as a yes," Duncan replied, a grin tugging his lips up at each corner. There was no ignoring the shadows hanging beneath his eyes, the same that also spoiled my face. We were exhausted, but even in this state, the concept of sleep was displeasing. "The rest of the storage I found has been ransacked. By rats or people, maybe both. We shouldn't let it go to waste."

"What would Nathanial think if he could see you now? Duncan Rackley, solving problems with a bottle of wine," I said, vividly remembering how Duncan poached bottles from Abbott Nathanial's store cupboards as a youth, but more recently during our short stay in the Abbott's attic room.

"Old habits die as hard as sinful ones," Duncan mocked, forcing the aged voice of the kind-hearted Abbott.

My smile was short-lived as I remembered Nathanial being torn to pieces before our eyes by the gryvern. And I had just left one to face Rafaela's judgement. The possibilities of whatever outcome she'd come to haunted my mind.

If Erix was guilty, it would at least solve the issue of who killed Gabrial. And if he was innocent, that person could still be among us.

"Go on, I need something stiff to settle my mind," I said. "Get to opening it."

Duncan's brows rose, a mischievous grin pulling at his lips. "And if it is something stiff that will solve issues, I have a better idea of what can be offered."

I didn't react to Duncan quick enough. By the time I dragged myself out of my mind somewhat and plastered on a fake smile, it was too late. His dark brows furrowed, painting concern across his handsome face. "Ah, I think I've overstepped."

"I'm sorry," I said, dropping my chin in defeat to my chest.

"Don't be." Duncan towered above me as I slouched in a moth-eaten chair. The fabric had certainly seen better days and smelt like damp mould. But at least I was able to make myself sit in one place and not pace around, like I wanted to do. "Here, you need this more than me."

Duncan bit his teeth down on the edge of the cork and tugged. The pop was satisfying. So was the spray of red liquid that escaped onto his lips. One swipe of his tongue and the droplets were gone. He pulled a face, dramatically widening his eyes. I watched as he determined if the taste was good enough.

"Has it spoiled?"

"It'll do," Duncan confirmed, although the furrow of his thick brow suggested otherwise.

With a lack of confidence, but an overwhelming desire to drown out my thoughts, I snatched the bottle and took the longest gulp.

Duncan's reaction wasn't misplaced. It tasted vile at first, burning down my throat – something wine shouldn't do. But the aftertaste was when the flavours of fruit revealed themselves beneath the sharper tang that only age could be blamed for – the buzz spreading through me was exactly what I needed.

"And you're sure there aren't any more of these?" I asked, waving the bottle at him like it was a bone to a dog. "This one isn't going to last long."

Duncan's dark curtain of hair had fallen before his eye as he shook his head. He combed his fingers back through it, tucking it neatly behind a curved ear. "Just the one, so make it last, darling."

"How unfortunate," I replied, knocking back another gulp, not caring for the dribble that escaped down the side of my mouth, coating my chin in sticky, red liquid.

"Do you want to talk to me about it?"

I shrugged, not sure where to even begin. "We don't need to."

"But we can. Share the burden I can see haunting your mind." Duncan urged my knees apart with his legs until he stood between them. Then he knelt. Groaning slightly as his knees met the cold, hard floor of the room. He was just shy of eye height in this position. It gave me no excuse but to look at him. "This is what I'm here for, darling. Allow me to shoulder some of your woes."

I knew this was coming. I was just glad I had some rush of wine to aid me in picking a worry to start with.

"It feels wrong not acknowledging Seraphine and the Asps' deaths," I admitted, still hearing Gyah's comment ringing in my head. *No one grieves an assassin.*

"What happened was not your fault."

"Then whose?" I asked. "If I had not gone to see them, then they would be alive."

Duncan's fingers dug into my thighs. It was a pleasant grip, one that sent a shiver up my spine. "There is no good taking the blame for another's actions. Robin, I don't want to hear you take it again."

"But it's true. They died because I was there. It is a fact, and I appreciate you trying to say otherwise, but you can't deny the truth."

"Those monsters could have taken you, Robin, but from what you described, that wasn't their purpose. They went to Imeria to destroy it. There is no saying whether your presence at the castle drew them there or if something else did. And until we know, speculating isn't going to help. I want you – no, I *need* you to stop putting yourself as the reason for all the bad that happens around you. You didn't invite the Draeic to Imeria, nor did you command them to do what they did. Seraphine, the Asps, their blood is not on your hands."

"Perhaps not my hands, but it stains my land," I replied. "My court."

There was no good admitting that I still didn't believe him. Even now, I fixated on Berrow and how my presence here would only bring more danger to these streets. I promised to free and protect the fey who followed me blindly here. My promises of protection and safety should not have been made.

"I wish to honour them. Without the Asps, without Seraphine, there is no saying how life would look right now."

"Then we shall do just that." The muscles in Duncan's jaw tensed as he regarded me with fierce determination. "But first, you need to rest."

"*First*, I need to see that Aldrick dies and Duwar's name is forgotten alongside him."

A storm passed over Duncan's face at the mention of the Hand's name. Sparks of purple light danced in the dark points of his pupils. "His time will come. That, I can promise."

We both hated the man for differing reasons. However, even I knew just how Duncan felt, considering it was Aldrick who lied about his birth parents, using the idea of one day getting the name of the person who killed them, when that was something Aldrick never knew.

"Tomorrow, I want a plan." I sat up, knuckles paling as I gripped the neck of the bottle harder. "Decisions need to be made. We are still steps behind Aldrick, constantly racing to catch him but finding out we are still miles away. I don't think it is right that we wait. The time to act is now. Especially because the courts are unsafe, I don't even know if Seraphine got out the message to her Asps across Wychwood before she was..."

I couldn't say it. Didn't need to.

Duncan swallowed hard, the lump in his throat bouncing suggestively. "Then that is what we shall do. But tomorrow. It can wait until then. Just because you are not out there, doesn't mean your allies are not furthering plans. The world doesn't stop if you do, Robin. For you to be at your best, you need to rest. And this time, promise not to leave me in bed alone."

It was on the tip of my tongue to tell him about the dreams I met every night. Should I burden Duncan with yet another reason to hold concern for me, or keep him in the dark, just to lighten his own loads? The choice was easy.

"I promise," I replied, leaning my forehead to his. "No more parting."

Duncan's grin had the power to draw away my worries, if only for a fleeting moment. "Good boy. I'm glad we agree on something."

"Thank you... for making me give Erix a chance to speak," I said, before quickly taking yet another swig. This was the largest gulp, so much so that I almost hoped the cruel red liquid choked me. It would have saved me from the path the conversation was about to take.

"I didn't make you do anything. Only encouraged you on a path that I knew was important you took. Closure isn't something we all get the chance to take, I didn't want you to waste such an important moment." Duncan rubbed both hands from my knee and up my thigh. His fingers gripped slightly as though letting me know he was here and not going anywhere. "It was a blessing he was there."

"I know, but it still takes a moment to get used to the fact that my old lover saved my new lover from certain death."

Duncan flinched before me.

"Lover?" Duncan questioned, forcing a grin to hide his reaction. "Is that all I am to you?"

"No," I replied, shifting forward in my seat to lean into him. The movement made my head spin, revealing that the wine had its desired effect on me. "That title is only one on a very long list I have."

Duncan exhaled through a smile as he forced himself to stand, using his hands against my thighs as leverage. With one confident swipe, the bottle was no longer in my hands. "I understand a lot has happened between Erix and you. But I think it is healthy for this, and this, to consider forgiving him." Duncan placed a finger on my forehead before moving it to the space above my heart. His touch left a warmth on me as he pulled away. "There is no good to come from carrying hate-fuelled grudges. Believe me, Robin, look how I turned out."

Empty-handed, I picked at the loose thread on my trousers. It was that or I'd bite at the already ruined skin around my nails. "I don't hate Erix. Is that what you wish for me to admit to you?"

"Yes, actually it is."

I gaped, surprised that was his reply. "Why?"

"Because you are far too important to allow such an emotion to poison you."

I swallowed hard, fighting the urge to snatch the bottle back. "Erix means... meant a lot to me. Another man would feel he had some sort of possessive territory over letting the one they loved spend time alone with the one they had loved before."

"Trust," Duncan answered simply. "I trust you implicitly. Respect. I harbour enough respect in your own decisions and the ability to take care of yourself. My job isn't to suffocate you but to encourage you to act in your best interests. My upbringing was not like that, so it is my duty to carry those lessons with me for the rest of my life. And my pleasure that you are the one I can do that for."

Duty and pleasure. Those two words sparked another voice to fill my head.

"You are my duty, and my pleasure."

The urge to touch Duncan overwhelmed me. I needed to act before Erix and his invading presence completely took me hostage. So, I pushed myself from my seat, knees and body aching from the lack of sleep, and melted into his welcoming embrace. I breathed him in deeply. Sandalwood mixed with the newly added tang of red wine. In the dark that waited when I closed my eyes, I could easily picture the attic room with its mounds of books and discarded, empty glass bottles of holy wine. That was his scent. Familiar and warming.

"Any monstrous past lovers you need to warn me about?" I asked in jest, knowing nothing could be worse than a gryvern. "I can't be the only one with such heavy baggage."

"You are and will only ever be the one of importance. The rest, nameless and faceless, were simply means to warm my sheets. There is no one from my past that you need to concern yourself with. Well, except Aldrick, although perhaps we leave him out of our conversation for the rest of the day."

"Oh, come on," I pleaded, neck aching as I looked up at him and he down at me. "Not even one scary ex-partner?"

Duncan huffed a laugh, his nose screwing up as he leaned in. "As if Kayne would have let them get that close."

Mood ruined. It was amazing how a single name could draw me away from the moment. Maybe Duncan noticed my reaction, or it was the sudden lift of my hands leaving his back that exposed it.

"I have arranged for some warmed water to be brought here. There wasn't much, but enough for you to lie and bathe. You can thank Althea when you next see her. What do you say?"

"Are you suggesting I smell?" I asked, painting my expression in mocked offence.

"We both do," Duncan replied, voice tempered.

"Then let's hope we can both fit in the tub."

Duncan tensed beneath my gaze. He took a shuddering breath, deeply inhaling through his nose.

"Where there is a will," he said, nostrils flaring, hands gripping my thighs with a silent need for me. "And there is a certainly a way with the thoughts currently occupying my head."

The water was tepid when we'd climbed in, but now it was borderline detrimental, to Duncan at least. I rather liked the cold. It was second nature to me, more comforting than I could explain. Yet Duncan showed no sign that he was bothered. Instead, he pulled my naked body atop him and used me as a blanket as we lounged in the brass tub together.

"One memory keeps surfacing of us in Finstock when you could hardly turn your gaze away from me as I was the one who bathed."

I laughed, wafting my hands through the cloudy water to create small waves that lapped against Duncan's muscle-carved leg. "Where else was I to look?"

"Believe me…" Duncan's cock, which was currently pressed into my lower back as I lay between his legs, twitched. "I would have felt pure jealousy if you had given the brick wall of my old room more attention than you did to me."

I rolled onto my front, not caring for the rub of our skin nor the splash of tepid water that fell beyond the curved lip of the tub. "Do I even want to know what you thought of me back then?"

"I thought you were trouble," Duncan replied confidently, one brow raised above his mischievous glare. "And I wasn't wrong. Not one bit."

One of the many things I loved about Duncan was how my fingers tangled willingly in the coarse hairs across his chest. When they were wet, the hairs stood out more like a thin carpet of masculinity that set a fire deep in the pit of my belly.

"Interesting. We shared the same first impression then."

Duncan's lips parted into an exaggerated O-shape. "Are you telling me you didn't wish to throw yourself into the tub at that very moment? To have your way with me?"

"Nope," I said, pouting. "In fact, given the chance, I would've frozen the water you submerged beneath and left you for dead. But in hindsight, I would never have discovered the best fuck of my life if I did that."

"Now that is a compliment. Although Robin, I'm beginning to believe you only require me for one thing."

"I need you for lots of things, Duncan," I replied quickly, smirking to myself. "But right now, I want you to pluck me from this tub and take me to bed."

He had tried his best to distract my mind, and it had worked to an extent. However, there was one thing I was ready for now, and that was to truly be with him. Connected, in flesh and bone, for the final hours of our time alone.

Duncan leaned upward, water sloshing around him. His stomach tensed and hardened into six perfectly compact mounds. He took my face in his hands and added pressure to both cheeks. "Ask me again, but this time do it properly."

I also loved this side of Duncan. How his joking mannerism could shift to something more powerful and demanding.

"Please…" I began, widening my eyes to give a sense of false innocence. I batted my eyelashes dramatically, looking up through them at him. "Remove me from this bath and take me to bed, pretty please."

"To sleep?"

I shook my head. "Eventually, but not straight away."

Duncan didn't wait for further explanation. He gathered all his strength and composed himself as he moved from beneath me. A wave of water lapped into my face. I laughed, feeling the well of excited glee fill my lungs like air. Suddenly, arms wove beneath me, and greedy fingers dug into my skin. The weightless feeling that followed was pure euphoria. In return for Duncan holding me, I wrapped my arms around his neck and held on for dear life.

My damp thighs did well to grip around his waist and squeeze. His hands, perfectly placed beneath my ass, held me up. Duncan didn't say a word as he padded from the bathing room, leaving wet footprints on the aged oak floor as he trailed toward the bed chamber. I kept quiet, too, enjoying the easy rhythm our hearts fell into when our naked skin was pressed together.

Only when Duncan stopped, just before the bed within the simply decorated room, did I say a word.

"What are you going to do with me?" I asked, heart practically leaping in my throat.

"Not what you may expect."

Suddenly, I was in the air, swallowing a scream as my body fell and crashed into the feather-stuffed mattress. It took a moment for the world to still and my mind to catch up with what had happened.

"Did you just... throw me?" I asked, accusation drawing each word out and increasing them in pitch.

"I did."

I was on my front, with hardly a chance to move, when Duncan's guiding force overwhelmed me. "Tonight, it is about you."

There was no time to ask what Duncan meant when rough hands urged my knees apart, allowing a cold breeze to kiss up against the centre of my ass. All I could do was inhale sharply.

I exhaled a guttural moan, his name coming out of me in a breathy pant.

"Take the pillow, Robin, and bite down on it," Duncan commanded.

I opened my mouth to reply, but only a string of sounds came out. Suddenly, wet fingers were on me. Searching and tracing across my ass cheeks. Duncan urged them apart, trailing a nail around my centre. Around and around, growing closer to the sensitive skin that would turn my body to fire and melt me from the outside in.

"Bite down," he said, cutting through my weightless pleasure. "Unless you wish for all of Berrow to hear you? I wouldn't mind if the answer was yes."

Fire coursed across my chest as excitement bubbled up within me. I did as he asked. Sinking my teeth into the pillow, I bit down hard.

"Good boy," he praised.

My skin was damp from the bath with Duncan. But it was nothing compared to the wet glaze of Duncan's spit which glistened across my ass as his tongue lapped at it, like a cat to milk. Over and over, his devouring touch hypnotised me. I was lost in a sea of indulgence. He drew shapes and symbols with his tongue, making sure there wasn't an inch of skin left unexplored. Now and then, Duncan would introduce the soft graze of his teeth or the sharp suck of his lips as it left a bruise behind.

A mark to claim me – not that one was required. I was his, entirely.

I reached back and gripped his hair, holding him in place as he continued devouring me. My nails scratched his scalp, and I was certain Duncan growled.

There was nothing more I wished, in that moment, than to watch him. I wanted to look at Duncan's ravenous, spit-slicked face as he ate at me like a piece of the ripest fruit. But I didn't wish to ruin the moment with movement. I dared not do anything but expel groans into the pillow stuffed between my teeth.

"You taste divine, my darling," Duncan said. "Do you enjoy when I fuck you with my tongue?"

I released the pillow, ready to give him an answer when said tongue dove back into my sensitive entrance. Instead of words, my scream of pleasure was the only answer I could give, the only answer he needed.

Duncan's hand reached beneath me and took my hardened member into his grasp. My enjoyment intensified to a new, higher realm, as I became a tool in his hold. I was his instrument, and Duncan played me with confidence. His touch conjured a song of sounds that I had no control over keeping in.

Between his furious, passionate kiss that licked and nipped and the voracious rhythm of his arm as he tugged at my cock, I was moments from exploding.

The feeling came on so suddenly that I lost the will to maintain a breath. It swelled inside of me, uncontrollable. I buried my head into the pillow, muffling my cry as the rush of pleasure burst out from me.

My entire body trembled as the feeling overtook me.

Duncan pulled away slowly, only when he was certain the wave of pleasure had been drawn out to its fulfilment. I fell onto my stomach. The wet smudge of cum spread across my abdomen and the bedsheet. But I couldn't care for anything but the feeling that Duncan had gifted me – and how I wished to make him feel it in return.

The heavy weight of a body flopped onto the bed beside me. I lifted my head an inch from the pillow and looked at Duncan through tired, narrowed eyes. His face was lit with pride. My eyes fell from his pink, bruised lips to the glistening of spit that covered his chin.

"That was fucking incredible," I said, breathless considering I hardly did anything.

"You are incredible," he said, mischief rolling like thunder in his eyes. "If I had to survive off you alone, I would live for an eternity. You're the only sustenance I require, my darling."

I swore that I could've gone again, encouraged just by the hungry way he looked at me. "And I would gladly be the one to provide you that sustenance if it's like that every time." I replied as I rolled myself onto my back. The room seemed to spin as though a lingering climax still had me in its grip. "Now would be the apt moment to gush about your godly touch and equally godly mouth."

"But you look tired," Duncan smirked, as if that was exactly what he wanted to happen. "Who knew biting into a pillow could be such *gruelling* work?"

"If I had the energy, I would smack you with the same pillow just to shut you up." My laugh was natural, not forced.

"Then you should ride the wave of your exhaustion and get some rest. Come dawn, you can resume your threats when you have more energy to expend. Although, I have some other ideas of what you can do, which include a pillow put beneath your knees and not stuffed between your teeth."

For once, I longed for the idea of sleep, just so I could wake again and do this over.

"Until tomorrow then," I said, using what little strength I had left to lean up on my elbows so I could press my lips to his. "If you can wait that long to bury yourself inside of me."

"Trust me, darling. I could wait until the world ends if it means experiencing such a thing." Duncan welcomed me into his arms, his chin and mouth still glistening as though they dripped with honey. "I love you, Robin Icethorn. So much."

"And I," I said, eyes flickering between his. I wished for his soul to hear what I was about to say, so I searched for it before finishing. "Love *you*."

It didn't take long for me to fall into sleep. Wrapped in Duncan's arms, our flesh pressed together as one, I found sleep. And this time, I didn't fear what was waiting for me.

Oh, how wrong I was.

The dream snatched me before my head even hit the pillow that still bore my bite mark on its skin. I expected welcoming darkness and empty thoughts, but as I disappeared from the world of reality, I was greeted by something far more sinister.

Dark, billowing hair whipped around a face of pale ivory skin. One side of the female's head didn't dance with her hair because it was shaved down to the scalp. This dream, although similar to before, felt noticeably different from the others. It was clearer – vivid and real.

I heard myself speak without knowing I'd even opened my lips. "Jesibel?"

CHAPTER 22

Jesibel stood before me among wisps of dark shadow. They coiled around her frame like vipers, striking at skin mottled with bruises. Her arms were wrapped around her waist, doing little to cover the torn and stained clothes that hung off her body in tatters. She just stood there, staring at me with wide eyes, torment etched into every line across her skeletal face.

"Jesi?" My voice filled the strange space, her shadows seeming to dance in tandem with the noise. I listened as her name echoed as though I'd shouted it into a barren cave.

The sound was strange and haunting, but *truly* real.

She didn't reply. I watched her mouth intently, ensuring I didn't miss a single movement. Jesibel just stood and watched me.

Even in this dreamscape, I tried to convince myself that this was all the vision was. A nightmare dragged from the darkest corners of my subconscious. Jesibel couldn't be real. This was just a haunting image of what I believed she'd look like in the clutches of Aldrick.

My arm itched as my eyes fell upon the torn skin on the soft part of her arm. Her wound was angry, violently spewing blood and other unknown yellowed liquids that screamed of infection. Her mark was in the same place Aldrick had drawn blood from me all those weeks ago. I reached a hand to grasp my forearm, only to find that there was nothing to touch.

I looked down, and there was nothing but darkness. I was merely a part of it – a part of *her* shadows.

"Listen to me carefully."

My attention snapped upward, and Jesibel was inches from me. Even without a body, I could feel her presence. The rancid taste of copper invaded my mouth, forcing its way down my throat and choking me. I reached up to grasp my neck, but I had no hands, arms or body to command.

I belonged to Jesibel in this odd place – I was her toy to play with. Her dream to terrorise.

A patchwork of bruises covered her face, spreading like a necklace across her neck. Heavy, dark circles beneath her carved eyes accentuated her emaciated skull. She looked more like a mound of bones with damaged skin stretched over it.

Unlike the other times Jesibel had been in my dreams, this was different. She wasn't listening and watching as she worked through my mind. Jesi was no longer just a bystander. She commanded the dream as if it wasn't mine to begin with.

"I tried to save you," I pleaded, forcing all my will into creating a voice in a place where I should not exist. "I came back, just as I promised."

"Forgive me, Robin…"

Although she was speaking, her lips didn't move. Her face was stoic. Almost… calm. Which was the opposite of how I felt. I drowned in her shadows. Jesibel's eyes were endless and without focus. It seemed she glanced straight through me whilst also seeing me completely.

"I'm doing everything to save you. Please don't haunt me. I promise I'm trying, Jesi. You are the reason behind all this, I have not given up yet."

"I know."

My blood thrummed, which was an odd sensation, considering I didn't have a corporeal body here. Her response was not meant to taunt me. I expected my consciousness to craft Jesibel to hate me for failing her, for allowing Aldrick to reach her before I could. If only I'd brought the prison break forwards, perhaps I would've got to her first.

"Listen to me carefully, Robin. Now isn't the time for wallowing in your self-pity." Jesibel's voice was stern and scolding, snapping me out of my stupor. Her shadows reached out for me, twisting among the mass of black that encased my body. *"You can't trust me. You can't trust those around you. I need you to do everything in your power to–"*

"I am!" I snapped, shadows recoiling from my fury. "I'm doing everything."

"No. Forget me, Robin. Do not come looking."

Jesi was fading. Her skin became translucent, flickering as though she was the sun obscured behind dark clouds. If I had hands, I would've reached out for her and kept her in place. But I was forced to watch as her form bled away from me. "Don't trust them." Her voice broke in my skull, like the crack of a whip. "Trust no one."

Her warning was as clear as the sky during summer.

"Who?" I asked. "Who can't I trust?"

Her mouth parted, the skin at the corner of her lips ripping like paper. Fear sliced through me as Jesibel's entire body contorted in on itself. I wanted to move back, but I was powerless in this place. Jesibel didn't make a sound, but the muscles in her neck bulged, and veins burst across her pale face. She was trying to speak, her lips moving in the same formation over and over. But the word she wished to say, the name that would answer my question, betrayed her.

"Jesibel, I cannot forget you. I will not," I said, hoping those words were enough to calm her – or calm myself in whatever was this dreamscape punishment I'd clearly made.

If I was in control, I had to wake up. I couldn't bear to watch anymore. Seeing her throw her head back and forth, her black hair sliced to her scalp with grease, blood and gore. I wished to shield myself from the horrific view laid out before me. This didn't feel like a dream or a nightmare.

She stopped so suddenly it frightened me more than her suffering. Her bloodshot eyes locked with mine, her hands bent into claws. "Beware of the–"

Jesibel was torn backwards by an unseen force, ripped from the floor and dragged into the dark unknown, all before she could finish what she was about to say.

I bolted upright in bed, gasping for breath. My hands grabbed greedily for my body, just to make sure it was there. My skin was damp to the touch. Even the sheets of the bed had gripped to my skin in places slick with sweat.

Just as my mind caught up with reality, I caught the tail-end of a noise beyond the building. I first believed it was just the remains of the dream, but the noise repeated to prove me wrong. It wasn't Jesi's success at warning me but something else.

It was the trill cry of a bird, mocking Jesi's cry.

"It's okay, darling. I've got you," Duncan said, leaning up on his elbow with tired, heavy eyes. I melted into his firm hand, which drew circles across my back. "You've had a nightmare. You are safe."

I fixed my stare on the blanket of night sky beyond the window. How long had I been sleeping? The candles had burned out completely, but the day still seemed leagues away. "It was awful," I gasped, burying my face in my hands.

"Talk to me." The bed creaked as Duncan forced himself to sit up. "I'm here to help, so let me."

I exhaled into my shaking hands, unable to rid myself of the dream. Even the taste of blood still lingered in my mouth. I ran my tongue across the insides of my cheeks to check if I had bitten them during sleep.

Duncan gave me a moment to compose myself. Then I drew free of my hands and faced him.

"I'm fine," I forced out the lie, unable to convince myself with my shaking voice, let alone Duncan.

"You're quite obviously not fine, Robin."

My sticky legs clung to the sheets, so damp I thought I'd pissed myself from fear alone. Luckily for me, and Duncan, it was only sweat. "There isn't even peace for me in my dreams these nights, that is all."

Or peace in waking, for I soon remembered the last time I woke in Berrow from a nightmare. Different arms had waited to comfort me, arms belonging to Erix. Of course my waking mind went straight to him, it liked to punish me no matter my state.

"I just need a moment," I exhaled. "Once the dregs of that dream pass, I'll be okay."

Duncan was clearly not satisfied. He'd seen me struggle to sleep, lying awake some nights, or those I did sleep I'd wake looking more exhausted than before. And yet, those times he didn't pry. That luxury had long gone. "Why do you not want my help–"

"Duncan, please! Just… just give me a moment?" I snapped, unable to hold back my sudden fury.

"I'm only trying to help," he said, his hand pausing its rubbing motion on my back. "What good am I to you if I cannot do even that?"

My mind spun, the desire to run from this conversation a siren song I couldn't ignore.

Duncan swallowed hard as I jumped from the bed, leaving his hand hovering in the air where my back had been only seconds before.

"I just need to breathe."

The silence Duncan responded to me with was more painful than a knife to the chest. Instantly, guilt overwhelmed me. I shouldn't have spoken to him like that. I was exhausted and shaken, but he didn't deserve that.

"I'm sorry." I stood before him, chest heaving with the urge to hold back my sobs.

"Don't, Robin, you don't need to apologise to me. I understand." He didn't need to tell me he was hurt. I could see it in the wince of his forest-green eyes, the downturn of his mouth at its corners.

Even in the face of my mistreatment, Duncan *still* had my best interests at heart.

Selfishly, I turned my back on him and paced toward the window. It wasn't Duncan who experienced my wrath next, but the window that wouldn't open no matter how hard I pried at the handle. Time and weather had merged the wooden frame with the windowsill. The more I forced it, the more it refused to budge.

"For fuck's sake," I cried out, slamming my palms on the glass. The wave of anger came as suddenly as the first, and left just as fast. I pressed my head to the cold pane and exhaled, watching my breath fog beneath my lips and blur the view of Berrow from beyond.

"I need some air." I turned from the window to see Duncan standing helplessly beside the bed. The landscape of mountainous muscles across his stomach and chest were taut as he regarded me. He gripped the bed sheets enough to shield his modesty, trembling from his own anxieties.

I was a puzzle of missing pieces, one he wished to put together but never would be able to.

"I thought we agreed you would not leave me again," Duncan said, attempting to offer a smile.

"Are you planning on stopping me?" I replied, unable to control the torrent of emotion in my voice.

I hated how I sounded, but I couldn't change it. My defeat and exhaustion were in control, and I couldn't do anything but allow it to puppeteer me. They say you took your pain out on the people you loved the most, but Duncan deserved more than this version of me. That is why I had to leave.

"No, I won't stop you, Robin. You know that."

Did I wish for him to say otherwise, or was the disappointment conjured by something else? "I do."

"Get the fresh air you need, and I will be here waiting for you, ready to talk this through when you are ready."

It was on the tip of my tongue to thank him, but I couldn't say it.

I rushed to clothe myself before I changed my mind. It would be easier for me to crawl back into bed with Duncan, but I forced myself to keep moving.

"I won't be long," I said, as if he'd asked. Duncan didn't say a word, instead he just nodded.

Part of me wanted Duncan to remind me what happened the last time I walked out on him. Maybe it would have the power to cut through my tantrum and stop me. But Duncan kept silent as he watched me from the edge of the bed.

He only spoke when I gripped the door handle and turned it. His voice was loud above the screeching of the worn, tired metal.

"Robin, just promise me you'll come back to me."

The pain in his voice almost buckled my knees beneath me.

"Always," I whispered, my voice calming as my strength dwindled.

"All I want is to help you, Robin, but I can only do so when you want it from me. So, when you are ready, I will be here to talk about what has upset you. If you don't wish to share it with me, then I will not ask again. But promise me, you will come back."

"I said I will."

"No," Duncan growled deep within his throat. "Promise it."

I felt as though his reaction was born more from just my reaction to the nightmare. And from the way his gaze moved to the door I stood before, as though settling on something in the distance that neither of us could see, I wondered if he thought of Erix, too.

"I promise," I said.

I forced myself out of the room, down the creaking stairs and out into the cold street of Berrow. My feet carried me away from the house as I embedded myself into the silence of the town as its new occupants slept. Not that I cared for the cold, but I naturally drew the cloak around my shoulders until the torrents of winter winds were kept at bay.

It was easier to count my steps as I walked aimlessly through Berrow. Counting kept the visions of Jesibel buried. But it wasn't only her face that haunted me. In waking, it was Erix. I found my mind demanding to know if he'd left. Did I want to know that he had gone again, or did I wish to find him lingering in the dark room within the abandoned house I'd last seen him in?

Neither thought filled me with any warmth, neither question I had an answer to.

I kept walking, kicking mounds of snow and ice that had drifted into piles at the edges of the path. Only the moon guided me through the town, not that I cared about getting lost.

It was only when my feet were tired, and my mind finally felt like my own, that I heard the noise again. The sound that had been both within my dream and welcomed me when I had woken from it.

The squawk of a bird. Not entirely uncommon during the late hours, but usually I'd expect the hoot of an owl. Whatever this was sounded different – familiar.

And it was close.

I slowed my footsteps and lightened my weight. It was as I rounded the corner of a side street in Berrow that I saw *him*. Huddled within a cloak, just like I was.

"Kayne?" I said, wading through the shadows into the alleyway. "Problems sleeping again?"

The Hunter didn't seem surprised to see me. He drew back his hood and exposed the grimace that always seemed to be plastered across his freckled face when presented with me. "Sleep hasn't been kind to either of us recently, has it?"

Something about his words cut me deep.

"What are you doing out here?" I asked, already knowing he could ask me the same. Issue was, I was king, and he was still an ex-Hunter. My goings didn't matter as much as his.

"Night-time stroll to clear the head. I could ask the same of you though, Robin. Are you expecting to find someone else out tonight?" he asked, brushing past me with a harsh shoulder as he walked back out onto the main street. I looked down the alley, searching for someone or something else. But Kayne was alone – at least he was now.

"I don't know what you are suggesting," I replied, voice as cold as the winds ripping around me.

"Perhaps you came to find Erix and thank him for saving Duncan in a more... private manner?"

My eyes narrowed on him, just as Kayne's smile widened. "What did you just say to me?" His accusation felt like a slap to the face.

Kayne was already creating distance between us, but it didn't take much for me to catch up. I reached out and grasped his forearm before he could run away from the conversation. My fingers gripped his skin, hard. In the dark part of my mind, I enjoyed his grunt of surprise.

"Get your *filthy* hands off me!"

I made sure they dug deeper. "Your attempts to irk me with your comments are wasted."

Kayne shrugged himself out of my grip, his face was flushed scarlet, lips pulled into a firm white line. "What do you want, Robin?"

He spat my name at me like it was a disgusting, spoiled piece of food in his mouth.

"A simple night-time stroll to clear my mind, and yet here you are, ruining it with your mood. Dare I ask what gets you out of bed?"

He flashed me a sickly smile. "What does it matter to you what I do with my time? You aren't my keeper."

All my pent-up anger came rushing out at once. This time it didn't shy away from it, or hold guilt for the person at the other end. Better Kayne than Duncan. "I asked you a question. I suggest you answer it."

Kayne stepped in close. His breath itched at my face, his towering posture making me smaller before him. But I didn't feel small, not with the power readied beneath my skin. I didn't so much as flinch as his boots cracked into mine. Kayne lowered himself until his nose was inches from mine, glaring down the length of it as he regarded me. His shallow breaths came out in silver-lined clouds beyond his pursed lips. "You don't trust me, do you?"

"Should I?"

Kayne's laugh sliced directly through me. I watched as his gaze flickered around me as though he searched for something. When his attention returned to me, his voice was louder and more confident. Each word he spoke felt as though it came directly from the centre of his chest. "What would Duncan say if he knew his beloved and his longest friend disliked one another?"

"He already knows, why don't you go and ask him?"

There was no denying the way his eyes widened a fraction, proving my reply was news to him.

"But it's nice that you finally found the confidence to admit it aloud," I added. "Do you feel better getting that secret off your chest?"

"You don't deserve him," Kayne hissed suddenly. I flinched as his spit landed upon my cheek, but didn't dare to brush the droplets away.

I broadened my shoulders, trying to match his physical prowess. "And you do?"

"Yes!" His eyes bulged. "More than you could even begin to understand."

There was no warning before strong hands pushed at my chest. Pain jarred up my back as I landed on my ass, the skin on my palms ripping across the stone and ice.

A growl erupted from me as I pulled on my magic. The cobbled ground beneath my splayed, bleeding hands cracked with ice. Even the winds rejoiced with my desire to hurt Kayne back. But the magic's glee lasted only a moment.

"Hurt me, go on, and you'll have to explain yourself to Duncan. Will you lie and come up with a justifiable excuse to victimise me with your magic? What will he think of you for being the one to hurt, or worse, kill his *closest* childhood friend?"

The freezing winds calmed, and the ice melted. My grazed palm stung as the cold infiltrated the cuts that crisscrossed them. "You cannot manipulate me, Kayne."

He knelt down before me, eyes glowing from within. His voice calmed and was now only a whisper. "Here, let me help you up off the floor. It's not place for a king now, is it?"

I drew my lips back, flashing my teeth up at him. I looked at Kayne's hand as though it was a snake, ready and poised to strike me.

"Robin?"

Kayne's smile faltered as my name rang out over the night. We both turned to look for the owner of the voice. I didn't need to see her to know who it was, her voice was steel sharp and familiar.

"Is everything okay over there?" Althea Cedarfall asked, fire flaring suddenly as it bloomed within her hand like a rosebud. It cast light and shadows across her pinched expression, then over the scene: me, splayed out on the ground, and Kayne hovering above me.

I acted fast. I took hold of Kayne's hand before he could pull back. His weak gasp revealed he never expected me to accept his offering. He quickly shifted his weight to support me as I pulled myself up, using him as my anchor. Disgust laced across Kayne's face as the melted ice and blood smeared across his own hand before I pulled away.

"Who knew it was so treacherous out in these streets?" I replied, grinning at the concerned Althea and the fearful Kayne. "Thank Altar for Kayne. If I was alone, I could've really hurt myself."

"Yes," Kayne laughed, shuffling awkwardly from one foot to the other. "You could have."

"So, not sleeping is an issue we all have then, Althea?" I asked. "Seems to be the common theme tonight."

Her wary gaze swung between Kayne and me like a pendulum.

"I thought I heard you outside and, funnily enough, I was right," Althea replied, wide, distrusting eyes coming to settle on the Tracker. "It was either me who came out looking, or Gyah. And I think we can all agree that I was the preferred option, wasn't I, Kayne?"

The bud of flame became a tower in her hand, making the Tracker wince. His face paled to a sickly pallor, eyes diverting to the ground.

He may not have feared me, but I couldn't say the same for his reaction to Althea, or the promise of Gyah.

"All is well, Althea," I said.

She didn't believe me, and nor did I want her to. Her clear, judging disbelief twisted her face into a scowl. It had the effect I wished it to have on Kayne. All his bravado had slipped, and he was quieter than I had heard him before.

"*We* didn't mean to wake you," I added. "Did we, Kayne?"

He kept silent, knowing that saying the wrong thing would end up with him as a pile of ash.

"Well, you did."

Kayne swallowed hard and took steps away from me. He mumbled something beneath his breath. It was a mixture of an apology and a goodbye. Althea's amber stare followed him until he was out of view, and his footsteps were no longer audible.

Just like that, he was gone.

"Wish to talk about it?" she asked, eyes tracking Kayne until the shadows swallowed him.

I shook my head, looking over my shoulder. Perhaps I wasn't the only puzzle with missing pieces. There was no working Kayne out. "Not tonight," I said. "I should get back to Duncan before he comes looking for me."

"Robin…" Althea pressed. "I can sense your distrust for the Tracker, it's so potent that I can taste it."

"Don't worry." I smiled at her. "I have *everything* well under control."

CHAPTER 23

The pungent smell of boiled potato and meat stew seeped into my skin, lingering like an unwanted guest. My fingers were sticky with the brown sludge-like liquid. It splashed across me each time I dunked the ladle into the cast-iron pot and slopped it into a bowl offered out before me.

Regardless of the stains across my tunic, I was thankful to be helping. Putting myself to work among the people of Berrow – my people – gave me a sense of worth. Purpose. And that was exactly what I needed to take my mind off unnecessary worries. Spending time with the civilians of Icethorn not only focused my mind away from my list of anxieties, but also kept my fingers out of my mouth and my teeth away from my nails.

They had become my repeat victim.

"We're nearly all out," I called over my shoulder as I sloshed another spoonful into the wooden bowl of a gruff-looking man with sandy curls and hands the size of plates. He thanked me quietly before shuffling off toward Gyah, who worked at my side, handing out lumps of crusted bread.

"That is the second pot we've gone through," Althea chimed from the burning stove behind me. "At this rate, we will need to request further supplies from mother before the week is out."

I cringed at the thought of asking for help from the autumn court. But it was required, so I welcomed the carts brimming with supplies with a smile. What sort of king was I to the people when I could do little more than dish up stew with a forced smile whilst their lives were still at threat with each passing moment?

"Robin?" Gyah prompted. "Focus."

I shook my head, forcing a smile suddenly at an older fey woman with a nest of grey hair and eyes that matched. "Sorry, my mind's running away from me. Here you go."

She bowed, eyes glittering with admiration I didn't feel like I could accept. "Thank you, my king."

Gyah waited until the woman claimed her bread and moved on before accosting me with her accusation. "Something is bothering you," she said out of the corner of her mouth, careful of those listening in.

"How long have you got?" I huffed, offering her a pathetic grin before dishing out the stew to the never-ending line of fey. I recognised many of the faces from Lockinge and the journey to Icethorn. Now, though, the faces were fuller, their eyes not so tired.

"Althea told me you're still struggling to sleep."

The words hung between us, the silence treacherous. It had been three nights since Jesibel had invaded my dream and each night since she'd returned. Actually, sleep was easier now, but that didn't mean I wanted it. I almost preferred the chaos of seeing Jesibel. The silence, the space without her, made everything worse.

"Don't trust them."

Three words that were on the verge of driving me to the point of insanity. I looked across the bustling room of the old town hall and rested my eyes on Duncan. He was flocked by a group of burly looking fey men and woman, with stern glares and gritted jaws. He had busied his days gathering a small band of them, people keen to help protect their newfound home. He trained them in physical combat and they helped him with controlling his power. Most of his mornings were spent convincing new recruits, and his afternoons were busy training for the inevitable fight to come.

Although he was always only a short glance away, I still felt like I hadn't truly seen him in days. We were ships passing in the night, barely getting time to be together.

"Oh, you know," I replied. "Apparently sleep isn't a luxury until the world is saved from a mad man and his demon pet."

"There are draughts that can help with that, you know," Gyah said, tearing another piece of bread into six smaller chunks, the muscles bulging in her sleeveless tunic.

"I'm tired to the point of exhaustion, I could fall asleep now. That's not the problem."

"Then what is?" Gyah pressed.

"Do you have a draught that will deal with Aldrick? If I could take that, I would."

Gyah huffed, well aware that my worries were not misplaced. "Good point. But, you know, we've been talking. Don't be pissed at him, but Duncan has told us about your nightmares. He's worried about you."

I warmed at the sentiment, glad to hear Duncan's love for me was obvious to those around us. "Even when I dream, I don't feel like I'm sleeping. It's been like this since we left Lockinge, and I know I'm one more pathetic night's sleep awat from my sanity cracking. But... it's getting better. Slowly but surely."

"It's been going on *that* long?" Gyah's nails pinched into the hard crust like a hot knife through butter. With one great tug, it split in two, crumbs falling like rain on her boots.

"My subconscious has a way of punishing me for failing someone. Now I dread closing my eyes for fear of another berating."

"Robin, why haven't you said something about how long this has been going on?"

I pursed my lips as I contemplated my answer. "With everything going on, I didn't think it was important to divulge my personal issues. As if there aren't more pressing matters to worry about. And what could be done about it? Not even a stiff drink has the power to fend the nightmares away."

Gyah's lips pulled into a taut line. I saw her cheeks flutter as she chewed the soft insides of them. This was a habit I noticed a lot more than before.

"Something is on your mind now," I accused.

Gyah didn't tell me I was wrong. "Did this Jesibel ever divulge her powers to you?"

I shook my head, almost pouring an entire ladle of stew onto my boots instead of the bowl before me. I mouthed my apology to the young woman who moved along to Gyah swiftly.

"Believe it or not, there wasn't much of an opportunity to discuss such things during my intimate stay in Lockinge's prison."

Gyah nodded, her golden eyes still scrutinising me. Althea swept in with the new cast-iron pot hanging like a pendulum between two strong arms. Her muscles bulged, the freckles across her skin rippling, as she heavily discarded the full pot of stew before me.

"This is the last of it," Althea said, hardly breathless. Flour was smudged across her cheekbone. She attempted to clear it with the back of her sticky hand, only to smear more on the attempt. "It is going to need to stretch to feed the last of the line. Not so heavy-handed this time, Robin. Make it last."

My face warmed at Althea's reaction to my stew-covered boots.

"I'll try my best," I spluttered through a yawn.

Althea and Gyah shared a look that brimmed with concern.

"Remind me to ask Elinor for a draught to help you get a proper night's rest," Althea said. "Your nightmares are now punishing the rest of us with your snappy mood."

The concept of a draught – dreams or not – actually sounded heavenly. Just a few hours without worry and I'd be back to normal.

"But what if they are not that?" Gyah added quickly. "Dreams, nightmares, terrors. We all know them well, but never do they repeat. Our minds don't work like that. Nor do they make their victim look like an exhausted sack of shit, as our dear Robin does."

I flicked my ladle at her, splattering her dark leathers with droplets of stew. "Watch it."

Gyah raised her hands at her sides and gasped. "No, please," she mocked. "Not the spoon."

"Would you two stop." Althea laughed, echoing my chortle. She threaded her arm around Gyah's waist and held her. Seeing them so close warmed me from the inside out.

"I'm serious about this," Gyah said, frowning as she plucked a lump of what I hoped to be overcooked venison from her dark braid. "I think this is more than just dreams."

My blood ran cold in my veins, sending a strange wave of numbness down my arms. "What are you suggesting?"

"This is speculation, but Jesibel could be doing this to you. By choice, or not."

Althea's brows furrowed. "You think she's a–"

"Dream walker," Gyah interjected. "Yes, I do. Robin said Jesibel was originally from the Icethorn Court. Dream walking was a rare ability but one only privy to those Icethorn natives. It's possible she has those abilities just as Althea has with the flame and Robin's little icicle fingers."

Althea leaned in, hiding her smirk at Gyah's description of my powers. "It's certainly possible."

They both seemed pleased with Gyah's suggestion, but I felt nothing but dread. If that was Jesibel, then she was truly warning me. It wasn't some dream conjured from my worries about her safety and condition. She truly was broken and weak. Her body was no stranger to pain from the marks, blood and bruises.

Worst of all, she had seen everything. Jesibel had torn through my memories, devouring information about the Nephilim and our whereabouts.

Our plans.

Dread pierced me, deep to the marrow.

"This has to stop…" I started but quickly lost my words. My mind raced for a way to prove that Gyah was wrong. What it meant if she was right was terrifying. "Jesibel shouldn't have access to her powers. The iron cuff around her neck should stop her abilities. Unless..."

"Unless it has been taken off her," Gyah finished for me, working out what was worrying me. "Fuck, this isn't good, is it?"

"No." Heat cracked from Althea's skin. "If what you are saying it right, that means Jesibel is being used as..."

"Bait." My heart fought its way into my throat, attempting to block the word but failing. "Aldrick is using Jesibel as bait. He knows seeing her like that will make me want to save her. She has even told me not to trust them... I didn't know who she was speaking of, but it must be Aldrick. She is – has been – warning me not to fall for it."

"And are you?" Althea said, eyes drinking me in. "I know you, Robin. Regardless of the meaning behind Jesibel's dream walking, I don't think for a second that you will give up on her."

A gust of wind screamed through the double doors as they were thrown open. Our heads snapped toward the noise to see Kayne standing between them as he searched the room. I knew who he was searching for.

He raised his hand, sleeves rolled to his elbow, exposing a sea of freckles across his slender arm. Duncan lifted his chin as though he sensed eyes on him. He beckoned Kayne to him with a smile.

"I won't give up on her," I replied, watching as Kayne sauntered toward Duncan. I hadn't told Duncan about my interaction with Kayne those nights ago. Althea hadn't brought it up, either. "Which is why we need to do exactly as Aldrick wants us to do."

Althea cocked a hand on her hip and rested on it. "Falling straight into his web does not sound like the smartest of ideas."

"No," I said, forcing my stare from Kayne as his hand lingered far too long on Duncan's shoulder. "No, we make him *think* we are falling for it when, in fact, we do the complete opposite. News from Oakstorm and Cedarfall has been quiet on the Aldrick front. He hasn't acted since he took Elmdew. Every morning we wake up expecting news of his next move, and nothing. He is waiting for something... I just haven't worked it out yet."

"The last time he had that lost look in his eyes, he was planning a prison break," Althea muttered to Gyah as they both regarded me.

I dropped the ladle into the pot, not caring for the warm liquid that splashed up my arm. "We can't sit around waiting anymore. I can't."

"And you suggest we..."

"I need to find Rafaela." I wiped my hands down my trousers and sidestepped around the pot with the goal of getting outside. "Can you get Duncan and... Kayne? We all need to be ready to discuss the next steps. Together."

"So, the King of the Icethorn Court has learned the importance of teamwork," Gyah jibed. "Well, I *am* impressed."

"I live to please." I faked a bow and rushed out of the town hall, leaving Althea and Gyah to finish service. Before I met the cold air of the street outside, I turned back to find Duncan staring at me. His eyes were alight with a question, and I hoped the look I gave him in return promised that I would give him answers soon. And I would. But first, I needed Rafaela's acceptance. Although I already knew, given the chance of destroying Aldrick for his part in Gabrial's death, she'd jump at the opportunity.

Aldrick had access to magic, to fey and an army of Hunters. But the one thing he didn't have was a Nephilim. If anything, the warriors set us apart. It was time to utilise our strengths – even if the risk was so great that we may not all make it out alive.

* * *

"The risks outweigh the rewards, Robin Icethorn," Rafaela said, her voice reverberating around the cluttered room. "However, I stand with you. If this is our only chance of stopping Aldrick, then it must be taken."

"I don't like it," Duncan glowered. He stared at his clasped hands resting on the table before him. The whites of his knuckles were stretched with tension. "You are giving yourself to him willingly. Why not tie yourself up in a red bow and burst out of a box? That would be a better surprise."

I gritted my teeth. It caused me great discomfort to hear the panic in Duncan's voice, and I knew he was right. But we were talking about a desperate situation, there was never going to be an option that pleased everyone.

"Duncan, it will happen quickly. He will be so focused on the fake version of me that he'll not expect it when I actually appear. I will kill him before he has a moment to register the deceit. Would you rather we wait for Aldrick to make the first move? Because so far, that hasn't worked in our favour."

"I would rather you were not the ploy," Duncan said, slamming palms on the table. "Anyone else, but *not* you."

"Believe it or not," Gyah grumbled, spinning a dagger with her index finger. "I am with Duncan on this one. Robin, your plan is well thought out and clear, but if he invades your mind and discovers the illusion you have weaved, it will be over for you. He will kill you, weaken Duwar's gate, and we will be one more person down in our efforts to stop him once and for all."

"What if this is *our* once and for all?" I asked, growing frustrated. "I didn't ask you here to vote or deliberate my plan. What I hoped for was your support."

I looked to Althea, silently pleading for her seal of approval. She wiggled forward in her chair and leaned on her elbows as she spoke. "When Robin asked me to break into a human prison and save hundreds of captured fey, all without being caught or killed by Aldrick and his band of crazed human cultists, I believed he had lost his mind. But I buried those worries and focused on how I could help him. I trusted in his judgement, and because of that, we are all sitting here together. Yes, we all agree this is dangerous, but not impossible. If it works, we save hundreds of lives."

"No, it is much bigger than that. We save the world." Rafaela stopped her pacing, white ruffling as she straightened her posture. "Aldrick is a weak, tired and bitter old man. His power is great but not undefeatable. It wouldn't take much force to end him, we simply need the means to get close enough to do it. Giving him access to, what he thinks is, a force he's yet to poison, is exactly what can distract him."

"You haven't faced him yet," Duncan hissed, as snakes of lightning sparked across his narrowed eyes. "Aldrick is strong. All it would take is for him to invade Robin's mind for a moment, and he will become the puppet master. He will take what he desires and do it over, given the chance. We have seen what has escaped the gate your Nephilim are protecting. What will emerge next?"

I stood abruptly, demanding everyone's attention without asking for it. "Enough."

No one uttered a sound. I looked to the seat Kayne should've occupied if he'd not conjured an excuse not to join our meeting. I wondered whose side he would've taken in this conversation. It wasn't impossible to imagine that he would have advocated for my plan, enjoying the risk I put myself in by doing so.

For the first time, I actually longed for his presence. I could've done with another person rooting for me.

"Seraphine and her sister worked for Aldrick and, all the while, kept their minds from his grasp. If they could do it, so can I." I raised my chin, forcing the confidence that I felt inside to radiate outwards. "What we need for this to work is Mariflora. Doses strong enough to keep Aldrick from controlling us. There you go, a resolution to the problem you keep coming back to."

"Then it will be me," Duncan snapped, gripping my hand. "I can't let you go alone. I'll offer myself to do this. If you are to *become* someone else, I will become you."

"No," I felt the urge to laugh as I refused.

"Robin has already asked me to partake in this," Rafaela added. "And I have accepted."

"It was not a suggestion," Duncan said, desperation dripping from his voice, gaze snapping between me and the Nephilim. "I'm telling you both: I am coming with you or this fucking plan ends here."

"I can't accept that of you," I said, breathless at Duncan's offer.

"You do not need to. I know what it is I am offering, and I don't take it back. We do this together. I'll have your back, and you'll have mine. And if it comes to it, I will do anything to give you the time to complete the task."

We fixated on one another's eyes. I searched his for regret at his offer, and he searched mine for something else entirely. Althea, Gyah and Rafaela faded into the shadows of the dimly lit room until I believed it was only the two of us, all until one of them cleared their throat.

"Whilst you debate who is prepared to throw their lives before Aldrick, I will send word ahead of our arrival in Aurelia. Mother will wish to meet us. I can then prepare a visit from the fey with the abilities we require for this to work." Althea pushed up from the table and stood, a determined scowl set on her face.

"We leave for Aurelia tomorrow. I don't want to leave it any later than that," I confirmed. What I wished to say was the longer we waited, the more chance Jesibel had to haunt my dreams. There was no telling what information she could glean out of me next – that was, if she came back.

Althea tipped her head in agreement. "I will prepare one of my soldiers to ride ahead within the hour. They will have at least a few hours' notice before we arrive in that case."

"Which will give me time to ready the fey I've been training to protect Berrow when the time comes. I hardly imagine they believed it to be so soon, but I trust they are ready to defend their home and themselves." Duncan stood now, still gripping my hand, which I was thankful for.

"My purpose is to prevent Aldrick from collecting another of Altar's keys," Rafaela added firmly, her wings flinching at her back as she spoke. "This is why I must be the one to go with Robin, not you, Duncan."

She was right, no matter if Duncan refused it.

There was an unspoken detail to my plan, one that I'd discussed privately with Rafaela before this council meeting began. I'd glossed over when explaining my plan to the group, because I'd promised Rafaela not to share it.

Rafaela was the only one with the knowledge of these keys. Which meant she was the only one who knew how to destroy them. For the sake of not letting that information spread further than it needed to, I vowed to keep it between us.

"We will continue this discussion when we make it to Aurelia," I said, although one look at Rafaela and we both knew that that discussion was pointless. In fact, it would be the topic of how to stop Duncan coming. "If everyone doesn't mind, I need a moment with Rafaela before we prepare ourselves."

Everyone got up and left – everyone but Duncan.

He came to stand before me, worry set deep in his forest-green eyes. "Please, Robin. I know you, which means I know what is going on in your mind. I cannot just sit by and let you put yourself in danger."

I lifted my hand and rested it upon Duncan's carved cheek. He leaned into my touch, closing his eyes and sighing. If he expected me to tell him he was wrong, I didn't.

"I'll meet you outside," I said, brushing my thumb over his jaw, enjoying the bristling of the dark hairs that had grown in the recent days. "Please, give me a moment with Rafaela alone."

I could sense Duncan's reluctance, but I was safest with Rafaela above anyone else... until the tide shifted, and she was forced to act in a manner to protect the world.

Duncan gritted his teeth and nodded, although it clearly took him great effort to do so. He shot her a look, then left. I waited for the slam of the door to prove he really had gone.

"Are you having second thoughts?" Rafaela asked softly, reading my mind.

"No, not about the plan."

Rafaela scrutinised me, as if she had the power to flay my worries out of my mind. "Then what else is there to discuss?"

"Erix." His name fell out of my mouth awkwardly and rushed. Three days of not speaking about him, trying everything to pretend he did not exist. That was all I could last. "You never told me if he was innocent of Gabrial's murder."

Although I guessed he wasn't.

I had avoided asking Rafaela how her interaction with Erix had gone for fear that the others would know I cared about it or that I wished to admit to myself that I cared at all.

"I have not told you, because you do not *need* me to tell you the answer," Rafaela replied. "You already know of his innocence."

I hung my head, chin to chest, relief blossoming within me no matter how hard I tried to squander it. "Good, I'm glad."

That still didn't solve the issue of who betrayed Gabrial, but at least it proved Erix was in control of himself.

"Robin, I do not need, or require, an understanding of your relationship with this Erix, but I can tell that the past still haunts you just as it does him. I saw into his truth. I know the guilt he harbours and the pain he is riddled with. But, without a doubt, Erix is not to blame for what happened to Gabrial."

"Then that person is still out there," I replied, trying to scrub my mind of everything Rafaela had just said about Erix.

"For now," she replied, causing shivers to spread across my spine. "All things that hide in the shadows reveal themselves eventually. One way or another, it will come to light. And when the one to blame reveals themselves, I will be ready."

I exhaled a sigh riddled with guilt. "Thank you for standing by me. I understand."

"Do not speak too soon," she replied, placing a hand on my shoulder and squeezing enough to tell me she was here. "Succeed in your plan, and then you may thank me."

Because if I didn't see this through and come back victorious, Rafaela had been tasked to ensure the power inside of me would never fall into Aldrick's grasp, both in life and death.

"I will leave shortly to collect the labradorite stone we require for the transfer," Rafaela said in a hushed voice.

I swallowed down the bile in my throat. I'd almost given myself up when accepting the Icethorn key, and now I was giving it to Rafaela. But I trusted her. Rafaela's entire purpose was to protect the key, so there was no better person to give up the power to. At least, as she'd promised, for a short time.

Unless Aldrick won, then she would destroy it, but that was something she'd vowed me to keep to myself. It went against everything she was made for. But we all had to do things we were not comfortable with in the face of impending doom.

Some more than others.

CHAPTER 24

The moment we passed over the border from Icethorn land to Cedarfall, I felt discomfort's longing hum within my body. Although the feeling came over me suddenly, it didn't linger long. I massaged at the dip at the centre of my chest and willed the tugging to calm. Leaving my court behind felt as disconcerting as a thorn lodged in my hand. And the further we rode from it, the easier the thorn dislodged until I no longer felt as though a hand was gripped around my heart, squeezing at it viciously.

Althea offered me a tight smile. It screamed with understanding, yet I couldn't help but notice how straight she sat on her ivory mare or how her cheeks were flushed with colour again. Being back within her family's lands reinvigorated her. Althea practically glowed, haloed by the orange and red tones of the setting sky we rode into.

Gyah sliced through the sky above us in her Eldrae form. She sped through the sea of gold, her nimble, black-scaled body dancing through wisps of cloud like a serpent. She disturbed flocks of sparrows, even snatching one in her maw for a quick snack. I was confident I recognised her laugh beneath the rumbling roar she emitted, and the giggles that came from Althea only confirmed it. Gyah attempted to fill the journey with some more entertainment than our fleeting attempts at conversation or, worse, my own thoughts.

Kayne, who rode at the back of our group, seemed wary

of Gyah. Perhaps it wasn't kind of me to smile every time he flinched or gasped as she glided down above us, but I couldn't help myself.

Duncan wasn't relaxed, either. Hours into our journey from Berrow to Aurelia, he was on high alert, constantly watching our surroundings for a threat. Even though that was the very reason Gyah flew above, guarding us from the sky.

The little conversation I had attempted with him had failed quickly. It was obvious that he was solely concerned with the horizon. He watched it, waiting expectantly for us to be greeted by more demonic creatures that crawled through the weakened gate in Irobel.

Since the attack on Imeria Castle, there had been no further sightings of hellish monsters. A fact that should have made me feel more at ease, but I'd learned that silence was not always a good thing.

"You see those stones there, your border markers. They're the same material with which the Defiler's gate was constructed." Rafaela encouraged her amber-haired stallion to the side of mine. They were similar in size, but the mare I rode on began throwing her head from side to side. My palms burned as I pulled tighter on the reins to control her. "Explains how the powers of your courts are kept separate."

Labradorite, Altar's bones.

I craned my neck and looked at the oddly shaped stone marker dusted with snow just off in the distance. I saw them in a different light now. Deep in my mind, I recognised them for what they were now I had the knowledge.

"One day, when this is all over, I'd very much like to go over those texts in Irobel that you mentioned," I said, pondering what other knowledge had been lost to us.

"Labradorite is an ancient mineral. And like all old things, it has many purposes." Rafaela looked ahead, but not quick enough for me to miss something that passed behind her stare.

"Such as?" It was better discussing such things, it kept my mind off what awaited us in Aurelia.

"Well, the Nephilim also have uses for the stone. Although rare of an occasion, it is not unheard of for our elders to bind a Nephilim within them."

My stomach jolted from the clear discomfort creeping at the corners of Rafaela's eyes.

"What do you mean, bind?" I asked.

"Duwar is strong. Aldrick's not the first being who has been invaded by the Defiler and... influenced. Those Nephilim who turned against their own were not killed and given eternal peace with the Creator. Instead, they were bound – imprisoned in labradorite and kept from existing in life or dying. Unless the stone is destroyed, of course." She shot me a look, one that spoke of our secret plan. "Nothing comes back from that. Being bound is a punishment revered at the highest level."

"That sounds awful," I muttered. "How the simple beauty of a stone can be turned into something so... evil."

"Even the prettiest of flowers can harbour the deadliest of poisons. Caution against even the most beautiful things in life might just be what saves you, trust me."

I soured at Rafaela's words, recognising the way she patted the pocket on her jacket, suggesting the piece of labradorite that no doubt lurked within. As she'd promised, she left Berrow briefly and returned with some, all before anyone but me noticed her disappearance.

"Without trust, I have nothing," I replied. "I especially need it if we are going to see that Aldrick is stopped."

"And we will," Rafaela replied, facing forward to our convoy.

"It would be foolish to think that Aldrick's not prepared for anything we throw his way," Duncan said, all without glancing our way. "What happens if he manages to open this gate, can we *trust* there is a way of solving that problem?"

"My power is the key," I replied before Rafaela could. "If Aldrick can open the gate, then we sure as hell can close it again. The old saying 'lock it and throw away the key' springs to mind."

Rafaela winced but hid her discomfort with a huffed chortle. "Your ability to look on the brighter side is an honourable trait, Robin. Even with everything you have faced, and have *yet* to experience, I hope it never fades."

"From the way you speak, it seems as though you believe I'm going to succeed."

"We are going to." Rafaela kicked her heels into her stallion's side and spurred it forward. "Because there's no other choice."

We stopped only briefly during our journey; it was all Althea allowed.

Duncan guzzled from my waterskin, some spilling over his lips and chin. He looked at me, face flushed and eyes wide, lips glistening with water and every thought was driven from my mind as a fire kindled in my belly. We ate dried meats and filled our bellies, gave our legs a break from the aching ride in our saddles. If I had the chance to speak with him privately, it was taken from me when Althea demanded we continued forwards. Even after we resumed, all I could think about was getting him alone. Time had been unkind since the night I'd left him and found Kayne. There was so much left unsaid, especially with what was to come.

From the way he continued to glance at me, I wasn't alone in my thoughts.

Kayne noticed too. I felt his stare bore into the back of my head. He hung back and seemed more at ease once Gyah had been sent ahead to scout the path to the city. The taut grin was set into his freckled face like a jewel. It didn't waver and only seemed to brighten the closer we grew to Aurelia, the city of gold.

Evening had fallen across the world, bathing us in a blanket of darkness. We navigated Cedarfall's landscape with only a conjured ball of light held aloft in Althea's hand for guidance. Without its proud glow, we would never have seen the group of shadowed figures reveal themselves. There were so many of them, each peeling away from the tree line ahead, making themselves known.

"Halt," Althea called to us, panic edging the single word. Rafaela and Duncan positioned themselves before me, a shield of wings and lightning encased in flesh.

Althea moved from our group to greet our visitors. It didn't take long for them to be recognised as Cedarfall guards as her ball of fire cascaded light across them. I felt the tension lessen as Althea confirmed what I thought. Soldiers sent by her mother to escort us to the city, all garbed in autumnal shades and silver, with their faces obscured by the leaf-like design of their helmets.

There were countless armoured figures. The closer we drew to them, the more seemed to slink from the shadows of the forest's edge, into the halo of Althea's light.

"Mother hasn't skimped on our protection for the final stretch of our journey," Althea said, looking directly at me.

The swarm of faceless Cedarfall guards circled around our group as we entered the dark tunnels beneath the tree line. Althea still kept ahead, but the line of soldiers didn't allow anyone to leave the perimeter they'd encased us within. It surprised me just how quiet they kept.

Although the soldiers refrained from much more than the sound of clinking armour and the heavy footfall of their mounts, I couldn't ignore the many that looked toward me. Whenever I would catch their heads turned in my direction, they would promptly turn away again. Not being able to see their facial expressions, which were masked by intricately crafted metal, only added to my growing unease.

Queen Lyra Cedarfall took the protection of her court

seriously, whereas I'd left my own people to fend for themselves. The contrast highlighted just how far behind I was as king.

I was quick to blame my discomfort on the likeness the soldiers had with Erix. They bore the same armour, adorned with the same colours he wore with pride. Deep down, there was a part of me that wished I had the chance of one more conversation before he left Berrow by my order.

Focusing on the back of one soldier, with his broad shoulders and familiar frame, I couldn't help but think of my old guard. His voice haunted me, taking me back to when I first saw him riding into the Hunters' camp, haloed by the golden light of day that danced from the designs of his armour. For a moment, encouraged by the silence, I allowed myself to remember him in that way. And, for the first time in a long while, I felt the tickle of a smile pinch at my own cheeks.

Duncan caught me smiling and returned one over his shoulder, directed at me. I didn't shy away or attempt to hide mine. I wasn't ashamed of my past and the feelings that came with it. Instead, I recognised it, welcomed it, and looked toward Duncan, my future, and felt grateful that I had one.

"How're you holding up?" he called back at me.

I shrugged, fighting the urge to yawn or complain about the ache in my thighs. "Like I wish I had taken you up on your offer to ride alongside you."

The thought of being held up by two strong arms, with the hard muscle of a stomach and chest at my back, warmed my soul.

Duncan's eyes narrowed. Within the dark of the forest, they seemed black and never-ending. "Careful, we have an audience around us."

I swore I heard Althea mutter beneath her breath, and something resembling a laugh escaped Rafaela. My cheeks warmed as I focused on my fists, which gripped the leather saddle. I couldn't stop myself from beaming.

The more time passed, the more I longed for nothing more than to climb from my mare's back and stretch my limbs again. Each thud across the uneven, leaf-strewn ground encouraged the song of discomfort to intensify across my back. I was certain every joint would crack with relief when we finally reached Aurelia.

We all bore signs of exhaustion, from our slumped postures to the echoes of yawns that plagued our group. All but Kayne. Every time I looked back, I expected to find that he'd vanished. Instead, he was still locked in the competition of silence with the surrounding soldiers. He sat straight-backed and wide-eyed as though he could not relax. His gaze drifted across the soldiers with a glint of expectation, likely counting his moments until they recognised his past and slaughtered him for it.

Not before long, a noise broke the silence. It was loud and shrill, close enough that its sudden presence shocked me out of my exhaustion.

Our group ahead slowed to a stop, searching around the dark for what had caused the sound. Althea lifted her orb of fire until the underbelly of trees glowed with ominous shades of amber and gold. Her light exposed the entanglement of branches, but also the cause of the shriek.

A bird sat perched on a branch above us. Iron-tipped claws pierced the wood's skin, causing it to bleed with amber sap.

"Lucari?" I muttered, pulling numbly upon the reins, causing Rafaela to do the same before her stallion knocked into me. I narrowed my gaze and looked up at the hawk as it glared down from its perch like a queen would from a throne.

Kayne's companion waited above us as though it was always meant to be there. It glowed in the reflection of Althea's light, which turned its beady eyes to small coins of gold. Lucari squawked once in warning before launching from the thick branch and gliding down toward Kayne's outstretched arm.

"Looks like she found her way home," Duncan said, concern evident in his chosen tone.

"And that she is still alive at that," Rafaela glowered.

An icy chill speared down my spine as I watched Kayne calmly welcome his bird. It wasn't the reaction I expected. There was no relief or surprise on the Tracker's face. Only a wide grin that seemed to grow until it twisted his face into a mask that sparked unease in my gut.

"There you are, my girl," Kayne cooed, running his finger across her yellowed beak. "Why, haven't you been a busy little thing?"

"Kayne," Duncan grunted whilst trying to steer his stallion back around to face him. "What's the meaning of this?"

Something was wrong. I recognised the dread as it encased me. Duncan trotted toward his friend, who still paid no mind to anyone but his hawk. "Don't you see, Duncan. Lucari has found her way back to me."

"Yes, I see that."

I watched as Duncan lowered his hand to the sword at his hip, knuckles paling.

"Fantastic, your bird has finally returned. But the reunion can wait. We must keep moving," Althea called out, but her voice was buried beneath the roaring in my ears.

Kayne's lips were moving as he whispered something to Lucari. Then, when his attention lifted from his missing – and presumed dead – hawk, he looked directly at Duncan. His smile faltered; the creases around his eyes softened. "One chance, Duncan, you have one chance to do what is right."

It became so quiet that a pin drop could've been heard within the dark forest.

Rafaela's feet thudded onto the ground, so disturbingly loud, I felt it vibrate through me.

"What are you talking about, Kayne?" Duncan asked.

"You know, deep down," Kayne answered, eyes brimming with tears. Except they weren't tears of relief of being reunited with his hawk. Nor were they a sign of sadness, but something else entirely.

It was regret.

"I'm giving you one final chance to do what is right. Stand by me, Duncan." Kayne reached out his spare hand, fingers outstretched as though he beckoned Duncan toward him. I wished to reach out and grasp the back of Duncan's cloak to stop him from moving any closer, but he was just out of reach.

I felt the soldiers shift around us, likely sensing the same strange atmosphere that had befallen us, ready to do anything to protect the fey from the Tracker and his hawk.

Duncan didn't answer Kayne. His silence clearly offended Kayne, whose face pinched suddenly into a furious scowl. When he spoke, he no longer did so calmly. He screamed, spit flying beyond his thin, freckle-lined lips. "Everything we have been through, all the years we have spent together, and you still pick *him.*"

Kayne snapped his reddening eyes toward me. I felt his hate like a wave, nearly powerful enough to rock me from my mare's back.

"Kayne, you are speaking in riddles! What's going on with you?" The air crackled with lightning as Duncan lost control of his own emotions. I felt his confusion and embarrassment as though the air was laced with it. "Now isn't the time to finally admit your misplaced jealousy."

Kayne ran a hand down his hawk's neck, bristling feathers to her delight. She expelled a sound, a rumbling shriek that I'd heard before. I blinked and saw Berrow under nightfall, Kayne lurking down an alley.

"I heard her…" The words flowed out of me as realisation came to me. Kayne looked to me, although his expression was impassive to my accusation. "Lucari. I thought I heard her in Berrow."

"Congratulations, Robin Icethorn."

My eyes narrowed on him, I was no longer bothered to conceal my distrust. "Lucari was never missing, was she?"

The Tracker rolled back his shoulders as he expelled a quivering breath.

"Answer *him*," Duncan growled.

I waited for Kayne to reply and confirm what I'd already decided, but when he spoke again it wasn't to prove me right or wrong.

Smiling from ear to ear, with ruby-stained eyes and skin paler than it had been moments before, Kayne shouted out words that flayed me open, from neck to naval. "Long may Duwar rule."

There was a terrifying silence that lasted only a second whilst Kayne's words fell upon the group like flakes of snow. Then chaos erupted as the soldiers swarmed.

Not toward Kayne.

No. The soldiers attacked *us*.

CHAPTER 25

Everything happened so quickly.

My mount shrieked, rearing to kick hooves at the soldiers who raced toward me. A hiss cut through the air, a blur of metal shot in my direction, followed swiftly by a wet thud. I became weightless, the force of the mount bucking knocking me backwards. I flew from the saddle, until the stirrup tangled around my ankle. Instinctively I tried to turn my body, eyes scrunched closed as the ground came up suddenly to greet me. But I was stuck, my mount falling down with me.

My lungs emptied upon the harsh impact with the ground, but the jarring pain was nothing compared to the weight of the horse atop me.

For a moment, I felt nothing but the panicked urge to breathe. Then the agony followed. I wanted to reach for my head, but my arms were trapped beneath me. Ringing filled my ears, the tang of blood rupturing in my mouth.

Chaos claimed the forest, a wave of bodies and blades crashing as one. It took a moment for my sight to steady from its constant swimming.

I clawed at the ground, trying to move, but couldn't shift beneath the force pressing down on me. Looking back, I saw that my mare was splayed across the lower half of my right leg. Its hulking body wasn't moving, its chest was still and lifeless. Bolts of metal had pierced its muscular torso, each wound oozing dark gore onto the forest bed.

It had saved me, and died for me. But there was no time to grieve the animal or contemplate its final act. I had to get free.

First, I tried to wiggle my toes but felt nothing but agony at the attempt. At least I could feel my foot, that was a good sign that the damage wasn't terrible. With my free leg I kicked at the animal's back, trying to pry myself free, all whilst magic clashed ahead of me.

A flare of stark blue light bathed the dark belly of the forest. The air splintered with the sudden heat before dispersing. I snapped my head in the direction to see a Cedarfall soldier running toward me, blade drawn, the desire for death pinched across their face.

I tried to call on my power, but my pain choked me. All I could do was lift my hands as if they had the power to stop a sword.

The air cracked with warning. As suddenly as the man was running at me, the next moment he was nothing but a charred husk of flesh and bone. Lightning cut through the forest, a whip of purple light that devoured him, melting armour and scalding the body it should've protected.

Blood misted the air, raining down across my face. I clamped my mouth closed, not before some invaded me, spoiling my tongue with the sour taste of ruin.

"No one touches what is mine!" Duncan bellowed, his voice stern yet dripping with fear. I found him, snakes of power crackling around his fists. His gaze snapped to something I hadn't yet seen, followed by another burst of blue light that shot across the dark forest. Like the first to die, another soldier faced the same end, a bolt hitting their chest and sending them flying into the dark of the surrounding forest.

A wave of strength came over me at the sound of his presence. From my position on the ground, I couldn't see anything but the rushing of feet. Unless Duncan conjured more of his lightning, we were bathed in darkness. Only the terrible sounds of a struggle told me that we were completely fucked.

"Robin," Duncan gasped, eyes laying upon the dead horse across my leg. His teeth gritted, his brow furrowed and then he gave me a command I couldn't help but follow. "Get up. Your people need *you*."

A feral cry tore out of me. Determination filled my body until I had enough strength to get free. I felt the sudden relief as the weight pressing down on my calf was lifted. I thought I'd done it myself, from the sheer need to help my friends. But looking back, I found Rafaela standing before me with the slumped, dead horse now spaces behind her. She was panting heavily. Her dark skin illuminated with gold light that emanated in pulsing waves from the hammer she held.

"Can you move?" she asked, words rushed. Her free hand was outstretched for me, the other gripping firm around the handle of her weapon. I saw the splatter of flesh across the flat surface – Duncan wasn't the only one to kill someone.

I brought my leg upward, recognising the sharp pain that encased my ankle like an unseen bracelet. "Twisted, not broken."

"Good. You can fight on it."

I opened my mouth just as a shadow peeled from behind Rafaela's wings. There wasn't time to warn her. Rafaela was torn from her feet and yanked into the air, snatched away from me. I scrambled to follow but thick serpents of root and tree wrapped around her limbs. They twisted around her wrists and legs, wrapping tightly around her waist until her wings were bound and her hands trapped to her side.

She was like a fly, caught in the web of a spider. Except no spider could control trees and foliage like this. Elemental power was rare, and I'd never seen someone command the earth to do their bidding before. It was as though the branches had come alive of their own accord.

Her hammer thudded headfirst into the ground beneath her and tumbled uselessly onto its side. Its golden glow died the moment it left Rafaela's touch. If it wasn't for the root that pressed over her lips, I was certain she would've erupted in shouts of fury. Her eyes screamed with that emotion – unspent rage that she couldn't access.

I threw out my power, thrusting arrows of conjured ice toward the living foliage that continued to encase Rafaela. Some embedded into the vines, while others smashed upon impact and rained to the ground in clouds of crystal.

"Duncan," I cried blindly for him. "Help her!"

Blue light flashed once again. This time it didn't disappear without having an effect. I threw my arm up and blocked the debris that exploded toward me. Duncan's lightning had caught a tree to our side. The cracking sound vibrated through my bones, the heat boiling the air.

I braced myself, lowering my bleeding arm to glance back up. But it wasn't Rafaela I saw this time, others demanded my attention.

A wall of masked soldiers charged toward me. I saw them perfectly. The forest was alight with fire that had sparked in place of Duncan's lightning. The irate flames danced off the armour, striking fearsome shadows across the ground.

Anger filled every vein, every vessel, until the storm inside of me was strong enough to ravage a world.

There was no time for questions or wondering how we'd got to this point. I had to focus. I swallowed the sharp ache in my ankle as I brought myself onto my knees. The soldiers continued to stalk toward me, with Rafaela dangling far above them in a cocoon of tree wrapped entirely around her. Duncan was nowhere to be seen. I feared what had become of him, but there was no point worrying until my enemies were taken care of.

I slammed my palms into the ground, letting every ounce of my power free. Leaves crunched beneath my force and turned promptly to shards of glass as I forced the inner cold to spread across the forest bed. Ice devoured *everything* in a wave of mist and vehemence. I forced so much power into the attack that I forgot to breathe properly, not that I needed it.

My magic fuelled me.

"Restrain the king!" one soldier cried out before my mist met him, consuming him whole. Another stepped forward, their hands raised, eyes glowing with an unnatural green sheen. That's when more roots emerged from the surrounding ground, coiling and dancing like vipers. They met my attack, the booming crack of elements colliding sending a colossal wave of force outwards. I felt the impact deep in my bones. Even my teeth slammed together, sending a sharp vibration through my skull.

So this was the person responsible for Rafaela's imprisonment. The same roots she dangled from like a puppet on a string above us now raced toward me. I pumped more strength into my ice, freezing as many of the roots as I could.

But more kept coming.

I barely had time to lift a hand before the ground burst directly beneath me, and the thick roots forced themselves upon me.

My life, and those of my friends, depended on me. I scratched and clawed at the successful root that had claimed my left hand. Forcing my power – not against the root but into it – I froze it through until it snapped with ease. But as before, the more I broke, the more that encased me.

"Nice little trick. Shame I always hated the concept of gardening." Althea threw herself before me. Her red hair was wild around her head, a crown of flames in its own right. She wasted no time in sending an arch of ruby fire toward the band of soldiers. It broke their line as they threw themselves out of harm's way. Some moved quick enough, but the soldier with the strange power was so focused on keeping Rafaela and me bound that they met Althea's fire willingly.

Their scream of suffering was a song to my ears. It was a song of pure, extreme agony as flesh burned and metal liquefied.

No longer trapped by the insistent earth magic, I pushed myself up to standing and gathered my power to hold off the rest of the soldiers who raced to take the place of those who died. There were so many of them – more than just who'd escorted us here. More had been lurking in the forest, out of view, waiting for... Kayne.

He betrayed us.

A new type of ferocity raged within me. I gathered his name in my lungs before shouting it out across the landscape. "Kayne! You fucking coward."

My power cast outwards, knocking enemies back, all to create a clear path for me to find him.

"Where are–"

Lucari burst into view, silencing me. Althea screeched as the hawk blurred through the air and flew into her line of sight. The hawk tangled itself within Althea's hair, claws outstretched for her face, iron tips slicing flesh, rendering her powerless.

The conjured fire spluttered, like a candle blown by a weak wind. Once again, the forest was bathed in shadow.

"No," I screamed, the air turning frigid before me. My eyes snapped around the panic, trying to make sense of where Althea ended and the hawk began. Even if I wanted to cast shards of ice upon it, I couldn't do so without risking Althea.

"You called for me, Robin." Kayne's voice rose from behind me.

I spun, teeth bared, a growl working out of my throat. Blinded by the need to hurt him, I didn't expect his hands until they were around me, grasping at my throat. He kicked out at my twisted ankle, forcing it to give way.

I was back on my knees before I could so much as conjure frozen winds.

Kayne's touch disappeared as suddenly as it arrived, although I still felt his presence linger upon my skin. I lashed out with my arm, preparing to thrust my magic into his flesh and shatter him. But nothing happened. My power didn't respond, its presence silent and forgotten.

"Did you really think I wouldn't have planned for this?" Kayne towered above me, his face dusted with soot and grime. "How does it feel to be the powerless one now, Robin Icethorn?"

It wasn't Kayne's touch that lingered on my neck. Lifting my hand, I found the answer. A band – a cuff of iron – had been locked in place.

Powerless or not, I still had the means to elicit pain. So I took it, jolting forwards, clawing down at Kayne's chest until he fell backwards. I drew my fist back, arcing it down upon him, knuckles cracking against something hard.

"It was you," I screamed, spittle falling out of my mouth. "It was always you."

Kayne couldn't reply as I rained my fist down upon him. All the pain in my ankle, all the helplessness caused by the lack of my power, I took out on him.

"I'll kill you," I bellowed.

His eyes met mine before another punch could crack into his face. "And if you do, who will stop Lucari from prying the eyes out of Althea's skull?"

I stopped, enough to recognise Althea's cries which still thundered behind me. It was a risk, but there was something joyous about the way Kayne looked when he said it that told me he was telling the truth.

My moment of hesitation gave him the chance he needed. He shifted his weight, spinning me onto my back until he was the one to straddle me. I thought he was going to beat me, like I had done to him, until the world spun again and I was on my stomach, facing Althea. Lucari continued to claw at her face just as Kayne suggested. My friend had thrown herself into a ball on the floor, her head was covered with her arms, skin glistening with gashes spewing dark blood.

And the only way I could help her was by not fighting Kayne. "Stop it," I pleaded. "Please, Kayne."

He whistled, surprising me with his word. Lucari stopped her attacking, instead flying to perch on a nearby branch. From the shadows of the tear, more soldiers ran forwards, overcoming Althea before she had the chance to right herself.

"Don't fucking touch her." I fought against Kayne's weight, but he pressed his knee into the soft spot on my back, causing me pain every time I moved.

"Duncan," I cried for my love, waiting for him to strike Kayne down with his power. But the forest had stilled – the battle no longer waged. At least the noise told me we still had a chance, but the silence I was met with hurt me more than any wound Kayne could give me.

Duncan didn't respond.

"Are you going to be a good boy and stop your struggling?" Kayne asked.

"That depends," I said, struggling for breath.

My view of the forest ahead moved again as rough hands spun me onto my back. I was forced to look up at Kayne, seeing the dark forest crown his dishevelled face. "I will be the one to remind you that you're on your back, and are in no position to make demands. Do you hear that?"

I bit down on my tongue, refusing to answer him.

Kayne smiled, the corners of his mouth cutting from ear to ear. "No, exactly. I won, Robin. Finally, I have bettered you. Go on, shout for Duncan again. See if he'll come to your rescue this time."

That's when I noticed the sheer amount of blood on Kayne's hand as he drew his thumb up to his temple and cleared a bead of sweat.

"What have you done to him?" I seethed.

"Me? I have done nothing. You're the one to have doomed him. I tried to make Duncan see sense, but you'd blinded him. I gave him a chance to do the right thing, to remember the cause that once brought us together. His death, *all* their deaths, will be on your hands."

I forced upwards, not caring for my ankle or the iron at my neck. Kayne had my wrists pinned down, but I still had my teeth. I tried to sink them into any bit of flesh I could find, or even smash my forehead into his – anything to get free.

Kayne hardly flinched as my teeth caught the soft flesh of his arm. In fact, he laughed, as if he enjoyed it. "A little help please."

I didn't know who he was speaking to until more hands were on me. As Kayne's accomplices dragged me away from him, I didn't stop fighting back. I wouldn't stop – not for the sake of everyone I loved.

"Oh, I bet you wished you could have done that to me weeks ago," Kayne glowered, pacing before me. My eyes found the mark I'd left on his arm, and I smiled, blood-slick teeth on show.

"You're not wrong."

"Oh, I know I'm not. I even thought you were finally going to crack and hurt me the other night. But you never had it in you. Whereas I do. I have waited for this, almost thinking it would never happen." He flicked with his hand, and suddenly I was forced back to the ground. "Ah, look at you, on your knees before me. What a beautiful sight this is... from this angle, I can almost imagine what Duncan liked about you."

His use of the past-tense made me sick.

"Fuck *you*–"

My jaw cracked as Kayne's knuckles met it. My head snapped to the side, but that was all I could move as the many hands still held me up. The inside of my cheeks filled with blood as I yanked my teeth from my tongue, leaving gouged, leaking marks behind. Not one to waste, I gathered it and spat it directly at Kayne's feet the moment I could.

"See that the rest of them are dealt with," Kayne instructed a soldier who stepped to his side. "Not a single one is to be left alive."

I watched with sickening horror as the soldier removed the Cedarfall helmet and revealed something entirely different beneath. I hadn't even contemplated how Kayne managed to get our own people onto his side – but they were never fey.

Of course not. The man was human, clear from the curve of his ears and the hateful sneer he laid upon me.

"The Hand will reward you greatly for this, Kayne," the man said, slapping his meaty hand upon the metal breastplate and leaving a bloodied handprint over his heart. Hunter. All of them were Hunters dressed in the clothes of our allies. "Finally, you have proved yourself worthy with your loyalty."

"Go," Kayne snarled, forcing the Hunter to scuttle away in a hurry.

"Yes, sir."

Kayne brought his dirtied, bloodied fingers to his mouth and whistled. A shrill call replied, then Lucari flew so close over my shoulder that I felt her iron-tipped claws graze the side of my face. I watched him fuss over the hawk as she perched on his shoulder, offering her praise as though she were a child impressing a parent. "Such a good girl. My patient girl. We will both be rewarded, you and I. Just look at the bounty we have for the Hand."

His eyes settled back on me.

"What have you done to Duncan?" I spat, tasting the copper of my blood and the ash that fell from the burning forest. If I had access to my magic, this entire court would've faced the wrath building inside of me at the thought of Duncan hurt.

Kayne winced, then gestured to a slumped body on the ground behind him. "See for yourself."

My body threatened to give way, but I bit down further into my tongue to keep myself upright.

Duncan was splayed out on his back, his body one of many, scattered among fallen Hunters that I hadn't noticed him until Kayne had pointed him out.

"No," I breathed, pain lancing through me, draining me of all my strength. "You haven't... he isn't–"

"Yes, he is. Look at what you've forced me to do, Robin. Surely you can at least see that?"

I dragged my eyes from the body, up to Kayne. "You killed him."

"This would be the moment to say your goodbyes to Duncan. You'll not see him again."

"He'll never forgive you," I shouted, throat aching, eyes stinging. But I refused to cry – refused to show weakness to the traitor before me. Instead, I would turn the agony inside of me back on Kayne. He was a monster, he betrayed us – but he loved Duncan, too. I could see that he struggled from the slight pinch of his mouth, and the way he couldn't look at Duncan for a single moment. "He loved you like a brother, and you've betrayed him."

Kayne shrugged, cracking knuckles to give himself something to do. "What good is asking forgiveness from a dead man?"

"He loved you!" I screamed again, unwilling to consider the possibility of Duncan's demise.

"Not in the way that mattered," Kayne snapped, eyes flaring wide. "I never asked for him to see me as his brother. I wished for more. For years, I have longed for him. Then you came and bewitched him. Ensnared him like a wounded dog caught in a trap."

I turned my head, daring to admit aloud what I had wondered all this time. "All of this… all this death and deception because you were *jealous* of me?"

Kayne's shadow cast over me, then he leaned in close. Lucari screeched in warning, her amber eyes flicking over me with hunger. I expected Kayne to deny me, to conjure another excuse as he had all these weeks.

He didn't.

"Yes," he whispered, lips dusting close to my ear. "And if you are wondering if I feel bad, I don't. I never shall. Because now neither of us can have him. And once you have been handed over to Aldrick, my life will be blessed far greater than anything Duncan could have ever provided me."

"You're pathetic," I said, my voice barely a whisper. "You desperate, disgusting prick."

"Says the king, powerless and alone, who's on his knees before me. Since Lockinge, I have waited to see you beaten down. Aldrick encouraged my patience, told me to wait and I would be rewarded with this very moment. He knew this was how it would come to an end, and he was right. I can honestly admit it was worth everything just to see you like this."

"You've been lying to us... since Lockinge?" I asked, unable to ignore the stinging in my heart.

"Indeed. From the moment we escaped Aldrick, I have been waiting. How else did Aldrick escape the city before we ambushed the castle? The attack on Imeria Castle? Jesibel? Even that fucking Nephilim, Gabrial, the nosey bitch..." Lucari flexed her wings in pride, chirping happily at the mention of the dead Nephilim. "Everything I've done, everything I will do, was to see this moment. I'm a man of faith, Robin. Did you actually believe I could turn my back on all I've ever known, just because you swept in with ideas of grandeur? Unlike Duncan, it takes more than a pretty boy to distract me from my path."

His freckled fingers clasped my face and squeezed. The pain was nothing compared to what I felt inside. In fact I relished in it. And there was so much I wished to say. Names and curses I longed to hurl at Kayne. If my hands weren't bound or my power drawn away by the iron around my neck, I would've thrown every ounce of my strength into hurting him over and over.

But there was nothing I could do but listen as he divulged his betrayal, his deception. He'd been patient and got what he wanted, and so would I.

"Should I offer my congratulations to Lucari?" I asked through gritted teeth.

"Well, of course, how else would I have kept in contact with Aldrick and my fellow Hunters? Between her and those pesky dreams – oh, you know the ones – I've been in communication with him. And he is rather impressed with me."

Jesibel. Dream walking. I had often found Kayne awake at ungodly hours, looking as exhausted as I felt.

And I scorned myself for not trusting my gut. All this time, Lucari had never been missing, Kayne's hate for me was more than just surface-level distrust. I should have known, and my hopes to be wrong had led to the demise of those I loved.

"So, this is it, then?" I asked.

"Oh no, you are required for so much more."

"Indulge me for a moment, Kayne." My body shook, my skin itching with the desire to fight. "Now you have no one left to stop you. What happens next? Are you going to take me and hand me straight over to Aldrick yourself? Because I can imagine just how praised you will be when you do so."

Kayne dropped his hand from my face and raised it sharply before me. I flinched, and he laughed. I thought he was going to strike me, but instead he rested a caring hand upon my shoulder. The circular dance that his thumb began made my insides knot, bile burning my throat. "You're going to join me on the journey to Elmdew. But I promise to atone for the sins you believe I have committed. Once Aldrick takes what he requires and kills you, I'll make sure your body is returned to those with enough care to bury you. Perhaps they may even be kind enough to entomb you beside your dear lover."

I searched for a lie in his wide stare but found only honesty. Fear crept up my throat and threatened to strangle the air from me once again. "What makes you hate the world so much that you would aid the end of it?"

Kayne pondered the question, chewing on his lower lip as he did so. Before he could reply, we were greeted by a rush of roaring winds. It coursed through the forest, dousing the flames and returning the underbrush to darkness. Riding the wind was a grumbling roar that tugged at my soul. The trees bowed beneath the force, screeching and groaning as though they cried out in alarm.

The calm expression on Kayne's face, as the winds pulled back at his ginger hair, told me he wasn't shocked at the strange power that radiated around us.

It left as suddenly as it arrived.

And all around the forest, the Hunters exploded in cheers of delight. I felt their excitement buzz through the very ground at my feet as they danced and whooped.

"It would seem the second key has been successfully collected," Kayne announced, making the cheers intensify. "Aldrick will be disappointed it wasn't himself that dealt the final blow. But I'm certain he will feel fulfilled to know another has been eradicated. We are one step closer to saving this ruined world."

I blinked and saw Elinor Oakstorm in my mind's eye.

"Is that a tear I see?" Kayne asked, brows furrowed.

"What have you done?"

"Everything required of me." Kayne caught my pesky tear and cleared it away with his thumb. "You don't even know who it is you cry for, do you?"

From stubbornness and fury, I refused to answer him. I dared not speak aloud Elinor's name for fear it would curse it. Selfishly, I wasn't prepared to know that Aldrick had pushed at the Oakstorm borders and killed her when she had not long found her freedom.

"You'll pay for this. All of this," I sneered, no longer able to see him through the goblets of tears that filled my eyes. "Elinor didn't deserve…"

"Elinor?" Kayne barked a laugh, one his Hunters echoed back at me. "You believe Elinor Oakstorm is the one who has fallen to our cause?"

My mouth dried as I saw the deranged joy in his eyes.

No. *No.*

Kayne narrowed his eyes on me. "You've just worked it out, haven't you?"

I couldn't speak – wouldn't.

"Robin, if it wasn't for your wish to visit Cedarfall, it may well have been Elinor who was dealt with first. But *you* wanted otherwise. You drew us to the Cedarfall Court, and we simply took the opportunity to ambush it when it was least expected. Queen Lyra Cedarfall's death is because of you. Now, time to get up."

Even if I wanted to, I couldn't move. What Kayne had just revealed had me refusing even myself.

"You're lying," I whispered, silently pleading that my accusation was right.

"Actually, for the first time I'm being rather honest with you," Kayne said, his chest puffing out as pride spread across his face. "The Cedarfall Court is dead. And you shall be the next to follow."

CHAPTER 26

My wrists burned as the rope binding them rubbed viciously and without peace. But the agony was nothing compared to knowing I'd left behind Duncan, Althea and Rafaela to their promised end at the Hunters' hands.

I tried to focus on counting my footsteps but couldn't reach the count of ten before my mind trailed back to their bodies. Kayne had ignored my attempts at pleading, which left my throat dry and sore. Then he had a cloth knotted around my head and stuffed between my teeth, stopping me from making much more than a muffled gasp.

There was no distraction from my truth of failure I'd been forced to leave behind.

Night had fallen upon Cedarfall, blanketing the sky with impenetrable obsidian. Still, I looked to the starless sky and prayed to anything or anyone that listened. Because there was one person Kayne had not found yet – Gyah, and I had to believe she'd return.

I focused, trying to discern her fearsome body among the cloak of night. But time passed, and she never revealed herself. I soon added her name to my list of grief, wondering what kept her from us.

Had she fled in time, or died just without us knowing.

It didn't take long for us to reach Aurelia, the Cedarfall city which lingered beneath the monstrous golden-leaved trees. And it wasn't the same as it had been the last time I'd seen it.

Once a city of fey, it was now overcome with the enemy. As the band of Hunters, led by Kayne, paraded me into the fey city, I knew it had been lost from the amount of humans I saw filling the streets.

Cedarfall had fallen, just as Kayne said. And the city now belonged to the enemy.

With each footfall, I ground the golden leaves to dust, itching at the sound my destruction made. Everywhere I looked, I witnessed what had become of Aurelia.

The streets were empty of life, the ground now littered with the bodies of fey. Beneath the sweet kiss the trees graced the city with, I could smell death lingering. Pungent, the scent smacked into the back of my throat and stung my eyes.

Hunters, marked clearly by the stark white handprint of their leader upon their chests, swelled throughout the streets, ransacking homes and buildings, even so much as burning them down. I watched as some kicked at the bodies of the fey, whilst others buried swords through them, over and over, just to ensure they were truly dead.

And for so much death, I sensed the atmosphere of excitement.

The rope at my wrists relaxed. I tore my gaze from the destruction to Kayne, who spoke with another at the barricade that had been erected at the city's entrance. At first, I thought the barricade was constructed from mounds of silver until I noticed the horrifying truth. Cedarfall soldiers, dressed like the Hunters who'd tricked us, lay in heaps. Blood oozed from the piles, creating rivers of red that spread far beneath the Hunters' boots. They didn't care.

"Halt," Kayne announced.

I stared daggers through his head, wishing to slay him in a thousand different ways.

"Before we proceed further into the city, have our enemies been dealt with, and I mean all of them?" Kayne asked a willowy blonde Hunter. Her face was stained with dark smudges of brown that matched the gore she cleaned methodically from the sword outstretched across her lap.

"Those that matter have," she replied. It was obvious from the lack of attention she gave Kayne that she believed to have greater authority than him. She paid more attention to her weapon than him. "There are a still a few fey remaining in that pompous building in the city's north, but it will take only a few hours to deal with them."

"We don't have the time to spare," Kayne spat, snatching the sword from her and throwing it to the ground.

She stood quickly, finally addressing him, pressing her face close to his as she seethed through bared teeth. "Do you require a reminder of who you speak with, *deserter*?"

Lucari screeched upon Kayne's shoulder, distracting the nameless Hunter from his hand, which disappeared into his belt where the handle of a small knife waited. In a blink, Kayne drew the blade free and sliced it across the woman's neck. She was dead before her body hit the ground.

"Let that be a reminder as to who Aldrick favours," Kayne said, sheathing the blade without bothering to clean it. "Who's in charge here?"

Another Hunter pointed downward at the body of Kayne's victim. "No one... now."

His posture straightened, his face easing from its mask of anger. Kayne stepped into the position of command like a snake shedding new skin. "Wrong answer, the right one is that I'm in charge."

I watched as the Hunters shared a look, one screaming of trepidation. I almost hoped they'd turn on Kayne just to save me an eventual job, but that wish dwindled when they submitted to him.

"It is imperative we leave for Elmdew and return the keys to Aldrick." Kayne pulled on the rope at my wrist, making me trip over my feet. They laughed at me as I almost fell atop the dead Hunter.

I made sure to look them each in the eye, hoping they saw the dark thoughts I beheld for each and every one of them.

"What has become of the Cedarfall key?" Kayne asked, reminding me of the terrible loss this city endured.

"Daveed has already left with it," another Hunter answered. I memorised his face as I did with all those around me. He was young, with his chin and cheeks speckled with white-tipped spots. Dark circles surrounded his blue eyes, making them sink into his skull. Unlike the other Hunters, his clothes hardly fit him. A human boy, likely thrown into a world of promises made by the Hand. And, unlike those who circled him, I sensed guilt across his face. He didn't smile, nor did he spare much of a glance at the surrounding dead.

"The teleporter?" Kayne said, unable to hold back his sudden fury. "He left without us? I was told he would wait, who gave the command – was it you?"

The young boy flinched away as Kayne drove forward. He cowered beneath raised arms, pleading through a snot-filled nose. "Please, please don't hurt me. Sir, I'm sorry. I didn't give the order, I only know of it…"

Kayne paused, hovering an open palm above the boy as though frozen in place. Then he lowered it. "Pathetic. Is this an example of those who wish to fight for the Hand and the future he promises? Boys like you would have never passed initiation. Desperate."

The young Hunter scampered away from Kayne on an awkward footing. Those watching on laughed; even Kayne cracked a smile. "See that the boy is flogged for his weakness. It may toughen him up. In the meantime, someone tell me when Daveed will return."

"By morning."

The answer didn't please Kayne, but this time I watched as he swallowed his anger. "It will have to do. And do you know *why* he left before we arrived?"

"Truthfully, those who were in charge didn't think you'd succeed…"

"Well." Kayne mocked a bow. "I do enjoy exceeding expectations. If I'm forced to wait until morning, then something must be done about him. I have been cursed with his presence too long already. See that he is locked away until the teleporter returns."

"Yes, sir."

Kayne stepped to me. I flinched as his pale, freckled fingers drew toward my mouth. With rough hands, he pulled the cloth from between my teeth, ripping the skin at the corners of my mouth deeper.

"I would suggest you act carefully going forwards, Robin," Kayne warned. "There is no one left to save you. Perhaps, depending on the accommodation these fine Hunters seem fit to provide, you should get some rest." His voice lowered. "I hear that the extraction of the key is rather… uncomfortable for the person experiencing it."

I drew my head back and thrust the hard part of my forehead into Kayne's nose. The sound was beautiful. Kayne rocked back, hands slapped across his face as he choked on a curse. "How was that?" I snarled. "Equally as uncomfortable, I hope."

A trickle of blood slipped down my forehead, catching in my brow. Sweat made the cut sting with vengeance, turning the pain into a throb all across my skull. Not that I cared – nothing seemed to matter anymore. Seeing the smudge of Kayne's own blood spread between his cupped hands was worth every ache.

"Lock him up, hurt him, do whatever it is you wish," Kayne commanded the crowd of Hunters. "But make sure, come morning, he still breathes. I want him to experience every ounce of suffering that waits for him."

With his final words, Kayne swept away, clutching his bloody nose, Lucari following in flight. That left me to drown in the wave of Hunters who suffocated me where I stood, all before I could fight my way free.

* * *

Far above me, Lyra Cedarfall's body swayed in the night breeze. Her neck was bent at an ungodly angle, tied by three thick knots of rope. The noose was the only thing keeping her up, the rest of her body weighed down by death.

She'd been stripped down to the thin garment that would have once been pure white. It, too, danced in the winds, turning her into a vision of a phantom before my very eyes. The dress was torn and stained with blood. Her wild locks of red hair would blow away from her face, exposing the wide, all-seeing eyes and gaping mouth. Only then would I turn away. Unlike her husband, who hung to her left side, or the line of red-haired children hanging to her right, Lyra was the only one whose arms showed signs of mutilation. Two angry slashes marked both wrists. Her hands and fingers were almost black with dried blood. Her death hadn't been caused by the noose around her neck, not like her family's. Lyra had been bled dry, forced to expel the Cedarfall power – the key – until she was nothing but a husk.

The Cedarfall family was dead, every one of them. Faces I'd seen at the banquet during my last stay in Aurelia. I thought of Orion, killed by Hunters and now reunited with his siblings and parents. But mostly, my mind drifted to Althea. I saw her in all of them.

I had no tears to shed. Grief was not the emotion that claimed me as I watched them move from side to side above me.

It felt like violence – the burning need to set the world on fire with Cedarfall power, just to get vengeance for this heinous crime.

My wrath devoured me from the inside, searching for a way out. It was all-consuming, but I had to keep it in. There was nothing I could do with the emotion here. Buried in the narrow, deep dungeon carved into the ground. A place to be left and forgotten with only the prison bars crisscrossing, out of reach, above me. There was little room to move. Only enough for me to shuffle on my feet but not to sit or lie down on the sodden ground. All I could do was look skyward and watch the haunting dance as the wind toyed with the bodies of the slain Cedarfall family.

There was nothing I could do but wait until Kayne returned for me. Altar protect the poor soul tasked to pull me out of this dungeon. I might not have access to my power, but I had my will and boiling desire for revenge. For Althea, for Lyra and her family. For every soul who had been killed as the Hunters invaded the city and claimed it as their own.

I would fight, tooth and nail, in their memory.

It was easy to lose track of time within the dungeon. It slipped away from me like sand through parted fingers. The horror of watching the hanging, dead bodies of those I'd known lost its power. I grew numb to the view. The pendulum sway within the brisk night winds entranced me, hypnotising me to the point of exhaustion.

At some point, I must've fallen asleep leant against the wall. I woke abruptly to my name, ready to fight the instant my eyes opened. I first thought it was Jesibel warning me from my dreams as she had many times before – warnings I didn't listen to. But when my name came again, I recognised the voice, despite the hissing whisper it was spoken in.

I'd recognise it in this realm and the next.

I blinked away the sticky sleep that clung to my eyes as I peered toward a face looking back down at me through the dungeon's bars.

"Good, you're still alive, little bird."

"Erix?" His name clawed out of my throat; my voice was painfully hoarse. My nails scratched the narrow stone walls surrounding me. If this was still some terrorising dream, then the pain should have freed me. Even as they bent back and the rough stone tore at my fingers, the vision of Erix didn't fade away.

"What have they done to you?" He growled, reluctantly taking his eyes off me as he scanned the area out of my line of sight.

I dared to welcome the relief that rushed over me, and yet I couldn't find the words to answer him.

"I *am* going to get you out of there, but I need you to be patient." Erix's eyes glowed with his promise. I couldn't help but believe him, cling onto the determination he emanated. "Can you do that for me?"

The pleading desperation in his steel-silver eyes was palpable. Erix radiated his urgency in undulating waves.

I opened my mouth, forcing something out. "It was Kayne. He... They're all dead."

There was no need to specify who exactly Kayne had seen killed. Duncan, Althea, Rafaela; I'd not seen them since I was dragged away from the forest where Hunters had been left to finish them. Perhaps I referred to the swaying bodies of Althea's family that danced in the breeze just beyond Erix's protruding clawed-tipped leather wings.

Erix flinched, his lips pulled taut. "He will pay for his deceptions, don't worry."

Our gazes locked, and I felt every shield of vehemence crumble within me.

"I'm so scared." The revelation burst out of me in a sob.

Erix's face pinched into a scowl that gave a view of the berserker that lurked within. His lip pulled back from his teeth, revealing the sharpened canine. "I will not let anyhing happen to you. Do you hear me?"

I held his gaze, witnessing the mask of sadness that did little to hide Erix's own fury. The berserker lurked within him still, and I cared little if Doran's death meant Erix had full control over himself or not. There was an entire city of Hunters. He could tear through them all, and I would never think of them again.

I nodded, swallowing down bile. "I hear you."

"Good. Wait for me to return," Erix said, fingers gripped around the bar far above me. "You will know when the time comes, but I need you to be ready. Remember our training, you are going to need to utilise every ounce of it."

"No," I half gasped and shouted. Erix didn't pull away as I reached up to him, my fingers barely grazing his own. "Don't… you can't leave me again."

"Little bird," Erix breathed, his shoulders sagging from the weight of the world he carried. "I never left you. I never will."

The walls could have closed in on me at that moment, and I wouldn't have cared. "You came back for me."

"Always. No matter what has happened, you are still my duty." Erix unravelled his grip on the dungeon's bar and stood tall. I watched his every move, holding my breath as he surveyed the surrounding area before speaking a final time. I thought he was going to say the final words that always followed when he referred to me as his duty.

And my pleasure.

Instead, Erix said, "Our allies live."

Then he was gone, the powerful burst of his wings forcing winds down upon me. I squinted against the torrent, feeling the fresh breeze brush the hair from my sodden forehead.

Our allies live. His words played over in my mind.

It wasn't long before the sky answered my pondering. Stark, white-blue lightning forked throughout the dark, revealing a swell of clouds that rivalled the obsidian of the night. I lifted my head as the sky opened and droplets of ice-cold rain fell upon my face, mixing with my tears.

Our allies live.

CHAPTER 27

The song of impending fatality filled Aurelia's sky. I didn't need to see it to know the Hunters were under siege. I heard it in their raw-throated screams and begging pleas, before their bodies sizzled beneath the fire or they were silenced with steel.

The attack persisted until the sky had brightened behind the swell of dark thunderclouds that sparked with the warning of lightning. Still, Erix hadn't returned for me. Time stretched on uncomfortably. I swallowed the desire to shout for him or cry out a name of someone I'd thought dead. Although the flashes of fire and the bursts of lightning suggested Duncan and Althea had survived, until I saw them in the flesh, I wouldn't allow myself to hope.

I sobbed when Gyah sliced through the sky, roaring hell-fury across Aurelia. Even from my distance, I could see her maw stained with blood and the mound of flesh trapped between her teeth. There was no stopping me as I screamed her name, begging her to come and free me. The feeling bubbled through the ground and burst out of me without the ability to stop it.

The Eldrae released the corpse within her jaw, which soon revealed itself to be the body of a Hunter. I felt the ground shudder under the impact as it fell from the great height. Then Gyah was out of sight, roaring once again, chasing after her next meal. And yet, within her cry, I felt as though she called out for me.

The patience Erix asked me to keep had grown thin. I couldn't stand to listen to the unknown battle that raged above ground. My heart threatened to burst if I didn't help. Blood swelled beneath my nails as I clawed at the narrow walls pressing on either side of me. I attempted to climb up the slick-damp wall and grasp the bar. After the umpteenth try, I hung from the rusted bars as the aged metal sliced into my palms. When I dropped, I howled with a mix of frustration and desperation, my twisted ankle sparking pain up my leg.

Until the iron cuff was removed, my healing and magic would be kept away. And if I wanted to do all the dark things that harboured in my mind, I'd need to be at full potential.

For a moment, I confused the sound of pounding feet with my heart, which was clogging up my throat. Once the sounds had desynchronised, I stopped my struggling.

It was a set of feet. One person.

This was it. Erix was coming for me.

I prepared myself, jaw aching. Would it be Erix, or perhaps Duncan would've found me first? Rafaela would tear through the city to find me, tasked with saving me or keeping me from Aldrick's grasp.

But none of them gloomed over my cell, peering down with a stare overcome with the need for death.

Kayne was back. I fought the urge to cower from him, to force my body into a ball so he couldn't reach me.

"You are going to do as I fucking tell you!" He panted, face pale against the smudges of ash and blood that covered him. The skin around his nose was bruised and swollen. Dirt, and a burnt smudge of rust, was spread across his neck as though bloodied hands had grasped for it. "Do you understand?"

I traced every detail of him, devouring it all. His panting, frantic breathing. The way his eyes left me and flickered across the unseen landscape. Beads of sweat coursed down his grime-covered face, attempting to clean a path through it. I even glimpsed Kayne's constellation of freckles beneath.

"How do you feel watching everything you've worked for burn around you?" I asked, staring daggers through him as Kayne fumbled with a key from his pocket. He almost dropped it in his rush as he thrust it into the old lock that kept the bars in place.

He mumbled something under his breath.

"I asked you a question," I said, surprising myself with how calm I felt. "How do you feel knowing you've failed?"

"No!" Kayne screamed back at me, slamming his fist into the lock. I heard bone crack and skin rip. "This isn't the end. I'll drag you to Elmdew if I have to. I'm so close..."

He swallowed his words, unable to focus on anything but unlocking the gate. Stone chipped beneath the force of the iron gate that Kayne threw open. There was nothing keeping us from one another. Kayne watched me for a moment, glaring down into the dungeon space as he considered his options.

"This ends now," I said, fists balled and ready at my sides. "It's over. I would suggest you get a head start with running before Duncan finds you."

Or before I get my teeth into you again.

Kayne flashed a bloodied dagger and pointed the tip toward me. "I should have killed you myself. It would have saved me the hassle of weeks of lies and secrets."

"But Aldrick needs me, so you wouldn't dare–"

"I couldn't give a fuck what that fey scum wants. It's what *I* want that matters. And that is to see you dead. Once you are gone, that wretched spell you have placed on Duncan will break. He will come back to me. I will free him from you."

Kayne's frantic, demented expression hid nothing of his intentions. I could see from the wide set of his unblinking eyes that he believed everything he spat upon me.

"All of this deception, all of this death, because you loved a man who never loved you back." I couldn't hide my deranged smile. "You sad, little man."

My words hit their mark.

Kayne lunged down, one hand free and the other gripping the dagger. There was nowhere for me to move within the narrow space. No place to hide or shield myself from his attack.

But that was never my intention.

A feral sound tore out of me as I thrust my open hand toward the blade. It was close enough to reach as Kayne swung blindly, all in the hopes of hurting me. And he did, because I allowed the edge to slice into my palm. I felt the echo of pain, but it was kept at bay by the adrenaline that turned my blood to fire.

I wrapped my fingers around the dagger and squeezed. The momentum caught Kayne off guard as he leaned himself into my hole. I reached up with my spare hand and smashed my closed knuckles into Kayne's shattered nose. It popped again beneath the impact. The weak bone breaking easier than before. Kayne reeled back, scrambling away from my now-open cell. I didn't make the mistake my last attack had on him, this time, I left more than a bruise.

The dagger slipped out of his grasp, falling to the muddied puddle beneath my feet, just out of reach from both of us.

If he wanted to hurt me, he'd have to get me out, or come in. Either way, I liked my odds.

"Duncan was never yours," Kayne screamed down at me. He was like a child, gripped in the thralls of a tantrum. "He was mine, and I waited patiently for years, knowing that one day Duncan would see me in the light I wished. Then you came and trapped him in your web. It is my duty to free him. To protect him from your kind, just as we vowed in our oaths to the Hand."

I squared my jaw, teeth grinding across one another until the bones in my face ached.

"Free him, then," I begged, preparing myself for my next move. Kayne needed to act fast because the feeling in my hand faded. The pain was demanding to let itself known. "Get it over with, Kayne. Do what you have to, just break this fucking spell. I'm waiting."

Something caught Kayne's attention out of my view. He smiled, lips curled upward as blood oozed down his face, smudging across his skin until it looked like he wore a mask obscuring his nose, mouth and chin.

My breathing hitched as he moved out of my line of sight, toward what had caught his attention. I hardly had a moment to steady myself before he slunk back into view, a torch of burning fire gripped in his hand.

The glow of furious flames reflected off his sinister expression. I saw his intention gilded in his eyes. He lifted the torch away from him and held it horizontally over the entrance to my narrow dungeon.

"Aldrick may punish me, but at least I will be known for being the one who killed the Icethorn King. Tell me, Robin, will you burn, or will you melt?"

I winced as the fire dripped from the oil-sodden tip of the torch. Burning ash fell upon my shoulders like snow, hissing upon impact.

"Come on, then," I shouted, panicking but refusing to let him see. My sliced palm slapped against the brick wall as I tried to scramble up toward the exit. My feet slipped across the smoothed stone, my weak fingers unable to grasp anything. I'd rather fight in my last moments than stand still and wait for the fire to consume me. "I die knowing you will suffer. And in the next life, I'll find you and make you pay tenfold for everything you've done."

Biting down on my lip, I refused to snivel for Kayne to spare me. Steeling myself, I stopped my clambering and tried to control my breathing.

"I've often wondered what it would sound like to hear you scream for me."

I let the smile creep across my face. "I'm surprised you haven't heard it before, every time Duncan fucked me."

Kayne faltered, hissing spit through clenched teeth as he stabbed the burning torch toward me. Heat licked over my skin, and I thought it was going to be the end. But then he withdrew.

"Indulge me for a moment, Robin," Kayne forced out. "If you survive this, will Duncan love you when that face is a ruined mess? When your skin is a map of scars that rivals the constellation of marks across your lover's skin? Would Duncan wish to bed you, or will he finally have space for another?"

I wouldn't entertain him with the reply he wanted. Instead, I spoke with calm clarity, which mirrored the rush of serenity that cooled my body and numbed my panic and pain. "It may not have been enough for you, but Duncan did love you, Kayne. As a brother. Do not punish him because it was not what you demanded of him. That was never his fault. It was *yours*."

"No." Kayne's lip curled upward, exposing his blood-stained teeth. "This is all because of you–"

The fire winked out as though it was a candle blown out by an unseen wind. Kayne looked down to the smoke-curling tip, surprise working across his face.

"He is all yours," the unseen, deep voice said. The baritone voice warmed my skin, tickling across my consciousness until it conjured an image of a man, half gryvern and half fey. "Duncan."

Hearing Erix shocked me, but knowing he spoke directly to another person I couldn't see had the power to sharpen every one of my senses.

Kayne thrust the splinter of wood outward as though it was a sword made from deadly metal. He gripped it in both hands, pointing it before him.

"Robin was right." Another voice joined the fray, one I expected. Duncan. "I did love you."

"Duncan, please hear me out," Kayne pleaded, eyes filling immediately with tears. "This isn't you! Aldrick has told me… he has said this will break the fey's sway on you. I can help you. Once Duwar is free, you will be shown the light again–"

"I've heard enough," Duncan replied. I could almost taste his dismissal when he spoke. "Erix, see that Robin is taken far away from here. I don't wish for him to see what happens next."

My chest thundered alongside the sudden clang of power that filled the skies. The thick, grey clouds burst with blue light as Duncan fuelled and called upon his power. I couldn't see Duncan or Erix, but in my mind's eye, I had a clear image of them both standing side by side. The chaotic thought was almost hard to believe. But it was real, even if I could only see the horror rise across Kayne's face... Both men, my past and present, faced down the threat to my life as one.

I heard the heavy footsteps on the ground above me. They froze Kayne to the spot. He shook like a leaf captured in the wind of a storm. Then Duncan was there, standing beside the mouth of my cell. He glanced down at me, horror darkening his expression, his eyes glowing with power. "I will come back for you, darling."

The sudden urge to scramble out of the dungeon toward him was overwhelming. I longed to reach for him and encase myself in his protective embrace.

I gritted my teeth, reading the future in Duncan's eyes.

"Make him pay," I commanded.

"I will. I'm sorry I didn't listen to you," Duncan said softly, regret twisting his face into a scowl. "You're in pain because friendship blinded me. Robin, you are safe from Kayne, *we* will ensure nothing happens to you again."

His voice, although loud and demanding, was for me and me alone. Each word crackled with his power, burying Kayne's pleading as nothing more than background noise.

"Wait," Kayne pleaded again. "Just let me explain–"

"This ends tonight," Duncan said, drawing his gaze from me. He looked to Kayne, who swung the fireless torch like a sword before him, tears, snot and spit lacing down his panicked face.

Duncan offered a single word, humming with his dark desires. *"Run."*

Kayne didn't waste a moment before he threw the cold torch at Duncan and sprinted away from view. The splinter of wood bounced across his powerful chest, but Duncan was running before it hit the ground.

The sight of the swaying, dead Cedarfall royals was once again in perfect view. No longer obscured, it reminded me of the severity of Kayne's deception. I scrunched my eyes closed and refused to open them again.

"Do not be afraid, little bird." I peered through one eye to see Erix leaning on his front on the floor above me and offering me a hand. His nails were pointed into claws, his skin as grey as stone. "No further harm will come to you. I swear it."

I didn't waste another moment. My slick fingers gripped around Erix's firm hand and held on. I cried out, almost surprised at the pain my mutilated hand gifted me. Part of me required the pain his grip on my sliced palm provided – it made this moment feel real.

The joints in my arm screamed as Erix pulled me out. His leather-stretched wings flapped, providing him with the extra strength he needed. Once I was half out of the narrow dungeon, he took another hand and gripped the material of my shirt. My belly grazed the harsh stone edging as he yanked me to freedom.

We both lay on our backs upon the ground, panting. The rain was falling harder now, splashing its fresh kiss upon the skin of my face. Erix was at my side, looking at the ominous storm clouds, but I sensed he knew I was looking at him. I wondered if he wished to look back at me or if he didn't out of respect for Duncan.

"Tell me when you feel ready," Erix said finally, whispering beneath the crash of Duncan's thunder, "and we will leave. Unless you wish to lie here forever, then I will allow it."

I watched as the droplets of rain splashed across the sharp structure of Erix's face. They fell on his skin and ran down his hollowed cheeks as though he cried.

"Thank you," I breathed out slowly, feeling the tension in my chest unravel. It was the only thing I felt like I could say.

"Never thank me," he whispered.

"But I will. Thank you for not listening to me. For coming back…"

Erix rolled his head and faced me. I didn't need to explain what I meant. In the glow of his silver eyes, I could see he knew exactly what I spoke of.

He flashed me a smile, but it was brief. I waited for him to say something, but his silence continued. Then his eyes fell upon the iron cuff around my neck, and he released a taut breath.

"There is a small band of Hunters left alive. They've hauled themselves within the capital building. Do you have the energy to help eradicate them and reclaim the city?"

My body was mine once again. I sat up, weak but willing to fight. "More will return by morning. We must be ready."

The Hunters had spoken about a teleporter who would return to Aurelia to take me to Aldrick. By the time they returned, we had to be prepared.

This was our one chance, my initial plan still had life left in it yet.

"First, I need to get that cuff from your neck," Erix said, eyes fixed on the bolt that hung above my collarbone. "I'm going to need your power to see that this city is taken back… for them."

He looked over his shoulder to the dead Cedarfall family.

I stood, uncaring for the pain and the tiredness embedded in my bones. Glancing down at Erix, it was my time to offer him a hand. He looked at it as though it were the strangest of things. Then he took my offering, held my gaze, and smiled mischievously.

"Yes, for everyone who has lost their lives because of this mad petition of demons and gods."

Erix's jaw gritted. "Just like the old days."

"Just like the old days," I repeated as he towered above me. Inches apart, I allowed myself a moment to inhale him. A scent my body recognised and my soul had missed. If I stared into his eyes, I easily forgot the rest of his changed appearance. It was like looking into the man I had once known, before he left me in bed alone on that fateful day.

"Quick," Erix muttered, his gaze flickering across every inch of my face. I felt my skin warm where his eyes graced. "Before there isn't a single one left for you to enjoy yourself."

My mouth watered at the thought of a fight. I glanced again at the dead Cedarfall family. I felt their fire course through my body. This was for them.

"I'm ready."

CHAPTER 28

Althea severed the rope from her mother's neck, the muscles in her arm tense with every saw of the blade. Once it finally snapped, Queen Lyra's limp body fell into her daughter's arms before being carried down to the ground and laid out beside the rest of the Cedarfall family. And not once did Althea cry. No tear escaped her defiant eyes. It was not sadness that billowed from her in powerful waves. It was *fury*. Hot, melting vehemence trapped within the casing of flesh.

They didn't need to die. As I watched the unnecessarily grotesque scene, I knew that Aldrick could've taken the keys without the need for murder. But he did it anyway, because this was all a game to him. A sign. And with every life lost, and the promise of more to come, I wanted to repay it back to him tenfold.

Gyah waited off to the side, never once taking her eyes off Althea. She held the pile of folded white sheets to her chest almost protectively. That pile lessened with each Cedarfall Althea freed from the noose at their necks. One by one, the bodies were then covered. Harsh burns marked their skin, left by the rope. The blue tint of their flesh and the wide, bulging eyes were finally covered when the sheets fluttered down over their corpses.

There was no hiding the horrific image of their bodies that could conceal the truth scorched into my mind. I still saw their deaths clearly, and refused to forget them.

Dawn had arrived, bringing an air of peace with it. The sky, still bruised with ominous clouds, no longer flashed with lightning. Everything seemed so still.

The giant trees of Aurelia shed their leaves, casting the city in a bed of gold. Even the earth grieved for what was taken from them. The air was still thick with the scent of charred wood and flesh, piles of Hunters' bodies collected swarms of flies, whereas the dead fey were gathered like twigs and used to build pyres throughout the city.

Each one burned with Althea's crimson fire, the rightful end of a Cedarfall fey.

Lady Kelsey, Althea's aunt, sobbed among the crowd of survivors. She'd been among the small group of fey who'd barricaded themselves within the manor. After Erix freed me from the iron cuff, we cut through the remaining Hunters who'd also fled into the manor. The hallways toward the great hall in which Kelsey and the rest of the fey were hiding were soon littered with shards of shattered, ice-hardened flesh of the Hunters I'd fought. It was over for them before it could begin, and I was disappointed – disappointed I couldn't take out my pain on more, destroy more, wound Aldrick as he had wounded us.

In time, I promised myself, he'd meet an end worthy of the monster he was.

My heart stung as I heard and watched the grief. I pressed my bandaged hand over my chest, hoping to keep my heart from bursting free from my ribcage. If I had tears left to shed, my face would've been sticky with them. But I was empty – a vessel of nothing but power that demanded to be released.

But I would wait until the time was right.

Throughout the crowd of survivors, there was a symphony of wailing and screaming. As we watched the last of the Cedarfall royals lowered to the ground, everything went still for a brief moment. Then every set of eyes turned to Althea, seeking the one thing desired in a moment of chaos.

Guidance.

The Cedarfall Court and its crown belonged to Althea now. All that was missing was the Cedarfall key that Aldrick had taken. But the snivelling, magic-wielding human, who took tenancy in the dungeon I'd not long left, would help us get it *back*.

"I can't bear to watch this anymore," I whispered, tightening my hold on Duncan's steady hand.

He tugged on my arm in gentle suggestion, pulling me into his side. I turned to face him and buried my face, eyes closed, into his chest as he coiled his arm around me.

"I've got you," he said, voice monotone with heavy emotion. "I'll always have you."

I hated how he sounded, as though his grief was lodged in his throat. There was no question, he felt some guilt toward what'd happened – Kayne's deception.

Duncan had said little about what became of his friend after he chased Kayne through Aurelia. From the whispers I'd heard among the survivors, Kayne had been dragged through the city by his ankle and dumped within the manor. What happened beyond the closed door with just Duncan and Kayne was still a mystery, and I was almost happy to leave it as one. I did, however, know that Kayne was dead. The Tracker's blood stained a path from the place Duncan took him, that was enough for me.

Duncan hadn't been the same since he returned from that room. Quiet, distant, although never straying far from my side. Although he held me up as Gyah lowered the final white sheet across Lyra's body, I sensed that, somehow, I helped hold him up, too.

I hated Kayne for what he did, but more so for what he had done to Duncan.

I swallowed my thoughts and focused on this moment, not wishing to give Kayne's memory any more power. I had more important things to focus on now.

Like killing Aldrick, reclaiming Altar's keys that he'd stolen, and righting all the wrongs that threatened to tear Wychwood apart.

Above the stillness, someone cleared their voice, followed by stern cut words.

"This would be the moment I have to say something, but I admit I am struggling to find the right thing to share with you all."

I turned back to look at Althea, who stood with shoulders back as she addressed the crowd, Gyah standing a step behind her, a constant shield at her back. I could see the grief Gyah carried in her golden eyes, it almost concealed the desire for vengeance that mirrored what festered inside of me – *almost*.

"You may expect me to encourage you, or perhaps spark strength back into your hearts with the promise of revenge. But I cannot lie to you. I cannot or will not make promises I am not confident I can keep." Althea Cedarfall washed her gaze over the mounds of her dead family before her. We all watched as her face softened by the time she regarded her mother's crowd again, her eyes glistened with unspent tears.

It was her crown now.

"Cedarfall has been violated by evil. Poison. Our enemy saw a moment of unsuspecting weakness and pounced. And so many lives have been stolen from us because of it. We can all agree, Aurelia will *never* be the same." Althea's voice cracked, Gyah stepping forwards in response. But Althea raised a hand, signalling she was okay, that she could continue. "*My* city is scarred, mirroring the marks left upon our own hearts, our souls. I know that there is nothing I can say, nothing I can do to help heal you, or give you back what was stolen from you. Nothing that will fix…" Althea choked again, chin dropping to her chest, shoulders heaving as she took a hulking breath in.

I stepped forward instinctively, but Gyah was there in a blink, taking Althea and pressing a kiss upon the wild red curls stuck to her forehead. This time, Althea didn't make her stop. Gyah's affection had the desired effect, allowing Althea to gather herself to finish speaking. "Nothing that will fix me."

Gyah whispered something to Althea, whose forehead creased with lines as she nodded in silent agreement.

I was surprised when I felt my heart crack. I'd thought it'd already shattered beyond repair, but seeing my friend in such a state of grief made me ache for her. We locked eyes and I mouthed my words of encouragement.

"You've got this."

Althea's jaw tightened, the resolve in her hazel eyes sharpening. She nodded, faced the crowd, and continued.

"This is not over," Althea bellowed so suddenly the air sparked with heat. "We will not submit as the enemy may hope. Not now, not ever. As long as Aldrick continues his campaign against the realms, more lives will be taken. Our enemy tried to destroy Cedarfall just as they did with Elmdew. But the pain doesn't stop here. Innocent people will continue dying as long as our enemies breathe. But like the smoke that coils and dances in the wake of the Cedarfall's mighty flame, I will stop at *nothing* until they suffocate. I will burn them out of their hiding places, scorch everything they hold close, so they know the suffering that is our flame. Not even the winds will dare collect their ashes. The ground will regret them. The water will refuse to wash their memory away. I promise – *promise* to see this dark time come to its end. Nothing can extinguish our hope, not even Aldrick and his band of twisted, hateful followers. We will rage, we will consume, and we... *will*... devour anyone else foolish enough to stand in our way."

If Althea's speech had been given at a different time, under a different circumstance, I could only imagine the explosion of applause that would have followed. Instead, the crowd was silent. But no one cried in the quiet that followed, no one uttered a word.

Instead, they all bowed. A wave of respect, cresting like a wave across the crowd, all whilst Althea watched on.

I looked through the crowd and found Erix without meaning to. He hung at the back like a shadow, his arms folded over his chest, wings gathered at his back as though he carried a flag. It seemed he sensed that I watched him, for his silver eyes tore away from Althea and found me.

My breath caught in my throat, Duncan squeezing my hand in response to the fleeting sound.

Rafaela stood beside Erix, her face set into a grimace as she leaned on her golden hammer for support. She, like the rest of us, showed physical signs of exhaustion after our fight.

I was just glad to see they were all alive – my friends. And it was all thanks to the silver-eyed guard beside Rafaela. Duncan had revealed as much.

"There is so much I wish to say to him," I whispered.

Duncan turned, and followed my line of sight. "You and I both. If it was not for Erix, we wouldn't be here. Cedarfall would have fallen to Aldrick's attempts, and more would have died. Erix saved us, he saved you. For that, I am indebted to him."

Erix had been following our party the entire time since we left Berrow. He'd not made himself known, out of the respect that he believed I wanted him to leave. But his hesitation, his overwhelming sense of duty, kept him close. And thank Altar he had. Because he was able to slip in and save Rafaela, Althea and Duncan – before slaughtering the Hunters who'd stayed behind to destroy them.

Without Erix, Cedarfall really would've fallen to Aldrick. Without Erix, I would've lost everything.

"As am I," I replied.

Erix looked away first, and I reluctantly followed.

"Robin, I want you to know I will never forgive myself," Duncan said, as the crowd swelled, going to pay their respects to the dead. "I should've listened to your concerns. Kayne got this far because I allowed him to, because I was too blind to think my... friend was capable of changing."

"Don't," I said.

"No. I need to say it, Robin. I'm so sorry."

Discomfort clawed up my spine at Duncan's revelation, but I fought to bury it. Hearing the guilt in his voice, the inability to hold my gaze when he spoke, only broke me down further.

"Even I wouldn't have foreseen his betrayal, Duncan," I replied softly, longing for Duncan to believe every word I said in reply. "Kayne tricked us all. No one is guilty but him."

Duncan winced, brows furrowed. The scar on his face deepened, as did the lines across his dirt-covered forehead. I wished to reach out and touch his face. To draw him down to my mouth where he could forget his regrets. "Kayne got his comeuppance," I added. "Don't allow him to haunt you, Duncan. If anything, it won't benefit you. We must not be distracted now, not with what we have left to do."

"I hear you, my darling. But it will take time."

I wanted to remind him that time wasn't a luxury we had. No matter how I wished it was, until Aldrick was destroyed and his poison cleansed from the realms, we couldn't hope for anything but the moment we were given.

"Do you want to free yourself from your burdens?" I asked when Duncan looked down to his broken knuckles. He kept doing it, ever since returning from that room where he and Kayne had shared their last moments together. "If you keep it all in, you'll find that your guilt eats you from the inside."

"Kayne hurt you. Guilt isn't what I feel for his death. The only thing I'm guilty of is wishing so desperately that I'd killed him before he had the chance to—"

Althea's voice raised in volume, silencing Duncan before he could finish. It seemed she wished for everyone in Cedarfall, living and dead, to hear what she had to say next. Duncan swallowed his words and pinched his mouth closed. I caught the feathering twitch of his jaw as he fought hard to keep himself quiet.

"I understand you have all been through a lot, and it is unfair that I ask anything of you. But I must. I ask that all fey with access to magic stand up and fight. Fight for those you've lost, and those you do not wish to be taken. Will you stand with me, as your queen? Avenge the Cedarfall name, and ensure we have one when this is all done?"

A beating sound began. I looked around and watched as fey slammed fists into their chests, a thud that soon became a booming song – a song of acceptance. Althea swept her eyes across the crowd, and for a moment, I saw the hint of a smile grace her lips. This time, when her eyes filled with tears, she let them loose.

Pride swelled within, watching my friend accept a fate that had unkindly been handed to her.

"Just as a Cedarfall is born from the flames," Althea called out, each word striking into the heart of the crowd, "may they return to them."

Althea waved her hand before the line of bodies at her feet as though gesturing farewell. Fire bloomed within her open palm, then fell in arching, golden waves upon her family until her blaze consumed each one.

No one left until the wind claimed the Cedarfall family's ashes, and the ground was left eternally scorched.

"Are you confident that is what you saw?" My question echoed across the throne room. It wasn't exactly empty, but for the grand size of it, the room should have hosted far more than the few of us. "It is important that we know every detail exactly if we are to make our next move."

Lady Kelsey turned her red-rimmed eyes upon me. "I watched my sister's murder. Every detail will haunt me until I am returned to the fire. Of course I am sure."

I bowed, sorry that we even had to have this conversation.

"I didn't mean to offend you, Kelsey." I hoped she registered the apology set in my expression. "I'm merely trying to understand it. If Aldrick is using the labradorite to extract the keys, then he is aware of the rites royalty conduct during the succession of an heir. If we can get it back, then we can give the power back to Althea."

"It would make sense," Rafaela added. I was thankful for her taking the weight of Kelsey's eyes off of me. It had only been hours since her sister was cut down from her hanging place, and already I'd offended her with my careless comment. "Aldrick cannot use the keys to open Duwar's gate until he has all four. This is as much a rescue mission as it is a mission to keep him from completing the task."

I shot her a look, knowing the undercurrent of meaning beneath what she'd said. It was part of our plan, a plan that still had life in it yet. We either succeeded in getting the keys back, or we destroyed them.

But for the sake of not inspiring panic, we kept that part to ourselves.

"Aldrick has access to an abundance of labradorite in Elmdew. If he is fashioning boxes to collect the keys within them, it makes sense why the power has not manifested physically within Elmdew and here. He has successful captured it long enough to wait to get the rest."

It didn't feel right to describe it as a box. Kelsey had recounted what had happened, watching the Hunters cut through Queen Lyra's wrists where they collected her blood within a box of labradorite. Not a drop spared, she had said.

Lyra hadn't screamed or fought. She made no sound as she expelled Altar's key alongside her blood. Now wasn't the time to remind the group that Aldrick didn't need to kill them to take the key – I trusted they all knew it deep down.

"It took hours," Kelsey sobbed, her words barely audible as her hands muffled them. "I begged them to stop. Althea, I never wished to leave her in her final moments... but I failed her."

Althea raised a hand and silenced her aunt. "Now is not the time for concerning ourselves with what has happened. I don't wish to hear any more. We focus on our path ahead."

Kelsey bowed her head, eyes smudged with kohl that ran down from her lathered eyelashes and left rivers of black down her grief-stricken face. She didn't utter another word, but her muffled cries carried as background noise inside the room.

"Labradorite is not indestructible," Rafaela continued to explain, aware that the entire room required her knowledge of the stone. Just like our knowledge of the keys, it seemed Altar wished to remove the true purpose of the stones from our history. Perhaps the gods wished to keep us in the dark to protect us, but all it had done was make us more vulnerable. "It is malleable. The Nephilim have used it for prisons, weapons and even the heart of our concerns, the gate which keeps Duwar locked away."

"For now," Althea said quickly, her gaze fixated on a spot on the floor before her. "We understand Aldrick's intentions and know what he wishes to achieve. He may even claim the third key if we continue sitting around talking about it. Or, we act before he makes his next move. Robin." Her eyes settled on me. "You are safest with us, but Elinor is currently in her court alone. I have already sent word to her, told her to prepare her borders for an inevitable attack."

I nodded, swallowing down the lump in my dry throat. "And we are sure that Aldrick cannot use the keys?"

It was a question for Rafaela, one she answered freely. "There was a reason Altar made four. Because only a god can access the full power of four, and regardless of what Aldrick thinks he is, he is no god. To our luck, we only have his magic to contend with, and the force of his Hunters."

Three powerful raps sounded on the closed doors. No one needed to accept the request for entry, for the door burst open. I turned and watched as Duncan and Erix entered, side by side. In the middle was a man I had hoped to see.

My knees almost buckled as I set my eyes on him. "Eroan."

He bowed, black hair tipping over his eyes. "My king, it is good to see you."

"And you."

It took effort not to run to Eroan, the kind-hearted tailor who had greeted me with such warmth the first time I'd visited Aurelia. Relief at seeing him alive was all consuming. I'd hoped that I would see him again, but not under such circumstances, and certainly not as he pushed the wooden, wheeled cot before him. As much as I was glad he was alive, it was also because I required his unique skills.

And as I settled my eyes on the outline of a body upon the cot, covered in a sheet, I knew I was closer to the next step in my plan.

"Just in time," Althea said plainly, resting each elbow on the edges of the gilded throne as she surveyed the new arrivals. "Eroan, I trust you have everything required for this?"

"I do," he replied, although his hesitance was evident in each word. "It will take time, but I will do everything that is required of me."

I left Rafaela's side and paced directly toward the cot. There was no time for niceties as I offered Eroan a weak smile, trying everything in my power not to focus on the dead body he carted before him.

"I must ask myself, Robin. Are you sure this is what you want?" Eroan laid his tired eyes on me. Black as jewels, much like my own. Although he lived within the Cedarfall Court, Eroan belonged to Icethorn. Like Jesibel, I recognised my court in the blue shine within his black hair to his stare – as cold as ice.

"I appreciate your worry, and understand that this is a hard task, but I thank you for trying." I placed a hand on the man's shoulder. "Yes, I am sure. It is our only option. Turning Aldrick's plans back on himself, giving him a taste of his own poison."

There was a reluctance in his expression as his eyes trailed across me, searching. "Please, tell me there is another way."

I shook my head. "This is the only way."

Eroan sighed, gathered his emotion and boxed it away, leaving only a stern mask of determination lathered across his face. "So be it."

I mouthed my thanks before turning back to the room. "We will have a short window to infiltrate Elmdew and deal with Aldrick. Going under the guise of a surprise worked for him with Elmdew and Cedarfall, and so it will succeed for us. Gyah, have we received word back from Elinor? Is she aware and ready?"

Gyah prowled forward from the shadows of Althea's throne. Her hand lingered on the new queen's shoulder, offering her the reminder that she was there, which had the desired effect from the way Althea's face brightened. "No word yet. And there is no time to wait for a reply, either. If we wish to use the human teleporter, we must do so before Aldrick has enough time to understand that there is a problem. We can only hope that Elinor receives our request and acts immediately."

I swallowed down my fears, feigning confidence in my plan. "She will. Elinor will do anything to protect her people and us. I believe it. And what of the Asps?" I turned to Lady Kelsey. "Have any been located among the Cedarfall survivors?"

Kelsey lifted her chin, broadening shoulders as pride practically glowed from her face. I knew the feeling was born from knowing she had something to offer toward the retribution of the family taken from her. "As they are my expertise, yes, I have had success in communicating with them. Without the assassins, I wouldn't be standing here…" There was more Kelsey wished to say, but one look from Althea kept her on track. "This is the first time the Asps haven't requested payment for their aid. They, too, have lost family and will stand by us. And thanks to them, the tonic you require to keep that *leech* out of your minds should arrive shortly."

"Good." My body trembled. "That's good."

Everything was falling into place. If the Asps provided us with stores of Mariflora, we could keep Aldrick out of our minds long enough to finish the task of destroying him. But the other issue was getting close enough, and that relied on Eroan, his magic and the body upon the cot.

I didn't want to ask the next question, but the answer was important to our chances.

"How many of Aurelia's survivors have agreed to come with us?"

Duncan cleared his throat. "Enough. Close to sixty, the rest will stay back and protect what is left of the Cedarfall Court."

"As I have said before, my people have lost enough," Althea added sternly. "I do not wish for them to put themselves in harm's way. I regret asking them to step forwards."

"With all due respect, Althea, you did the right thing." Duncan was careful with every word and the tone he used. "Your people would refuse anything but the chance to help. They, much like you, feel as though they have nothing left to lose. And there is nothing more frightening than someone with nothing to lose... trust me."

Althea's eyes sparked with flame. "I don't disagree, there is nothing more terrifying than that."

My blood cooled as Erix spoke next. It was the first time he'd uttered a word since he removed the iron cuff from my neck. He walked directly toward Althea, sparing me only a quick glance as he passed. He stopped when he reached the throne, then bent his knee and bowed his head.

"My duty started in this court," Erix said to Althea alone, although he spoke with undeniable conviction. "It was my honour to serve your family, and it would be an honour if you allow me to do the same for you, my queen."

"Stand," Althea commanded. "Please, Erix. I don't ever want to see you bend the knee to me."

Erix stood tall, his leathered wings flexing naturally at his sides. Physically, he was not the same man who last served the Cedarfall Court. But his soul had not changed, deep down, it was still him.

I was glad for it, happy I finally recognised the truth.

"My life is yours," Erix said, clear and stoic.

Althea's brow softened, her hands tightening on the sides of her chair. "If you wish to continue your service to the Cedarfall crown, you will do as I ask of you, no questions."

"Anything," Erix replied, almost choking on the word. "Name what you need of me, and I will see it done until my last breath."

Althea looked over Erix's shoulder – directly at me. "You are to protect Robin Icethorn. Stay by his side, at all times, and keep him alive. He is *your* responsibility as his guard, that hasn't changed since my mother gave you that command, and it will not change now."

I felt every drop of blood inside of me cool. I dared not move a muscle as they both looked at me.

"Robin does not require me anymore," Erix replied, all without looking at me.

I was thankful he didn't glance back at me. If he had, my knees might have failed me completely. How I fisted my hands, his words cutting deep.

"He has Duncan Rackley to protect him now. Robin has his power–"

"And he will have you," Althea persisted. "If Robin is still determined in his desire to be the lamb sent to the slaughter, it will be with as much protection as I can offer at his back."

Even if I wanted to agree with Erix, I couldn't form the words.

"Althea is right," Duncan spoke for me. His sudden presence was beside me, a shadow over my shoulder. I was so focused on Althea and Erix that I hadn't noticed. "Erix, you have Robin's best interests at heart, as do I. If you refuse Althea's request, I may just never forgive you. He needs you, and I need you. You have proven your loyalty over and over, that is all I could ask for. So please, I know I'm in no position to ask you to do this, but I will get on my knees and beg if it comes to it."

I couldn't believe what I was hearing, or how Duncan's plea warmed my soul more than I was brave enough to understand in that moment.

Duncan took my hand in his and squeezed. His grip was soft yet firm. As his thumb began tracing small circles on the back of my hand, my thoughts calmed enough for me to say something.

"They're right, Erix," I added. "I need you."

Even the weakest of spring breezes could have toppled Erix over. We all watched as a wave of relief cascaded over him. He straightened, pushed back his shoulders and lifted his chin until he looked down the sharp arrow of his nose at me. "Then I will prove myself to you again."

I smiled honestly. "There is no need, you've already done that, as Duncan has said."

Althea stood from her throne abruptly. A black band gathered her mess of red curls into a bun and swept it off her sharp face. Still covered in muck, blood and other soils of war, she provided her final decree to the room. "Erix, Rafaela. Gather those who want to fight and get them dressed in the Hunters' clothes. Aunt, you have an hour to get as much Mariflora tonic as the Asps can supply. I want every person in this room to waste not a moment in preparing for our strike."

"I will see it done," Lady Kelsey said, pride burning in her eyes for her niece. "My queen."

Althea bristled but made no comment on how that could be an issue. "We must fortify our minds, or this will be over before it truly begins. Go, with haste, we should not waste a moment. Robin, Eroan, you can use this room to complete the final task you have to do."

The room was already emptying before she finished speaking.

"I will work as fast as I can," Eroan said, glancing toward the covered body laid out before him. "But understand that a glamour is a sensitive and delicate thing. It can be as weak as powder upon one's face or as strong as a mask. I will need time to ensure this works."

"Eroan," Althea replied softly. "Do your best with what time is given. You may just be the reason we save the realm."

I sensed determination swell within the slender frame of Eroan, he straightened, lifted his chin as cold eyes set with focus. "Then I will not let you down."

"One last chance, Robin," Althea said to me. I could hear my breathing as the room emptied. All but Althea, Gyah, Duncan and Eroan, who fussed around the sheet-covered body as Roan rolled his sleeves up to his elbows in preparation. "If you tell me you have changed your mind, we will find another way. It hardly sits well with me knowing that you are going to put yourself in this position, but I understand why you must be the one."

"And I will," I said firmly, trying to mirror the outward resolve that Althea exuded. "We all have a part to play. This is my plan; I understand the dangers. I cannot allow anyone else to do this."

Rafaela caught my eyes from across the room. There had been a change to our plan, but I hadn't shared that with anyone as a promise for her aid. Before, I was to give up the key before infiltrating Aldrick's lair. But if there was any time its power was useful, it was now. Rafaela had a contingency plan in case it all went wrong.

"I will be by your side, friend, every step of the way." Althea placed a hand on my shoulder, standing at my side, offering me a meek smile.

"Which is why I have the strength to even take the first step," I replied. "For you... for your family."

Althea pursed her lips and exhaled a long, taut breath out of her nose. She wrapped her arms around me and pulled me in close. As I inhaled, all I could smell was fire. It was both pleasant and unpleasant.

I didn't pull away.

"I'll miss this face." Althea's eyes trailed across every detail of my face. I sensed her drink me in with her gaze. "How long will it last?"

Her question was not for me, but for Eroan.

"It is reversible only by the one who crafts the glamour," Eroan answered. "As long as Robin comes back a victor, and I'm still breathing, it will be reversed."

"Then you better stay alive," Duncan added, casting a hateful look at the bundle of flesh hidden beneath the sheet. "You've just become the second most important man in my life."

Eroan couldn't hide his blush.

I hadn't allowed myself to dwell on the new addition to my original plan. It had always involved a glamour and infiltration. But the face I was to take had only become a recent addition to my ever-changing plot. In my mind, there was no other option. It was practically handed to me on a silver platter.

"Let us leave them to concentrate," Gyah announced, urging Althea toward the exit of the room with a firm hand. "It's frowned upon to interrupt the artist who works on their finest piece."

Eroan waited for the great doors to clang shut behind them before addressing me again. "I'm ready to begin when you are, Robin."

"Let's begin then," I replied, focusing entirely on the covered body, not prepared for what I'd see when the sheet was finally taken off.

"Are you sure?" Eroan persisted. "I ask only a final time."

"Not at all," I replied honestly, forcing a wavering smile. "But this is my only option."

"I'm here," Duncan said. "And I'm not going anywhere."

I wondered if he would feel the same way when this was done.

"I am going to stay, too," Erix said, voice as sharp as steel. "Little bird, you are not alone."

Altar. Hearing those words were all I needed.

"You are going to need to sit for this," Eroan said, edging his songful voice with command. "It's best you are as still as you can be, so please try your hardest for me."

I did as he asked, taking a seat in a chair provided.

Eroan rubbed his hands together. Then, with disgust drawn over his narrow face, he tugged at the white sheet covering the body and pulled it away. The material rippled onto the floor like water. Everything was silent as I took in the body laid out before him.

Until now, this idea had been a grand one. But looking at Kayne's lifeless body filled me with nothing but dreaded regret.

CHAPTER 29

My guttural howls of agony drowned out the encouragement Duncan provided me. I heard him beneath my breathy moans and tight-lipped gasps, but that didn't mean I listened. The more Eroan worked on me, the louder I became, until all of Wychwood likely heard my screams.

The process felt as though my bones shattered and my skin was being continuously split apart. I dared not open my eyes for fear I'd find my flesh melting over Eroan's hands as he brushed tender fingers over my face, like the paintbrush of an artist.

"Can you give him a moment?" Duncan snapped.

I squeezed his hand, barely registering the click of his fingers beneath my force. If it wasn't for the precautionary band of iron clasped around my wrist, there would've been nothing stopping my power from rising to protect me.

"No." I heard the fury embedded in Eroan's reply. He was breathless, as though he climbed the face of a mountain. "If I stop, there is no saying how disjointed the glamour will be. Please, allow me to... focus. Or leave until it is over."

"It's fine," I hissed through gritted teeth. "I'm fine."

Of course it was a lie, but Duncan couldn't refuse me.

Instead, Duncan leaned his forehead into my shoulder. I risked a peak and saw no blood, melted flesh or destruction. There was nothing to suggest I should've been in so much torture. Eroan's fingers were feather-light, but where he touched, it was as though he left ruin in his wake.

347

Gritting my teeth, I leaned into the pain and focused on the body before me. Kayne's head was turned slightly to face me. His wide eyes were all-seeing. His skin was an ashen grey. I expected him to blink or move. He didn't. Every now and then, Eroan would turn back to look at Kayne, pausing his work and studying the lines of his face and the details that one would only see up close. Freckles, old scars, the tone of hair and the length of eyelashes. Those moments of painless peace were short-lived. Eroan reached for me again, fingers prepared to mould my face into one that no longer looked like mine I focused on keeping my heart beating.

If I wanted to succeed, this had to work. The glamour was about to make me look like Kayne, to steal his face and use it as my own. Our key into the heart of Aldrick's base – close enough to kill him.

"It may have been many years since, but I remember when your father was sitting before me at your mother's request." Eroan's words distracted me as his thumb smoothed across each of my brows. I felt the hairs bristle and settle. If I'd seen my reflection, I would likely have watched as they changed from black to auburn. "It was never my place to question your mother at the time. She was my queen, I would've run to the ends of the earth for her. But for the years after, I pondered why she had wished for me to glamour a human Hunter. Of course, now I understand."

"He told me." I winced, not at the pain this time, but from the way the mention of my father and mother dredged up a mental discomfort. "He changed his appearance to hide from his past…"

"Having a glamour worked upon you is not a forgettable experience, as I am sure you understand."

I lifted my chin, guided by Eroan's vice-like grip. He studied me down the length of his nose, shifting my face from side to side before continuing again.

"Can you tell me more about them?" I asked, feeling pathetic to do so. "It might help distract me from–" I swallowed my words as a gasp burst out of me. Eroan forced his fingers into my temple, working my skin like soft bread dough. I felt as though my skull would split. "This fucking torture."

Eroan winced, but did as I asked without question. "I remember his face; the one Julianne commanded me to conceal. Your father was a handsome man. It was not impossible to imagine what had captured your mother's fascination. There is so much about you that looks like him, from your full lips and slender brows, just as your father's had been. I see your mother, too, more so if I am honest, which hurts me to conceal. She was a beauty others would go to war for. The kindest face, the sweetest soul."

I blinked and saw the emotion crack across Eroan's long, focused face. A bead of sweat rolled down his temple, mirroring his finger that fell from my own. "I... love hearing about her. Please, tell me more."

"Your cheekbones," Eroan continued, resting a gentle finger upon them. "They are sharp as the mountainous range north of our homeland. I remember when your mother was young, her cheekbones inspired poems from besotted men and women. In fact, if I dare spill her secrets, I remember one girl who particularly enjoyed cursing the apples of Julianne's cheeks red with kisses. She was a lady-in-waiting from Elmdew, and your mother was still a princess. Ever the scandal at the time."

My chest warmed as a smile bloomed over Eroan's face.

"By the sounds of it, you knew Robin's mother well?" Duncan asked from his perch beside me.

"Of course. Knowing her was one of the greatest honours of my life."

"What else?" I pleaded, grimacing at the unseen fire that devoured my skin.

"An Icethorn-born always had the darkest of eyes. Black as night. It was said that the Icethorns' eyes made even the rawest of obsidian jealous," Eroan replied. "Close yours for me now. I'm nearly finished."

I did as he asked, glad that the end was near. Eroan's hands covered my eyes and pressed down. It was no surprise as I cried out, the pressure was unbearable

Before I drowned in the strain, Duncan closed his lips to my ear and whispered. "Breathe, my darling. You've done so well."

By the time Eroan retreated, I was exhausted. I fell forward, leaning on my knees as I tried to catch my breath.

"Do you wish to see?" Eroan asked. He wiped his hands down his silken shirt, leaving damp stains upon the material. Once his palms were dry, he produced a small, clasped mirror from his pocket. It was no bigger than his hand and was golden, speckled with azure jewels.

I took it from him. My fingers shook slightly as though the weight was too much to bear. No matter how I convinced myself otherwise, I wasn't prepared to meet my reflection – not my reflection, but the face of Kayne staring back at me.

If I wasn't completely marvelled by Eroan's gift, I would've been sick at the sight.

"I shall begin working on the Tracker's body next," Eroan announced, sharing a glance at Duncan. "I know the face I will create well, so this glamour will not take me as long. Dare I admit I wish he could feel the discomfort I'm about to give him?"

"If it makes you feel any better," Duncan replied. "Kayne certainly felt a world of pain for what he has done."

Eroan exhaled heavily, his pink-stained lips quivering. He steeled his expression, flexed his fingers together and moved for the dead body without another word.

I didn't wish to look at Duncan for fear of what I would see as he took my unfamiliar face in. Now my wonder had faded to a simmer, I longed to lift my nails to my skin and scratch every detail off. Remove every detail that didn't belong to me.

"Don't look at me," I said, words fumbling out of my mouth.

"I'm going to look," Duncan whispered. "Do you know, it does not matter what you look like to me. I know the truth behind the lie. I know you."

Duncan encouraged me to lift the mirror again. His two fingers held the weight of it, lifting the glass surface into view. "I don't want to see it any more than I have to."

"Then look at me," Duncan urged. "Robin, look at me and nothing else."

My head didn't turn.

Duncan knew he wouldn't encourage me with words. Instead, he got on his knees before me and took both of my hands into his own. I studied his face as he fought to hide his reaction.

Instinctively, he grimaced, and that made me feel repulsed. Even he couldn't hide his reaction, no matter how his words tried to suggest otherwise. And I couldn't blame Duncan for his reaction. He currently faced the man he'd once believed to be his brother. A man who had betrayed us. A man Duncan had killed. The bruise marks around the real Kayne's neck revealed how he had perished. Yet Duncan had still not spoken a word about it.

"I'm sorry it ended the way it did," I said, drawing my hand down his cheek.

Duncan's eyes narrowed, and he rolled back his shoulders. "I'm not. I'm only sorry I didn't figure it out before. It would have saved a lot of pain. Friend or not, he hurt you before he revealed his true nature. That should've been enough. You are far more important than anything else, remember that."

"And now you are forced to stare into his face until this is over," I replied, smiling before realising who exactly smiled back at Duncan. Which was why his lips hardly so much as twitched.

"As I said earlier, you're no longer the *only* important person in my life," Duncan replied. "So is Eroan here. His survival is as important as yours. The moment we win, and we will, you are coming back here, and Eroan is going to pull every one of his threads apart until he returns you back to me."

"That I shall," Eroan answered, turning away from the table. He was finished with Kayne's face. "Stay safe, Robin Icethorn. I'm no king, but I say that as an order. I cannot give strength to the thought of losing you, when I have so many more stories just waiting to share about your mother."

"Then I will have to come back," I replied, standing from the chair with the aid of Duncan's offered hand. "When this is over, I could do with someone of your knowledge and loyalty in Icethorn to stand by my side."

Eroan's tired face lifted in a smile.

"It would be my honour. And, must I say, I am very much ready to return to Icethorn." Eroan bowed. "I've missed my home. Now, is there anything you need of me before I take my leave?"

"Only that you will need to pack a bag," I said, offering my thanks with a smile. I felt my adoration for him swell in my chest. "Your home awaits."

"Thank you." Eroan bowed deeply again, his voice muffled in thanks as his sobs finally overtook him. Without another word, he left, sweeping from the room on quick feet.

I stepped forward, pulling free from Duncan's hand, as my eyes fell back on Kayne's dead body. My knees wobbled, but I gripped the edge of the table to steady myself as I saw what was now upon it.

It was my face that rested among the white sheets. Not Kayne's. Dark, obsidian eyes. Locks of midnight hair fanned out around the head. Skin as pale as winter's first snow. The subtle point of ears that belonged to a fey, not a human.

"Uncanny," I breathed, reaching for the point of cheekbone that stretched the surrounding skin. It was cold to the touch, but real. The image of my face did not fade away or ripple like disturbed water to reveal the image beneath.

It stayed there, unwavering.

"And beautiful," Duncan added. "Although, seeing this is my greatest fear, brought to life."

He turned his back on the table, rather facing Kayne's face then seeing the death on mine, whereas I couldn't do anything but look. I marvelled at the face that I knew so well. I replayed Eroan's comments about my features and how similar they were to my deceased parents'. Hearing his words in my mind was enough to dilute the horror of looking at my face upon the dead body before me.

"You know, this might just work," I said, speaking my thoughts aloud, recognising hope swell in my chest. "I hardly dare admit it, but it might."

"All we need is a moment of distraction. A way of getting close enough to Aldrick to kill him, reclaim the keys and end this twisted desire for a demon god."

"Simple yet effective."

"That indeed, but you must remember one thing. Presenting Aldrick with what he believes to be *your* dead body is only going to anger him," Duncan reminded. "You are going to need to be ready for that."

My stomach flipped at the thought. I tore my attention from my face and looked back at Duncan, whose eyes beheld a clashing storm of concern.

"That is exactly the reaction I hope for," I muttered. "There is nothing more distracting than anger. I want Aldrick to feel it, to lose himself in it. I will be ready when he does."

Duncan narrowed his dark-forest eyes at me, and the corners of his lips turned upward slowly. "Careful, Robin, such promises of danger will excite me. I want nothing more than to turn all of this pain toward Aldrick, so he experiences what it feels like to lose."

As did I.

"Tell me it will work," I said, needing to hear someone else believe it was a possibility. "One more time."

"For our sakes, I hope so. But if anyone can do it," Duncan replied, keeping his focus on his boots this time, "you can. It is our only chance."

I looked away, worried he would see the dark thoughts pass in my mind. This wasn't our only chance; it was our *last* chance.

And I would make every moment count for the people I loved.

Duncan, Althea, Gyah and even Rafaela, all who'd paid the price to help me. But Erix, too… I would do it for him. And I would do it for me.

CHAPTER 30

The sun burned through the final smudges of ominous cloud. I looked up, and all I saw was endless blue.

There was no relief from the heat that warmed the Hunter's leathers I wore. I felt my skin prickle beneath, itching for the promise of fresh air. My entire body seemed to exude sweat. It took great effort not to run a hand through the ginger curls plastered to my sticky forehead.

My foot thumped the ground as we waited for Rafaela to return with the human teleporter. Our one ticket into Elmdew rested on the shoulders of the boy we'd kept prisoner for hours. And the longer we waited, the thinner my patience grew. I couldn't help but dwell on the time that we had wasted. It was mid-afternoon, hours after the teleporter had returned to Aurelia, and still we had not left for the spring court and the retribution that awaited there.

Perhaps I was frustrated because, with each passing moment, my confidence in my plan dwindled. If I waited long enough, I feared I'd give in to the niggling thought that it was better to give up.

I chewed on the insides of my cheeks, trying not to dwell on what was to come. Lucari chirped on my shoulder, iron claws digging into the padded leather. What I would have given to knock her away from me just to feel my power return, freeze her small body and break her just as Duncan had with Kayne.

I flinched every time she moved, expecting that she'd discover that I wasn't her loyal Tracker, but a sheep dressed in wolf fur. Lucari's lack of distrust gave me some hope. If I could trick the hawk, then Aldrick should never be the wiser. And with the Mariflora's sharp nectar currently threading itself through my body, and another vial of it hidden within the inner pocket of my jacket, Aldrick wouldn't have the chance to invade my mind and discover the truth behind this illusion before it was too late.

"I can feel your heartbeat in your hand," Duncan said, voice muffled by the helmet he wore. Across the front of it, a white-chalked handprint had been dried across the metal. The symbol of Aldrick, the Hand.

A symbol he once wore with pride, but now he could barely look at without grimacing.

My breath lodged in my throat as I looked at him. Even with his face mostly obscured by the Hunter's helmet, seeing him dressed in the dark brown leathers with a multitude of blades threaded among the straps that enhanced his broad structure reminded me of when I first met him.

"Just don't let go of me," I replied. It must have been strange for Duncan to hear my voice falling from Kayne's lips. He did well to hide his discomfort, but there was still a wariness to his glance. Since Eroan had altered my face into this image, Duncan hadn't got close enough to kiss me. Nor did I try, even though that's all I wanted. With what we were about to face, I longed to feel his reassuring mouth on mine. But in the same breath, I couldn't face the thought of him laying his lips on this face.

My lower stomach flipped as Duncan winked at me. If it wasn't for the helmet, I would have seen the scar upon his face tighten. "Never," he said, lowering his face slightly toward mine. "I'm here to stay."

I glanced back over at the group, searching, hoping the person I looked for had suddenly appeared.

Duncan read my mind, exposing my unspoken worry aloud. "Erix will come. He made a vow to you, and I trust him on it."

Excuses flooded to my mind. They all were conjured to throw Duncan off my trail of thought. I didn't like to imagine how Duncan might leave, knowing Erix occupied my mind. And it was pointless to lie. To tell him I was not looking for Erix would have been an unfaithful act.

"Will he, though?" I asked. I hadn't seen Erix since before the glamour was put on my face. It was as if he was evading me for reasons I wasn't brave enough to contemplate.

"I spoke with him, Robin. He has assured me he will come. Erix desires nothing more than to help. But there is something he must do first."

"And that would be?"

Duncan's thumb continued its circular dance across the back of my hand. It may not have been the affection I desired from him, but I willingly accepted the calming effect he offered.

"We need numbers. Erix believes he can add to them but needs time to–"

"Places!" Althea silenced Duncan as she called across our small band of fey. Like me, each one of them was dressed as a Hunter. It was our turn to dress as our enemies and trick the unexpecting. "Rafaela has the human boy."

I looked out toward the pathway that led back to Aurelia. Sure enough, Rafaela was there, walking side by side with the powered human.

The sun glowed across her skin, light catching in the pale hue of her wings. Rafaela's wings weren't folded away but were wide and proud at her back. The larger, grey-toned feathers trailed across the ground behind her. At her side limped the human. He was young and thin, no more a child than a man. His pockmarked skin and hairless face revealed his naivety. That, and the way his posture screamed with his lack of confidence.

I almost felt guilt for needing to use him. He was the enemy, and yet he was far from a threat the closer he got.

The human's eyes were trained on the ground as he strode in line with Rafaela toward us. He gripped his arm as though it were broken, rubbing it up and down to soothe himself. Fear wore off him in undulating waves.

"Why does he walk freely?" Gyah called, authority booming out toward Rafaela.

Panic surged through me as I took the boy in again. Gyah was right. He had no chains binding his wrists or tethering him to Rafaela. There was no evidence he wore iron to prevent him from using the powers that had been given to him. He could have teleported away already, warning Aldrick of what to expect.

"He is not our prisoner," Rafaela replied calmly, one hand on the hilt of the great hammer that balanced feather-light upon her hip. "I trust Daveed will not flee. Believe it or not, but he *wants* to help."

I had known that Rafaela had spent time with the Hunter. He was human, and she represented the physical form of the Creator. Never did I imagine she could sink her faith through his shield of disbelief. But, with the boy looking up at her with fiery awe, it was clear she had succeeded.

"I do," his small voice said. "This is my choice to help, not something imposed on me by that madman."

I actually believed him, felt his emotion in his reply.

Tension hummed throughout our group as they joined us. I realised quickly that Rafaela's open wings were more of a warning to us that she protected the boy. Her knuckles tightened on the handle of her weapon, the squeak of flesh against leather piercing the silence.

"Then I thank you for your support," I said, offering him a smile, trying everything to make it reach my eyes.

Daveed glanced timidly up at Rafaela, who was focused on Lucari perched on my shoulder. Her lips peeled back from the gleaming white of her teeth as she watched the murderous hawk with hungry intent. Rafaela had made it clear what she desired to do with the bird that tore Gabrial to shreds. She just hadn't been given the opportunity – *yet*.

"Tell them what you've shared with me, Daveed," Rafaela said sharply, speaking to Daveed all without taking her narrowed eyes from Lucari.

"I… I'm sorry. For all of it," Daveed croaked, his high voice cracking like stone. "I never wanted this, a lot of us hadn't."

"Be more precise. Help them understand *why* we can trust you."

Daveed took a deep breath in as his cheeks flared red. "The Hand is not giving us a choice. I never wanted this life, and I don't want it even now. He… makes us do as he wishes. I can hear him in my head every time he is close. Whispering for me to do things I… I…"

"Take your time," I said as Rafaela placed a hand on his shoulder. I watched the calming effect it had on him.

Daveed took another deep breath in and blinked to clear the haze of panic haunting his sky-blue eyes. A chill spread up my spine as I waited for the boy to continue. His bruised face was scrunched in turmoil as he faced unseen battles within his mind.

"How did he capture you in his web?" I asked, drawing his attention to me. "The promise of power, or the promise of a world in which you would thrive. Which one is the answer?"

Daveed grimaced as though my suggestive comment had physically struck him. "Neither. They took us from our homes. In the room of mirrors, he killed us with a blade of blood, but we did not die. He made me into this…" Monster. He didn't say it, but I knew that was what was coming. "Aldrick turned me and used me. I just… I just want to go home."

"You will go home as soon as this is over," Duncan promised, oozing a fatherly calm. He strode forward with the confidence that made others stand back. "I understand what has been done to you, for the same has happened to me. You are pulled on both sides. But if you help us as we ask, I vow to get you home myself."

"Daveed has a family," Rafaela added, wide-eyed. Those four words had as much power as the ice that crackled in my blood. We all knew the importance of a family. Some more than others. "Aldrick has threatened them if Daveed does not comply. By aiding us, he is proving himself in a measure that we cannot begin to understand."

Duncan nodded, lips pulled into a tight line as he regarded the Nephilim. "I will ensure that you return to your family, Daveed."

"No," Daveed barked. "The Hand promised... he said he would kill them if I ever went back."

"That will not happen," I added, feeling his panic slam into my chest. Rafaela wrapped her arm around the boy's quaking shoulders and held him close.

"Together." Duncan took my hand once again. "We will make sure Aldrick is never in a position to threaten anyone again, human or fey."

The young boy hardened his expression. He held Duncan's stare, searching for any reason he couldn't believe him. Then he bowed, satisfied there was nothing sinister to uncover. We all witnessed as Duncan's words fuelled Daveed with a confidence that was previously lacking.

Daveed squared his shoulders and puffed out his chest. "Make it hurt," he said. "When Aldrick faces his judgement, I want him to know how it feels to die."

"Aldrick will know pain unlike anything he could imagine," Althea added, sympathy hidden beneath her mask of fury. I saw it through a crack of emotion that lasted only a moment. "That is a promise."

We all felt the scolding heat in her words.

"How many of us can you take at one time?" Althea walked through the parted crowd, a helmet carried in the crook of her arm. A long blade tickled the ground at her side. Garbed in the leathers that fitted her slender, hard body, she looked all the warrior with a whip of red hair twisted into a braid across her shoulder.

"Three," Daveed replied, doing his best to hold her gaze. "Four, at a push."

"Three will be sufficient. I'd rather you did not burn out by trying to take too many. If that is what you can do without pushing yourself, then there is no good to come from depleting your energy." One wave of Althea's hand and the group of Cedarfall fey split into groups of that number. I recognised Lady Kelsey among them. There was no stopping her from joining our small army, she too thirsted for the same revenge as those she stood among.

"But Daveed, understand that if you betray us, it will not only be you that burns but the home Aldrick stole you from."

Daveed flinched at Althea's warning. Rafaela's wings folded slightly around him.

"I know you have no reason to trust me," Daveed said firmly. "But I promise… I promise you safe passage into Elmdew."

Althea watched him for a moment, then stood back. "Then we are at an understanding. As soon as you deliver us safely into Elmdew's borders, I want you to get out of there. Return here and my people will protect you. Aldrick will kill you first if he knows you are the one dropping enemies behind his lines."

"You must take us directly to Aldrick," I said, trying to cool my tone. "It is important that he doesn't suspect anything."

Daveed buzzed on the spot, wringing small hands before him.

"No harm will come to you," Duncan reassured him. He reached into his pocket and withdrew the spare vial of Mariflora tonic. "Aldrick's attention may be diverted when we deliver the false body to him. However, that is not to say he will not have the chance to invade your mind. Take this, it will keep him out."

"Duncan, no." I longed to reach out and snatch the vial from his hand. "There isn't any more to replace this."

"I cannot and will not allow Daveed to risk himself on our behalf. The tonic is for him."

"But…" *But what?* I couldn't tell Duncan he was wrong, because he wasn't. Daveed was a child, and he needed the protection more than anything. But that didn't stop my internal panic, however, I could control how I acted in the face of it. "There is no knowing how long the tonic you've taken will last. What if it fades, and you need another dose?"

"Aldrick will be dead long before the tonic I've taken fades," Duncan replied. "Because you are going to finish this. Swift, just like we agreed. In and out."

"In and out," I repeated, trying to convince myself that it would be just that easy.

Daveed's hand shook as he plucked the vial from Duncan's thick fingers. He popped the cork, the sound vibrated through my bones. I watched the vial empty as Daveed knocked it back. The small, protruding lump within his throat bobbed as he downed it in one.

The glass smashed on the cobbled path at his feet. "I'm ready."

"Then let us not waste any more time," Althea clapped, commanding us all into action. "Daveed, the next part is up to you. Get us into the nest, so we can burn it from the inside out."

His smile was sinister, matching the thoughts coiling within me. "With pleasure."

It was hard to breathe as we waited for Daveed to return. Each length of time between his teleportation grew longer. When he finally would return, he looked more exhausted than when he left. His face had paled to a deathly white, while his eyes were ringed with a dark crimson.

There was no warning before the air crackled, split and popped into a bundle of unfurling light as the human boy revealed himself. Each time, although I burned holes into the ground he would materialise back to, the shock of his return didn't dilute. Perhaps it was more relief that he returned rather than surprise at his sudden appearance.

Althea and Gyah had been among the first group Daveed took. I'd made one final plea to Althea and Gyah before they left. *Don't come for me until you find them.* Save Jesibel and the other fey he has imprisoned. Leave Aldrick to me.

I hoped they listened.

Unlike my pending destination, Daveed delivered the small, disguised army to another place within Elmdew. From what Daveed had revealed, the capital city, Rinholm, had become the heart of Aldrick's efforts. The dead king's castle was being used as his base of attack, so that was where we would go.

I wasn't stupid though. There was no knowing Daveed hadn't delivered the rest of them to Aldrick. With the deception that I'd grown accustomed to, it was easier to distrust the boy. My conscience reacted naturally to that emotion. Each time the air split, and he stepped through the spindle of light, my concerns only grew.

But Duncan trusted him, so did Rafaela. I had to lay faith into that for now – until I was proven otherwise.

Rafaela was the last to be taken to Rinholm. A heavy, black, woollen cloak was draped over her shoulders, barely concealing her wings. Her presence demanded attention whether they were hidden or not. No garment would conceal her for long. One look from the wrong person, and they would see the tips of grey feathers or the awkward bulge of a golden hammer protruding from the cloak like a bone out of skin. Which was why Daveed would drop her off far from Rinholm Castle. She would wait for our agreed sign before revealing herself.

"It is my life's purpose to worry about you," Rafaela had said before she departed. Part of me wondered if she spoke so slowly to give Daveed time to recover from his last jump. It was a term he had used when describing how his newfound power worked. He could only travel to a place he had physically visited before. "Do not concern yourself with me, Robin. I shall be fine."

I knew she was still displeased I'd not given her Altar's key that lingered within me, but even she knew we'd need that power.

"Until we are all reunited, I'm afraid the worrying will persist," I replied, taking her hand in mine. Our grip on one another was strong. We stepped in close, connected as one.

"This is only the beginning. The first hurdle of many more to come. Stopping Aldrick will not undo the damage he has inflicted on the realms. He is merely a wall through which we must travel to get to the next. Remember, he is only one weak old man. We only give evil strength if we hold on to the fear of it… so be strong."

Rafaela's words occupied me whilst Daveed split the air and beckoned her through. It left Duncan and me alone. Except we didn't utter a word to one another. There was comfort in just having him by my side. Even if he said something, I don't think I would have heard it over the roaring in my ears.

Not long after, Daveed returned. Duncan had to catch him as he stumbled out of his spindle of light.

"You've done well, Daveed, careful now. One last trip to go." Duncan offered his praise as he righted the human boy before turning his attention to the sheet-bound body at his feet. Until now, it had lain across the ground, hardly more than an afterthought.

Kayne's limp body collapsed over Duncan's shoulder. If this was another time, under different circumstances, I might have admired his unearthly strength. But I couldn't spare much attention to the dead body nor the visible pain that sliced across Duncan's dark gaze.

"Once you take us to Rinholm, I want you to *jump* as far away as you can," I said, focusing on the panting human who could hardly stand up without burdening his weight on his thighs.

Daveed blinked slowly, eyes heavy and mouth drawn thin with tiredness. "If I can manage it."

"For your sake, I hope you can," Duncan grunted as he balanced himself with the added weight of the dead he carried. "Let's go."

"Wait," I snapped, and they both stopped to regard me.

"What is it?" Duncan drew his eyes up and down me.

"Erix isn't coming, is he?" I asked, wishing I had the strength to not let his abandonment hurt me.

Duncan's silence spoke volumes. If it wasn't for the helmet covering his expression, I was confident I would've seen him wince. "No. Erix isn't coming, Robin. I'm sorry."

Shock lanced through me, a frigid wind of destructive power. I stared at his dark-green eyes through the slits of metal. "You knew all along?"

There was a pause. "I did."

My nails bit into my palms, but I hardly registered the feeling. "Why didn't you just tell me."

Duncan swallowed, resolve masking his emotion. "Because you didn't need the distraction."

"Then Erix is no longer a man of his word," I said, fighting the words out past the lump suddenly in my throat. "I should have known. You heard what Althea commanded of him. He should be here; he is meant to protect me. It's his duty, and his pleasure and…"

Duncan wrapped his arms around me, drawing me close. His kiss worked into my crown, warming my body with a wave of pleasant shivers. "Erix hasn't turned his back on you yet."

A part of me wanted to cry into Duncan's chest, but something stopped me. "It doesn't matter. Daveed, take us."

"Erix will–"

"I don't wish to discuss him anymore. Enough of my energy has been wasted on trusting people who never deserved it in the first place. Erix, Kayne. They don't differ from one another."

Duncan reached out for me. I sensed his want to say something, but I pulled out of his reach.

"Daveed, do it," I command. "We leave now."

I saw the human boy hesitate out of the corner of my eye. I caught how he looked at Duncan as though searching for a command.

"Now!" I felt my power rise to the emotion I felt. Lucari chirped, digging her iron claws into me, my magic dispersed before it even had the chance to show itself. "*Please.*"

I gathered the storm of dark emotions and took it in my hands. There would be a time soon enough when I would release it. Like a rabid beast chained and baited with bloodied meat, I dangled the promise of vengeance before me. It was Aldrick who hung on the hook.

As Daveed thrust his hand downward, peeling the air in two and drawing it apart like curtains with the arrival of dawn, I walked past Duncan. He watched me like the hawk perched on my shoulder.

"Enough men have lied to me, Duncan. Please think again before you consider joining the list of their names," I warned.

"Please, Robin. I don't want to go like this."

I grimaced at the sad edge to his deep voice. It would have been easy to turn back to him and give in. Instead, I forced my feet forward, closing into the spindle of shimmering light. "I don't wish to discuss this anymore, I need to focus, just as you said."

"Robin!" Duncan tried a final time.

"My name is Kayne," I barked, recoiling at my hateful tone. Duncan didn't respond.

I felt all the parts of the man I had to play slot into place. There was no time for remorse. No time to dwell as Duncan's heavy steps sounded behind me. There was only Daveed and his power, and the man I was prepared to kill on the other side of it.

CHAPTER 31

The air was crisp with the sweet floral scent of flowers. From the moment we slipped out of Daveed's spindle, it was as though a wall of fragrance slammed into me, ridding the stench of burning bodies and ruin from my nose with one inhale.

I inhaled deeply, unable to stop the pleasant smell invading my nose and spreading its presence down the back of my throat. I swallowed hard, trying not to cough on the pungent aromas.

Daveed fell to his knees upon a bed of daffodils the colour of freshly churned butter. Their green stems snapped beneath his weight; his fingers smeared with pollen as he dug them into the ground to catch his breath. "I'm sorry – I'm so tired."

Panic gripped me as I surveyed our destination. Aldrick wasn't in sight. In fact, no one was.

"You can do it," I hissed, scanning the surrounding area for threats besides the tangling of tall, stemmed flowers around my ankles. "Come on, we are so close. I told you to take us to Aldrick, it's important we–"

"I... I can't." Daveed's back arched as he spluttered his excuse to the ground.

"Robin, give the boy a moment." I cringed at the ice in Duncan's tone, then at the memory of my own.

"We don't have a moment," I snapped at him, wide-eyed. "He was supposed to take us to Aldrick. Does this look like we are in..."

"The gardens." The young boy muttered, breathless and meek. I choked on my reaction as I saw smudges of blood leaking from his ears. "These are the gardens set at the back of Rinholm Castle."

I threw my gaze across the expansive view around me. Much like the sea of daffodils that Daveed currently lay among, there were other patches of colour spread across the flat landscape. Towering crimson tulips bowed in the slight breeze. Lilac hyacinths swelled among one another like bunches of ripe grapes ready for the picking. Ahead, I could see stone walls that had been built into a partition of arches. Vines draping with colour pulled at the ancient bricks, leaving little of the natural stone behind the vivid green and dew-wet flowers.

"Then we are close *enough*." I scanned the garden, knowing deep in my gut this was not the destination we needed. But I couldn't take out my panic on the young human, not after everything he'd done for us.

I forced a smile, letting my frustration simmer deep inside of me.

Daveed lifted his face and stared directly through me. His skin was almost grey, his wide eyes rimmed with red, irritated veins. "I'm sorry, but I can't do it anymore."

I laid a hand on his shoulder, softening my expression. "You've done excellently, Daveed."

Duncan spoke too in a voice laced with understanding. "Rest now. When you get your strength back, I want you to return to Aurelia. The fey waiting there will keep you safe. Can you do that?"

Relief smoothed all the turmoil from Daveed's face. He gritted his teeth as his arms shook to keep him from falling face-first into the bed of flowers. "If you want to reach the Hand, you'll need to walk north from this point." Daveed's worn gaze travelled in the direction he spoke of. "You will hear Rinholm before you see it. Aldrick is in the old king's throne room. In his room of mirrors."

"Room of mirrors?" I asked, cringing at the thought of seeing my reflection again, or what lurked beyond it.

Daveed nodded, lifting fingers and wetting them on the blood at the side of his face. "He never leaves it."

"Then that is where we will go," Duncan said, looking north, a determined scowl set into his brow. With a great heave, he shrugged Kayne's body over his shoulder into a better position before looking in the direction Daveed had spoken of. "You've done well, Daveed. Be safe."

The human boy looked at me, and the softness dissolved into something harder. Perhaps he waited for me to add my thanks. "Your name will be celebrated when this is over," I said.

Daveed's lips twitched into a smile. "I'm only glad I was given the grace to allow myself to choose the right side of history."

I knew he referred to the other Hunters who never got the chance. Those we'd killed during our rampage through Aurelia. I swallowed the tang of regret, my nose tickling as pollen invaded it. With each swallow, I felt the sticky residue cling to the back of my throat with defiance. Spring was beautiful for many, but not for me.

"By sundown, Aldrick's poison will no longer threaten another life again. Yours, your family's or my family's." My heart hammered in my chest, threatening to break free. "Rest now, just as Duncan said. Then return to the fey. Thank you, Daveed, for everything."

Lucari chirped, perhaps sensing my discomfort. I tugged on the leather band tied around her claw, which I'd gripped around my fist like a leash.

"Good luck," Daveed called out, voice cracking with youth.

"You, too," I replied, walking ahead, carelessly stamping over unnamed flowers, which bled across the dark leather of my boots. Duncan kept up the pace behind me, his silence propelling me forward.

* * *

Daveed was right; I heard Rinholm before I saw it. As I traversed the sprawling glades of flowers, each neatly arranged and separated into patchwork sections throughout the garden, I caught the rumble of thunder. At least, that was the only thing to explain it. Except, there wasn't a single cloud in the bright sky, nor was the sound Duncan's conjuring.

I slowed to a stop. Duncan joined me at my side, his arm brushing mine only slightly.

"Is that...?" he asked, voice buried beneath another explosion of sound.

We both looked up to the pale skies around Rinholm's crown. My mouth dried as horror washed over me. "It is."

The three monstrous Draeic circled Rinholm like birds enclosing prey. Tension snapped at the leather cord as Lucari attempted to take flight. Her small wings were powerful enough to cause me to wrestle against her.

"At least there is no doubt Aldrick is inside," Duncan said, tightening his hold on the corpse across his shoulder. "We're close."

My power rose as I watched the creatures twist through the sky in a never-ending loop. Something drew them to Rinholm, and deep down, I sensed it, too. A pulling influence that I didn't wish to pay attention to. Reminiscent of when I left Icethorn and recognised its siren call. This feeling was similar but much quieter. Less like the pounding of a drum in my chest than the soft, lulling whisper-like waves lapping against my soul.

"We should've expected nothing less," I said, biting down the fear I felt for the Draeic's presence. "Let's continue. We don't know how long the Mariflora will last, and since you gave up your final dose, it's better we end this before you put our efforts at risk."

Duncan flinched, recoiling from my words as a sour expression pinched his face. I sensed he wished to say something back. Part of me wanted him to. Whatever retaliation was promised by his parted lips soon dispersed, and he took up walking ahead of me the final distance to Rinholm's boundary.

That would've been the moment to tell me not to worry, but even Duncan knew those words would be wasted. I should be worried – for him, for me and for our plan. His act, although valiant, didn't matter, considering Daveed never made it into Rinholm castle. Now, that choice left us vulnerable.

The castle was smaller than I expected.

It was less a behemoth of stone like Imeria, and more a modest manor set in the heart of acres of fields. The castle wasn't surrounded by a city like Aurelia, either, or embedded into the mountain face like the ruins of mine. It was nestled away from civilians and would've once been a place that encouraged peace among its visitors.

As we stepped beneath the hulking shadows cast down from the Draeic that flew high above us, I couldn't help but recognise that peace was far behind us.

I straightened my back as the hive of Hunters revealed themselves beyond Rinholm's main entrance. The metal gate towered skyward, its design reminiscent of vines and flowers in full bloom. At its top, the vines developed sharp-pointed thorns. I imagined it kept anyone from climbing over because the design continued as far as I could see on either side.

Like the plump, coin-sized bees that danced among the hedge of drooping snowdrops, the Hunters spread themselves out as we took our final steps toward the castle's gate.

"Lost?" a grizzly voice asked.

I felt the weight of his dark eyes as he looked from me to Duncan and then to the pointed-ear body flung across his shoulder.

"The Hand has been expecting our presence," I spoke out, forcing as much of Kayne's confidence as I could by deepening my voice and keeping the trembling at bay. I wasn't scared of the Hunters. No, I was fearful of what I would do to each of them if I lost control. Thank Altar for Lucari's iron claws, as they kept my power at bay.

I looked at each one of them, memorising their faces. As their eyes fell on the illusion of the fey body that Duncan carried, I recognised the boiling tempest of hate inside of them. Oh, how I wished to give them something to justify such an emotion. But I *had* to wait. Their time would come once Aldrick was dealt with.

It was a fleeting thought, but I wondered how many of these women and men had been forced into this position, like Daveed.

I ground my teeth together as the man released a barking laugh. It was soon silenced as Duncan discarded Kayne's body to the ground with a careless thump. Even with the gate between us, the Hunter jolted back. My face looked blindly toward the skies with glass eyes and lips stained blue with death.

"Going to take more than a corpse to let you in 'ere."

"Then you be the one to tell the Hand we have delivered the Icethorn key to him, and you won't move out of the fucking way." This fury was the easiest to call up. "I'm sure he'll praise you greatly for keeping his bounty from him."

I was certain I saw fear in the Hunter's face as he looked down at the body again. "Is he that the Icethorn boy... dead?"

I didn't know what pissed me off more. Being referred to as a boy, or dead.

"Stone cold," Duncan growled, asserting each word with the attitude he once imbued as Aldrick's general. "Hence the delay in our arrival, the scum put up some resistance."

Panic overcame the guards as they worked out the issue at hand. "Has he bled?"

The question would have been strange, but knowing that Aldrick bled his victims left little room for hesitation as I replied.

"Not a scratch." I blinked and saw Queen Lyra strung up by thick rope around her neck with gashes across her wrists like jewellery crafted from rubies.

I wondered if Duncan recognised the relief across the Hunter's face. I noticed it. Then, without another word, the gates opened. Duncan stepped over the glamoured corpse without sparing it another glance.

I followed, keeping my chin raised. "Someone pick it up and follow."

They scrambled like a pack of wild dogs for the chance to be the one to deliver such a bounty to their master. It took three of them to carry it inside Rinholm, each Hunter wanting a piece of our success.

"Where is the teleporter lad?" another Hunter asked as we entered the cool shadows of Rinholm's main atrium. I didn't need to press him further to know he spoke of Daveed. "He left hours ago–"

I kept my gaze forward, focused on the back of Duncan's head. "That pathetic excuse of a Hunter? Was it you who sent such a tired, weak boy to collect us from Cedarfall? He could hardly stand when he returned to us. *Pathetic.*"

"If you've got a problem, bring it up with the Hand. I'm sure he would love to hear you moan," the Hunter replied, smiling in jest as he looked at Duncan.

"We shall do just that," Duncan replied. The heat in his voice had the Hunter swallowing back his laugh. Even he sensed Duncan's authority as though it oozed from his very skin.

He was playing his part well – an act he was well rehearsed in.

I felt the urge to smile. Not because I cared if the Hunter believed us, instead it was the tickling presence that spread throughout my skull. The further we paced into Rinholm, turning down its long corridors and passing through the barren, silent rooms, the more the feeling intensified.

Aldrick. He reached out for my mind, looking to unveil our secrets before we reached him. But, unlike before, his presence was only a brush of a feather. I could picture the tendrils of fingers prodding and poking, but this time I was in control. In fact, it was an almost pleasant feeling. The Mariflora worked, just as the Asps promised. It kept my mind as my own, allowing Aldrick to only grace it as a visitor, rather than invade it completely.

Duncan turned his head slightly. Through the slit in his helmet, I saw his eyes grace me. He felt Aldrick, too.

"I would've expected Rinholm to be a fortress," Duncan said, speaking on something I hadn't noticed yet. "Where are the rest of our numbers?"

He was right. Rinholm was empty. The further we walked, the more I expected to see walls of Hunters, but there was barely a soul in sight.

"Is that bitterness I sense? Are you pissed that you've not been trusted as one of his chosen?" the Hunter retorted with a snort. "Maybe the delivery of the Icethorn boy will put you in his good graces, and you'll be given a new purpose – initiate."

"That would be an honour," Duncan replied.

"What if Rinholm is attacked?" I asked. "Shouldn't the Hand be more protected in case of a fey invasion?"

"Have you not seen the fucking monsters the Hand has collected?" Although his tone dripped with sarcasm, the Hunter looked at us like we were stupid. "The Draeic protect him. The only fey that grace these halls are dead ones."

My blood chilled to ice. I tightened my hands to fists, the leather gloves squeaking beneath the force.

"I thought he would've kept the fey close, considering he needs their blood to give us power," I said, mind whirling quickly to come up with something to say without prying too obviously. "He promised me magic if I brought Robin… the Icethorn key to him. Doesn't he need the blood of the fey to give it to me?"

"The Hand gives us all the opportunity to be changed," the Hunter replied as the group ahead slowed before two closed doors. They were made from carved wood, depicting all different types and shapes of wood-toned flowers. Much like the main gate we'd entered through, it was clear the decoration continued inside the castle. Even the muddied, worn carpet we trod across had peonies woven in shades of blue, pink and purple. "Don't worry, the Hand keeps his prisoners elsewhere, but close enough."

If the missing and captured fey weren't in Rinholm, then Althea and the rest of them had been brought here for no reason.

I'd put them in more danger. We had plans to stop Aldrick, whilst they found Jesibel and the other fey and got them to safety.

There was no time to dwell on the panic as the doors before us creaked open. Sudden light blinded me from within the room ahead. I lifted a hand to my brow just to shade my eyes from the sudden burst of it.

"Enter," a meek voice croaked through the glare. *"Enter."*

The second command filled my mind. It was strong and forceful, but it did little to move my legs. My will was my own. If it wasn't for Duncan, who stepped forward, I would've likely stayed rooted to the spot, revealing that Aldrick's magic didn't work on me.

"Master," Duncan's voice carried, sharpening my senses. "We have arrived, as promised."

The Hunters who carried Kayne's glamoured body entered the room first. Their rushed footsteps echoed across the smooth stone floor like the pattering of rain. I forced my chin up as I followed them. Duncan hung back until I was at his side. It took great restraint not to reach out and clasp his hand.

Lucari screeched with glee and launched herself into the air. I let go of the leash and allowed her to be free, glad for the itching of magic that quickly returned. I watched as she glided toward Aldrick at the far end of the grand room. From the folds of heavy woollen blankets rested across his lap, he lifted an aged, thin arm which shook violently as he welcomed the hawk.

I heard his broken, gravelly voice greet the hawk, fussing over her. But their reunion mattered little as I cast my attention around the room. Drinking in my surroundings was important to what was to come.

A room of mirrors. Daveed had said it, but I'd never imagined such a place until seeing it with my own eyes. Every wall and even the ceiling had been covered with mirrors. All different shapes, designs and sizes fit together like a puzzle until little of the original stone was left visible. I tried not to stare at my reflection as I paced toward Aldrick. I was faced with hundreds of Kayne's faces reflecting back at me from all sides, the mirrors revealing every inch of my stoic expression, one that didn't belong to me.

"He returns to me, my most trusted warrior. How I have looked forward to seeing you. My son found his way back to me and comes bearing the greatest gift of all."

I stopped just shy of the throne and bowed until I faced the floor. "Master, we're sorry for the delay. Turned out the fey weren't too happy with my deception."

"I imagined as much," Aldrick said, taking in a rasping breath. His throat clicked as though it was filled with sharp stones. "It is I who should bow to you, Kayne. But alas, my body is not as forgiving as yours."

By the time I straightened, Aldrick was frowning at the dead body carried in the Hunters' arms.

"I would have liked to have been there to watch the life drain from that boy's body." Aldrick stopped talking aloud. Instead, he forced his piercing will into my head. As before, when he spoke with his mind, the voice brimmed with clarity and boomed with youthful strength. The far opposite of how his physical form portrayed itself.

"*At least I will be present as his blood drains until he is left as nothing more than a husk, with not a drop to spare.*"

"I will also enjoy watching that," I said. "Very much so."

Aldrick was swaddled within a cocoon of blankets. They pooled around the throne he sat upon, shrinking him into a weak image of the man I'd last seen. Wrinkled skin hung from his bone-sharp face like sun-dried scraps of leather. His eyes were glassy and distant as he looked at me. Across the little skin that he didn't hide beneath his coverings, I recognised the faint lines of scars. Marks that hadn't been there before. Likely gifts left from when Seraphine pushed the gilded mirror atop him during our escape from Lockinge all those weeks ago.

"One of many rewards I will grant you," Aldrick said through a scowl that deepened the many wrinkles marring his face.

I dug my teeth into the inside of my lip until I could taste blood. Duncan shuffled nervously behind me, likely sensing as Aldrick forced his presence back through our minds. I wondered what the Mariflora would show him. Whatever it was, he withdrew briskly and showed no signs of distrust toward us.

"Are you well?" Aldrick rasped. "I sense a sombre mood that follows you."

"I'm sorry," I said, forcing my voice to sound like anything but my own. Eroan's glamour didn't run that deep. "I mean you no disrespect. I suppose locating the right words proves difficult when faced by you. After all this time, I never thought I would have made it back."

"I never doubted you," Aldrick replied. "Without your efforts, I would never have made it out of Lockinge." My mind sang with his forced entry. "*You have been there every step of the way to ensure we are not stopped. I understand the weight of a lie, and you have been buried by them.*"

It stung, even now, to know how deep Kayne's deception had rooted, and for how long. "I did what I had to."

"That you did, and with the return of Duwar, you will be a general of the highest order. It is your reward for your persisting loyalty."

Lucari eyed me from her perch on Aldrick's arm. Her talons pierced his flesh but didn't draw blood. Aldrick didn't care or seem to notice.

"Come, kneel before me, let me see you for the saviour you are."

I stepped in closer, feigning admiration, whilst I prepared myself to finish him. There was nothing stopping me from killing him, no Hunter stepped in my way.

The few Hunters who had come into the room couldn't stop me or my power. I sensed Duncan's energy as though it buzzed around my ears. Part of me wondered if it was my imagination or if his own electrifying power leaked into the room's atmosphere.

"*Wait,*" his inner voice cut sharp. I snapped my body, forcing myself to stop before I revealed that he had no sway over me.

I couldn't help but feel like he was testing me, or playing with me like food on a plate.

"Yes, Master?"

"I wish to show you something," Aldrick announced. "Would you entertain an old man?"

I kept rigid at the stop. "I couldn't refuse you." At least until he gave me the command, then I'd use it and act.

"*No, you could not.*" There was no denying the force to his magic, as though he willed to bend me to his command. I had to pretend it had that effect, otherwise, he would catch me out before I had the chance to strike.

"Bring the Icethorn's body," Aldrick spoke to the Hunters carrying Kayne. "Let us show our guests what their efforts have aided in."

Lucari shot away from Aldrick but didn't return to me. In fact, she flew in circles around the room just to stay away. I waited for Aldrick to notice, but he was focused on the sudden appearance of more Hunters who moved, emotionless, to the back of the throne and pushed it. To my surprise, it moved. Wooden wheels screeched across the slabs as Aldrick was wheeled toward me. I hardly moved out of the way before one wheel ran straight over my foot.

He really was physically weak. A hint of the man I'd faced before, no threat besides his ideals and magic. Both of which I was firmly protected from.

"I don't much like surprises," I said, the words tumbling out of me. "Take Robin as proof of that."

Duncan inhaled sharply.

Aldrick raised a shaking hand, flecked with liver spots. Those pushing his wheeled throne stopped. He was now at my side, between Duncan and me. From his perch among the mounds of blankets, he glared directly into my eyes.

I refused to look away. He was so close that I couldn't breathe without inhaling the stale stench. If I reached out my hand and touched his thin skin, I would've allowed my ice to devour him.

I lifted my hand slowly. Duncan moved, but I couldn't care why. Not as I focused on Aldrick, who watched me expectantly.

"The gate should be no surprise to you," Aldrick said, so suddenly I almost stumbled back.

Gate? I couldn't let the surprise show on my face, but Altar knows it raced within me. But Rafaela had shown me the gate was on Irobel, protected by her people. "Oh, of course. I would like to see it."

"Then come, see what I have forged whilst you have been collecting the third piece of my puzzle."

My legs betrayed me. I couldn't dare so much as lift my eyes from the spot on the floor where Aldrick had only just been.

"Perhaps I will allow you to be the one to pierce the Icethorn's flesh. We will watch as the third key is bound, and my gate weakens with its addition."

"And it works, this gate of yours?" I asked as dread sliced its fingers down my spine. I couldn't control the bite of panic that coated each word like thick honey.

"The Draeic are drawn to it for a reason. It calls to them like a beacon," Aldrick replied, wheels screeching in chorus with his tired voice. "Their presence here alone confirms our victory is closer than ever before."

I locked eyes with Duncan. He'd pulled the helmet from his face, revealing moon-wide eyes that reflected the same horror that turned my limbs to stone.

"End this," Duncan mouthed to me, but Aldrick was already back in my mind, forcing his will. *"With haste, follow me."* Like the puppet I was to play, I moved toward him before he had the chance to see that I hadn't followed.

I caught something in my peripheral. Movement in the mirrors behind Duncan. My knees almost gave out as the figure of brimstone, fire and shadow stepped forward.

Duwar. It was here. Duncan noticed my change in expression. I saw it in the rise of his dark brows and the softening of his eyes. Panic surged through me as I felt the demon god boring through my soul with its fiery stare. Before my knees gave way, I snapped my attention back to Aldrick.

He had his head turned slightly, regarding me through a side-eye. I sucked in a breath, hissing through gritted teeth.

"Kayne, the creation of our gate is a success. Because of you, because of the information you have shared, Duwar shall be freed and the world will be ours to claim."

CHAPTER 32

We'd been deceived from the moment we arrived.

Rinholm wasn't empty of Hunters as we had been made to believe. Because, as we followed Aldrick through the castle, the hallways and rooms became thick with bodies. The stench of stale, sticky skin infected the air, successfully burying the sweet kiss of spring.

They were like statues. Unmoving and frozen, guarding the inner castle like a forest of waiting soldiers.

Duncan kept close to me. Even if I wished to reach out, I dared not. I could have brushed my fingers across his waiting body behind me, but any connection could've given us away. His solid presence was a shield at my back, and I was thankful for it. With the countless eyes following our every move, I couldn't do anything but keep my gaze set on the back of Aldrick's thinly silver-haired head as his presence parted the walls of Hunters like a rock did to a river.

"Pardon the audience," Aldrick said, turning his face slightly until I glimpsed his hooked nose and drooping chin. "My creation requires the best of our numbers to protect it. Each man and woman has been hand-picked and would sacrifice themselves willingly to ensure the gate is safe from those who would wish to see it destroyed."

This is what he was doing. Protecting the one thing that really could destroy the world as we knew it. Not the gate on Irobel, but here, in Wychwood – made by the madman himself.

"And you trust them all?" I asked, eyeing the stoic and still bodies.

A shiver coursed up my arm as a smile twisted Aldrick's face. "I have peered through every thought and every memory that occupies their minds. There's not a shadow that I have not infiltrated. Each of these brave humans has laid themselves bare for me. I trust them all, not because they have earned it, but because I have judged them and found them worthy."

"Does that answer your inquiry?"

"Yes," I replied aloud. If Aldrick heard the frozen sharpness of my voice, he didn't react to it. "It does indeed."

We finished our short journey in silence. I took the time to map out our surroundings, or the little I could see through the haze of Hunters standing around us. All I could do was memorise the turns. Keeping a trail clear in my mind for a way back... if that was ever an option. The second I killed Aldrick, we would have a wave of Hunters ready to fight for him. I was suddenly thankful for the proximity of our friends, even if I didn't know where they were. When the time came, I would need them close.

The castle walls receded, giving way to an open garden brimming with light. If there had been doors to exit through, they had been long removed. From the jagged walls, it seemed something had torn them free with force.

The garden beyond revealed itself slowly the further I followed Aldrick into it. I couldn't see much through the multitude of bodies, but I could hear everything. As I stepped out into the cooler air, I ducked with a gasp as the Draeic made their presence known. It was above this place that they flew in their endless circle, chasing one another's tails in a circle of dark, scaled flesh.

"Only Duwar's enemies should dread his hounds. Creations born of chaos power that even I cannot comprehend." Aldrick pierced through my mind, searching for something, I was sure of it. *"You are his champion, Kayne. You have nothing to fear from them."*

Aldrick saw the fright in my mind, an emotion even I couldn't hide. But it wasn't only the monster's presence that scared me.

The faint pulling that I'd felt when we first arrived had returned. Perhaps it never disappeared, but I simply grew used to its call. Now, stepping free into the open garden within the heart of Rinholm Castle, it spiked with intensity.

Like the Draeic, the gate they flew above called to me, for I was its key.

Four mounds of dark stone speared through the earth and reached up to the heavens. Labradorite. Altar's bones. Even from a distance, I could understand their sheer height and size. Decay spread beneath them. Like blood pooling from the body of a victim, the stones drew the life from the grass bed, turning it brown and wilting flora until they were unrecognisable.

I blinked and saw Gabrial's vision. It was as if this scene had been plucked directly from it and recreated before me. She'd shown me the gate the Nephilim had protected in Irobel, but here one waited before me. Different in location, but the details were all the same.

But how? Aldrick said this success was down to Kayne, but Kayne had never seen this vision, and nor did I share it with him.

More questions overlapped others, and I knew I was missing something in the path to Aldrick's success.

Hunters pushed Aldrick's chair, wheeling directly through the circle the stones created. Whispers of silver-grey mist twisted around his chair, disturbed by his presence. I hadn't noticed the sea of it hanging inches from the floor, as though repulsed by it.

Duncan kept me walking, his firm hand pressing into my back. I didn't care if anyone noticed anymore. It was the least of our concerns. Instead, I took the quiet to filter through every conversation that Kayne had stolen information from. He had always been there, stealing knowledge and sending it to Aldrick, but he wasn't the only one – that was clear now.

Kayne knew of our plans to infiltrate Lockinge. It was Kayne who tipped off Aldrick for our move to Aurelia. Jesi had been taken solely to punish me for Duncan's affections. What else had he gleaned from me and shared with Aldrick?

"Would you care to do the honours? I would, but as you can see, my body is not as it once was," Aldrick asked, arms open as he beckoned me toward him. At the side, his Hunters fussed over Kayne's body. He was placed delicately at the base of one stone pillar and left slumped against it.

"I would," I said, drawn forwards like a moth to a flame.

"I remember all the things you wished to do to him. Now is your chance. Even if his soul has departed, you can still leave your mark on the king's skin. You have been patient for this moment. Come. Bleed the Icethorn King dry. For Duwar, and for your future."

"For Duwar," I muttered, stepping away from Duncan, whose fingers dropped hesitantly away.

Like the interior of Rinholm, its exterior was decorated with Hunters. All around the outer edges of the garden, a line of them waited. Hundreds of them, far more than the two of us could take. But as long as Aldrick died, I would follow in death happily.

They just stood still and watched. I felt every eye burning a hole through me. I risked a quick glance around. There were too many for me to take. There was no telling if the Hunters were powered with fey blood or mundane, but regardless, I couldn't comprehend the number of them.

I wondered if they recognised the internal battle I suffered. Was it plastered across my face as each step toward the gate was like wrestling against the tide of an ocean? The curls of mist were corporeal, like fingers gripping onto my boots, trying to get a hold of them. My footsteps grew heavier the further I walked, and I was certain I felt a heavy vibration from the ground, as though it growled in threat or hummed softly in greeting.

"Isn't the gate useless without the final key?" I asked, wishing to stall Aldrick with my questions. "Elinor still roams free."

"All is in hand, Kayne. Thanks to your insight, we were ahead of the Oakstorm's attack on our eastern borders. The summer court is fractured. It wouldn't surprise me if their queen were returned to me by her late husband's supporters. From what I have learned, Doran would have been an interesting man to break bread with. It is a shame someone of his ilk was taken from us too soon."

I wasn't surprised to learn of Aldrick's knowledge of our plans. Part of me wondered if Kayne had revealed Elinor's reasons for the attack on Elmdew. Did he already know that it was meant as a distraction for this very reason?

"Tell me what you need me to do with him," I said, biting my nails into my palms to still my panic. "And I will do it."

"Bleed him," Aldrick rasped. "Altar's bones will contain the Icethorn power. Just as ribs house the heart or the skull shields the brain, the stones will devour the key. Stain the ground red. Feed the gate."

I knew that the death of a fey wasn't required, but was an extra layer to Aldrick's desire to be destructive. All it would take was the skin to touch that stone for long enough, and the key would slip free.

Which was why I couldn't allow myself to get close enough, even if it lured me.

One look at Duncan and I caught the shake of his head. His dark forest eyes were wide, pleading. They screamed for me not to do it.

"Surely you would prefer to be the one to do it?" I asked, sauntering toward the slumped body. The second I took a blade and cut into Kayne's skin, this would all be over. "I brought him for you. I wouldn't want to take such an important moment from you, Master."

"I flayed the Elmdew King and his consort." Aldrick frowned as he spoke. It was the first time I noticed his impatience. "Once you skin your first fish, you have skinned them all. I admit I allow you to do this because Robin is past the point of putting up resistance. It is not as enticing when their minds are quiet."

I swallowed hard. "I don't have a knife on me."

Aldrick clapped his crooked hands. "Supply Kayne with a blade."

Before the command was completed, the Hunter closest to me shot forward. I tried not to allow my hand to tremble as I reached out and grasped the hand of the plain dagger held out for me. As my fingers curled around the leather-wrapped blade, I felt a shock of warmth. It was warm, the leather slick and sticky as it fitted into my palm.

Warm, hazel eyes glared back at me. The helmet did little to hide the bridge of freckles and a strand of fire-ruby hair. Her heat alone revealed who hid behind the Hunter's outfit.

Althea Cedarfall, I'd recognise her in any life.

"Kayne, there is one more person I'd like to witness this success, someone who deserves to see Robin Icethorn cut open." Aldrick gestured behind him, directly toward where Althea stood.

I thought it was all over, but one moment she was there, the next, she melted back into the wall of Hunters she had come from. Before I turned my back on them, I looked across the line. I searched for others who seemed out of place. Gyah, or Lady Kelsey. But among the line-up, I couldn't identify Althea again. I just had to hope they were all there, like Althea, waiting to attack if the time required.

It wasn't Althea who Aldrick had gestured to, but someone else.

Two Hunters forced the frail body of a fey out of the crowd. My heart lodged in my throat, and I was powerless to stop my reaction.

Jesibel limped ahead, a dirtied and torn dress hanging from her limp body. Just as I'd seen her in my dreams, she looked terrible. Gaunt and thin, skin marred with unknown substances, her cracked lips forged shut.

It was a miracle she was still standing. In fact, if the two Hunters didn't hold her up, I hardly imagined she would be.

"A gift, Jesibel," Aldrick called, gesturing down to the corpse before me. "All your help led to this. Do you see now that your constant attempts to resist me were wasted, for nothing? Robin Icethorn, your king, is dead. Now you can watch as he bleeds out before you."

I couldn't move, couldn't do anything but look at Jesibel. Her gaze was fixed to the corpse, unblinking, skin pale as death itself. Duncan sensed my hesitation, hearing the name of the very person I'd have done anything to save.

"Kayne, you may begin."

A cacophony of emotions burned through me. Fury, pain, anguish and sorrow. I longed for Jesibel to look up and meet my eyes. But her grief, her guilt, was so thick I could feel it even with our distance.

"Kayne?" Aldrick leaned forwards in his chair.

I was losing control, everything blurring before me. Slowly, I lifted my eyes and locked them with his, and watched Aldrick recoil slightly. "Is there a problem?"

"Yes." It was all I could manage. Duncan tried to get closer to me, sensing how close I was to losing my sanity.

Aldrick might not have known it, but he'd just paraded my one weakness before me. He didn't need his magic to ruin me, his actions against Jesibel had already done that.

But she was alive. That had to count for something. And I vowed that it would stay that way.

"You must have been so disappointed to have missed the murder of the Cedarfall Queen," I said, voicing the confidence with rolled-back shoulders and a raised chin. It was easy to see Aldrick as the weak man he was. Curled up in a chair, with the inability to raise even a hand from its armrest. I glared down at him, hearing the leather of the warm blade squeak in my grasp. "Perhaps you would like me to describe it to you?"

I was vaguely aware of Duncan opening his mouth to say something, but no sound came out.

Aldrick's lips pinched into a thin, tight line. I felt his power press into my mind again, searching as the beginnings of distrust were planted. The Mariflora kept his will at bay but did little to dilute his vile presence.

"I do hope that is not regret I am sensing," Aldrick said.

"Regret?" I echoed, feeling my power swell in my chest. All I could think about was giving Althea enough time to get Jesibel to safety. That's why she was here, I had to believe it. Althea had found what I needed her to, and she knew how it would affect me.

"No, not regret," I forced out louder. "I just thought you might like to know what you have achieved?"

Aldrick's eyes traced me, then pressed a bent finger to his lips. "No. I do not care how she perished. What matters is the Cedarfall key was collected and brought to me. That is where her power now resides." Aldrick pointed to the large stone at the north of the forged circle. "As you will soon watch, it is like watering a flower on the brink of death. The stone will devour the key and hold it. If you were cursed with fey heritage, you would sense the gate. It grows stronger with the presence of each key."

Oh, I felt it. The humming beneath my feet and the way I longed to reach out and dust my fingers across the stone at my back. It called to me, the song of power even I couldn't explain.

Perhaps this is what enticed Aldrick. The whisper of Duwar promising power.

"Death seems like a steep price to pay." It was hard not to smile at Aldrick, especially when one of his Hunters was currently moving through the crowd. I knew, without a doubt, it was Althea, getting closer to Jesibel, using Aldrick's distraction as the time she needed.

Aldrick was entirely focused on me, sensing the oddity to our conversation. He leaned forward, grasping the arms of his chair as he attempted to make his frail body look larger.

"They could have opened the gate for Duwar freely," I said. "No one needed to die for this, did they?"

"The fey chose to stand against us. All the death is merely a means to an end," Aldrick seethed, spit dampening the neckline of his stained tunic. "Enough of this. Kayne, finish the task, or I will take your hesitation for weakness and act accordingly."

Without taking my eyes off Aldrick, I lowered myself to my knees. Out of the corner of my eye, I saw Duncan hesitate. If only I could infiltrate his mind and tell him what I knew. That our allies were around us, that I couldn't act out until Jesibel was removed to safety. Although we were not alone, Jesibel was still an unknowing shield before Aldrick, placed so perfectly I almost believed he sensed our deception.

But from the look of surprise across his face, Aldrick had no idea what was to come.

My fingers wound through the dark hair of the dead body. I tugged it hard, pulling the head back and exposing the white of the neck. My neck. Aldrick's eyes seemed to light with excitement. It was like he was a child, looking at the most delicious of treats. He followed the slow lift of the knife as I brought it to the skin.

"That's it," Aldrick breathed, relaxing back into his chair as his tongue traced his lower lip. There was a hunger in his expression as his eyes focused on the dead body I drew into my lap. "Allow the blood to fall upon the stone, and it shall do the rest. Let us all watch as it leeches the Icethorn of everything that made him who he was."

But that wasn't it. I was in control, and I sensed the draw. It was my choice to give in or ignore it. Rafaela had told me as much.

Kayne's body had stiffened in the hours since Duncan killed him. Eroan's glamour did little to conceal the necklace of bruises that encircled his neck. I brushed the sharp edge of the blade against the bruises, pressing the edge into flesh.

I risked one glance toward Althea. She was close now. I longed to watch as the excitement drained from Aldrick's face when he realised his failure. If only I could memorise the moment the realisation struck that he had been deceived. Witnessing that would make this all worth it.

Duncan must've figured it out, because I saw him look to Althea.

Angling Kayne's neck toward the stone, I felt my skin prickle with its proximity. I could not react, not yet.

I drew the knife across Kayne's neck. His skin split with ease, like a sack of grain did when cursed by a knife. Aldrick's focus was entirely on the show before him that he didn't notice Althea sweep in and take Jesibel away. I almost expected Jesi to fight or cry out at the suddenness of it, but she made no sound, her lips never parting.

Just a few more minutes, just long enough for Althea to get far away from her, I silently urged myself.

Cold blood poured over my hands, staining my skin crimson. Powerless blood. From the gash across Kayne's neck, it spluttered and splashed across the waiting stone, the sharp tang scalding the back of my throat.

It was as though the entire audience of Hunters inhaled at the same time. Anticipation was as ripe in the air as the rot that scented it. I focused on Aldrick and the sickly grin that twisted his face into one of horror. Then, ever so slowly, that mask slipped.

"More, give the stone more."

His command was clear, but I ignored it.

Sharp as an arrow, his eyes snapped to me. I'd disobeyed his order.

"Were you expecting something to happen?" I asked, releasing my hold of the hair and letting Kayne's body fall limp to the ground at the stone's base.

Aldrick lashed his power into my mind, over and over. But it had no effect. I heard his commands but brushed them away as though they were the weak wings of moths. He longed to find out what was happening. He focused all his power and might into controlling my mind, and he howled in frustration.

"So close," I tutted. "Yet *so* far."

Thunder rumbled as dark clouds spread across the blue expanse, devouring it entirely. The booming rumble made the Draeic whimper like scorned puppies. The world grew dark. A sudden fork of blue-white lightning cut across the sky.

"General Rackley," Aldrick growled, turning his attention to Duncan, whose body was sheathed in sparks of white light. "Have you returned to avenge your parents with the power I gave you?"

Duncan shrugged, eyes bleached white with power. "Something like that."

Aldrick looked back to me, unbothered by the flesh-made weapon that was Duncan.

"You," Aldrick spat.

I smiled, dropping the knife and encouraging icy winds to billow around me. "Hello again."

His scowl deepened, focus plastering his wrinkled face as he forced more of his power into my mind, but to no avail. "Aldrick, this ends now. If you haven't figured it out, you've failed."

A storm of emotion brushed over Aldrick's ancient face. His wrinkled lips pulled back, revealing stained teeth. A bead of sweat traced down his face as he continued stabbing daggers of his power into my mind. Each one snapped and broke. His efforts were wasted.

My glamour meant nothing. Aldrick knew what I was – *who* I was. I heard my name screech through my mind as he pleaded to take control of it.

"Robin Icethorn."

The force retreated as though scorned by fire, sent scurrying away like a whimpering mutt.

Aldrick looked between Duncan and me. Tension hummed thickly in the distance between us.

"I admit, I am both surprised and impressed," Aldrick said, his voice almost buried beneath Duncan's thunder. When his voice invaded our minds again, it was not to take control. In fact, it was not meant for us at all.

"Stop them."

His army of Hunters exploded into action. A wave of leather bodies thrashed toward us. Lightning whipped across the sky, and winds screamed throughout the gardens. Better they focused on us than Althea and Jesibel – they needed to get out of here.

And for that, we needed to prolong the distraction, and I had *just* the idea for it.

I welcomed the attack. As the bodies swelled toward us, I kept my eyes focused on Aldrick, who disappeared behind the wall of leather and flesh. But he still lurked in my mind, trying to get through, failing every time.

"You shall die." I let my promise fill my thoughts until it was the only thing Aldrick could hear. *"The failure you are."*

Then I let my power free, every scrap of it, including the full force of the key Aldrick so desperately desired. Winter didn't belong in the spring court, but I invaded it with a single exhale, claiming this land as my own.

CHAPTER 33

My back pressed into labradorite stone as the Hunters continued their attack. Magic-fuelled humans and steel-carrying Hunters came in waves, each one I forced back. Bodies froze to ice, shattering like glass. Flesh scorched then exploded as Duncan called down his lightning. On we fought, killing many, and yet more came. Soon enough, I felt the rough edge through my jacket, scratching at my skin. The discomfort reminded me I was very much alive, and this was very much happening.

The ground trembled with the stampede, the air alive with the cry of battle. I steadied my footing, calling forth the power that lurked within, and brought it to the surface. The force split through my skin and exploded in a wave of furious mist that shot forward across the garden. Whatever it touched turned to ice. I felt every rotten blade of grass and flower shatter beneath the force. The first wall of Hunters didn't care for the cloud of mist that greeted them until it was too late. My starved power clung to flesh and spread like a plague. The first humans it graced didn't have a chance to cry out. My ice claimed them. Their bodies froze to the spot so suddenly that the Hunters behind them couldn't slow down. Humans barrelled through my wall of frozen statues of flesh. The bodies of my victims exploded in smatterings of blood and skin.

As long as they ran toward me, giving Althea and Jesibel time to evacuate, that's all that mattered. I'd let Aldrick watch as I destroyed everything he'd worked for, and then he would follow.

I inhaled the cold sharply, drawing it back to myself.

Snakes of pure light crackled at my side. A Hunter, who scrambled carelessly over the pile of dead comrades, gathered himself and ran toward me. He made it a few steps from the barrier of frozen corpses before he joined them in death. A burst of light struck him, tearing him from his feet. One moment he was racing toward me, the next, his body cracked into another oncoming group of enemies. Melted flesh smeared across those he hit. Even from a distance, the smell of charred hair, meat and skin suffocated me.

"Are you all right?" Duncan panted, placing his body before mine. It was shrouded with bursts of hot, blue light that charged the air around him.

"Excellent," I replied through a smile. "But they'll keep attacking until they are freed from Aldrick's control. We either kill every single one of them or the strings that tether them to him."

I couldn't locate Aldrick amidst the bedlam, but his cry still rang out through my mind. The more time passed, the more frantic and desperate his pleading became. He was losing and he knew it, the sound was a joyous thing to hear.

"Take the Icethorn heir. Duwar will bless the brave warrior who sees his blood is spilled upon the stone!"

"Lies," I spat. I could've given my power to the stone if I wanted, and Aldrick knew that.

"I need to get you out of here," Duncan said as he sent a chain of his lightning into the Hunters closest. The spark of light shot between four bodies before fizzing back into the static air.

He didn't see the threat of a blade coming in from his side. But I did. I conjured one of my own, spilling my power into a spear of ice that grew into a sword. The cold bite burned into my palm, and I welcomed it. I thrust the cold edge into the belly of the Hunter who lunged for Duncan. The force ripped the ice from my hand.

As the Hunter fell to the ground, she landed upon the spear and forced it deeper into her belly. She didn't move again.

"I'm not going anywhere until Aldrick is dead," I replied, grunting as I gathered a pressure of frozen wind between my palms before sending it into the chest of another Hunter who drew close. "Duncan, I'm not leaving you, either. We started this together, we end it together."

I expected him to refuse me, but he didn't.

An arch of fire exploded in the distance. It moved with grace and control. It drew the attention of the Hunters and drew them toward it like moths to an open flame. It eased the wave of those who tried to reach me.

"Althea?" Duncan breathed, now pressing his back to mine. I felt his deep voice rumble through him. We moved as one unit, throwing power out to anyone who drew close enough to cause risk.

Another burst of unnatural flame answered Duncan's question.

"She must've got Jesibel out of here," I exhaled, relief swelling in my chest.

Time was a strange concept when all I could do was worry for my life and the life of the man I loved. Knowing we were together made us fight harder and smarter. I growled through my exhaustion, grappling with the adrenaline that would soon wane. Every step we fought our way from the labradorite stone was slow. It felt as though we were kept in place. Stuck in a web with dwindling hopes of getting out.

Aldrick's fuelled commands would quieten, and I grew hopeful that Althea or Gyah had reached him. But the Hunters didn't stop, and Aldrick soon returned with more demanding pleas.

"Kill the Icethorn. Duwar will reward you. Do. Not. Stop."

I wished to form words of encouragement to share with Duncan, but I couldn't hold a breath. Even the desire to shout for help, as the wave suffocated us, I couldn't so much as gasp as I threw arrows of winter outward and conjured ripping winds of ice to devour those who got close. And they did. Each attempt was getting closer. Fingers grasped at my skin, and swords were thrust out toward me in the hope they would cut flesh and spill blood.

The Draeic beasts didn't discriminate over who they attacked. Their powerful wings forced gusts of scorching, stale air upon us as they dove and picked people from the ground and took them skyward. It was another reason I'd drawn all of Aldrick's warriors, beckoning them forwards to become a shield of flesh – just like how Aldrick used Jesibel. He could control his followers, but not chaos-made monsters from Duwar's realm.

I delighted in the terrified screams as bodies were sliced in two by serrated teeth and plucked between the Draeic as they fought each other to devour the limbs. Blood fell from the sky like rain, splattering across my hair and face as I continued my fight.

As much as I wished I was limitless, that wasn't the case. Exhaustion soon crept up on me, a silent assassin. I longed to throw out my power, as I had at Imeria, but I couldn't. Not as the crowd around us was filled with my allies. So, I kept my magic gathered and intimate. Which allowed the Hunters to press closer with each passing second.

A swell of enemies coursed forward as one. Duncan cried out, trying to carve a path through them. But it was no good because every Hunter we killed, another two took their place.

It seemed the tide was changing, and not in our favour.

Until something slammed into the ground before us, sending bodies flying in all directions from the force. The comet of gold and grey blurred with speed and barrelled into the unexpecting Hunters who pushed toward us.

Dove-grey wings unfurled, and a golden hammer swung in one wild move that popped skulls like grapes between teeth. By the time Rafaela righted herself, the smooth edge of her weapon was coated in chunks of bone and gore. Her skin glistened with the blood of those her fall had killed. The cream robe she wore had stained to a dark crimson that would never truly be cleaned from it.

"You did not give me the signal!" Rafaela shouted as the flat head of her hammer split the skull of a Hunter with ease.

Her presence alone rejuvenated the adrenaline within me.

"I haven't exactly had the chance!" I grunted, ducking as a blade passed over my head, but I thrust pelts of ice forward, tearing the skin from the face of my attacker.

"Focus," Rafaela cried, twisting her wings and knocking multiple humans down with little effort. "Don't let the gate taste your blood. It will not stop drinking until you are empty."

"You said it didn't need my–"

Rafaela's eyes flew wide. "I have said a lot of things that are not true, Robin Icethorn. Keep your blood away."

If I had the time to contemplate her words, I would've perhaps faltered beneath the realisation that she'd lied to me.

Aldrick was right, and I'd unknowingly put myself in danger.

I swallowed hard, hyper-aware of the labradorite behind me. Its presence seemed to be the only thing to offer a sense of calm patience. It was waiting for me, stalking my every move. My false sense of control slipped away like ash on the wind, carried so far away there was no hope I could claim it back.

I opened my mouth to question her, but Rafaela worked her way through the crowd as more Hunters attempted to overwhelm her. And it was working, cleaving me a path to get far away from it.

There was no chance but to take it – until my window to move was swallowed by a wave of leather and flesh.

Feral, skin-flaying screams split the air. Thunderous roars responded. I couldn't look up at first, not as a Hunter grappled onto my jacket and pulled with all their might. Stumbling over my footing, I almost fell, but Duncan reached out and grabbed my shoulder. His grip pulled hard backward, giving me a moment to thrust another spear of ice straight up from the ground beneath the Hunter. It pierced, at an angle, through his chest and neck. He hung there with wide, all-seeing eyes. It took a moment for death to claim him.

"We are close to victory," Aldrick screamed, forcing his voice into every mind. I'd enjoyed the knowledge that he was lying before, but now the truth hit me as hard as the fist careening into my jaw. I wondered if it was my deep-rooted exhaustion, or the Mariflora that was weakening, because, for the first time, I felt his innate demand. For a moment, my soul wished to bend to it.

My head snapped to the side, teeth cutting into the insides of my cheeks. I blindly reached up, watching as Duncan fought with a sword he'd taken from a Hunter at his feet, trying to reach me. He swung it, two hands holding firm. Lightning twisted down the metal of the blade until it glowed a furious red.

I fought, tooth and nail, to get out from beneath the Hunter atop me. I bit at his hands and arms and gouged my fingers into his eyes. He shook me violently, slamming my back against the ground with such a thud my breath evaded me.

"Robin!" Rafaela's muffled cry reached me. Her voice was laced with fear for the first time, she knew we were close to failing.

Someone growled. The air hissed with the cut of steel. I barely had a chance to close my eyes before blood exploded over me, raining onto my face, into my mouth. When I opened my eyes again it was to see the headless body swaying to the side, falling off me.

"No man touches what is mine and comes away with their head," Duncan growled, standing just shy of where I lay, his blade dripping fresh blood.

I took his hand, and was hoisted up. "Thank you–"

"ROBIN!" Rafaela screamed again.

I turned back to find her but could no longer see her among the sea of Hunters. As I scanned the crowd, fey roaring with each burst of their magic, I noticed that Althea hadn't announced her location with fire for a while. Nor had I seen Gyah in her Eldrae form. All around me were the angry faces of our enemies whose bodies no longer belonged to them but to Aldrick, who pulled the strings from his unknown location of safety.

I forced three words into my mind. *"This must end."*

"You know what is required. Give yourself up freely," Aldrick replied quickly, as though he had waited for me to reach out. *"Hasn't enough blood been spilled? If you stop, I will call back my warriors. No one else needs to die today."*

Duncan snapped his head to me. His wide eyes revealed he had heard Aldrick. "This is not–" his teeth parted as he emitted a growl, hacking through the arm of a Hunter before pulling his blade back and driving it through their soft belly– "the time to be the hero, Robin. Give him what he wants, and we all die. Aldrick does not know mercy. We have a plan, *your* plan, stick to it."

Deep down, I knew Duncan was right. I couldn't trust a word Aldrick said.

"Give the gate your power. One sacrifice to save them all."

Another scream lit the air. Then another. And another. But they were different. It wasn't the keening cry of death, or the song of agony as fey and Hunters fought. This was a sound that once haunted me.

I risked a glance and saw the sky filled with winged creatures. Like flies to rotten meat, they swarmed the three Draeic. The cloud of grey limbs slashed and picked at the demons whose roars no longer sang with terror but bled with their own fear.

Gryvern. A cloud of claws and fangs attacked the Draeic. I felt a drop of blood land upon my upturned face. I lifted a finger to my cheek, and it came back black.

My lips curved upward, and my chest swelled with hope. It took moments for my mind to piece together the strange, unexpected puzzle that was the gryvern's presence.

Erix sliced through the sky among them, hands curved into monstrous claws. His growl was low and trembling, matching that of Duncan's thunder. Steel-cold eyes locked with mine. There was no hesitation as he found me within the crowd from his height.

As tides do, this one changed back in our favour.

"Oh, Aldrick, I'm afraid you are in no position to compromise with me." I coated my mind with ice and forced the reply back to Aldrick. *"Look up."*

I thrust out my power, pulling on the dregs that lingered in the deep pit inside me, and pushed outward. The cold blast of winter wind coiled around me and forced the Hunters close enough to fall back.

It let up space ahead of me for a moment, and then Erix was there. Standing inches before me, with his blanket of thin leather wings blocking out the enemies at our back.

"So, you disappeared and found me an army," I muttered, wishing to reach out and grasp him, just to check he was real.

Erix took me in his arms, holding me as though a soft breeze could've torn me away from him. "Forgive me, I had a feeling we would need help, and I had some *siblings* I thought I should call upon."

The gryvern cried out in unison. I sensed their glee within the high-pitched nature of their noise.

"You can control them?" I asked, trembling at the thought.

"No time for explanations now," Erix replied, flashing two sharp canines that overlapped his lower lip. "When this is over, I will tell you everything."

Duncan cried out, his voice pitched with pain. I glanced over Erix's shoulder and watched as Duncan disappeared into the wall of Hunters. Even as he drowned within the bodies, he fought for his life. The crack of a jaw as his fist connected. The snap of a bone at his elbow jolted into someone's face. Then he was gone, just like that. Gone.

"I offer this to you one more time, give your power, or Duncan Rackley dies."

"No," I screamed as my power became a blizzard, drowning out all other noise. My heartbeat filled my ears, my throat and even shuddered painfully through my bones.

Erix sensed my action but was too late to stop me.

Then I ran, thrashing out deadly cold before me, Erix following at my back, wings propelling him forward.

I threw myself into the same wall of hands that took Duncan from me. I clawed through them, caring little as my nails tore with flesh. My skin burned with the frozen kiss of ice. Anyone who touched me would feel pain until it was my last chance.

Erix was never far behind. He forged a path at my side. The tipped talons on his wings swung and stabbed, his claws turned skin to ribbons and his teeth buried into anything he could reach until his face was masked in blood.

"Give him back to me!" I couldn't help but plead.

"Give up the key," Aldrick replied, calmer than he'd been before. Hearing his tone frightened me the most.

"Don't hurt him. If you do, you'll never get what you want."

His soft chuckle vibrated through my mind. Goosebumps puckered across my arms as it rang like a bell through my skull.

"Fight them, Duncan," I shouted, my voice rough as shattered stone.

I could no longer see Erix. I looked around at the glaring faces of Hunters with their greedy hands and fingers that pinched my skin and pulled my hair.

"Aldrick," I bellowed aloud with as much vigour as I could, wishing for my voice to tear across the crowd and pierce him where he sat.

"Stop."

The word was final. It was meant both for me and for the army of Hunters.

My knees hit the bloodied mess of the ground. There was no warning to put out my arms, so my face took the brunt of the fall. Everything went dark and quiet. I dared not open my eyes for what I might find. I waited, curling my body into the foetal position, waiting for more pain, more hands and fists and nails and blades.

Nothing.

"Here lies a king, cowering in a pit of dirt and death," Aldrick sang. "What a sight."

The mass of Hunters had moved. Now, they waited in a circle around me. There wasn't that many of them left, we'd been so close, but I was blinded by the need to protect Duncan from a fate that I couldn't bear the thought of him falling to.

Death.

Aldrick was there once again, mud splattered up the wheels of his chair and sticky among the woollen blankets across his lap. Besides that, he was untouched. Unscathed, whereas I felt like my soul had been flayed from my body.

"I will admit, Robin Icethorn, you really had me for a moment. The glamour, the body, all of it. I would be lying if I said I wasn't impressed."

I pushed myself up enough that my chest peeled away from the wet ground. Gathering a lump of bile, I spat before him. "Fuck you."

"Now, *there* is the human lurking inside. Rough around the edges and flawed. It must have been so terribly exhausting playing pretend all this time. I would not be surprised if you have had enough. Here…" Aldrick offered out a hand, palm raised to the sky, still filled with the gryvern's screams. "Allow me to help you rid yourself of the responsibility the *key* gives you."

I scanned the crowds, looking for a sign of Duncan. Erix. Althea. Gyah. Rafaela. Anyone who might help. While the sky was still a battleground for the gryvern and Draeic, everything on the ground seemed so still.

"What have you done to *them*?"

"Does it matter?" Aldrick replied. "Give me what I want, and I will give you what you want. Seems like a fair trade."

He was asking me to trade the world for the sake of a few people – and yet, they were my world.

"I'd rather die." I stood slowly, hoping that Aldrick did not see my legs tremble. It was only the two of us within the circle. No guards protecting him. Only his daring, but that would do little to save him.

"I can arrange that. You die, and I take the key, or you give it freely, and I take the key. Cooperation is not something I am concerned about."

I lunged toward him, feet slipping across the slick ground. My power had depleted, but that didn't matter. I would tear his throat out with my bare hands. I was so close, my nails a hairbreadth from his wrinkled skin, when another voice rose from the crowd.

"Little bird."

The wall of Hunters peeled away, allowing Erix to pass through. He moved awkwardly as though his legs were not his own. His face was painted with apology and fright; both emotions were in clear conflict with one another. "This is not me. I am *not* doing this."

"Your guard does not lie to you, this is my doing."

"Get your fucking hands off me," Duncan screamed as he, too, followed out of the wall of Hunters. He was being dragged, his hands clasped behind his back, a blade pressed to his throat. Still, he fought, even with death a literal swipe away.

Duncan was forced to his knees, held down by a small group of Hunters. And I watched as Erix came to stand above him, claws grasping at his chin and neck. I saw his hand tremble with hesitation, but they didn't move away.

"Mariflora." Aldrick mocked me from my mind. Then he continued out loud so everyone could hear. "Highly effective when ingested by a mortal but rather useless to monsters. And look what you brought to the fight, one cut from both cloths."

My lips parted, expelling a feeble gasp. "Erix, I command you to resist him."

Erix's silver eyes twitched, his mouth drawn in a pinched line.

"Robin," Duncan said, demanding my attention to meet his. Our eyes met, his verdant gaze brimming with defiance. His chin was raised, his shoulders back as much as the bindings allowed. Muck coated his face, deepening the hollow of his cheeks and the etching of the scar down the side of his face. Now, more than ever, it looked like a permanent tear engraved into his hardened expression. "Let it go."

I didn't know if he spoke about my power or him. But knowing Duncan, he'd rather die than hand anything over to the very man who ruined his life.

"One thought, that is all it would take, and your beloved dies," Aldrick grinned wildly at the revelation. "There is no more fight left. No more bloodshed. One thought, that is all it will take, and it is over for Duncan Rackley."

I didn't know where to look. I was being torn between Erix under his spell, Aldrick smiling and Duncan looking almost peaceful as he faced his end.

"Robin, don't you dare listen to him. Do you hear me." I recoiled as Duncan shouted at me. Spit burst out of his mouth as he snarled his own demand. "My death is not what matters. I *do not* matter!"

"You do," I exhaled. "To me."

I dared to look away as tears filled Duncan's stare. He refused to blink and provide them with escape.

Erix fought against Aldrick's control. His entire body shook like a leaf caught in a breeze. Yet, still, his claws didn't retract from Duncan's neck.

"The choice is yours," Aldrick said calmly. There was something about his tone that reminded me of my father. It was paternal, as though used to trick me into doing what he wished. "Think wisely about your decision. The lives of those you care about rely on what you *do* next."

I glanced at the labradorite stone. The Hunters had deposited me right at the foot of it. As I had before, I sensed its thirst for me, more so now that my body was cut open in places, wounds leaking blood. As though it understood the conversation and sang with its longing for me to give it what it desired.

"You speak of life as if it is important to you," I said, turning my focus back to Aldrick, hate sparking in my gut, the desire of his blood a song I couldn't ignore either.

But he was no longer alone.

"No, no." I leaned forwards, screaming at her.

This wasn't happening.

Jesibel sauntered from the line of Hunters like a wisp of smoke. Bare feet, her dress barely clinging to her, dark eyes wide with a feral agony I recognised.

Aldrick turned his body to look at the person who moved with free will, sensing my distraction. Although, he wasn't surprised to see her. "Come to me, that's it."

Like with Erix, Aldrick was controlling Jesibel.

I thought she'd gotten away, that Althea had saved her. But here she was, as if she'd never left. Perhaps she had, but Aldrick's power reached far, like a leash, and dragged her back.

Jesibel didn't look anywhere but at Aldrick – her focus entirely locked on him.

"You say that Mariflora is useless to monsters, then explain what I am," Althea's shout rose from the Hunters until I spotted her. She wasn't on her knees like Duncan but standing among them. "What you have made me."

"Wait, fey," Aldrick commanded Jesibel, who stopped so suddenly and rigid I knew she was under his spell. But Aldrick didn't care for her, not when Althea had just stolen every enemy's attention in that moment. Including Aldrick, who almost forgot Jesibel was beside him.

Althea's face was masked with red hair that billowed in the

winds. The deepest ruby, as the colour of blood that covered most of her. "I'm a monster, and I am free from you."

"The last Cedarfall," Aldrick sneered. "Perhaps I should rectify that."

"I welcome you to try," Althea hissed, her eyes smiling with equal want for that very thing.

What happened next was so quick I refused to blink to miss it. Jesibel moved – the first sign she was not under Aldrick's spell as I first thought. She leaned into Aldrick's ear and whispered something.

His eyes flared open, a shout gargling out of his throat as he spun back on Jesi, likely surprised at what she said, or that she could even say anything without him commanding it.

The air split with light just beyond Jesi. I saw the small frame of a familiar boy for a second, then he was gone, taking Jesi with him. Aldrick stared at the empty space, shocked at what he'd seen. But it wasn't empty for long, because the light parted again, flashing the determined scowl of Daveed the teleporter, followed by the ravenous Althea Cedarfall.

She'd traded places with Jesibel. Seconds, that was all it took.

"Boo," she snapped at Aldrick, who didn't even have time to lean back in his chair before she attacked.

Althea clapped her hands on either side of Aldrick's face, silencing him. Her thumbs dug into his eyes and squeezed. His scream was a song of pure agony. There wasn't time for him to send out a command to his followers, not as pain overcame him.

I watched, arms pinned helplessly to my side, as dark gore streamed out of Aldrick's eye sockets and slipped into his parted mouth. Aldrick choked on his blood. He grasped at his neck with liver-spotted hands, attempting to claw at his skin for a reprieve.

But there was none to be found for him. His time, as we all recognised, was over.

"This... this is for my family," Althea whispered into his ear as fire blossomed across her hands and spread across Aldrick's face. The bright spark of furious crimson engulfed his skin, masking his silent scream in the roar of burning flesh.

"*Stop her–*"

"Burn," Althea bellowed her war cry above the final command Aldrick attempted. "You *bastard.*"

CHAPTER 34

Aldrick's body sparked like aged, dried kindling, rupturing in flames until every inch of his skin was engulfed in them.

I felt nothing for him as ash peeled from the bundle of fire and drifted skyward on the spring breeze. Through the haze of licking, hungry fire, I couldn't take my eyes off him as his flesh melted and bones charred black.

Grunts echoed around us as the Hunters regained control of their own minds. The once steady wall was now a mess of shouting Hunters with stark, pale faces and blinking, distant stares.

I wished it took longer for Aldrick to die, but even the universe seemed to want his soul with such desperation, he left the realm of the living too quickly.

Althea didn't release her dark flames as she withdrew from Aldrick's charred husk and faced the crowd.

"I will give you all the same opportunity, so listen carefully," Althea called out, whips of flame hissing like serpents from each of her fists. "Now your minds are your own, will you continue to fight against us or lay your weapons down and stand beside us?"

Figures slipped from the line of Hunters, scratched and battered but alive. I noticed Gyah stride forward, a deep gash sliced above her brow, blinding her left eye with blood. Lady Kelsey followed, limping with the aid of another fey who had joined us from Aurelia. One by one, the humans allowed our kind through until the middle of the gate's circle was filled with us.

Arms engulfed me, pulling me tight into a hard chest. Beneath the harsh tang of death that covered him, I still smelled Duncan. His hand cradled the back of my head, his lips pressed atop it.

"It's over," Duncan whispered, voice muffled into my hair. "It's fucking over."

I wish it was, but I knew that we were far from the end of this story.

Aldrick was evil, but he, too, was a puppet to a master. Duwar was still the threat, we couldn't forget it.

"Is it?" I replied meekly. I forced my eyes closed. My fingers wound into the material of Duncan's jacket, and I held firm. "Aldrick may be dead, but the gate still stands. Duwar is still a threat."

"Robin is right." I pulled away from Duncan enough to see Rafaela. She used her hammer as a walking stick to keep herself upright. Her wings were torn and thin, feathers had been ripped out in clumps by the hands of those who attacked her. One hung at her side, unmoving, unlike its twin, which twitched with energy. "For as long as the keys play a part in the realms, Duwar will always have a chance to return."

This was the part of mine and Rafaela's plan that we'd not divulged to anyone. The price I'd offered to pay for her help.

Althea continued calling out to the humans, not knowing what was brewing in the centre of the gate. "I will regard you all as victims of Aldrick's control until you give me a reason to think otherwise. Lay down your weapons. No one else needs to die today."

There was a clatter of metal as weapons were thrown to the ground in surrender. Many of the humans fell to their knees with their hands raised behind their heads. Those who continued to stand, hands still gripped around a blade, were targeted by our forces, who surged back toward the crowd to deal with them.

I saw Erix then, standing in the same place he'd held Duncan. His heavy breathing and hunched frame told me of his exhaustion.

He had one hand pressed against the side of his head. He must have felt my eyes upon him because he looked up then. The gryvern – *his* gryvern – screeched in the sky above us. A cloud of grey skin, coiling and twisting among one another in a bundle of black blood-covered bodies. Not a single Draeic was left in sight.

Had they fled as Aldrick's control had slipped from them? Did Duwar even recognise the failure waiting for it?

"It wasn't me," Erix mouthed. Each word clear even from a distance. "I wasn't in control."

I blinked, parting my mouth as I formed my reply. *"I know."*

Erix was no stranger to being controlled by sinister people. Doran had used him to hurt me, and Aldrick almost succeeded until Jesibel…

Where was she? Daveed had teleported her to safety, but I still needed to see her, the desire was burning inside of me.

"It's now or never, Robin," Rafaela whispered at my side. "You know how we can save this realm. This must be done before the chance is taken from us."

I sensed panic edging her words, the way her knuckles paled as she gripped tighter to her hammer. I sensed there were more reasons as to why she wanted the keys destroyed – forever removing them from the game board that was this world. Her purpose was to protect them, and yet she would happily default from the Nephilim and go against them, for this one purpose.

But she was right. As long as the keys were in play, the gate was always under threat to be opened. Duwar would find another person instead of Aldrick, and attempt their campaign for freedom. The only way of preventing it was making sure this gate, or any other, could never be opened.

I locked eyes with Rafaela and nodded in silent agreement.

"What is the meaning of this?" Duncan moved his body before me once again, but I pushed at his upper arm.

"Duncan, please," I begged. "Don't stand in my way."

"All well and good asking that of me, but what from exactly?" he barked. His blood-splashed face was twisted in confusion as he took hold of both of my arms and held on. "How can I stand in your way if you do not tell me what it is you're doing!"

Rafaela winced as she hoisted the hammer above her shoulder where it rested. "Aldrick is not the first and will not be the last whose mind is infected by the will of the Defiler. Gates will be erected, and Duwar will not stop his campaign to be free. But the gates are useless if there are no keys to open them."

"They need to be destroyed," I said, aware everyone was listening. "The keys. Duwar will never have a chance of freedom again."

It was the *only* way.

Duncan's face shifted between emotions. He wrestled with what I told him. Before he could refuse or say anything else, I stepped in close and pressed both hands onto him. On tiptoes, I raised my aching body and placed a kiss on his hesitant lips. "I need you to stand by me. It will be one less person I'll need to ask for forgiveness when it is over."

"This was always the plan, wasn't it?" he said, looking between Rafaela and me.

I nodded, glancing at Rafaela and wishing I could borrow some of her defiance.

"Why?" Duncan breathed. "Why did you keep this from me?"

I shrugged, unsure which excuse to pick from. "This is my choice. The key is in me. For as long as it dwells inside me, or any other Icethorn – we threaten the lives of the people we are sworn to protect."

He knew I was right, deep down, they all did.

Duncan looked to Rafaela, distrust thundering in his verdant stare. "How dangerous is it?"

We both noticed the grimace on her expression. She did well to hide it. "The labradorite is the second vessel strong enough to contain the key. If Robin binds the power into the stone, *I* can destroy it."

"You are asking Robin to do exactly what we have just fought against Aldrick to prevent." Duncan's entire body hardened into a shield before me. "No. I can't let you both do this. Not until we have all discussed every option. This is not only your fight but also ours. All of ours."

"This *is* the only way," I pleaded.

"Perhaps so, but I love you enough to make sure you make this decision with a clear mind. We have time to make it," Duncan spoke softly, although there was no ignoring the demand that lurked beneath each word.

"Erix," I called out, noticing Duncan wince as I did.

In seconds, my guard was there. It seemed it was my turn to take control of his mind. Doran had done it, then Aldrick. I refused to let him suffer in the hands of another again. But for that, I had to play the game of monsters.

I dropped my hands from Duncan's stomach, reluctantly tracing my fingers down his frame.

"You called on me, Robin?"

I nodded, locking eyes with Erix, not able to look anywhere but at Duncan. "Restrain Duncan."

"Robin, wait." Duncan tried to stop me, but his attempt was futile. "Think about this."

I had, over and over, so many times.

"I do not understand…" Erix said, looking between me and Duncan. "Why?"

"Do it. Don't let Duncan out of your hold until I give the command. Have your gryvern stop anyone, friend or foe, from getting near me. As your king, am I clear?"

I expected Duncan to fight, but he didn't.

"Yes," Erix said, grimacing as he stepped toward Duncan and took a hold of him.

Since when did victory hurt so badly? Because right then I felt nothing but pain, like a thorn in my heart. I tore my gaze from Duncan, unable to witness the anger that coiled in his eyes when he looked at me.

We all knew he could've fought free, Erix wasn't exactly holding him tightly. But it was the meaning of my action that hurt him. But I silently vowed that this would prevent true destruction from ever gracing Wychwood. I did this to save them from a future always under threat.

I knew little of how Erix controlled the gryvern, but suddenly they screeched in threat and broke apart, flying down to the ground. The Hunters scrambled for their weapons again, and even the fey gathered at their sides at the new threat.

Althea locked eyes with me before the gryvern thudded into the ground, creating a wall between us. She'd not heard this conversation, as her focus had been on gathering the chaos left after Aldrick and controlling it.

I sensed the question in her eyes, but there was no time to answer it.

Erix pulled Duncan away, deeper into the circle of the gate. The mist had returned, twisting around their ankles. Both men looked at me with similar expressions. I couldn't stand to punish myself with their attention any longer. I knew this decision was the right one. They would see.

It was the only way, just as Rafaela had confirmed, to finally stop this.

"They will hate me for this," I said to her, allowing my inner anxiety to spill out of me.

"Hate is the other side of love," Rafaela replied. "My people will also hate me, but it is the only way. You are saving their lives. Doing this will prevent Duwar from ever returning to this realm and laying waste to it. It is not only the right decision, Robin. It is the *only* decision."

Destroying the gate was temporary – more could be built. But without the keys, a gate was nothing but stone.

"I hope you are right." I faced the labradorite before me. *Altar's bones.*

"I give the stone the Icethorn key, and you shatter it?"

"Precisely," Rafaela confirmed.

"If only Aldrick had been alive long enough to see this," I said, reaching out and pressing my palms into the sharp edge of the stone's surface. I felt it sing beneath me. The stone trembled to life beneath my touch. It drew me in with such force, I knew that trying to remove my hands would result in a battle. "It would have been one of life's greatest pleasures to see as he watched all his years of hard work crumble before him."

It was an odd feeling, the blood seeping out of my wounds to creep toward the stone, defying the laws of nature. Ice crept over my fingers the more I pushed it out of me and into this vessel. It crackled across the dark stone slowly, spreading and devouring. I opened the power deep within me and pushed it harder, expelling the pressure into the stone. There was no need to spill blood, it helped with the extraction, but I could've done it without it. As Aldrick had said, the key could have been given willingly. He just chose otherwise.

It wasn't my innate power that flooded out of me, but the wild storm that dwelled deep inside. The presence of cold, which filled me the moment I'd accepted the Icethorn power all those weeks ago, awoke.

I closed my eyes as the sensation overwhelmed me. The stone flickered its unseen tongue, tasting the Icethorn key. Then, its teeth peeled back and sunk inside it, latching on like a leech. I cried out. The sudden pain was overwhelming, all-consuming.

I tried to call out for help, but my body refused me.

"Do not stop, not until it has it all!" Rafaela shouted, but her voice seemed quiet.

At what cost?

My mind pleaded for me to pull away, but I feared the stone had me shackled. It pulled and pulled, sucking the power out of me. I felt the marrow in my bones shiver, my veins knot and blood hiss.

I squinted through the wild winds that tore around me. Rafaela fought against it, hammer poised and ready. Her braids whipped like snakes around her skull.

As the stone drew the Icethorn key out, I witnessed a new horror. A vortex of dark smoke turned the middle of the gate into a sea of shadow. All but one stone was alive, fuelling the gate, opening it.

Deep inside me, I felt the gate crack. Like a door being forced, but not completely, just enough for someone to peer through the crack on the other side.

"I'm... opening the gate!" I shouted, my throat raw and bloodied. "Rafaela, what have you done?"

"You are not, I vow it."

Erix and Duncan were swaddled in the shadow, trying to reach me. My scream had made them forget orders. Duncan, now free from Erix's hold, ran into the centre, my name sliced across his lips. Behind him, Erix flapped his wings and became airborne. He looked down at the reaching waves of shadow that tried to pull him back down.

Duncan couldn't have escaped it. His powerful arms cut through the walls of shadow and mist that slowed him down, trying to fight his way toward me.

The darkness rose up to his waist, then his chest, then to his chin.

Deep in my bones, as the stone continued to drink the Icethorn power from me, I sensed it crack open like a door on hinges that desired oil. I tried to pull back from the stone, but it was too late.

One moment Duncan was there, the next, he was gone, slipping beneath the wave of shadow and not coming back out of it.

And I knew, without question or thought, where he'd gone.

The gate had claimed Duncan. It had pulled him from the small slip my power had encouraged open. Without Elinor's key, it wouldn't have been enough to free Duwar. But his presence leaked out into this realm and captured what he desired.

I locked eyes with Erix, who flew out of reach of the shadows. For a moment, the world went quiet. I saw into Erix's wide eyes and read his intention.

Erix didn't hesitate. His silver eyes dropped from mine, and then he was gone, diving into the swell of shadow beneath him.

Like Duncan, I felt Erix's soul leave this realm and slip into the one that waited through the crack in the gate.

The key's presence was fading within me. I felt it, the final will of the power clinging onto me. I reached out my will and held onto it, entering a competition with the labradorite stone. I refused to give it up. If it took the key completely, Rafaela would destroy it.

Duncan and Erix would be lost.

Forever.

The gryvern dispersed with Erix's disappearance. Wherever he had gone, his command on them didn't stretch. The creatures scattered, clawing through the air and fleeing from the gate.

Althea was suddenly visible, standing just out of reach from the gate's boundary. She was shouting, commanding no one to pass into it, human or fey. All the while, her attention was on me. I would never forget the look on her face. I was sure it would haunt me for all of time.

"Stop resisting, Robin," Rafaela commanded. "Finish it, give it all and I can break it."

I hissed through clenched teeth as I expelled my desperation. "I can't... I need to keep it open."

"They're gone!" Rafaela's hands twisted around the handle of the hammer, her biceps protruding as she kept it hoisted. "Before anyone else is put at risk, give the gate the key and let me destroy it."

I refused to listen, refused to believe they were gone. I didn't deserve to feel the sadness that stabbed through me. Not when there should only be room for guilt. "Give them more time."

"No," Rafaela spat. "You do not understand the threat this poses for the future. Finish this, or I will destroy *you* alongside the gate."

Her threat was wasted, I didn't care. How could I fear for my life when my actions had already destroyed me? I wouldn't wish to live if I came out of this without Duncan. Without Erix.

Despite Rafaela's warning, I held on for as long as I could. Rafaela promised me this was a choice, to give the key up – she was wrong.

"Do not resist it, Robin." Her screams coiled with the winds that became one.

Come back to me. Come back to me.

"I – I can't."

I will not give up on you. Come back.

I felt the grasp of the key weaken, loosening its grip one finger at a time.

Cold tears stung my cheeks. I refused to blink for fear I would miss something within the shadows of the gate.

The force pulling me into the stone weakened. It was as though it repelled me. Now the stone had the key, it no longer wanted me. It had what it thirsted for.

I understood then why death was a kinder option than experiencing the extraction I'd just been through.

I stumbled back, legs giving way as I fell into the bloodied mud at the stone's base. The shadows reached for me now. I reached for them in return, wanting to slip through the crack in the gate, to follow the two men who'd been taken from me.

Rafaela brought the golden hammer up above her head. It caught the fading light across its golden head.

"Forgive me," I spluttered into the shadows. Then Rafaela brought her blessed weapon down upon the labradorite plinth. It cracked, fractures running across the stone in veins. Golden light burst outward.

Three attempts. That was all it took.

Pelts of stone exploded outward. The rain of debris fell upon me. I felt my skin split as the stones sliced across it, but I had no energy to lift a hand to shield myself. Nor did I care.

Rafaela moved to the next stone and the next. She destroyed the keys with grace and ease. The Cedarfall key broke first, and then the Elmdew key, which required more force than the rest.

Only the final stone, powerless and keyless, was left standing.

Rafaela fell to her knees. She pawed into the ground, hammer discarded at her side, wings splayed out around her like a tattered blanket.

I scanned my eyes over the gate as the smoke that twisted around us melted into the earth until not a single sliver was left.

My breath hitched as my eyes fell on the bundle of two bodies in the middle.

No. No. No.

I dug my fingers into the sodden ground, dragging myself toward its centre. Toward the tattered grey-leather wings of Erix, who unfolded his body from the second body – off of Duncan, who lay motionless beneath him.

CHAPTER 35

No one refused me as I pushed a cot up beside the one Duncan's body rested on.

I hoped the sickening screech of wood against the stone floor would've woken him. It didn't. Nor did the slight thump as the cots bumped together. Without discarding my dirtied boots, I climbed on and curled my body beside his. I lay with my knees tucked up to my chest and sobbed.

My breathing was erratic. Tears scored down my cheeks, their presence leaving wet scars and turning my skin sticky. I felt the feather-down pillow dampen beneath my face. No matter how loud I cried or how my desperate fingers took hold of Duncan's stiff hand, he didn't wake up.

If not for the faint yet persistent flutter of his heart, which danced beneath his skin, I would have believed he was dead. Regardless of what the healers said – what Elinor Oakstorm confirmed with her own magic – Duncan was so still that it was hard to believe he still lived.

Whatever state he was in was no better than death. I'd lost him, and it was all my fault.

The gauze that'd been bound tightly around his midriff had already stained. It hadn't even been an hour since it was last cleaned and redressed, and already blood forged its way to freedom.

The wound across his abdomen refused to heal. Long gouge marks that had dug so deep muscles and bone had been exposed. I'd not seen it myself, choosing ignorant bliss over torturing myself, but Elinor had described the three long tracks like something had scored Duncan's stomach.

Two days. It had been two days since the keys were destroyed and Erix and Duncan had returned from the other side. Two days, yet the improvement to Duncan's situation was minimal. If Elinor Oakstorm hadn't arrived the night prior to Rinholm, I was confident we would have lost him. *I* would have lost him, for good this time.

"Duncan," I exhaled his name, defeated. "Wake up. Please, I can't face this future without you."

I watched the dark brush of his eyelashes for movement. *Nothing.* His lips didn't twitch, nor did his jaw tense. I dared not blink in case I missed a sign that he could hear me. Only when my eyes stung did I pinch them closed, burying my face into the cold skin of his shoulder.

"There is so much I wish to say to you, so many things I need to hear you reply. Please… just… fight this. For me. Come back so I can tell you how sorry I am. This is my doing. My fault. Don't you dare leave me until… until you get the chance to punish me. Just don't leave me."

What little control I had over my breathing was gone as quickly as it came.

Duncan wasn't kept with the injured fey. With the help of Elinor, a makeshift camp had been erected within Rinholm Castle's grounds for the rest of those needing help. Elinor had brought as many healers as she could from Oakstorm, even confirming more were on their way. Aldrick had hurt Elmdew and its people greatly in the short time since he had invaded, and many had not made it to see this day.

I couldn't help but see them as the lucky ones.

Like beetles, her healers scuttled around the camp day and night. It seemed the list of Aldrick's victims was never-ending. Every hour, more and more fey had been rescued from camps across Elmdew's lands. In droves, they were brought to

Rinholm to be cared for. Even the dead, and there were many, had not been left behind in the terrible conditions they were found in. Pens and cages that even the most feral of animals would not be put within.

I hadn't been allowed to see them for myself. Not allowed out of these walls. And I understood why.

I wasn't trusted.

Rafaela was dealt the same judgement. The stone of these walls were no different to shackles bound around wrists and ankles.

We were not trustworthy because of what our actions caused. And I didn't blame the brief sideways glances Gyah had provided me or how Althea had kept her distance from me in the days that passed.

As Elinor had reiterated, with a look that blended pity and disappointment, it wasn't that I sacrificed the Icethorn key that was the problem. It was that I didn't give Althea the chance to make the choice for herself. It was her right as a Cedarfall to claim that power, and I'd taken it from her. Regardless if she knew it was the right choice, it was hers to make, not mine.

And there was no denying that the destruction of the keys was the right decision, but the manner in which it was conducted was nothing but wrong. I was wrong. And the man beside me, whose shoulder was coated with my tears, had paid the price for my betrayal.

A wave of sickness bore over me. I clutched my empty stomach at the pain that coiled and twisted as though a serpent had taken residency in the place the Icethorn key once had.

"Jesibel is healing well." I spoke the words for the first time since the news had reached me. It was what drew me to Duncan. Selfishly, I required comfort even if I didn't deserve it. "She isn't speaking, but at least she is eating and sleeping, although the latter is only in short bursts."

I swallowed the urge to vomit. Even lying down, I felt the world tilt violently. "Whatever Aldrick did to her... it has affected her more deeply. No healer is able to fix the wounds that linger in her mind. Only time will tell if she will survive those..."

I'd been almost confident that Jesibel no longer had a tongue, considering she refused to talk. But after examination, her choice to not speak was her own. Elinor believed it was because she'd been used against her will to give our information to Aldrick – she'd likely wanted nothing more than to refuse him, and now that desire had caused her to not speak at all.

Of course, it was speculation, but there was no denying that she was hurt. One look in her eyes and it was as if Jesibel wasn't truly with us.

"Everything I've done was to save her, and I couldn't even do that. She is alive, but not with me. Like you. I hate myself for not working harder to free her. Instead, Aldrick used her against me, and she'll likely never recover from it. If I had not fixated on freeing Jesibel, perhaps Kayne would never have known her name. He would never have exposed my weakness to Aldrick. She... she would be happily returning to Icethorn with the hope of a future..." I took a deep breath in, mind falling to what I'd learned yesterday. "Althea gave her the second vial of Mariflora because Jesibel refused to leave Rinholm. That's how she distracted Aldrick enough for Althea to finish him. But... I saw her whisper something into his ear, so I knew there is still hope yet that she will find it in her to talk to me."

Familiar silence drew out in the moments after my exasperated monologue. Only the feather-soft breathing of Duncan responded. It was both enough and not. I needed to hear him tell me it was going to be okay. To remind me of what we had achieved. It was his opinion that I desired the most. Even if he looked at me with the same disdain and blame as Althea or plainly ignored me like Gyah, at least I would know.

It was the not knowing that ate me up from the inside – sinew, gristle and all.

Most of all, I wanted to know what happened to him when he disappeared through the gate. Getting answers out of Erix was wasted when he treated me with the same frosty emotion whilst still acting as my guard. He'd become a second shadow, hardly leaving me for a minute since he had saved Duncan, and yet barely being able to look at me.

It was strange how Erix could be so close, yet so far.

Erix had little to say about what happened when he dove in after Duncan through the portal into Duwar's realm. All he revealed was that it was a dark and quiet place. One moment they were buried in it, the next, they had returned.

I knew there was more to it. But every time Erix was pressed for more information, his silver eyes would dart away to someplace else. His gaze shifting as though his consciousness slipped back into Duwar's realm and the secrets he harboured from it.

If I had the energy, I would've demanded the truth. But who was I to force such things out of people when I had become the greatest liar of all time?

It was my lies that had torn us all apart – and saved the realms.

A steep price to pay, but I held onto the knowledge that it was the right thing.

I'd saved the world, but destroyed mine in the process.

Night had fallen over Rinholm when a knock rapped on the door, waking me from my light slumber.

My voice cracked as I replied. "Come in."

There was the screech of the door followed by a soft thud as it hit the wall behind it.

I looked up, eyes heavy with sorrow and exhaustion, to find Erix standing in the doorway.

"I have been asked to escort you to the meeting." Erix's voice was distant. Emotionless. I hated it.

"Let them wait," I replied, turning my focus back to Duncan, searching for signs that he'd improved in the time I'd been asleep next to him. There was nothing to see besides the sheen of sweat clinging to his forehead.

"They have been waiting, for two hours, in fact. Althea postponed the requirement for your presence for as long as she could," Erix said. "I recommend you come so you can get it over with, and return back to *him*."

My chest shivered with the thought of Althea doing something for my benefit. I wouldn't let myself believe she did so because she cared. It would hurt less to believe in such things.

"I can't leave him," I mumbled, brushing my fingers over the soft rise and fall of Duncan's broad chest. "What if Duncan wakes when I am gone? I can't bear the thought of it."

We both knew it wouldn't happen, but that didn't mean I wouldn't hope.

I had yet to look at Erix, but his lack of footfall suggested he had not stepped any further into the room than a single pace. If I glanced up, would I have seen pain painted across his face? Would he attempt to hide the way his gaze always flickered uncomfortably between Duncan and me?

"Let the healers return so they can care for him. Duncan will not be alone, I vow it. The moment the council meeting has concluded, I will bring you back to him."

I longed to refuse him, but I had no fight left in me.

My body creaked in tandem with the cot as I shifted to standing. The side of my body ached from lying in the same position since I'd arrived. Across my cheek, I felt the imprint of the sheets like fresh scars on my skin. These would fade, unlike the ones deep inside of me. Those scars were there to stay.

I silently bid Duncan farewell. Once I had my back to him, I had to ignore the violent urge to turn and clamber back on the cot at his side. Every step out of the room was harder to take than the one before it.

Erix watched me pace toward him with stifling intent. His nail-tipped hands were clasped together at his front, his wings shifting awkwardly in the Cedarfall uniform, which had been re-tailored to fit around his newly altered frame. Besides the thin-membraned wings, the grey tint discolouring his skin, and the points of his canines slightly overlapping his lower lip, he looked more the part of my personal guard than the gryvern, which made up half of him.

Maybe Eroan had painted a glamour across Erix. He would've had time after he tore the glamour from me, removing Kayne's mask for good. Eroan had the power to hide, or at least *dilute*, the gryvern within Erix. Or maybe I just saw him differently. In a new light, one not painted through a haze of hate or disdain for him.

"Shall we?" I gestured to the open door his body blocked. "I wouldn't want to keep them waiting. There is no need to give them more reasons to hate me."

Erix paused. Hesitation lingered in his stiffened posture. I waited for him to move out of the way. Instead, he looked down the point of his nose at me. Steel-silver eyes so wide they seemed to drink me in. "Are you okay, little bird?"

His question caught me off guard. I wanted to laugh because, of course, the answer was plainly clear. But I betrayed my control with my reaction.

"No, actually," I spluttered, pushing myself into his chest until my face was buried in the warmth of his torso. Erix drew his hands apart, in surprise or disgust, I couldn't tell. "I'm not."

Pinching my eyes closed, I inhaled Erix. His scent filled my nose and throat like heavy smoke. I felt stupid, cocooning myself into him when Erix refused to touch me in return. After everything, all the hate and regret, I wished he would just hold me. I wanted him to provide me comfort. Comfort which once lingered in his arms. Comfort he would have willingly given me before everything.

Before Doran, before Aldrick.

And before Duncan.

I didn't pull away for fear he would see the embarrassment stain my cheeks and neck scarlet. Just as I built the courage, two arms fell around me. Like an exhale of relief, wings followed, folding around my body and holding me upright.

"You are going to be fine, I promise." Erix's words were nearly unintelligible as he spoke them into my mess of black hair.

"How can you promise such things?" I allowed the tears to come once again. If it made me weak, then I was the most brittle of them all. And I didn't care if I held such a title. I deserved it.

"It is my duty, as your guard, to make promises others would deem impossible to keep."

Erix felt my change in posture. He freed me. I pulled back from him, almost stumbling back if his hand did not take mine to steady me.

"You know you could leave now," I said firmly. "There is no need for me to have a personal guard. I lost the one thing which gave me my title. You may think you are fulfilling a duty, but Althea won't force this on you. I'm sure there are more deserving–"

"Robin, that is enough."

I choked back on my words.

"I take my vows seriously. My bond is final. I protect *you*. It is what I desire and what I will stop at nothing to ensure. Regardless of what you say, how you act, you cannot push me away. I will not allow it." He traced a finger down my cheek, making me suck in a breath. "My duty and pleasure. Remember that."

"What are you going to protect me from now?" I asked, finding it difficult to hold his intense gaze. "Myself? It seems it is my decisions, actions and lies that cause more damage than anything else. Aldrick is dead, Duwar is locked away forever, the world has the peace it deserves. You deserve to find your peace, too, Erix."

Erix's stare left mine for the first time. It was brief, but his attention flickered to Duncan. His expression set in a grimace. When his eyes snapped back to me, all evidence of his emotion was gone. "I found it already, little bird."

Before I could question his reply, he stood to the side and gestured me to walk. "Before Althea comes looking for you herself, perhaps we go to them."

I was glad for the change of topic, although his final words haunted me.

"This conversation is going to be painful," I said. "Isn't it?"

"Like pulling a thorn from your foot. Once the task is dealt with, you will soon forget it and move on. I speak on all your behalfs, but you each cannot hide from one another."

"Althea hates me, and I don't blame her."

"And has she told you this herself? Because I hardly imagine Althea could *ever* hate you. Dislike, perhaps. However, an apology can be the greatest gift. It can heal rifts. It is the starting block of building trust. Believe me, I would know."

I forced a smile, thankful to have him at my back. Thankful to have him with me in any capacity.

"Erix?" I asked, voice pitching at the end of his name.

He exhaled. "Yes?"

I screwed my eyes at him, and his lips curled back into a toothy grin. Something warmed low down in my stomach. "When you are ready, will you tell me what happened?"

At once, his smile faded. Erix didn't need me to further explain what I was asking. He knew. As before, I expected him to refuse me. To tell me nothing had happened inside of the gate or for him to repeat the same muted story he'd already said, the one lacking details.

Something had happened during the short time Duncan and Erix had entered Duwar's realm. I remembered Erix's palpable shock even now, days later. When he looked at me, his eyes seemed to cut straight through me as though I wasn't there. Duncan was unconscious in his arms. Erix hadn't reacted when I shouted his name, he didn't even seem to notice when I waved my hand before his lost, all-seeing eyes.

Terror. I recognised it in his gaze.

Whatever had happened, Erix had come back in a state of shock and Duncan was gravely hurt. I didn't believe Duncan had hurt himself by the fall, which Erix had suggested was the cause.

But I hadn't pushed because it wasn't the right thing to do. There were far more important matters deserving of my focus. Especially now that Duwar's fate had been sealed for all eternity with the destruction of three out of the four of Altar's keys.

Erix gazed ahead, the burning sconces on the wall reflecting haunting light across the sharp lines of his face. The turmoil drew his expression into something unrecognisable. "If I am honest, Robin, I hope I never need to tell you what I saw."

My heart thumped in my throat. There was something in his reaction that called for my ice to crackle around the tips of my fingers. It was as though the power, beaten and tired like a hound cowering in its cage, finally felt the need to protect me.

A familiar lost expression riddled with terror shadowed Erix's face. I felt his refusal to look at me now as though it would stop me from seeing his horror plastered, as plain as day, across his face.

"But the information could help–"

"Please, do not ask me again," Erix snapped, his tone exasperated. "I... I am not ready."

I swallowed hard, forcing the calloused lump back down into the pit of my stomach, where it seeded and spread its roots of anxiety. Only when I brushed the back of my fingers against Erix's did he seem to snap out of the trance he found himself lost within. I was relieved when he looked back at me. Except, he made no attempt to smile.

"Whatever it was, whatever happened there… it is over," I said. "The gate has been sealed, and the only way to open it again has been removed from play. Nothing can harm you, or anyone else again."

Erix straightened, his fists tensing at his side. "I am not a pious man, little bird. But even I pray you are right."

CHAPTER 36

Althea waited beyond the door, pacing grooves into the ground. Only when she heard our arrival did she stop. I held my breath, expecting to hear her disappointment as she greeted me. Days' worth of silence unleashed as though she couldn't wait to release it upon me.

She watched me with a calculating stare. When she spoke, her voice shook ever so slightly. "How is Duncan faring?"

My shoulders sagged forward, unable to hold the weight of his name. I shook my head, dropping my chin to my chest. "Unresponsive, still."

Before I could look up, her arms were around me. A sob cracked free from my ribs as I buried my tear-slicked face into the mess of her red hair.

"I thought I was doing the right thing," I spluttered. "I never wished to deceive you or make you feel as though I acted behind your back. I'm sorry."

"Robin." Althea's voice was calm and controlled. "I wish I could tell you I'm not pissed off with you, but it is not in my nature to lie. But I have lost so much already." Her voice cracked. "I can't bear the thought of losing you, too."

I peeled my face from her hair. Althea's hands fell to mine, and we held onto one another, fingers coiled and firm.

"I'm so sorry," I said.

"For saving the world, don't be. For not including me in your plans, then I accept your apology."

It was on the tip of my tongue to explain why I'd kept it from her, but Althea spoke before I could say anything.

"We will have time to discuss everything, but first, I want us to be reunited. Our courts have always held a close bond. It would be foolish for it to break now. And, for what it's worth, I believe the decision you made was the right one, remember that."

"You have all the right to be angry with me," I replied, squeezing her hands.

"Undoubtedly," she huffed. "And I *will* make you pay. But after, and only *after*, we set the world right. The world your decision has made safe from a demon god. Not just now, forever."

Pride righted my posture. "I don't deserve you."

"I know, but I deserve you," Althea replied, retrieving her hands from me. She nudged my shoulder as we both faced the closed door. "Do not let Gyah know I am telling you this, but even she has fought your corner. I don't think she could have been prouder of you. Although, if she finds out I ever told you, she will suck the meat from both our bones."

"Sounds about right," I retorted. "With a tongue so sharp, it is no wonder you love her."

"What can I say." Althea winked. "There is something rather special about falling into bed, and love, with your personal guard."

Erix coughed into his fist behind us, reminding us of his presence. My cheeks bloomed with heat, and guilt crept across my consciousness.

I was thankful when Althea drifted on soundless feet toward the door and pushed it open. Inside, the room was bright with the scent of food. My stomach rumbled for the first time in days. The promise of a full stomach enticed me to forget Althea's comment.

"I will wait for you here," Erix said coldly.

"Take the evening off," Althea called over her shoulder.

"There are no longer evils lurking in the dark. Robin will be fine."

"You should know better than anyone, Queen Cedarfall. I made a vow. My word is bound. Robin, I *will* be waiting for you."

"For me, or him."

Erix's eyes settled on me, answering the question without a reply.

If Althea noticed the tension tying Erix and me together, like thick but frayed rope, she didn't say. Instead, she gestured for me to enter with a sweep of her hand.

"After you then, Robin."

I mocked a curtsy, echoing the title Erix had used for Althea. "How gracious, my queen."

One sharp punch from Althea into my shoulder had me stifling a laugh. Then we both entered, leaving Erix to disappear as I closed the door on him.

The three remaining heads of the fey courts sat around a polished wood table in the heat of a modest room. At the head of the table waited two thrones, each carved from ivory bone which seemed to glow in the dim light of the room. Delicate vines twisted around the formation of bone. Across it, buds of blush pink and purple flowers, each one wilting sadly with the lack of an Elmdew presence.

Althea sat at my side, back rigid and expression stern as she focused on Rafaela, the only one who didn't sit. Elinor Oakstorm was to my other side. I felt her look at me with a strange gaze which sang with longing. Her thin, jewelled fingers lay on the table before her, tentatively brushing up the long stem of her glass of amber-toned wine.

My glass was left untouched as my fingers busied themselves, plucking at a loose thread across the material of my trousers.

"Aldrick is dead. The Defiler is forever trapped within the realm with no promise of ever being freed again. I do not need to be the one to remind you we all have sacrificed much in this fight, but it is over." Rafaela practically shivered with glee as she spoke. "Your displeasure toward Robin is misplaced, if there is anyone you must be angry with, it is me. I made him vow to keep quiet, and he did as I asked. His compliance is what secured this allyship, and thus saved the realms."

The deed was done. Both threats had been removed from play, and the keys were destroyed. Which was what Rafaela had always wanted. What she and Gabrial had conspired to complete behind even their fellow Nephilim's backs. An act that the rest of the Nephilim didn't agree on, clear from her treatment since. I just hadn't had the chance to find out why yet.

"But they are not all destroyed, are they?"

Rafaela flickered her attention to Elinor who spoke over the rim of her glass.

"No, not at this moment," Rafaela replied.

"So, even now, you would you wish to see the Oakstorm key destroyed?" Elinor questioned, her stare boring through Rafaela. "It still lingers within me. Could this not pose a threat in our future, immediate or distant?"

"What good is a quill without ink?" Rafaela dismissed. "One key is useless without the rest. My fellow Nephilim likely prepare for my punishment. Cassial will not be pleased. I imagine it wouldn't change my outcome if I went against them and destroyed the final one."

"Then, for your sake, perhaps we go forward with the knowledge the Oakstorm key remains intact." Elinor smiled brightly, undeterred by Rafaela's tone. "I am complacent with the confirmation that this is over."

"Not entirely," I added. "Wychwood is bathed in unrest. Elmdew is without a leader..."

"And Cedarfall finds itself with a warrior for a queen," Althea finished for me, offering me a sideways smirk. "I think we will be fine."

"That isn't what I was going to say," I replied curtly. "It is going to take time and strain to help Wychwood heal. *That* is what we must focus on now. Looking ahead, not back."

"I think we can all agree with Robin on this matter," Elinor said, patting my thigh with her hand before returning it to her glass. "Our main priority is seeing the courts regain composure."

"Do not concern yourselves with Cedarfall, I will see all wounds are stitched and healed. Just as I am sure you and Robin have the ability to gather control of your own courts."

"And what of Elmdew?" I asked. "Is there a clear line of succession?"

My attention drifted to the empty thrones, wondering who would find themselves upon it next.

"There is a boy," Althea confirmed, voice as cold as the ice dwelling within me. "Barely walking. The young child was brought into the realm by surrogacy for the kings. His reign will not solidify for many years, so until then, his council must be iron-clad. For that, the three courts will need to lend aid to Elmdew."

"I agree, but what of the turmoil in Durmain?"

"Leave the humans to the Nephilim," Rafaela said, chin raised. "Your realm is not the only one which requires healing, nor is Durmain your responsibility. Aldrick sullied Durmain with his beliefs and thus left the once great Kingdom without a ruler. But now that the gate our kind have guarded is no longer a threat, it is likely my brothers and sisters will return to Durmain's shores to help rebuild it in the glory of the Creator."

"And this includes the Hunters?" I asked. "Not all of them have laid down arms willingly. Many will hide and wait for the next leader to emerge from the ashes of their newly titled martyr."

I had longed to flee Rinholm and help chase the Hunters from Wychwood myself. Even after Aldrick's defeat, I still felt like the fight was not over. We had won, and they sang about it, but why didn't I feel like it?

"The Hunters will be dealt with. As Althea began, those remaining will be given a choice. How they survive after making that decision depends on them."

There was fury in Rafaela's voice. Powerful as her golden hammer, obedient as her belief in the Creator. I had no doubt Rafaela and the Nephilim would comb the realms, providing antidote to the poison Aldrick had spread, whilst burning out the last of those who still wore his mark with blinded pride.

"What about you?" I asked.

Rafaela's brows furrowed at my question. Her battered, torn wings twitched just as my own fingers continued to fidget on my lap. "My actions and desires have affected you enough, Robin Icethorn. I would not wish for you to concern yourself with the repercussions I have brought upon myself. The punishment which waits for me is not a new concept. Gabrial and I knew it would come with our success. I welcome it gladly."

"But I do worry," I said, sitting forward until my ass was on the edge of my seat. "All this talk of punishment does not sit well with me."

"Is there anything we can do?" Elinor asked the questions likely running through all our minds. "Surely the Nephilim would listen if the heads of the fey courts petitioned for you?"

Rafaela smiled proudly, brushing off Elinor's suggestion with an exhaled sigh. "Not even the Creator could cleanse me of my sins, Elinor Oakstorm. My duty, my purpose, was to protect the keys, but I went against it. I took it a step further and ensured they were destroyed. Whatever is waiting for me, I welcome it."

She looked at me, and I was certain I saw tears swell in her striking eyes. "Gabrial will provide me with comfort. I go gladly, knowing I am a step closer to seeing my sister's face again."

Althea stood abruptly. Her chair clattered with a bang against the floor. "There is no denying my views on your decision and the position it put Robin in. But I can't condone sending you back to the Nephilim if death awaits you. Actually, I refuse it."

"Starting a war with the Nephilim over one life is not worth it," Rafaela replied, voice clear and proud. "And there is no saying if death will greet me. My people are just and fair. I appreciate your wishes to protect me, but I am not in need. Believe me."

I didn't believe her, that was the problem.

I sensed Rafaela's finality to the conversation, but the look I shared with Althea confirmed this was not over. Far from it, in fact.

We continued speaking for hours. In the windowless room, time was inconsequential as a concept. Only the melting of the pillar candles across the table and the ever-growing puddle of wax at their base was a signifier of how long we lost ourselves to conversation.

"Forgive me." Elinor stood, face contorting into a yawn. "It has been a long few days, and I imagine those that follow will be no different. It is not criminal to steal a few hours of sleep before I have to face my council. Still, I sense nothing but resistance from them. Once this conflict has been dealt with, I will continue with the one which rages in the heart of *my* court."

"Say the word," Althea said. "And I will help where I can."

"Doran surrounded himself with men whose narrow views did not vary. It will take some time to convince them of my rule, until I grow impatient and snatch it from underneath them."

"Weak men are fearful of powerful women," I said, echoing something my father had once told me. I couldn't help but wonder if he spoke of my mother.

Elinor placed a fleeting hand upon my shoulder. "Julianne would have told you, given the chance, I have always enjoyed a challenge. Now more so than ever."

My chest warmed at the mention of my mother. I wished Elinor didn't have to leave so I could finally take the chance to ask her everything she remembered of her. Now the Icethorn key no longer dwelled within me, I couldn't help but feel distant from her. It was as if the one physical thing tethering me to her had vanished.

As Elinor Oakstorm dismissed herself and slipped through the door, Rafaela also bidding farewell alongside her, Erix forced his way into the room under the muttering of apologies.

"Do you still struggle with the concept of personal space, Erix?" Althea threw her comment at Erix. It reminded me of a time, an easier one than this, when we were all friends without the horrible memories wedged between us.

My tired grin faltered as I looked at the frown that drew down Erix's face. He looked directly at me, hesitation lingering on his parted lips.

"Erix. What is it?"

The shadow in his eyes frightened me. It was as though he'd seen something horrifying, as though he faced his greatest fear and narrowly survived it – again.

Erix looked at me with wide, all-seeing eyes. My heart plummeted through my chest. Panic seized at my throat and squeezed. The look on his face seemed to reveal my fear. One I had faced multiple times.

Duncan's death.

I clapped my hands to my ears, refusing to hear the words Erix had to say. Except his words caught me off guard. They had me removing my hands slowly, lowering them back to my thighs as I tried to make sense of Erix's revelation.

"Duncan is awake."

CHAPTER 37

I stumbled over my footing, refusing to believe what I saw before me. Erix hadn't lied. For a moment, I thought he had. How could he have shown such an expression yet reveal such happy news? Was it his jealousy or bitterness taking physical form across his expression?

I would have berated him, but I had no time.

Instead, I ran. Ran through the foreign hallways and rooms. I ran back to *him*. To Duncan.

He stood at the end of the corridor, haloed with moonlight which swelled in through the grand window at his back.

"Tell me I'm dreaming," I said, taking careful steps forward. I feared I would rush and shatter the illusion I dared hope was real before me.

"I heard you calling for me," Duncan replied, his words slurred, voice weak. "Then, when I woke, you weren't there beside me."

Duncan raised and spread his arms, beckoning me to him. One moment I walked cautiously, the next, I barrelled into his hard chest.

"I'm sorry, I'm so sorry," I said, unsure if I was apologising for causing him pain now or what my action had caused when I opened the gate. His hand traced my back, and the other cupped the back of my head as I melted into him.

Duncan held me close, refusing to let go. "I never wish to hear those words leave your mouth again."

His skin was both hot and damp to the touch. He was slick with sweat, his breathing ragged. I was partially aware of the wound. It still leaked into the bandage around his waist, but his arms held me in place, soundlessly refusing to ever let me go again.

"You should be in bed!" I gasped, voice muffled in the moist flesh of his chest.

"Perhaps, but I came to find you."

A sigh escaped me. It spoke of my exhaustion, the cry of my soul as Duncan's physical presence finally sank in.

"I'm here," I replied. "*You* are here with me."

"Yes," Duncan replied slowly, drawing the lonely word out. "I certainly am."

Reluctantly, I pulled back. His eyes were hooded with shadows. The hair across his pinched forehead was clumped in sweat-damp strands. I reached out and brushed them from his forehead, only to feel just how warm he was to the touch.

"You look like shit warmed up. Let me get you back into bed before Elinor's healers blame me for your escape," I said, threading his arm over my shoulder. I instantly felt him drop his weight onto me.

"Sounds delicious," Duncan joked, eyes fluttering with heavy exhaustion. "However, I cannot promise my performance will be any good. You may be very disappointed."

My chest warmed with his attempt at a joke. I looked up at him, unable to do anything but beam with a smile as he pathetically winked at me.

"How about you focus on getting better first," I said.

"Oh," he moaned, rolling his tired eyes. "Killjoy."

I half encouraged and half dragged Duncan to walk back to his room. It was as though he was drunk on fever, laughing to himself as if unseen spirits whispered jokes into his ears.

All my worries faded with each step into the room. I glanced behind me to see if Erix was still there, but he was not. For a moment, I felt a pang of something painful in my chest, but it soon dissipated when I looked back to Duncan at my side.

Something caught my eye. A flickering of burning fire, glowing crimson. Frowning, I glanced at the strange light. There were no candles burning here, no light visible but the silver of the moon and the stars attempting to glow in competition.

But there *was* a mirror.

Duncan didn't seem to notice, continuing his focus forward to the promise of rest.

Over Duncan's shoulder, I glanced into the mirror reflection, which showed the misplaced light I'd seen moments before. And in it was a reflection so horrific, it skinned the flesh from my body.

I blinked, wanting to rid myself of what I saw. Wishing it would change and the cruel trick my mind played would go away.

It didn't, nor could I look away.

I stared at a body made of molten flesh. I propped it up with my shoulder, my arm wrapped around its sizzling, cracked flesh. Ram-curled horns like a crown atop a hairless head. Hooves thudded in time with Duncan's footfall, except the reflection showed prints of flame and rot left in its wake.

Soon enough, the mirror passed, leaving the glimpse of the demon behind me. My eyes bore into the brick of the castle wall as I focused on the child-like singing Duncan was lost to.

It took a second for my mind to slow down and shield me from the fear threatening to drown me. Then his words became clear. Each one stabbed into my chest, over and over.

"I am here. I am here. I am here."

No. I refused to believe it. My happiness slipped through my hold like sand through parted fingers.

Duwar. In the reflection, I had my arm wrapped around the demon god. The same one I had seen in the mirror in Lockinge, the same one which had poisoned every reflection in the room of mirrors Aldrick had constructed within this very castle.

This was different, so very different.

Duwar didn't stand at our sides, following us like a starving hound. He stood in place of Duncan. He was...

No.

No.

"Robin?" Duncan said my name in question. It had sway over me, the way he said it drew me back out of my mind. "Do you see something you don't like?"

My stiff neck ached as I turned to look at him in the flesh. Deep green eyes waited for me. His mouth parted, lips lined with a thin trail of spit. Duncan no longer sang, but the glazed look in his eyes told me he was still not completely here.

I couldn't reply, dared not make a sound for fear this would all be real.

"Is something the matter?" he asked again, voice deepening with worry.

We had stopped walking, the door to his room only a stretch away.

A storm built in my stomach, twisting it into knots. I felt bile slither up the back of my throat, threatening to burst out of me.

"I don't know," I replied honestly. "Should there be?"

For a moment, Duncan's gaze cleared. He straightened slightly, removing his weight from me as he peeled back. Then he kissed me. Pressed his sodden, heavy lips into mine. Our teeth almost clashed with the urgency. I tried to pull back, but his fingers encased my wrist and squeezed.

I wondered if he sensed my hesitation when he pulled away. I bit down on the insides of my cheeks as he regarded me down the line of his nose. If I didn't cause pain, I would have faltered beneath his stare.

"I am just so *happy* to be here," he said. No. It wasn't Duncan who spoke. "And it is *you* I have to thank."

A cold tear of ice rolled down my spine. I felt it run across every inch of my skin, spreading across my body in a wave of goosebumps.

"Come now, Robin," he said through a smirk. "Help me back into bed. I am going to need my rest."

I didn't refuse Duncan. I couldn't. Except, I knew without a doubt that it wasn't Duncan who spoke to me now. This was the demon god, Duwar. The reflection confirmed my greatest fears.

Duwar *had* made it through the gate.

The gate that had been closed, the keys destroyed alongside it.

And yet Duwar was here, before me, encased in the flesh of the man I loved.

Keep reading for an exclusive
bonus chapter for
A Deception of Courts,
told from Erix's point of view...

BONUS CHAPTER

Old stone crumbled beneath my hands as I clutched onto Imeria Castle's exterior walls. My talons dug into mortar as frozen winds buffeted my body as if even the elements wanted to drag me from my hiding place and punish me for being here. I found purchase, slotting my boots into the space of a missing brick, gritting my teeth as I focused on holding on, all whilst I peered into a bedroom and watched two men sleep.

This was wrong, deep down I knew that.

But I would not leave no matter how I longed to, no matter how many times I told myself to.

Robin had told me to leave him and never return, and I vowed it was a promise I would keep until my last breath. But all that disintegrated into nothingness the moment I heard his name being spoken about outside the window of the home I had claimed in Berrow.

For weeks now Berrow had been a place of silence and contemplation – somewhere I had clawed my way back once Doran Oakstorm returned my mind to me. Although I had not seen it with my own two eyes at the time, I knew he was dead.

Every waking hour I waited for his commands to fill my head once again – to return with more sadistic orders that I was powerless to refuse. But as the days went on, and the silence reigned, I found that I could begin piecing myself back together again, bit by bit.

Until my past came to haunt me.

Until *his* name sang across the once empty streets of Berrow.

For the first time since Doran vacated my mind, I thought he had return to punish me. Because the moment I heard one of the fey mention Robin Icethorn and what he had achieved in Lockinge, I found my body moving without thought.

I had left out the back of the run-down building, casting skyward with a single beat of my wings. There was no room for thought, only action, as I sliced through Icethorn skies until Imeria Castle was no longer a vision on the horizon, but a behemoth of grand design directly in front of me.

That is when I found him. My Robin, my little bird – the man who showed me purpose in life, then even when I destroyed his world, he could not find it in him to destroy mine.

I owed him everything, more than I even think I was capable of understanding. Which was why I knew the right thing was to leave, to stop watching through the narrow window as he curled his body around the back of another man, his life in the hands of another.

Did I stay to punish myself? No, I knew that was not the case. Because seeing him in bed with another did not hurt me as I thought it would. If anything, the vision was enough to settle the fire in my belly to a simmer.

That was the thing about love. It never stopped, never left – but if left unattended it mutated to something that even I could not explain. All I knew, as I focused on his back rising and falling with each breath, the way his bare feet tangled together and the distant yet powerful beat of his heat, was that if I could not love him, he deserved to experience that feeling from another.

There was peace in accepting loss in yourself, and the gain in another.

I was about to leave when Robin rolled over and faced me. Before he saw me peeking inside like some creep, I spun from the window and out of the way. My heart thundered in my dry throat, my foot slipping slightly until I almost fell.

A part of me wished he had found me lurking. As I clung to the wall, winds beating against my face, tearing nasty little hands at my wings, I wondered what would have happened.

Now was the moment I should leave. I knew that I could not return to Berrow, not if Robin had plans to return there. I would not want to put him in a position to be near me, to face me, to experience my company – instead, I would find another empty hole in this god forsaken realm and curl up into it.

At least I had this memory to take with me.

I was just about to launch myself from the wall when I heard a door close behind me. Holding my breath, knowing the risk if I made myself seen, I peeked back around the window and saw that Robin was gone.

All my hopes of listening to his desires faded for a second time. Instinct took over. He was alone, in a castle full of assassins and I could not just leave knowing that. I withdrew my talons from the mortar, pushing off from the wall until weathered stone crumbled and fell into the abyss below. Then I was flying, senses scanning the castle for signs of where Robin had gone.

I would find him – if only to become a shadow and make sure he was safe until he returned to the Hunter's arms. Or, at least, that is what I told myself, to make this sin not hurt as badly as it carved into my bones.

I could barely contain my heart in my ribs as I listened in on Robin's conversation with the feather-winged warrior he called Rafaela. I had never seen her kind before, but that did not mean I could not understand the threat she posed.

They spoke upon a balcony overlooking Icethorn's never-ending landscape. A blanket of greys, blacks and whites, a patchwork of land that was rightfully Robin's and yet every time he looked out across it, he winced. I hated myself for hiding in the shadows, listening in on a conversation that I had no right in hearing. And yet, I could not bring myself to leave.

His voice was everything to me. From the lightness of his tone, to the occasional dropping of sarcasm, or the way his voice softened when he spoke of topics laden with emotion. I missed that voice so much – I would have given anything in the realms to hear it spoken directly to me.

There was nothing more beautiful in this world than hearing my name on the tongue of the man I loved.

But this was more than I could have ever wanted, and my time of spying was over as soon as it began. Perhaps Robin felt my gaze on his flesh like a knife, or he sensed the same tugging in my gut that plagued me the moment I heard he was close, because he paused his conversation and looked directly toward me.

I threw myself from the spire of the tower above him, allowing my body to blend in with the night as winds caught my wings. I flew away – from him, the punishment I put myself under just being close.

I had allowed myself the time to be selfish, but now I could not afford it.

My wings took me north, directly past the line of thick clouds and up into the part of the air that hurt to breathe. I delighted in the light rush that overtook my skull, the way my limbs felt as though they did not belong to me. The higher I gained, the more the helpless feeling overtook me, until I almost forgot about Robin.

That was when the roaring sliced the night. A deep, guttural bellow that clawed me back from the brink of losing consciousness and falling to my death – because that was what I wanted in that moment. I knew, no matter how far I flew or which corner of the realm I found myself hiding in, Robin would always linger. Not punishing me with his memory – that was not want I wanted reprieve from. But reminding me of what I had done, and I could not trust myself to ever leave him again if our paths ever crossed.

I was a weak man – no, not a man, but a monster.

But so were the dark shapes that flew toward Imeria, hulking beasts of scale, claw and fang, wings so large they cast shadows upon the ground even in the dead of night.

Then I heard Robin, his voice crying out for the man he had left back in bed, fear lacing every syllable of the name: Duncan.

There was no time for thought, no chance for deliberating right and wrong, or the repercussions I would face for involving myself in Robin's life again. But even I sensed the danger as though it was my kin.

What my soul wanted to do was spear through the night and clash with these strange monsters that flew toward Imeria. But my heart, well, that gave me another command. And just like when Doran pulled his strings and made me do things even I could not comprehend in the moment, I folded my wings into my body and dove down.

Not toward the monsters. Not toward Robin, who let his winter out of his skin – he was capable of surviving without me, the weeks that had passed proved it.

But I flew toward Duncan, the man Robin loved.

I had once taken someone Robin loved from him, and I would not sit back and be complacent as the universe did it again.

Whilst Robin unleashed his fury across the night, sparking a pride so powerful in my chest for him, I flew back to the room, through the window and snatched the broad-bodied Hunter out of his bed, all before he knew what was coming.

My life only had meaning if *little bird* was alive. But I also knew that my life only had purpose if those he loved still breathed. Robin had lost enough to this cruel world, and I would not sit back and let the universe make him pay more of a price.

If this was the penance I was to pay to cleanse my soul of past mistakes, I would do it. For Robin, I would save the man he loved – and I would do it a hundred times over if I had the hindsight to know what was to follow these actions.

That was the thing about my love for Robin – it was content knowing that even after everything, he remembered he was worthy of it, and capable of giving it back. If that was to Duncan, the Hunter, then so be it.

It was my duty to ensure that continued.

And my pleasure.

ACKNOWLEDGMENTS

I want to start by thanking all my readers, new and old, for following along this journey so far. Whether this is the first time reading the Realm of Fey books, or if you have picked them up again to re-read these new editions, I hope you are all still surviving after the turmoil I have put the characters through. I wish I could promise that the pain and suffering is over, but we have one more book to get through before that.

The incredible Angry Robot team, once again I thank you all. It takes a village to make these books, and I cannot thank you enough for all banding around me, welcoming me into your ranks and guiding me along this journey. I really am one lucky author to be with you all: thank you for putting up with my many emails, questions and these crazy, dramatic books.

Hannah, my wonderful agent, of course I would not be here without you. And Laura, my darling friend, who put me on this path with her kindness and offers to help me. Then to all my friends and family: your encouragement is paramount, and without it I likely would never have finished my first book, let alone this one.

Ben xo

We are Angry Robot, your favourite independent, genre-fluid publisher, bringing you the very best in sci-fi, fantasy, horror and everything in between!

Check out our website at
www.angryrobotbooks.com
to see our entire catalogue.

Follow us on social media:
Twitter @angryrobotbooks
Instagram @angryrobotbooks
TikTok @angryrobotbooks

Sign up to our mailing list now: